# The Gadling Legacy: Haven's Fall
By Devany Wilson

# Table of Contents

CHAPTER ONE ........................................................5

CHAPTER TWO .....................................................19

CHAPTER THREE ..................................................35

CHAPTER FOUR ...................................................49

CHAPTER FIVE......................................................67

CHAPTER SIX.......................................................77

CHAPTER SEVEN .................................................94

CHAPTER EIGHT.................................................106

CHAPTER NINE ..................................................124

CHAPTER TEN ....................................................145

CHAPTER ELEVEN ..............................................158

CHAPTER TWELVE ..............................................171

CHAPTER THIRTEEN............................................187

CHAPTER FOURTEEN ..........................................200

CHAPTER FIFTEEN...............................................213

CHAPTER SIXTEEN ..............................................229

CHAPTER SEVENTEEN.........................................246

CHAPTER EIGHTEEN ...........................................259

CHAPTER NINETEEN ...........................................272

CHAPTER TWENTY...............................................284

CHAPTER TWENTY-ONE .......................................305

CHAPTER TWENTY-TWO .......................................320

CHAPTER TWENTY-THREE ....................................337

CHAPTER TWENTY-FOUR ......................................351

To Richard, for the other journey
this book took us on

# CHAPTER ONE

*"The ones who jump are proof that the fear of death isn't as strong as the fear of living an empty life. Every day, nothing. To get to the end and lay there without a single incredible memory over decades upon decades of living, to have waited all that time to set yourself free...it's a wonder there are any of us left at all."*

Alistanik slowly set the cutting knife down on the counter. The blade was thin, but near unbreakable. Since he opened his eyes that morning, he did every little thing as if it were the first time. A finely diced mound of green fronds was delicately piled in the palm of his hand, not a single fleck rolling off to the floor. The kitchen's arm whirred around, its interior sounds only adding a different tone of quietness to the room. With humanlike mobility, it plucked the knife up in its many-pronged hand and inserted the utensil up into a chute within the counter it protruded down from. During this, Alistanik poured the frond pile gently into a carefully cut rectangular leaf. He used to wish for conveniences like paper or for the blissful ignorance of not having read about such things. Things they would never have in Haven. As the years of his life went on, he found himself wishing less and understanding more. But as he hovered near the counter, enjoying this simple ritual, he did not allow himself to think of old wants and wishes. In the hallway behind him, one of his young sons wandered in, yawning and ruffling his hair.

"Go get ready to leave," said Alistanik, not looking away from his task.

His two children took so much after their mother, to others he looked like their reluctant caretaker. More people would have questioned their relation had their mother not been completely, undeniably in love with the gloomy young man before her accident. They were absolutely opposite him with his ever-creased brows, dark circles, and permanent sneer, complete with a short scar on his upper lip. Their difference in appearance was especially noteworthy as all the residents of Haven shared similar features. Everyone had black hair, gray eyes and freckleless, pale skin caused in small part by generations of living within the mountain, shielded from the direct sunlight. Alistanik was a Gray from the very last level down. Lidi was an Upper from the very top. It was her house they continued on in without her. To Alistanik, it was her world up there, not his.

He finished rolling the frond with the finely chopped bits inside, licked the leaf and waited for it to fully stick to itself. The leaves of bloodstones, their only source of food, became gooey when wet. Often they were used as a way to temporarily patch people up, for cringe worthy pranks, or for rolling improvised cigarettes. The people of Haven called these sitters as they induced over-sensitive motion sickness, but also calmed their nerves. The kitchen had seen Alistanik make enough of these. It had already superheated one of its prongs to light it for him. He took a couple of puffs, squeezed his eyes shut and let his head rest against the cool stone wall.

At the other end of the house, Marek, one of his sons, stood up on his toes to press the knocker pad in the upper center of the door. An artificial knocking resounded on the other side. Everything was made of stone: chairs, doors, walls and streets. Anything that wasn't made of stone was made of Thesmekkian metal, which was harder than stone. Knocking on any of this with soft bones was a sure way to send yourself to the med-fac. Marek held down the touchpad, following up with a swift kick he immediately regretted.

"Vik!" he groaned, fighting back the tears for his stubbed toe, "get up!"

There was a muffled stirring on the other side and Marek waited with his mouth hanging open, leaning closer to the door. He heard a loud thump and leaned back, shoulders slumping. He raised himself up and smashed the touchpad after each word.

"Vik. Get. Up."

The door finally whirred open just enough for his brother Vik to appear, burning a glare into Marek that made him momentarily forget why he was waking him up. Vik's favorite time of day was around the middle when the light shone through the circular Gate lodged into the top of their mountain. It would reflect off the Thesmekkian metal as a flashing signal to Vik that it was almost time to watch the sun pass by. It was already midday when Marek woke him.

"What?" Vik snapped after Marek didn't fill the silence.

"Dad says we're going somewhere."

"I don't want to go anywhere right now."

"What's wrong with you?" Marek finally registered Vik's subtle unrested appearance as he peered out from the dark room. "Did you have bad dreams?"

"Shut up."

"You're not worried about them are you?"

"I'm not a Gray, I don't care about bad dreams," Vik scoffed, rubbing his eyes.

"Don't let dad hear you," Marek said, hushing him, "he sounded pretty serious about going out. I think you have to."

"He's always serious. I don't want to go," Vik moaned, his head hitting the metal door a little harder than he would've liked.

"You tell him then," Marek said, marching away right after.

Vik slunk back into his bedroom far enough to slide the metal door closed himself, having turned off the automatic function long ago. A metallic ball small enough to fit in Vik's palm stuck halfway out of the wall, meant to be swiveled around for precise lighting. With a frustrated groan, he used two fingers to slowly rotate the shiny orb, taking care not to blind himself. After the light gently brightened to the dimmest setting he could see by, he sifted through drawers and piles of socks scattered about the room, searching for his shoes. They were three sizes too big and smelled like warm, sweaty feet, but his father said he would grow into them in the next few years. They couldn't withdraw fresh clothing since the last of those dispensers broke down many years before Vik and Marek were born and not even kids on the upper levels were given new clothes to wear. Their white and gray rayon outfits were made up of a short, thigh-length tunic under a flowy-legged set of overalls held up with a loop of fabric around the back of the neck instead of straps over the shoulders. These simple clothes were durable, but not childproof.

Vik swiped some socks off the floor, rammed them into the shoes and crammed his feet inside. His tunic and overalls lay on the floor, having slid off the countertop right after he'd set it there the night before. He easily slipped his feet through the legs with his shoes on and shifted around in what felt like a baggy cocoon. After flinging the loop over his head, he let go of the overalls and they fell to the middle of his chest, the sleeves engulfing his hands. Had he been the only child he knew with clothes in this condition, he would have refused to go anywhere. On his way out, he grabbed a belt he had made by cutting the end off of his blanket and tied it around his waist.

As he joined his brother and father in the kitchen, dragging his feet and tugging at his sleeves, Vik grumbled about Marek always getting to wear the clothes that fit best.

"When you wake up at midday, every day, you get what's leftover," Alistanik said, tapping his sitter out on the stone table.

He left the ashes where they were and ushered the boys outside. As usual, there were hundreds of people outside, indirectly soaking up as much of the midday sun as they could. Marek trotted over to the edge of the level and peered over the side, waving his arm for Vik to come over to him. Vik wasn't nearly as comfortable beside the edge as his twin, but he crept over anyway as their father always took a while outside their door to stare up at the Gate. Vik stood beside Marek with his head tilted up, body leaned back, and one foot far out in front of him.

"What are you looking at?" asked Vik, his voice wavering.

"I saw Edik and Kalan doing this the other day," Marek said, looking side to side before hanging his head over the edge and dribbling a huge glob of spit out of his mouth.

"What are you doing?" Vik gasped, a grin sliding over his face.

He whipped his head around to see if his father was about to stop them. As usual though, Alistanik's eyes were half open and he seemed to be having a hard time pushing his meager weight away from the wall he leaned against. The spitball nearly hit someone all the way on the bottom level, splattering in front of their feet. It was too far down to see that person clearly, but both boys laughed and took several steps away from the edge just in case the Gray below decided to come find them.

"Come on, boys," Alistanik called out from a short way away.

He had managed to stumble off from the wall and push his way passed several irritable bystanders. The boys jogged a few steps to catch up and trailed behind him in obedient silence, shooting glances at each other. They wanted to ask, but they didn't want to bother him. For six out of their twelve years, he'd been a completely different person: playful, fun, happy. This version of their father they followed closely behind was a hollow husk of the man he had been before their mother's death. Just a shadow waiting to disappear in the light.

On the fourth level, they passed the info board on their way to a house repurposed into a diner. The info board displayed things like the date, time, predicted weather and other such trivialities on a screen of glass with lights behind it. The diner drew in people from all parts of Haven, top to bottom, most coming for the creative variations on their only source of food. Alistanik was a regular customer, though it did little to lift his spirits. Even with all the variety, it was still bloodstones and water all day, every day.

"Why are we going to the diner?" Vik asked, arms crossed.

"It's you two's birthday," Alistanik said, matter-of-factly.

Vik uncrossed his arms and smirked at his already grinning brother. For four years, they'd done nothing for their special day. The last couple of birthdays, Alistanik would be in a near comatose state on the couch, still smoking sitter hanging between his motionless fingers. The boys would sneak it from him, run outside, and take as many puffs of it as they could between the two of them until their friends showed up. Their father's newer habits would take time to fade, but both boys lit up at the thought of getting their old dad back.

The automatic door buzzed open for them and burning, bittersweet aroma of bloodstones wafted out like a strong breeze. Inside the stone building were several tables and chairs scattered in no sensible order around the room. With it being around midday, most of the people were outside socializing and absorbing their dose of vitamin sunshine. They had no problems finding a place to sit inside. The three of them grabbed their chairs and Alistanik slid a table into the corner for them. He pushed it against the wall and put his chair against the corner, tucking himself against the two walls while his boys crawled up to their seats and sat quietly. The boys rested their arms on the cold table while their fingers drummed and twitched. Their eyes swam around, occasionally checking their father's face before darting off in another direction. Vik noticed some of the Grays in the diner watching them, shaking their heads, crinkling their noses, and whispering to each other without taking their eyes away from his father. The Uppers in the room were easy to spot not only because of their healthier skin, but because of their exact opposite reactions to the small family. A Gray living in his dead sieva's house on the top level with his rambunctious, Upper children and with nefarious connections on the bottom level, too. Alistanik was a blot on the bright Upper levels. Lucky for the three of them, fourth levelers were known for their neutrality.

"Look at all these handsome young men," the young woman cooed, batting her gray eyes and setting a poorly chiseled cup of rainwater down in the middle of the table.

Marek stretched a friendly grin back at her while Vik and Alistanik gave polite, tense nods and forced smiles. The waitress was perfectly average, nothing off about her appearance and nothing special either. Just like most inhabitants of Haven, she seemed to be cut from the same mold as a majority of the other female residents. The differences in every face were so minor, it took a trained eye to pick them out. Most children were of learning age before they could differentiate between two strangers of the same gender let alone recognize them again later. There were exceptions, but their waitress was not one of them. She flicked her long, heavy hair behind her shoulders and asked if there was anything she could get them.

"Could I get some wafers?" asked Alistanik.

"I'm sorry, sunshine."

"How about frond rolls?"

She shook her head.

"...A sitter?"

"No," she smiled even wider, "that man there got our last one."

If Alistanik had not spent as many years on the top level as he did, the waitress would have known he was a Gray just by looking at him. She would've known that he knew the man with the last sitter. You weren't a true Gray if you didn't know the man who could not be crushed, the giant of the fallen, Vojak. Vik and Marek were unaware of anything or anyone important, continuing to swing their feet around as they dangled just above the floor and making faces at each other.

"That's Vojak over there," said the waitress.

"Yeah, I know."

"Oh? You know him?" Her eyes lit up.

She snuck a peek over her shoulder at the Gray man twice Alistanik's age. Another waitress just as ordinarily pretty as the one beside them, her own twin, was swooning over Vojak with obvious desperation. She lit the bloodstone frond cradled between his teeth with a long, thinly rolled frond she had brought out from the kitchen, already lit. Even sitting down, he was obviously a mountain of a man. Bulky, towering, and gruff from head to foot, it should've been no surprise that he survived a fall from the ninth level. No one had ever lived falling more than three levels down. He fell five. In a society where no position is necessary, something like that is enough to push a man into a position of power. Social credibility, impressive feats, these are the currency of Haven.

"No," he said curtly. "Do you have anything besides rainwater?"

"No," she giggled, "But I could get you something else...in the kitchen?"

"Not today," said Alistanik irritably.

"Are you sure? Don't have to be shy here, sunshine."

"Don't call me that," he snapped, both his boys flinching out of their distractions.

"Well then. Enjoy your rainwater. We're almost out of that, too," she said, going from sweet to sour so fast, he thought he'd imagined the conversation up until then. Vik and Marek watched her march off, unaware of their father exhaling until his whole body deflated. Unbeknownst to the three of them, Vojak had noticed Alistanik's outburst, but that was the most he was willing to do about it. Alistanik was an undesirable on either side and in a way, untouchable. Vik picked up the water and swirled it around in the cup until some of it sloshed out, then took a loud sip.

"Dad," Marek started quietly, hunching over the table and whispering, "You're not supposed to act in anger."

Alistanik looked directly at him for the first time in several days. Marek straightened up, blinking and steeling himself before reaching for the water Vik had just set down. His hand quivered until it wrapped around the cold, solid cup. Alistanik was still as stone, watching Marek take his eyes away, focusing on the cup in hopes that the confrontation with his father would pass before it could happen. They all lurched when he slapped the cup out of Marek's hands. It bounced across the floor, spilling rainwater and shocking the all the other diners into silence. Vik jumped out of his chair and grabbed the cup, face flushed and unable to look around the room. His father had just lashed out in what would have been considered a small display of violence. He knew they would all be staring, but that's all they would do. No one hits in Haven. Normally, Alistanik would have been socially punished, but there was nothing more they could think to do to him.

Marek went rigid. The stone cup had smashed against his mouth. He could taste the faint copper of blood on his tongue and pulled his bottom lip inward to hide it from his father.

"Not supposed to act in anger…" he repeated his son through clenched teeth, "They are brainwashing you up here. Don't question why we're here, don't make a scene, don't get angry. How did you feel when your mother died?"

His question stabbed through both boys, digging into Marek's chest and bringing tears to his eyes. He fought them back.

"What is that right there?" Alistanik asked, pointing to his face and speaking a little more calmly, "What made you stop crying, huh? Are you angry with me?"

"Dad, stop," Vik whispered, glancing around.

"Their rules, boys, they're killing us…can't give orange pills to the dead, can't get angry, can't get out. It's being angry that'll fix everything one day. You don't understand," he shook his head and put his hands through his hair. "We've been abandoned, do you understand that?"

"Alright," Vojak said, having crossed the room without them noticing, "I think it's time to take your birthday party to your uncle Harlok, hm?"

"How'd you know about our birthday?" Vik asked quietly.

"Your uncle keeps talking about it," said Vojak, smiling with his cheeks and frowning with the corners of his mouth.

Marek hopped out of his chair without looking at his father, on the brink of tears. He and Vik rushed out of the diner.

"Wait here," Vik said once they were on the other side of the door. He rushed back in and shouted as loud as he could to his father, "I hate you!" before going back to his brother.

Alistanik tilted his chin up and after he was gone, smiled. Vojak didn't see what was so funny.

"What are you doing?"

"I don't have to explain myself to you," he said, glaring at him with his dark, black eyes.

"No, you don't. But if you're going to do what your brother's been saying, then just do it. But don't drag your boys over the rocks like this. You may have wasted your potential, but they still have the chance to be—"

"What? To be what?" Alistanik snorted, leaning closer to the giant man. "What does anything mean in here?"

"One day, they'll come back for us."

"The Thesmekka are gone. As good as dead and they've left us here to die too. We are in a hole in the ground. There is no forward, there isn't even an up. Our only hope is to push these walls down."

"We can't do that," Vojak chuckled lightly.

"Of course not," Alistanik said, looking anything but amused. "Not until we all start to understand."

"Understand what?"

"We've been abandoned."

"You keep saying that, but I don't believe it."

Alistanik finally deflated, waving his hand in the air to dismiss the powerful Gray. Vojak offered to sit with him and share his sitter, but Alistanik refused. The giant man shrugged, gave Alistanik a pat on the shoulder, and went back to his own table, knowing well enough after years of experience that talking someone down from wanting out was nearly impossible.

The boys ran in a great, wide circle, down the ramps toward their uncle's level. Haven was shaped like an upside down funnel, bigger at the bottom, with every level being a stone street winding around the interior walls of their shelter. Ramps united each one and there was a massive drop on every level except the fourteenth one. Fourteen was the bottom level of Haven and proof of how difficult blood was to wash off of stone.

12

Marek's face was flushed and he could feel his ears burning. Even his tears were too warm. After the boys fled far enough away, a row of elderly hecklers on level five attempted to flag them down for a good teasing, but they were on a mission. Lucky for them, the older ones weren't known for their attention spans or their desire to pursue moving targets.

Vik licked a salty teardrop then roughly rubbed his face dry. He was stomping down the levels, staring straight ahead and charging through a game some younger kids were playing in his way. It was midday and the carolers were singing on most levels. They had songs for every single thing they could think of. There was early morning singing, midday singing, evening and midnight singing, but there was also singing when events began, singing when someone died, and singing when someone was born.

Descending the ramp to level six, Vik and Marek felt soothed by the midday songs. Not completely, but the anger was fading. Some teens ran passed with a rock and were carefully tackled from behind before their pursuers hurled the rock down the middle of Haven and laughing, they all took off down the ramp after it to see who could get to the top. Games were played on every level, at all hours, and were often times dangerous. But the inhabitants of Haven had a skewed perception of death and injury. The med-fac could cure anything and everything, if you were alive when you got there. Bloody accidents, broken bones, even broken backs; cured within minutes thanks to the orange pills. The auto-arms in their kitchens even had some spares ready to be doled out, just in case.

Vik pulled his loose sleeves up and stretched his legs out as he walked. His too-big shoes wobbled a little on his feet. Marek did the same although, at least his shoes fit. They started squirming the closer they got to the non-Upper levels. It felt dangerous to be there without their father, though he was never the one to give them that impression. Uppers were always letting their children know how uncivilized Grays were, to keep away from them or they'd be snatched, and how much they hated Uppers for their health and position within Haven. Vik and Marek had been a little more resilient to these rumors since they had family on the bottom level, but they'd never met them.

On level eight, it was darker than they were used to for that time of day. The closer they drew to the edge the brighter it grew, but that was a dangerous practice. The buildings were exactly the same as they were on the higher levels, there were just a few more of them. Although there were more Grays than what was normal at the top, they acted the same as everybody else: walking, talking, smiling, gossiping, adhering to routines, going home to eat. Completely boring. With the feeling of danger greatly lessened, the boys stopped fidgeting and hurried on ahead, eager now to see their uncle. Level nine was just as disappointing, but level ten is where things became more interesting. As dim as late afternoon, they were the only Uppers in sight. Vik stumbled a few times, unable to see the ground as clearly. He noticed things weren't as smooth the further down they went. The building were chiseled rather than polished and the streets had been cratered all around. The info boards were brighter and more distracting than they were up top and it smelled different, less fresh and cool, more cold and muggy. The children still played game down there and they recognized them all. They wore the same clothes, though many of them bunched tunics around their necks and shoulders like a mounded up collar. Vik was starting to think the extra tunics and their paler skin were the only real differences.

At level twelve, the staring became noticeable. Grays of all ages and genders, in the middle of all sorts of activities, all of them stopped to gawk at the boys. They weren't glaring, they weren't even confused, but unease tensed up on every face long enough for the boys to see. Vik wanted to tell them not to feel sorry for him, that they weren't lost or anything.

"You don't think we'll see that one you spit at?" Vik whispered.

Marek shushed him, glancing around as if someone could've heard him. That would've been a good way to get held down by the other kids and stomped on. They'd heard that's what Gray children did to the ones they didn't like.

The decline to level fourteen was by far the worst. No one was going up or down levels, the ramp was completely empty except for them, and everyone currently in the streets had come to a complete, unnatural halt. Fourteen was the only level with a solid middle, a circle rather than a ring and everyone was staring at that solid space. They hovered, waiting for something. When they noticed the boys, many of them gasped, threw their hands over their mouths, or just nodded to themselves as if confirming something they already knew. A thin man stood near the edge of the middle area facing the ramp the boys had just descended, his toes lining up to the light forming a Gate-shaped circle. He was the only one who waited patiently, unwavering even when the boys came into view. A young girl ran across the light straight for them, her twin still clinging to the man's leg after a weak attempt at stopping her.

"Let it happen, girl…your father has seen it," a woman hissed at her, snatching her by the arm as she passed.

14

She jerked herself free and glared at her, "But *they* don't have to see it."

When she went up to Marek and Vik, trying to push them away from the gathering, they resisted.

"What's going on?" Vik demanded, leaning into her shoves.

"We can talk about it inside," she grunted from the effort of trying to move them, "Please, go inside. Please, go. Just go."

Marek conceded, but Vik only pretended until they reached the doorway. As it whirred open, he could feel a lurch in his gut and turned around, running toward the man he could just barely make out behind the light. His shoes slipped and shifted against the grainy street, no traction built into the soles. He stumbled forward, pushing off the ground with one hand, saving himself from falling. Running straight for the thin man, the moment Vik's body crossed into the circle of light a deafening bang jerked him back and an explosion went off between them.

Vik yelled and jumped back, covering his face. He felt something bounce off of his chest and flinched, throwing his arms in front of himself to block anymore of what flew at him. It had hit him hard enough to send him back a couple of steps. When he looked down and saw blood, he didn't know what to think. He patted his bloody overalls, feeling for a wound on his chest. Before he could determine whether the injury was as bad as it looked, he saw what had exploded between them. There, scattered around the circle of light were sprawling heaps of remains, barely distinguishable as human. His chest felt like it went under the weight of the mountain. When reality finally slapped him, he glanced up at the thin man wearing a face like his father's, without the scar on his lip. Scrambling wildly to his feet, he shot through the crowd and back up the ramp. Unable to think or breathe or stop running, he ascended the levels until reaching level five. He collapsed, trembling, in the middle of the street and screamed out as loud as he could. All of Haven heard him and stopped at the raw, gut-wrenching sound. That had been a person. *It could've been anybody*, he lied to himself. They had jumped from up high and dashed themselves into the ground in front of him. He had someone else's blood, bits of this person, all over himself. Vik tried not to think about that, but he vomited anyway. Everything forced its way out and the gasping between heaves felt like the first time he'd actually taken in air since he started running. Vik spit several more times on the street and was surprised no one was yelling at him. He could hear heavy footsteps barreling up and was surprised when Vojak scooped him up without hesitation.

"Where do you live?"

Vik could only point. Vojak marched briskly by the onlookers. Even the elders saved their breath until after they were out of earshot. The Uppers were captivated by the deluge of crimson red so rarely seen that high up.

They were steps away from his house when Vik's mind started doing the most ridiculous thing. It started coming up with all these reactions his father was going to have to all this. He's going to be furious about the overalls, he's going to be angry that they were anywhere near what happened, he's going to be this and that. But between all of those thoughts, his brain was chanting that his father was going to come through that door at any moment.

Vojak set him down inside and led him to the couch. Vik wobbled over to it like he'd never used legs before. He felt the rough ridge of long scars on Vojak's hand, unhealed by the med-fac. Vik's mouth tasted acidic and the more he tried not to touch anything with his tongue, the more aware of the acrid taste he became.

"Was that someone who jumped?" Vik finally managed to ask, his head wobbling on his neck like a person balancing on one foot.

"Yeah," Vojak said, squinting his eyes at him. "You sit there, give me your overalls."

Vik felt like the blood had soaked into his stomach and was surprised to see that his oversized tunic was stain-free. He stared at his own hand resting on the table while Vojak spoke to the kitchen's auto-arm and handed over the ruined garment. He hung his head, cursed under his breath, and went back to Vik.

"I need you to come over here," he said.

Vik senselessly obeyed and they went to the kitchen counter. Vojak lifted him onto the countertop and cleared his throat.

"I'm sorry about this, but it's not right to keep quiet about it." Clearing his throat again and nodding to himself, he lowered his chin and looked Vik in the eyes, "That was your father. You need to be aware of that now and sort yourself out in private here. You don't want people thinking you're weak, you don't want them to take your house from you, 'cause they will. They'll send you off to live with somebody as a reason for taking your house for themselves when we both know you and your brother are old enough to take care of yourselves."

The auto-arm redirected from the blood-stained overalls and proceeded to check Vik for injury, pressing a soft, spongy pad against his back, chest, and arms. Vik felt like someone was trying to shake him awake. Though reality was coming in and out of focus, he wasn't waking up. Vojak was rambling on, but all Vik could see was his mouth bouncing around beneath a shaggy beard. As if he couldn't translate the

16

Gray's words, Vik hopped down from the countertop and started calling for his father. He went into every room and looked in closets and even drawers, but Vojak didn't try to stop him. He waited by the kitchen's auto-arm, leaning on the counter.

"Who was that?" Marek gasped, running back inside the house on the fourteenth level.

The little girl chased after him, waiting for the automatic door to shut behind them. She trembled, her eyes swimming around the room, searching for anything. Her house felt foreign to her, abandoning her to something she wanted to be sheltered from. The auto-arm in the kitchen tapped on the counter, but they both ignored it.

"Who are you?" Marek snapped, focusing on her.

"Tayna, I'm your cousin. Harlok's daughter, you know who Harlok is?"

"Yes," Marek scoffed, "I know my uncle."

"Don't be angry with me," said Tayna, her eyes welling up, "I didn't do anything to you."

"How'd you know? Why was everyone standing around waiting down here? Did someone push him?" Marek started shouting by the end of his questions.

"No, stop yelling at me!" Tayna cried out, "My dad said his brother was going to jump today, he said he knew for sure and that everyone else would know what we could do if it all came true. Then I saw you guys, I didn't know you were going to be here, too. I've seen you before, so I knew who you were," her face flushed.

"That was my father?"

Tayna just held her breath.

"Uncle Harlok knew..." Marek shook his head, "Why didn't he stop him?"

Tayna blinked several times, shocked by the question. She never thought about her father's judgement in all her ten years of life, "I don't know."

The automatic door zipped open. Harlok's lanky figure sauntered into the room, set on a somber mission. He went to the opposite end of the room, as if in a trance, then darted back over to them with his fingers drumming on his lips. Blood stained his overalls from the knees down with a few flecks reaching higher.

"Dad?"

"Everyone was there," Harlok muttered.

"Dad, how many sitters have you had?"

"Today was my brother's big day," he answered.

Marek could feel his face burning beneath his warm tears, "You knew, why didn't you stop him?"

"I couldn't interfere in his happiness, not again. the first time I thought I was doing what was right, this time I have to do what feels wrong. Cause and effect, Tayna, remember this. This, today, was my punishment for stopping at the first veil all those years ago."

"Dad, I don't know what you're talking about," Tayna whimpered.

"This changes everything," Harlok muttered as an aside, then rejoined the conversation, "Not yet, but you'll know. One day, you'll see it. When you've made a mistake you can't come back from, when you've followed the wrong path and someone you love has suffered for it..."

"Come on, Marek," Tayna sniffed and then scowled at her father, "I'll take you home."

"...You'll finally see through to the other side, to the only way to set things right, and it will always come with a high price."

# CHAPTER TWO

When a man dies, maybe he thinks that's all he's doing. But not even dying is that simple. He's creating a ripple in the way things are and should be. Each morning, both young men woke up without their father and they didn't fully understand why. Their mother made sense. She was made of bone and blood, accidents happen. From a young age, death was a concept they'd been familiar with, but the motivation of a man is complicated for someone without the same experiences.

"Where are you going?" asked Vik.

"Out," Marek said, strapping the buckles on the shoulder of his shirt.

"Out of the house or...?"

Marek rolled his eyes, "Out of the house. I'm going to meet Mira on level three and we're going to spend the day with her family."

Marek finished dressing and stood in the doorway, staring back in at Vik. Sprawled across the couch, eyes half open, he was barely aware of his brother at all. Marek clapped his hands together once. The slap echoed with a twang off the metal counters and table, but absorbed into the cold, stone walls. All he got from Vik was a casual blink.

"You need to get up and get out of here."

"I'd love to..." Vik droned.

"No, couch stone, out of the house. Go see the guys, catch up with Ola or something."

"She left me," he said without breaking his daze. "Just a couple of days ago."

"Why didn't you tell me, man?" Marek said, genuinely surprised.

"I dunno," Vik shrugged, "I didn't really care."

"Vik," Marek said pointedly, "You need to get up and do something. I know you're tired of it here, but there isn't a choice and there never will be. You gotta learn to live with what you have. So stop wasting your life like this. Thessa forbid, maybe you'll enjoy yourself."

The automatic front door whirred open and Marek stomped through it, out into the crowded stone street. Vik watched the door clamp shut behind him and scoffed, shaking his head and relaxing even deeper into the couch. He stared into space with more awareness than he'd had all morning doing anything else. A few seconds went by and he slouched even more.

"Great. Now I'm bored with being bored."

Dragging his feet across the floor, he shuffled to the front door and set his forehead against the wall. He thought about going outside, not about walking out of the house, but the real outside. Agrona, the land outside the mountain. The land where the sun could be seen at all hours of the day. No cold walls and rocks under your feet. Vik heard dirt was soft and didn't break your bones when you fell. Food grew if you buried it and everything outside was supposed to be bright, beautiful...new.

The top level choir would be meeting soon, but he quit going to that weeks ago. They would gather in the morning, at midday and just after the sun stopped shining through the Gate, heralding the time to the other residents of Haven as only a group of people with nothing better to do could. Knowing chords and harmonies like they know their own names, the choir warmed up sometimes for hours before they actually needed to sing. The great thing about Haven is that they weren't wasting any of their time. No jobs needed doing that the machines and dispensers didn't already take care of and there was nowhere else they could be, even if they wanted. Vik left the group when he realized they only made his longing for the outside world worse.

Being in the library wasn't any better, but it was the first thing he thought to do outside the house. Trudging through the automatic doorway, Vik entered the stone and metal structure that housed all the knowledge the Thesmekka had rescued before sticking the survivors in a rocky vault for a couple hundred years. Several rows of glossy, metal tables stretched from one end of the room to the other, each with swiveling metal chairs attached at the base in comfortable increments. Aligning with the length of each table in the ceiling overhead ran a groove for the auto-arms to go up and down, delivering data to each reader as they requested it.

Vik flopped down in a chair too hard for throwing himself into. Jarred by his landing, he winced and rubbed his lower back, glancing side to side but no one was looking. Indented in the table was a screen covered in greasy fingerprints. He used the back of his sleeve and wiped it thoroughly before scrolling through the options with flicks of his own finger. After navigating through folders and subfolders, he stopped on, *Agrona: Brutes*, and sneered, choosing one of the options underneath, *Agrona: Fauna*. The auto-arm zipped across the ceiling after having retrieved the data device. It hovered over the table in front of him and

Vik leaned back so it could slip the tiny rectangle into the slot beside the options. The screen changed into a kaleidoscope of colors as it projected a hologram of information related to the fauna of Agrona, the world outside of Haven. Everything was deadly, dangerous or unpleasant. Everything wanted to eat him and he couldn't eat them back, according to the data he'd been reading since he was a child.

After almost an hour of attempted discouragement from all thoughts on leaving Haven, Vik couldn't bring himself to watch or read anymore. He slumped back in his chair enough that the auto-arm knew he was finished. It glided over with a faint buzzing sound, retracted the rectangular data from the slot on the table and dutifully dashed away from him, putting data back and waiting for another task. Vik watched the auto-arm with envy.

Outside on the street, he wound his way around the level heading back home. He could tell Marek he got out of the house without the guilt of lying. Mission complete. It was a beautiful day, at least it looked to be through the peephole above their heads. Plenty of people were out and about but of course they had nothing to do but meet up and amble around together. Gossip and intrigue ran rampant through the idle society and so most of the wandering mass met up to discuss their petty excitements.

"Did you see that Gray come up to the fourth yesterday?" Vik overheard a short man gossiping to his friends in their small group.

"No, but I heard Miksi handled it. Talked him down."

"I can't believe she wasted her time with him. If he's going to come all the way up here, he can at least go back down in a hurry."

His friends chuckled and one of them shook their head, still smiling, "That's stone cold."

This was the first that Vik heard about the event, but he wasn't surprised. The only person he'd talked to in the last couple of days was Marek and he wouldn't have told Vik about something like that happening. He wondered what Miksi said to the man to get him away from the edge. Lies were the only thing that could save someone ready to make the last leap. The higher up they went, the more they meant it.

Miksi was the leader of the Uppers. In her youth, she was the most passionate of the faithful, the ones who believed the Thesmekka were coming back for them. Her encouraging speeches made from the top level were the major contributors to Uppers being so hopeful as a group. She was also half of the reason residents of Haven were so divided as a whole. Harlok was that other half. Even though the physical leader of the Grays was Vojak, Harlok led them spiritually and emotionally. His accurate visions unified the Grays under the banner of fear.

On the way, Vik saw his friends Kalan and Edik along with their quieter brother, Ziven, who usually kept to himself. Ziven wasn't too popular, especially since he was rumored to be pursuing the scrimshander trade, the only actual profession in Haven.

The Haven dwellers had to improvise for luxuries since there was nothing frivolous. When a person died, or jumped, the scrimshander would make their scrimshaw then get permission from the family to take more than what was needed. All their bad deeds would weigh the departed down unless they had an acceptable scrimshaw to reside in and reflect on their lives, letting go of what kept them down. If the scrimshander was able to get more bones, they would make trinkets for themselves or others they favored. There weren't many scrimshanders in Haven as it was hard to find someone willing to pluck the bones from the dead and whittle them into tiny figures and baubles. Aside from the scrimshaws, usually the trinkets a scrimshander made for someone would be distasteful to don casually, even if the bones were made from the loved one of the wearer. A scrimshander was easy to spot by the plethora of skeletal items they would adorn themselves with.

That day, Ziven had been dragged out of his house in much the same way as Vik. He idled against a wall within sight of his brothers, fiddling with an off-white, rough ring around his finger. His two brothers were tossing a bloodstone between themselves, rotted and hard as a rock, occasionally tossing it to Ziven just to keep him on his toes. As Vik drew nearer, he slowed down and leaned back, scrunching up his face. The bloodstone rot had a stench too intense for hanging around too long. He waved to them as he passed by, getting hit in the back with the putrid food just as he worried he might. When he picked it up, he knew he'd have to wash his hands at least ten more times to get rid of the smell. He hurled it back at them and gave them a rude gesture as they laughed.

"Meet up with us later!" Edik shouted to him, "There's a show on the second tonight!"

"Sera's going to be in it!" Kalan added, loud enough that all of Haven heard.

Vik threw his hand over his shoulder and continued to his house.

They were unconcerned with how easy it was to hear everything from most corners of the hollow mountain. Everyone already knew Sera was the most beautiful girl of age, but the least attainable and the most aware of it. Standing out the way she did was only possible through her demeanor, as most everyone looked incredibly similar. All residents were born either twins or triplets with the same black hair and gray eye color,

22

with very similar features. Uppers were closer to the sun, but the paler Grays lived at the bottom. Sera was, of course, an Upper.

Once back inside his home, Vik stood over the counter, plucking a ripe bloodstone out of a metal bowl. Bloodstones, the only food anyone's ever eaten. The auto-arm swiveled around, dispensing a plate and a knife before moving to the far end away from him. This wasn't normal behavior, but the arm knew how Vik was by then. He wanted to do everything himself and even the machine thought Vik was troublesome when bored. It also knew as much as he did that he only snacked when he was restless. Cutting up the bloodstone was one of the few things he could do himself entirely for himself.

Vik hissed and jerked his hand away, setting the knife down as he examined his finger. The auto-arm twitched, but then remembered it knew better than to interfere. The poorly wielded blade had sliced a decent sized gash over the top of his finger. He reached out for the rag hanging nearby, hovering it over his wound. It bled, pouring red out like a faucet. The color, the crimson splash against the gray stone and metal all around, he couldn't take his eyes away. He imagined letting the blood run over the rest of his hand, down his arm until it spread to his chest. Vertigo pulled him toward his own hand.

The auto-arm began swiveling nervously, intentionally revving its normally quiet gears, almost grabbing several objects around it but stopping before it touched any of them.

"Sorry Havard," Vik mumbled, pressing the rag against his wound.

Immediately the auto-arm relaxed and let the end of it tap down onto the countertop. Vik chuckled to himself, watching it deal with its overwhelming anxiety.

"You shouldn't get so worked up, you don't want to short out."

He wiped the knife off and continued cutting up the bloodstone into various shapes and sizes. After managing to poorly recreate the circular top level of houses in Haven on the platter, he decided he was done and would eat them starting with the homes of those he liked the least. As soon as he set the knife down, Havard snatched it up and pushed it into the suctioning chute. Vik could hear it being cleaned and steamed but he was preoccupied with his ridiculous mission.

Vik crunched into a meaty slice as he tried not to think about the one thing he shouldn't think about. He had missed midday and would have to wait until tomorrow to see the sun through the Gate at the top of the mountain. The Gate was a Thesmekkian gift that showed them the outside, let air and rainwater in, but they couldn't reach it. The Thesmekka wanted to keep them safe in the mountain, in Haven. Vik

23

looked out from the doorway of his home. To everyone else they were just the stone streets on the top level of Haven, leading to the drop-off in the center that fell fourteen levels down. To Vik, it was the path his father had taken almost ten years ago, the path he thought about taking every day since. The bloodstone's pungent juices watered his eyes and made every bit of his mouth tingle, distracting him from his legs. They moved on their own, without conscious permission.

"Vik," Marek shouted to him, running up behind him, grabbing his shoulder and growling under his breath, "What are you doing?"

Vik jerked back, looked around and noticed a few people watching him anxiously. They carried about their business when they realized they weren't getting a show.

"I'm just standing here," Vik scoffed, "What did you think?"

He couldn't recall walking all the way out to the ledge, but he wasn't about to let him know that. His brother worried too much as it was. Marek tightened his grip and wouldn't let go of his shoulder.

"Let's just go inside," he said cautiously, "I have some good news."

Vik peeled himself away from the edge and followed Marek back through the front door of their house.

They got inside and Marek bit his lip, looking around the room, "You know what, I can just tell you later."

"It's alright," Vik said, flopping down on the couch, "I'm not upset about Ola. Go ahead and tell me."

Marek snorted, motioning outside with his hand, "Not upset?"

"Fine," Vik threw his head back and closed his eyes, slapping his hand over his heart, "I'm empty inside. My heart, it's done beating forever."

"Shut up."

"Just tell me the damn news already," Vik smirked.

"Alright," Marek puffed up his chest, "Mira is pregnant."

"Are you kidding?"

"She's going to be my sieva in nine months," Marek was grinning from ear to ear.

Vik jumped up and hugged his brother, lifting him off the ground just a bit before putting him back down, "Just think, soon, there's gonna be three copies of you pooping their pants all over the place."

Marek nearly choked, waving his hands around, "Just two, two at a time."

They celebrated with an assortment of treats all concocted over a couple hundred years out of sheer desperation for variety. The bloodstone, an all nutrition-encompassing wonder food, was capable of producing both the yeast and the sugars needed to turn itself into alcohol. The fronds were cut off, peeled, diced and rolled into a sitter, smoked for relaxation. And, through accidental neglect with a batch of fermenting bloodstones, a sort of vinegar was discovered only four years before the boys were born and thus pickling came to be. Pickles were all the rage in Haven. The feast laid out before them was one few would be proud of, but the residents of Haven were thankful for small gifts.

Two months went by after Marek's announcement, but nothing changed for Vik. Marek spent less time at their house and in seven more months, would be spending almost no time there at all. A siv always moved in with the sieva, unless there was an overwhelming reason not to.

Tossing the kitchen knife up and down in his hand to the serenade of Havard's unsettled gears, Vik lay on the couch on his back with his feet over the top and his head resting on the short table. His neck acted as a bridge between both pieces of furniture. He'd had a flying dream last night. No wings, just flying like the Thesmekka. So much of the dream had been spent flying around Haven, showing off what he could do, but when he finally launched himself up to the Gate he woke up the moment he crossed into the bright light.

The front door whirred up and Vik flinched, throwing the knife wrong. It bounced off the table beside his head and skittered across the floor.

"Don't do that," Tayna muttered, motioning toward the knife.

"Don't barge in here like it's your house," Vik wheezed, sitting up and squinting from the head rush.

"I do what I want," she teased, "I have something exciting to tell you."

"The Thesmekka are back?" asked Vik, reaching for the knife as Tayna sat beside him on the couch.

"Yeah, they're right outside, asking for you by name."

"Marek would be so jealous."

"Speaking of Marek, you're going to have to control yourself when you hear this. Don't run right out there and tell him you're going to join the Grays."

"Why in Thessa's name would I do that?"

"Because, they're coming up here today, in force."

"What?" Vik's heart sank.

"Not like that. Despite what you're told every single day, we're not violent people, Vik. We're coming up here with slabs of stone, bone chisels…"

"Bone?"

"Yeah, it's gross. But we've got to do what we can. We're going to dig as far into the walls as we can and stick the slabs in going up," Vik's blank expression prompted further explanation, "We're going to do this until we get up to the Gate."

"What?" Vik was caught between shock and tempered excitement. "The Grays are wanting to make a stairway…to the Gate?"

"Yes," Tayna said, beaming from ear to ear.

Vik couldn't breathe. He blinked about a hundred times, but his eyes still watered. Tayna waited impatiently for him to say something, but he just kept shaking his head.

"They'll never let you do this."

"Why not? How are they going to stop us?" Tayna scoffed.

"They'll do whatever they can."

"And all they can do is talk. All they can do is try to make us feel bad about it, but we can't be shamed into dying at the bottom of this hole. They're terrified of any kind of violence and even if they weren't, there are so many more of us. We could defend ourselves," Vik shuddered at the thought of a war erupting between the two halves, "Besides, they want us gone. As soon as they get over the initial shock of it, they'll realize that once we're gone, this is a great way to get rid of undesirables."

"Are they really coming up today?"

"Yes," Tayna smiled again.

"When?"

Jogging out the door, Vik peered over the edge and saw a hoard of Grays rounding the tenth level, still mostly obscured in darkness. Many other Uppers had taken notice and were watching them in the same way. Except Vik felt like in that moment, he could fly.

Harlok led the march and Vik's stomach sank just a little, but he wasn't caught off guard by it. What he was surprised by was the condition of his uncle. Vik hadn't seen him since that day ten years ago, but at the time he had looked like his father. When he saw Harlok marching ahead of the ambitious mass, he looked shriveled, stretched too tall, sickly. On the third level, Vik saw the broad-shouldered Vojak speaking with gentle hand gestures to Miksi. As the Grays passed them, the two leaders stopped speaking, moved aside, and watched quietly as the hoard trooped on without a word. Spread over the Grays, groups of three people held large stone slabs over their heads, the weight shared between themselves. They were like an army of ants winding up the inside of the mound.

"My boys are going outside one day," Tayna whispered.

"What makes them so sure of this?" asked Vik quietly, despite the rising noise around them.

"Fifty years, Vik. Did you know today is the fiftieth anniversary of the day they didn't show up?"

"I forgot that was today."

"Dispensers have been shutting down recently on the lower levels. I bet they haven't been talking about that up here though."

"No, I didn't hear about that."

"How long until the Gate shuts down next?"

"Don't say that," Vik gasped, shaking his head, "Besides, it's just a hole, it can't shut down."

"A hole made out of Thesmekkian metal. Are you sure about that? Have you ever wondered why it's so quiet out there?"

"You think we can't hear outside because it's a portal...?"

"It's just a thought," Tayna groaned and rolled her eyes at Vik, "Dad's giving a speech now."

The Grays who carried the giant slabs of rock dropped them near where the staircase would begin and returned to the gathered mass. Harlok wasted no time getting into it. He held up his boney, shivering arms and projected his voice as far as he could. It boomed out, not seeming possible from a body like his. The crowd stilled. Both Grays and Uppers settled their unrest to listen to what he had to say, even if one group was more eager than the other.

"The Thesmekka are gone."

His words echoed off the walls, resonating over the silent residents. Only when their momentum was gone did murmuring break out over Haven.

"We can argue over whether they'll return one day, we can argue over what's caused their absence, and we can even argue over whether or not they're still out there at all. But in the end, it's our survival that's the real question."

His speech continued on those tracks for several minutes. By the end of it, he was completely winded. Two of his devout followers helped him through the crowd and over to the pile of stone slabs as he waved Vojak over. The giant man gave Miksi a pat on the shoulder and strode over to Harlok, taking the chisel in his hand.

"This is from the arm of my brother," Harlok called out, "His name was Alistanik and he would've wanted this more than any of us."

Vojak held the shaped bone high over his head, showing the crowd his intentions before turning himself toward the wall and at chest height, chipping off the first pebble of stone from Haven's wall. The Grays erupted into cheering and briefly chanted, "for the fallen", much to the surprise of every Upper around them. Vik was quiet, but ever fiber of him cheered along with them until he saw Marek across the gap, in front of Mira's house. He was watching Vik the whole time. They knew this wasn't going to be easy for their relationship, both knowing exactly what the other was going to do.

Even though Harlok mentioned his brother, a man known to have lived on the top level, Alistanik's name did nothing to persuade the Uppers to join their efforts. Despite causing a rift between Harlok's nephews, Vik was one of the first volunteers from the top level. He worked side by side with the Grays for months, standing on slabs jutting out from staggering heights, higher than any Upper has ever been, while he chiseled into the next step. It felt incredible to be working on something for once in their lives. Vik would wake up when it was still dark and pick up where he left off. He was often the first one to start working in the morning. He devoted every day entirely to the stairway. His hands were calloused and every muscle in his body was in shock, but he hardly noticed these things until he went back to his house and tried to lie down in his bed.

Marek left a plate of bloodstone slices on his bed once he picked up on his routine. Even though he was spending more and more time with Mira, he felt like Vik had become a more frequent part of his life than he was before. Every day, he'd see him above the top level, but he knew Vik was too focused to notice anything around him. He knew Vik was too fixated to eat or give his body the rest it needed. Marek worried that by the time they reached the top, Vik wouldn't have the strength to carry on with it. Part of him wished he'd lose the ability to climb the stairs, but he knew Vik would never survive being trapped in Haven after everything he'd done.

"Are you thinking about Vik again?" Mira asked, her arm looped around his as they strolled across the top level.

"I'm sorry," he smiled, patting her arm with his hand.

"Don't be."

"I know how it makes your family feel, what he's doing, what side he's on…"

"I might not agree with what he's doing, but I don't think this is as much about sides as my family makes it out to be. There are a lot of Uppers who only wish the Thesmekka would return so that life here will change, so that something'll happen."

"…Are you one of those Uppers?"

Mira smiled and leaned her head on his shoulder, waiting almost too long to answer, "I've got you, sunshine. And there's a lot of change coming for us soon."

Marek squeezed her hand and glanced up at Vik one more time before they reached her parent's house, pausing in front of the automatic door as it gently whirred open.


Once the builders got to the last stair, the longest slab with the least amount of rock to chisel into, that's when things became less straightforward. The plank-like slab could only support one person at a time and that person needed to be very careful at the end. A rope had been crafted from tightly braided fronds and hair with a multi-pronged hook at the end fashioned from bones and a welded, warped piece of metal from some Gray's table. Vik couldn't remember his name, but he proudly explained how he made it, using the kitchen auto-arm's heating function over days and days until it finally started to bend. He'd been working on it almost as long as they were building the stairway.

It took several tries to toss it up through the Gate before it finally caught on something outside. Excitement rippled through the builders and onlookers alike as they went about choosing who would get out first. The one chosen to attempt climbing out slipped and tugged too hard on the rope, dislodging the hooks. He fell a greater distance than anyone had ever fallen in Haven, jumpers included. His scream rang out for so long, Vik had time to go through several impossible ways to try and save him before he crashed into the stone below. Vik had never felt too sorry for jumpers. He always thought, "they're the lucky ones" and "at least they got out". But that guy was at the cusp of real freedom. In all his construction over all those months, Vik had never been afraid of how high up they were until that moment.

The next to try a couple of days later was his cousin, Tayna. She was a short, thin young woman of about twenty years and had left her father in charge of her three year old twins. Tayna's siv was long dead and Harlok had voluntarily agreed to care for his grandchildren in her absence. They had tied knots in the rope and she was able to make it up with only minor difficulty. Once above the Gate, they could see her calling down to them but her voice was muted as if there were a barrier between them. Vik knew she'd been right and there was a real danger of being trapped there forever.

More people attempted the rope climb with a fairly high success rate until there were days where the stairway sat unused. Vik found himself watching the Gate again. He hated himself for the way his palms sweat and his gut lurched when he thought of that rope. It was the difference between jumping and falling that scared him. With an exit to Haven within reach, the hole in the middle of every level turned from a temptation to something darker. It looked deeper and everything seemed to slant into it.

After several days of internal pep-talking, Vik found some of his courage and journeyed up to the topmost step. He sat perfectly still on the outside, leaning his back against the mountain wall and staring with his eyes tilted up at the Gate. It was not a hole in the top of the mountain but a metallic portal that hung by strange, latched hooks. It took several more days after that discovery, but he managed to partially recreate the grappling hook he'd heard all about from its original maker. Havard acted like he understood exactly what Vik's intentions were when he came to him with the gathered materials, but the auto-arm usually understood both boys fairly well.

During the early morning, when the sun was barely leaking in through the Gate, Vik climbed the stairway with his new tool and made it to the highest step. He inched his way forward, holding one arm out to the side while he reached up toward the Gate. The Thesmekkian metal was sleek and a grayish purple underneath, curving smoothly into a perfect circle. Vik swung the twine underhanded and gripped the end as tightly as he could, wrapping it around his fingers to counter his slippery palms. After several minutes of having it ping off the latch, the bent hook found a place to lodge itself within the latching device. Vik tugged on it, but it didn't even budge.

In a moment of discouragement, he thought surely Thesmekkian devices were too well made to pull apart by poking and pulling at it. He glanced down at Haven beneath him and turned ghostly white. The twine slipped in his hands and his heart raced, but dread was what filled him up like a toxin. It went into every inch of his body. He couldn't stay in Haven, he couldn't stay down there in that safe, gray cave. Putting both hands on the rope, he leaned himself forward and then jerked back as hard as he could. He did this over and over again until he felt someone tap him on the shoulder.

"Can I help?" the man asked, "I'm Savan."

"We've met," Vik grunted, still pulling on the rope.

"I wasn't sure you'd remember me," Savan chuckled, "Here, give it some slack and I'll pull on the end."

Even with the two of them, nothing was budging. It wasn't until a couple of Grays joined the two Uppers that they were able to pop the latch free. They all exhaled loudly and smiled warily among themselves before Vik wound up to try for another. It took just as many attempts

30

the second time and he had to convince the Grays and even Savan to let him keep trying.

With a creaking clack, the next latch detached, then another. They had freed a segment of the Gate and with only two more to go. He stepped out to the very end of the platform and extended the line as far out as it could go, just barely reaching the latch to the left of the one he'd just detached. It was just as difficult as the first one and Vik almost lost his footing. He tried not to think about tumbling over the edge and falling to his death, but it became harder to swallow, his fingertips went numb, and he was suddenly all too aware of what he was standing on.

The latch to the right of the first one was all that was left on that side that he could get to with the man-and-a-half length rope. With one final tug, they pulled it loose and the whole Gate groaned. People down below had started coming out of their homes to see what Vik was up to at the top of the stairway. A few chunks of rock rattled loose and fell from the top of the mountain, but still no light shined through the solid wall itself. The walls of Haven were too thick to dig out of and grew much harder than any tool could handle the deeper in they went. After a small fuss, the Gate stopped creaking and settled for hanging just a little off its center. That was enough for him. They could build a couple more steps and just jump from the long step to the Gate. More than just those who were the smallest and quickest could now get out. People like Vojak would be able to escape after Vik's adjustment.

It didn't take long for the builders to extend the steps to the Gate, but with each person who successfully leapt from the stone slab platform the Gate groaned and creaked. Vik took a week to try and convince Marek to leave with Mira before it was too late. Marek was one of the faithful, one of the ones who still believed in the Thesmekka looking out for them and protecting them. He wasn't going to cave in easily. Promising to come back and see him when the babies were due, Vik left for the Gate, taking almost nothing with him except his father's scrimshaw and a pack of sitters.

Agrona could be seen above and below the off-kilter Gate, the sun shining in both directions through the metal ring. Vik made the leap onto the newly revealed topside of the portal. While he was halfway through he felt himself being pulled both back into Haven and up into the outside as others helped him and Haven did its best to pull at him from the waist down. Once on his feet, he planted them on the top of the black mountain, away from the Thesmekkian metal ring, and had to shield his eyes. The warmth was a smell out there, pleasant and earthy, feeling like each new breath allowed him to expel a life's worth of cold air from his body. His eyes stung, but they were hungry too. He let them squint out over the horizon. Every flavor of green was laid out before him, stretching out to the feet of another black mountain in the distance with a thin strand of smoke rising from its summit. The bright blue of the sky was whipped with white swirls and the wind carried so much with it, his senses overloaded and he sneezed until his head buzzed.

"You'll get used to it."

Savan was one of the people able to leave Haven after Vik tilted the Gate. He never wore shoes, his tunic was too tight and his overalls too loose, and he never took his necklace off. It was made of braided fronds tied to a tiny, detailed scrimshaw. The design of it meant something to him, but it was nothing Vik could recognize.

Savan put his hand on Vik's shoulder, urging them to get off the black rocks and out of the heat. Vik shook himself from his stupor, wiped his eyes and pinched the bridge of his nose, following Savan down the mountainside. They trekked into the fledgling settlement springing up from the nothing in the clearing. There was so much work to be done and for once, Vik was surrounded by likeminded people wanting only to make things happen, create their own lives, get their hands dirty. But before he eagerly joined them, he paused and imagined Marek standing there with him.

"Look there," Savan said, patting Vik on the shoulder and pointing down the mountain at the rest of the people.

"What am I looking at?" Vik said through his nose, feeling another sneeze coming on.

"Water pools up around there after the rain, so that's where we drink from," he said, making a circular motion with his finger, "and that's where we're building our shelters."

"What's that thing?" asked Vik, squinting down the mountainside.

"One of the shelters. You'll see it better when we get down there."

The occasional slip and stumble aside, traipsing down the graveled outside of Haven proved to be far easier than climbing up the inside. The only real difficulty was the oppressive heat. Halfway down, Vik and Savan were drenched in sweat and struggling to take deep breaths. Once they reached the bottom and wiped the moisture from their brows, Savan started excitedly telling him about what they'd found, what'd they'd made, and various other unimpressive facts. While he spoke, a swishing, rustling sound drowned out his voice. All around them was a wall of trees, each almost as tall as the black mountain itself. Many trunks were so wide that it took almost twenty steps to walk passed each one. The way they twisted, warping every which way, gave it an even

32

more sprawling feel, as though the bark got lost wandering across its own vast surface. Vik's entire house could've easily fit inside any one of them.

The arborous behemoths didn't reveal their greener sides until Vik looked toward the sky, where they floated alongside the clouds. Straight and narrow trees shot up from all around the towering giants, some of them leaking into the rocky clearing in tight clusters. These skinnier trees had no leaves and some even curled back into the ground, leaving both top and bottom buried with the middle arching up. The forest itself was dark, even with the sun shining overhead. The breeze swept by and lifted away most of the heat. Never had Vik felt so grateful to something he couldn't see.

"Has anyone gone through the trees?" Vik asked, peering into the woods as hard as he could.

"No. There are sounds that," Savan started to fiddle with his necklace, "I don't know. It just doesn't seem like a good idea."

"Sounds?"

"Yeah, you'll know it when you hear it," Savan seemed like he'd rather not think about it anymore, which only made Vik more curious.

"So, what needs doing out here?" Vik rubbed his hands together, smirking at Savan.

"Anything you can think of, but there is a real big need for rope. They've got all the stuff you need piled up over there, if you want to start braiding."

"What about farming?"

"Farming? I don't know, uh, we don't really need to farm..."

"What if something happens to our food dispensers?" Vik said, walking quickly over to the full bag of bloodstones slumped beside one of the sad lean-tos. "What if something happens to the Gate?"

A few of the Grays snapped up from what they were doing, their creased brows and shocked glares disapproving of the thought and the one who said it. Most of them shook their heads and mumbled irritably as they went back to their tasks.

Vik shrugged, "Why shouldn't we be prepared?"

"If you want to do that, then that's probably fine. If you know how to farm. What do you have to do?"

"You bury the bloodstones and they grow out of the ground," Vik said, glancing at the rocky dirt under their feet.

"Uh," Savan gently tugged at his necklace, "Are you sure?"

"I read it in the library," Vik stated confidently.

Savan wasn't convinced, but gave Vik a pat on the back and encouraged him to give it a try. Unfazed by the obvious differences in the trees and other things he'd read about in the library, he started digging into the rocky soil with his bare hands. It only took a few painful jabs for him to decide on a more intellectual approach. He sauntered by a large group of Grays toiling away, sawing at sticks with blunt rocks and wrapping woven vines around them to keep them together. They enjoyed the work, proudly sporting the blisters on their hands with light-hearted complaints, but there was one major problem. Nothing was really getting done. It took entirely too long to accomplish even the simplest task, but they were unaware of their unproductive pace, blinded by the euphoria of their new freedom.

Vik picked out a good sized rock jutting out from the dirt. Black and grainy with a wedged side, it would be the perfect tool for digging. Better than his hands, at least. Vik went back to where he had been digging, feeling the rocks on his heels through the thin soles of his shoes. A single bead of sweat rolled down the bridge of his nose until it settled on his cheek. It felt like someone had sprayed a mist of water in his face, but it was the heat that distracted him most. As he rammed the rock into the dirt, hitting stones with every blow, his skin felt like it was burning from underneath. Especially his face, which had already burnt to a dark pink.

The hole was barely deep enough to fit a full-sized bloodstone when his lower back gave a creak. This work was far more difficult than he imagined it would be. He glanced to the mountaintop and gave a sigh.

"If it's like this, Marek's never going to leave," he mumbled under his breath.

Looking over the lean-tos, the laboring Grays, and the few, meandering Uppers, Vik set his jaw and raised the jagged rock higher. He was going to make things better out there. They hadn't made much in the short time they'd been out there, but after about two hundred years of nothing new, every little thing counted. Vik glanced around and noticed that no one else was or had been doing what he was doing. No one else had tried to plant anything, he was the first one since they were put in the mountain. With renewed vigor, Vik dug a hole deep enough to bury his arm up to the elbow and stuck a bloodstone in, burying it right after. He gave the dirt a few good slaps then took a step to the side and started over again. With each new hole he dug, reality set in more and more. He was outside. He had a purpose. He was finally free.

# CHAPTER THREE

The flimsy lean-tos and sagging tents at the base of the mountain could barely be called an encampment. People were clumped together in groups working on bizarre projects with twigs, mud, and giant leaves. Vines spread out from the forest like veins, weaving in and out of the rocky soil. They were thick and ambitious, some reaching all the way through the clearing to the mountain's base. There were two semi-structures already set up, but a good shove would've put an end to their existences. No one knew how to build. No one had ever had anything to build with or any reason to learn. Vik would never have known the library had information on it if it weren't for Vojak and Miksi coming out of Haven that morning.

Vojak helped the forty year old Upper out of the Gate. They both stood at the top of the mountain for so long the gossiping came and went before they descended into the tiny settlement. Savan, one of the nine Uppers out there, was one of the first to greet them. Tayna, one of the thirty-three Grays, was the only one to put down her project and greet Vojak. Like they'd been storing up a life's worth of efficiency, the two unofficial leaders got to work finding out what there was to it, living out in Agrona. Tayna told Vojak what they'd accomplished so far without adding in any silver linings while Savan told Miksi what they were planning to do from there.

"Sounds like we've done a whole lot of nothing," Vojak grunted.

"…And we're not planning to do much to fix that," grumbled Miksi.

Tayna crossed her arms and looked around the encampment and Savan struggled through explanations, all of which implied they were learning and trying.

The sun rose from the other side of the mountain and was never directly visible until just before midday, but that was a familiar thing to them out there. They were used to it. The way it lingered directly over them for hours after that proved to be the real problem. As they listened to Savan and Tayna, shaking their heads at the creations around them, a disturbing sight caught their attention.

"What's wrong with them?" Miksi asked.

She pointed to a small group of people sleeping under one of the shabby shelters. They were all red and raw. One of them not yet asleep flinched away from the sunlight. Everyone was burnt to some degree, but those sleeping under the shade were unable to bear the pain.

"Oh, they're working during the darker part of the day right now," Savan hurriedly explained, "Their skin burns in the sun."

"Are they all Grays?" Vojak asked, knowing the answer.

"Not anymore," said Tayna.

"We should get those people back inside if we can," said Vojak, "or the sun's just going to keep making them sick."

"Go back inside?" Tayna asked, her eyebrows raised.

"Have long have you all been out here? A couple of weeks...and this is all we've got?" Miksi said, "This was idiotic. The most foolish thing any of us has ever come up with doing, building a stairway to come out here and burn in the dirt. A lot of good it did us, spitting in the faces of the Thesmekka."

Vik threw down his digging rock and tucked his father's scrimshaw necklace down the front of his shirt, "Why did you come out here, Vojak?"

"Good to see you again, Vik," Vojak chuckled, but it didn't break Vik's stride.

"I know why *you* did," he motioned to Miksi, "Can't wait to lecture us on our faithlessness?"

"Maybe I should," Miksi snapped.

"The Thesmekka abandoned us," said Vik, overly deliberate with every word.

"You don't know that," said Miksi defensively.

"You think we spit in the faces of the Thesmekka, coming out here? I hope we did. Living in there wasn't living. If I died out here right now, this last day of my life will have meant more to me than the last twenty-two years combined."

Several onlookers listened with smiles on their fried, worn faces. If he'd been a Gray, they might've cheered him on.

"You've been out here a day?" Vojak chuckled, "We better put you to good use then, before you start looking like the rest of them."

"What?" Vik was still shaking from his surge of energy.

"If you're ready to do what it takes, we're ready to get things done," Vojak said, "We spent the last week trying to figure through the complaints we've heard from some of the bloodstone runners."

Savan was the only regular bloodstone runner. The second person to go with him was always different, but so far always an Upper. Vik glanced at Savan and smirked at his slack-jawed, wide-eyed reaction to the fact that bloodstone runners were complaining. Savan was the only one who wouldn't complain about Agrona. Not to anyone. Even when he had to hike the black mountain every three days and crawl through the Gate of Haven to bring back bags full of bloodstones, each runner carrying one bag equivalent to half their own body weight, he did so without a negative word.

"You, you, and you…" Vojak said, lazily pointing at Vik, Savan, and Tayna, "…are going to be each project's, uh, what'll we call it, organizer."

"Leader sounds better," said Miksi.

"Alright, uh, how about team leaders? Thessa above…" Vojak wiped his bushy brow and glanced up at the sky, "You could melt rocks out here."

"Team leaders it is then," Miksi said, struggling with the heat as well.

Vojak proceeded to divide up the Grays among the three "team leaders" while Miksi had the overly simple task of splitting up the seven remaining Uppers. All but one of them were men and all but one of them went to Tayna, who was to preside over the most arduous projects. Despite the Upper's collective desire for less laborious tasks, they were the healthiest and the least damaged by sun exposure. Miksi was surprisingly unbiased in her placement of the other seven Uppers, unless her goal had been to make them the most valued workers in the clearing. Vik and the other newer arrivals were to gather resources from the clearing while Savan's group worked between bloodstone runs on more detailed projects like replacement shoes and clothing from those supplies.

Two twelve year old sisters sat hunched over the graveled dirt, idly picking out pebbles and playfully tossing the big ones at each other. Miksi took the two children aside, both Grays, and gave them an important task. They were to take a couple of sticks, wedge them into the ground, then find a long leaf to stretch between the two. This would form a simple shield from the sun over any stationary worker. Too many of them succumbed to the heat and sunburns every day. The twins leapt up from the ground and darted for the pile of sticks, digging through them for the perfect ones. Most leaves were easily as tall and wide as a twelve year old child and fell everywhere around the clearing.

With Tayna taking the helm of labor, Savan of bloodstone running and crafting, and Vik's team gathering, things started changing fast around the encampment. Vojak and Miksi had their unsteady alliance, but it didn't seem to trickle down to the people at all. As more Grays and Uppers came out of Haven every day, the tensions between the two groups just got worse, work slowed down, and two sides started forming in the clearing. The Grays refused to acknowledge Miksi and the Uppers politely ignored Vojak, each group going to their own leaders for everything they needed and every question they had. A week after Miksi had left Haven, the number of Uppers had reached almost as many as the Grays. Those who had been outside almost a month were constantly being confused for their opposite association by the ones who had more recently left the mountain. The resulting abrasive corrections did nothing to improve relations between the two groups.

Neither Vojak nor Miksi did anything to ease these tensions. They were focused on reaching their own personal goals, which upon completion would allow them to return to Haven. It didn't take long for Vik and Tayna to notice this lackluster motivation from their unofficial leaders. Savan always thought the absolute best of everyone and attributed their attitudes to disorientation in Agrona. Even when the first signs of violence trickled across the clearing the morning after a night of heavy rain.

"This wall brought the whole thing down on your heads. Next time, don't take so long to reinforce it," Vojak barked at a group of Grays, wiping his brow with the back of his arm.

"We weren't the ones who built it like that," one of the Grays shouted back at him.

"If the Uppers were building our homes like they built theirs, this wouldn't have happened," another Gray yelled, pointing to a group of Uppers.

"Build your own then!" An Upper with mud covering most of his body called out when he heard them talking about their work.

The other Uppers chimed in with similar shouts while the Grays continued to accuse them of discriminating until the gap between the two groups was only a few steps wide. Tayna threw herself between them, but the argument had grown too heated for her small presence to diffuse anything. She glanced to Vojak in a silent plea for help as she pushed against one of the most furious members of her team. All he did was cross his arms and watch the verbal battle play out from a distance.

"We should break them up," said Vik with a sitter bouncing between his lips, trotting up beside Vojak.

"Why? Let them get it out."

"What if they start a fight? Tayna's right in the middle."

"Is the heat getting to you? No violence is tolerated in Haven."

"We're not in Haven," said Vik.

"Go tell them that," Vojak chuckled.

As the two groups drew close enough to point their fingers in each other's faces, Tayna shouted as loud as she could over their own voices, but all of them were drowned out by a cry from the forest. Everyone turned to look at the wall of trees, everyone looking in different directions. The sound seemed to come out from behind every tree. The call only stuttered long enough to stun them before bursting into a full fledged screech, sending everyone to their knees with their hands clapped over their ears. Vik shouted silence, dropping to the ground along with his sitter. Grays and Uppers scrambled to the farthest point from the woods until they were all crammed together in the middle. Vik's eyes frantically searched every open space between the enormous, rugged trunks. The screeches multiplied, erupting from near and far but nothing emerged.

It wasn't until the nearer shrieks died down that a group of five creatures trotted to a concerned stop just outside the tree line. They were four-legged beasts about as tall as a man with long, thin tails covered in darker, wispy fur. The rest of their bodies sported a short, shaggy teal coat which ranged from darker to lighter shades between the five of them. Switching rapidly between panting through their long muzzles and sniffling with their mouths clamped shut through their wide nostrils, they paced on spindly legs as they examined the new state of the clearing. Deeming the encampment too crowded, they skittered off back into the forest without so much as a yip.

"Did you see that?" said Vik, brows raised and a stunned grin across his face.

"What was that noise?" Vojak groaned, hesitating to take his hands away from his ears.

"I can't believe that, what were they? I bet there's more of them out there…"

"Are you deaf?" Vojak bellowed, "Why would you want to go in there with whatever made all that noise?"

"I don't know," Vik shrugged, still smiling in a daze, "It's like we're just at the door to Agrona."

"Well get it out of your head," Vojak grumbled, "If you know what's good for you, don't go in the forest. We need you here, alive."

"Yeah, sure."

"I mean it."

"I know, yeah, I won't. I got it," said Vik, doing a quick head shake, appearing to snap out of it.

The act was good enough for Vojak. As soon as he was distracted by other things, Vik started walking toward the trees. He had seen plenty of images in the library of animals, from birds to bugs, but he'd never seen anything like that. He thought of Marek and felt renewed once again. If things like that came out of the woods, there's no doubt he would be impressed with Agrona. He just needed to work on keeping him out there once he was there. The settlement was budding, which was more than he could say for it a week ago, but it would still fall short of convincing his brother to stay.

As Vik stared out into the woods, his eyes skimming through the dim foliage in the hopes of another sighting, he locked onto a strange couple of trees jutting out in the distance. Squinting, Vik took a step forward, leaning his head sideways to try for a better angle at whatever it was. The two trees were only as tall as a person; both skinny but one only a fraction the width of the other and attached in the middle by what looked like an arm. Peering even harder, he realized he was looking at another pair of eyes staring straight back at him. Both trees twitched and spun around, disappearing deep into the woods in a flash.

The air shot out of Vik's lungs, but no sound went with it. He glanced side to side, but no one else was looking at the forest. In fact, most of them were actively avoiding even a glimpse in its direction after the echoing screeches shook them to the core. Vik broke into a sprint, stumbling to a halt when Vojak bellowed his name.

"I told you not go out there!"

"I saw someone," Vik called out, still feverishly scanning the woods.

Balanced on his toes, Vik was ready to bolt toward the trees to catch the figure he'd just seen. Vojak marched up to him, passed the startled gasps and muffled gossiping. He grabbed Vik's shoulder and spun him around, pointing his large finger in his face like he were a child to be reprimanded.

"We cannot risk going out there."

"That's what we said about Agrona," said Vik.

"Yeah, and what have we got so far? A sense of accomplishment. That's great. What about the dangers?"

"What dangers?" Vik chuckled, looking around, "There are loud noises and it's hot."

"Where are the Thesmekka, Vik? What happened out here? You think they went through the trouble of saving us from the Brutes, building us a sanctuary like Haven, then just got bored and left us? No, something happened to them and that *loud sound* we all heard out there, the sound that none of us know anything about, that could be one of the things that got them. You don't know, but you just want to walk out there before we have any means of defending ourselves from whatever might follow or chase you out? You are not a child anymore. Stop talking like one."

"And you're not my father. You don't get to tell me where I can't go and what I should do. I'm not scared of noises and I'm not ever going back to die in that giant hole."

"You're right, I don't care what you do," Vojak threw up his hands and turned to everyone else, "I don't care what any of you do. I'm going back to die in that giant hole and I invite anyone who'd rather die in there to come with me."

Vojak marched away from Vik, grinding the rocks under his mud-covered, Haven-made shoes. His footsteps grew crunchier as he neared the black mountain slope. Vik's muscles went rigid, holding him in place so he wouldn't catch up and drag Vojak back. The entire clearing watched him climb and remained silent as a few of the ones who'd been outside the longest dropped what they were doing and went home. From the top of the mountain, Vojak looked down and saw Haven. People under him were bustling around, laughing and talking. Out in front of him, across the vast green expanse, a mountain just like his sat with a trickle of smoke rising from the top, almost invisible to their eyes. But he'd seen it. He didn't talk about it, but there it was, calling out with a question he didn't want answered. His pulse quickened, but he clenched his teeth and stepped onto the Thesmekkian metal ring.

Vik struggled against himself. He couldn't think of what to do next, he couldn't figure out how to get Vojak back down from the mountaintop. As the giant Gray disappeared along with the few others following him, Tayna appeared beside Vik and put her hand on his arm.

"You can't go into the forest," she straightened when he glared down at her, his mouth falling open, "If something happens to you, if we find out the forest is really as dangerous as Vojak thinks it is, how many more do you think will follow him back to Haven?"

Vik gently pulled his arm away and wandered off to a pile of leaves freshly fallen from the night before. He ripped them up off the ground, folding them roughly under his arm, jaw clenched tight. After dropping them off in their appropriate pile, he repeated the task with various other supplies until there was nothing left to gather for the day. Most of the vines that wove into the clearing had been stripped up by then. Scooping up multiple handfuls of water from the rocky basins, he tried not to think about how his stomach would turn in a few minutes. He tried not to think about how far they were from actually living outside.

Tayna didn't talk to him again until the next day when she saw him digging in the dirt with a wedged rock. He didn't have to go deep before he found what he was looking for.

"What're you doing?" she asked.

"It didn't grow," Vik said, slumping to the ground and staring at the solid bloodstone in his hands. Tayna took it from him.

"It's softer," she said, offering a smile. "I don't think it's supposed to grow in a week."

"It's been two weeks."

"Still," she wavered, "I bet it takes longer..."

"Stop it," Vik said, waving his hand lazily in front of him, "You don't need to coddle me."

"I'll just watch you mope then," she scoffed, dropping the bloodstone in front of him, "I came over to ask you something about yesterday, anyway."

"Ask me then," he said irritably.

"Did you really see someone out there?"

Vik glanced up at her, squinting against the sunlight overhead, "I thought I did."

"I think you did, too." Vik jumped to his feet but she shushed him, "I had...a vision."

"What?" his tone dropped, excitement slumping off his shoulders.

"I saw people, other people. They were red and tan and there were a hundred homes spread out at the base of the mountain. I think I saw our future here. That person..."

"A vision," Vik interrupted. "Are you serious?"

"Yes," Tayna crossed her arms, "What's the matter?"

"The pebble doesn't fall far from the wall, does it...?"

"You would know," she said, scowling at him.

They parted ways and didn't speak again until the following morning.

After that day, Tayna became the go-to for the Grays. Despite all her help, they still refused to initiate conversation with Miksi and would never ask her for help or direction. Tayna may have been small in stature and voice, but her father's name carried weight even a world away. Every Gray knew her. She knew all she had to do was say the word "vision" and it would start all over again. They would flock to listen to her and take everything she said as if it were a certainty. Every single day, she fought the temptation. If she could help it, her father's abuse of power would stay in Haven where it belonged. She couldn't stop herself from having visions, but she could keep her mouth shut about it. At least, that's how she started out thinking, but the days were hard and worries festered with each strange noise that came from their vibrant surroundings.

"Vik, I want to talk to you," she said.

"Please," Vik wiped his brow after he finished coiling a pile of leaves into a roll and tucked them under his arm, "Grace me with your presence."

"I'm sorry about the other day."

Vik dropped his defensive posture, "What do you want to talk about? Not visions again…"

"No," Tayna sighed, "I was just wondering what you thought about all this."

"You mean, us being out here? You're not quitting, are you?"

"No, of course not. I'm talking about Agrona, the outside. Why were we taken away from this place? Where are the Thesmekka? And not that I want to see one, but where are the Brutes?"

"I've been thinking about that, too. I just can't come up with anything that sounds right," said Vik.

"Exactly," Tayna said, her eyes alight with intrigue. "There is definitely something wrong with what we know, you know?"

Vik chuckled, "Every time I said that to Marek, he would get so mad. I'd stopped thinking about it."

They continued dreaming up conspiracies and walking around with fat leaves over their heads, shading them from the sun. Every now and then while they spoke, Vik would glance into the forest to check for a face, but he never saw it again. The sun rose and fell over and over, but Vik never grew tired of his new life outside. His skin was burnt, his body was caked in mud and dusted with dirt, but he was invigorated by it. Only one thing would have made his life perfect. Only one addition to Agrona, but he knew it would take a miracle to convince Marek.

It wasn't often that he meditated, in fact, he couldn't remember the last time he'd sat down and cleared his mind. But, one rainy day, Vik finished smoking his sitter and flicked it out into the mud, and sat himself under the shelter he'd helped build with his own two hands. He closed his eyes and concentrated on sending his thoughts to the all-seeing Thessa, mother of the Thesmekka and creator of his people. He felt himself slip into peace, into a deep waking unconsciousness, completely unaware of the buzzing drizzle and vague grumbling around him. As he started to push the request for Marek to join him, he jerked at the flash of images in front of him. His eyes shot open and a second later, lightning streaked across the sky followed closely by a rolling thunder. Exhaling, Vik pushed the idea of images from his mind. It had

43

been a mix of his worries and the lightning. A daydreaming nightmare, nothing more.

*****

A second mountain towered above the ravenous forest, but it was far ahead of Haven in every way. This mountain was called Imperyo and the city spread out at its feet was Threshold. The surface of Threshold was covered in colorful rooftops, reds and oranges mixed in with browns, more vibrant in concentrated areas, with two house-sized bowls suspended above the roofs, attached together and supported by numerous stilted beams.

The most impressive structure was the thick wall that easily surrounded both the outer city and the black mountain, with room to spare. It was metallic grey with a smooth exterior but cracked every which way. Easily as tall as five or six men, it sheltered the inhabitants within its solid embrace. In a couple of places, a piece of the wall was missing or detached. Those spaces were filled in with wooden barrier constructed by the residents of Threshold out of branches, spikes, and tied together with a rope thicker than any the ex-Haven dwellers had ever made.

Outside the wall, people were working in fields that spanned the space between the metal barrier and the forest. More crops than anyone from Haven had ever imagined grew strong, with the help of the rich soil and tropical climate. On the opposite side of the farms was a giant crater. The biggest and strongest people trickled in and out of it all day long, carrying loads too heavy for most.

One dark pillar of smoke streamed out of the top of the mountain, lording over the vibrant hovels and shanties. It billowed from the hole like the breath of a volcano.

"Duzin should be back by now," said Zaruko, a tall, sun-touched man clad in drass-skin leather.

"It's barely morning, give him until sundown," suggested Gamba, Zaruko's most trusted friend.

"I can't smother it out of my mind," Zaruko confessed. "If there are still more of them out there, this could change everything."

"Or it may not. Don't fan your hopes too high. You need your eyes open to what's around you right now. This is just the kind of distraction your father would use against you."

"You don't think he knows about this?" asked Zaruko, pacing the stunted length of the room.

44

"We should be the only ones who know."

"I've heard that before."

"I haven't given up looking for our traitor," Gamba assured him, wiping the sweat from under his eyes.

"I know you haven't, but we should have an alibi ready. If they find Duzin that could be all they need to put an end to us," said Zaruko, flinching when a scream rang out that turned into laughter moments later.

"You think Lord Durako would go that far?"

"I think my father would do whatever it took to keep another group of outsiders from being brought into Threshold," Zaruko said.

Both Zaruko and Gamba were two of the few Impery living outside the black mountain, exiled for their sympathies for the people and their open objections to Lord Durako's method of ruling. Lord Durako was Zaruko's father, but for all their resemblances they couldn't be more different. Lord Durako did not see them as anything more than a danger to the future of the Impery people. Ungrateful guests, he would call the ones who disobeyed their laws. Lord Durako wanted to keep the residents of Threshold producing food and supplies under the guise of protection and real threat of punishment from his well-armed warriors. Separation was essential in Lord Durako's mind.

"Our superiority is diluded when we mix with anything other than our own people, as proven in the past," Lord Durako had said to his peers, convincing them of the need to separate from Sinovians.

But Zaruko wanted to open the mountain up for all, make it so that all could come and go freely, and bring protection out to the walls, to stop the threats before they reached their small city.

Zaruko had a small group of like-minded followers willing to move out of the mountain to support him. This was no minor sacrifice on their part. Outside the black mountain Imperyo, enormous beasts attacked from the sky, from the forest, and even sicknesses struck them from time to time. No one in or out of Imperyo had access to orange pills anymore. There was constant work to be done in the fields, in the quarry, in the market, and on their buildings to keep them from falling apart. But the exiled Impery had little to no part in these obligations. Instead, Zaruko and his warriors provided the protection that Lord Durako promised the people and never fully delivered. Durako refused to allow his people to risk their lives on a daily basis, just for Sinovians, the Impery's word for other races.

"Excuse me," said a deep, powerful voice from outside the hide covered doorway.

"Come in," called Zaruko.

"I don't think so," stated the rumbling voice.

Zaruko and Gamba exchanged a glance before shuffling outside to greet their visitor. It was Benne, one of the Sinovians they frequently met with. As a Brutemen, Benne towered above Impery and Sinovians alike. Even the Brutemen women easily met Zaruko eye to eye.

"I don't think you'll fit in there anyway," said Zaruko, offering an uneasy smile.

"I found this," Benne said, looking side to side as he slung a pack off his back, "There were unfriendly firefolk walking along the forest front all morning. They went into the trees, came back out, and left for Imperyo. We waited until they were gone and the balcony was distracted."

The pack that'd been obscured by his muscular physique was a bound bundling of branches, gathered from just outside the forest. Something was tucked into the middle of the cluster. Benne parted some of the sticks and started pulling a body out by the arm. Gamba snapped up straight and glanced around to be sure no one was noticing them. Their line of rundown shanties were out of the way of the main road through town. Despite this, a young man with bright blond hair darted out of sight after witnessing Benne's true cargo.

"Ridiak!" Benne bellowed, his booming voice chasing the speedy young spy, "Damn that boy and his mouth."

"Get him inside," Gamba whispered.

"It's Duzin," breathed Zaruko. "He's dead."

"I found him like this. They didn't burn him," said Benne, wiping his brow. "Why wouldn't they set fire to him?"

"They didn't want us to find him," said Zaruko.

"We'll take him out to the fields and set his fire free," said Gamba somberly.

"What's happening?" asked Benne, "Lady Nattina will want to know."

"We don't know now," said Gamba, motioning to Duzin.

"Tell Lady Nattina, there'll be New Ones here soon."

Benne's scarred, bristled brows stretched as high as they could and his mouth curled into a smile. He remained silent on the exciting news while he scooped up Duzin's body and nodded to Gamba. The three of them marched out the patched gate, heading across the Jabulian field to where the sunbloom buds reached their waists, their slender stalks and heavy bulbs bobbing in the breeze. Zaruko cleared his throat before spitting once on the ground beside them. Instead of saliva, two combustible chemicals splattered near their feet and he stomped out the small flame that sprung up.

A young Impery exile sprinted toward them, across the fields from the other end of the colossal, Thesmekkian metal wall. Her hair was braided like the Sinovian Jawnies and she wore beaded bracelets on her arms made of brightly colored clay and tiny strips of twine. They clacked noisily together as she pumped her arms.

"Zaruko!" she frantically shouted, trotting to a stop, "Zaruko, who is this? Who is it?"

"Go home, Josanna," Gamba said quickly.

"I will not," Josanna barked through clenched teeth, balling up her fists and jabbing her finger at Zaruko's face, "That's Duzin, isn't it? I told you we should act now. What are we waiting for, more of this?"

"How do you know…?"

"We all knew. Nattina, Harash, Reeta…Benne even knew," said Josanna, motioning toward him.

Benne scrunched up his face and stared at the sky.

"This isn't to do with any of that," Zaruko whispered, motioning for her to keep it down. "I need you to hold off for a while longer."

"Why?" she shouted, "It's there, right inside the mountain. We could let everyone know about it."

"Josanna, keep your voice down," ordered Zaruko.

"I'm sorry," she whispered, her face flushed and her jaw set tight, "but there is a Thesmekka in there and we know it. It's only a matter of time before they know we know it. Do you see why I'm having a hard time waiting on…whatever it is you're making me wait on?"

"You keep talking out in the open about it like this, someone's going to find out right now," growled Zaruko. "We're going to move on this when I say. Burn lightly for now."

"I'm going to fizzle out at this rate, Zaruko. I don't know if I can wait anymore," she grumbled. "I can't ruin my father's plan a second time."

"If you don't follow my orders on this, I'll do what I have to. Even if I have to put you out myself. This is bigger than you and your father, and you're not running things out here, I am."

Josanna glanced at the sizzling strand of smoke rising up from the ground near Zaruko's foot. She drew a deep breath, held it briefly, then spewed a jet of flames from under her tongue over Duzin's corpse. Benne leapt back from the bursting chemicals. He'd been teetering on the edge for most of their encounter already.

"He was a friend of mine. I'd want him sent off properly," she snapped as quietly as she could beside the crackling flames.

Zaruko crossed his arms and stared her down until she left. The smoke drew Imperyo's attention and Duzin was still recognizable when one of Lord Durako's men arrived at the scene. He feigned ignorance with little effort, confident there was nothing Zaruko could do even if he openly admitted to knowing how Duzin died. Zaruko's explanation of a drass dragging him into the forest satisfied the lazy investigator. His real purpose was to ensure that Zaruko wasn't going to press the matter. The Impery departed for the black mountain without showing the son of Lord Durako a hint of the respect he would normally deserve, if only he were more cooperative with his father.

"They're out there, I'm sure of it now," Zaruko glanced from the fire to Gamba and Benne, "I'm going to convince Durako to grant us passage into the forest. He'll let us bring the Sinovians here."

"I'm not sure that's possible," said Benne.

"It'll happen. As sure as the fire burns."

# CHAPTER FOUR

Another week had gone by and it was finally time. Vik took his father's scrimshaw from around his neck and dug a hole he deemed deep enough as far away from the black mountain as he dared to go.

"Even if I can't come back, you'll be outside like you always wanted," he whispered to the small, whittled bones before putting them in the ground.

Vik met up with Savan after Tayna wished him luck. They rolled up one large, makeshift bag each and tied them around their waists with the same twine that would hold them closed when they were filled with bloodstones. Not only was he going on a food run with Savan, but he was going to visit his brother and see the new babies that should already be born. There was still a chance he might be able to convince Marek to leave Haven.

Even though he kept his hopes high for Marek coming around to see his side, Vik was trembling throughout the approaching ascent. Nightmares had increased as the day for him to return to Haven drew nearer. Over and over again, he'd dreamt of himself falling from the Gate. He'd seen Marek covered in blood and himself standing over Haven's Gate, unable to see inside. The fear of being trapped, the Gate somehow closing over them, these thoughts shook him to the core. He tripped on loose rocks over the clearing and nearly slammed into a Gray carrying a large brick of dried mud. He knew he needed to get it together or he'd be distracted and stumbling all the way up. Despite all his worries, he had something louder nagging at his brain than the fear of being trapped. The new world was so beautiful, fresh and full of life, it felt wrong for Marek not to know it with him. He had to go back, no matter what fears he might have.

The mountain was made of black rock on the outside, slate gray on the inside, and it made the climb miserable. It was so hot, the air wavered over the ground they treaded on. Savan even wore wraps around his normally naked feet for the climb. Unable to see the mountain clearly only made the oppressive heat more obvious. It pressed on them, melted the water out of their bodies, turned the air thick and heavy, and made them dizzy. The black rocks under their feet would hiss and sputter when they were ground against each other, sometimes spitting burning droplets onto their toes. Savan chanted a small prayer for a breeze under his breath, but it wasn't until they reached the summit that they were graced with fresh air. Vik wasn't fully aware of how soaked he was until the wind illuminated every bead of sweat like beacons of light.

"Why..." Vik breathed, "...don't you do this at night?"

"Believe me, we need all the light we can get to go down through the Gate," Savan explained wearily.

"I see."

"Thank you for coming with me," he added.

Vik just nodded with his brows raised, unable to muster the energy for an audible response. Savan picked up the rope and wrapped it around one arm as he carefully, slowly descended. He used the knots and kept his arm coiled in twine. Vik felt ill watching him disappear through the Gateway. The hook jerked and wobbled against the metal it was anchored to, the twine creaked and strained under Savan's weight, and from that angle, the barrier was visible against the direct sunlight. It would occasionally surge with a pulse of energy, rippling across the opening like a layer of light before going invisible once again. Swallowing a lump in his throat, Vik took the twine in his hand after Savan had reached the top step beneath the Gate. A flicker of images passed over the back of his eyelids and he angrily shook his head, gritting his teeth and determining to do this despite his body begging him to go back through the sweltering heat. Even hiking barefoot back down, the sizzling black rocks were more appealing than dangling above the fourteen levels from that rickety rope.

Vik mimicked Savan the best he could, looping the twine around his arm and using the knots to support his own weight. As he dangled just above the topmost step, swinging himself to reach the stone slab with his toes, a water droplet sprinkled down on his head. It startled him and he gasped, throwing himself onto the stair and frantically running his hand through his hair. He sighed loudly and Savan steadied him from the adjacent step. Vik nervously laughed with his back pressed against the mountain wall, rolling his eyes while he glanced at Savan.

"It gets easier each time you do it," Savan merrily assured him. "But if you need a minute, we can wait here until you're ready."

"No, let's go," Vik said, his whole body quivering.

Vik and Savan strolled along the circular stone streets of Haven filled with running, laughing and screaming children. All of them slowed to a stop, overtly pointing and staring with their jaws hanging open. The adults were only slightly more subtle. They were no longer Uppers and no longer Grays, but some less pale, foreign element to their unchanging world.

The rain poured down from the Gate. What used to be a perfect cylinder all the way to the bottom level was distorted by the new slant of the Gate into a much more narrow oval instead. Like a thick curtain of rain. It would be caught in the drains on the fourteenth level and filtered behind their walls. Every level was wider than the one above it though the edges of the streets reached out exactly the same length and the fourteenth, the very bottom level, was completely flat. No edge of the street, no great hole in the center of it. Just drains and splatters of blood permanently staining the stone. Each level had small panels protruding from the edges, absorbing and reflecting light back onto the street that would otherwise have been blocked by the level above it.

"I'm going to go see my brother before we load up," said Vik.

"How long are you going to be?"

"I'm not sure, however long it takes…"

"You're going to try and convince Marek to leave?" Savan smirked at him.

"…Yeah. What's funny?"

"I wish you all the luck I can, Vik, but Marek's not leaving Haven. As long as I've known him—"

"You know my brother?"

"—I've known that he's more faithful than Miksi."

"Is that so?" Vik grumbled, glancing toward his house.

"Well, I mean, I'm not his brother, so you'll know him better than me. Of course," Savan rambled, regretting so freely voicing his opinion.

"I'll meet you back here when I'm done."

"Right," Savan nodded.

"With Marek," Vik added quickly.

"Definitely," he rushed to say, smiling encouragingly. "You know, I think I'm going to go see my grandfather. I'll wait for you if I beat you back here."

They parted ways and Vik tried to push Savan's words from his thoughts. He was going to walk in without a doubt. When Marek saw him, realized how dull life was in Haven compared to the new life outside, how happy Vik was, there's no way he'd be able to say no.

Vik sped to his house, attempting to ignore Haven for what he hoped to be the last time. A few levels down, he heard laughter erupting from a group of friends much older than himself. Around the corner, he could hear the entire gossipy story two girls shared about a boy they thought was cute and the level beneath Vik sounded like someone was playing marbles with a rock. Haven was a giant cave and everything could be heard from just about anywhere outside. It was different being surrounded by walls again, safer, but his world felt so small. The air was too cold, burning his throat and chest like his body was freezing, solidifying from the inside. He couldn't wait to tell Marek all about Agrona, how much better it was and how much they'd love it if they'd just come with him.

His blood pumped a little faster and his heart fluttered at the thought, but all of those feelings shut down the moment the door whirred open and he stepped inside his house. Vik had walked in on a gently intimate moment between Marek and Mira. They were sitting together on the couch, Marek's arm wrapped around Mira while she rubbed her own belly in a circular motion. They were whispering, but Vik couldn't hear. They kissed between smiles.

"And now I'm going to leave."

"Vik!?" Marek shouted, giving Mira a final smooch before hopping up off the couch.

The two embraced, gave firm pats on the back and then Marek hurried to the kitchen to get something for him to eat.

"It's good to see you, Vik," said Mira.

"You too. I can't believe you're still holding onto them."

"You're just a day early," she smiled, "Tomorrow's the day. We're heading down to the med-fac in the morning."

"That's exciting," Vik said with unconvincing sincerity.

"You look ridiculous," Marek laughed, unable to adjust to his brother's new look.

"It's called a tan."

"Is it hiding under all that red?"

Mira seemed completely oblivious to the world around her, smiling and staring at her belly, but she spoke to Vik anyway, "We finally came up with a name."

"Just two more to go," Vik teased.

"It's harder than you think," Mira said, feigning exasperation. She enjoyed everything about the process. Her friends grudgingly put up with her constant passive gloating, but they were happy for her. Especially since in these later months she became house-bound and they controlled when they would see her.

"What did I tell you before, just two at a time," Marek playfully grumbled from the kitchen as Mira winked and held up three fingers to Vik.

52

"What did you guys decide?"

"Garek," Marek called from the kitchen.

"Oh," Vik snickered, "how about, Gik and Gira as the other two?"

"Very funny…" Mira said, looking up long enough to glare at him.

Marek was quiet on the matter, but Vik knew he was too excited and proud not to say anything ridiculous. He had assumed the children would all be named after their parents or random, made up names. Marek took a cutting knife from the auto-arm, who was far more trusting of him over Vik, and easily diced up the two bloodstones. The pungent bloodstone aroma floated upward into Marek's face, stinging his eyes until they watered, muttering about the ripeness of that one as he wiped his cheeks with the back of his hand. While he cut them into slices, Havard waved the end of its arm back and forth over Marek's shoulder.

Vik grinned, "Havard, I've missed you out there. You wouldn't believe how different it is outside," he stepped to the other side of Marek and leaned against the counter, "Is there any way I could pull you off there and take you with me?"

Havard swiveled nervously in place then lightly pushed Vik away from the counter with careful, repetitive shoves. Vik made his body deadweight from the waist up and laughed mischievously while the auto-arm struggled to gently increase the force it applied to shoo him away.

Every auto-arm was made of three visible segments of perfect, Thesmekkian metal jutting out of the low counter barely hanging above their heads. It gracefully swiveled with non-robotic, fluid motions and used its delicate prongs to work around the residents like a third arm. Auto-arms never needed maintenance, cleaning, or supervision. They were always there for all of the inhabitants when they needed them, hyperaware of their surroundings at all times.

After Marek finished chopping up the bloodstone, the auto-arm dispensed a platter and Marek loaded it full. They took slices from the platter during lazy conversation. For every one the boys took, Mira had four. Vik could feel the effects the outside was having on him even as he ate with his brother and Mira. For once in his life, he worried that they were consuming too much. There wasn't a visibly finite amount of food out in Agrona and as a rule, they only ate as much as they needed to not feel hungry anymore. Vik felt the anxiety as he watched them eat and suppressed it as best he could. It was a new awareness he didn't know he had. Haven was different, the rules of one world didn't apply to the other.

Vik's teeth met the bloodstone slice and pushed through the thick skin. The juices sent needles through his taste buds and the pungency burned his nostrils.

"Do you need anything, sunshine?" Marek cooed to Mira, kissing her on the lips before she answered.

"Ugh, guys, I'm still eating…" Vik moaned. Mira threw the last bite of bloodstone at him and he caught it. "Don't waste food," he playfully lectured, popping it into his mouth.

"Just help me up," she said to Marek.

While they waddled into the bedroom, Vik took the platter over to Havard. He handed it to the prongs, always enjoying even the simplest interactions between them. The prongs clicked gently against the platter and then, when the grip was secure, it cautiously tried to pull the platter out of Vik's hand. Vik tightened his grip, but the auto-arm didn't use force to retrieve it. Gently rotating side to side, wiggling, tugging a little bit more, the auto-arm utilized a wide array of techniques to try and wrest the platter from him without resorting to force. Vik was always amused by its patient persistence and inability to resort to aggression against the dwellers in the mountain. Although no longer an official resident of Haven, Vik would always belong to Havard's house as far as it was concerned.

"Stop doing that," Marek said, emerging from the whirring doorway.

The auto-arm had frozen while Marek spoke and as if knowing it had won, waited for Vik to let go. The moment he released it, the platter was whisked away into a slot beside the one it had been pulled from. Vik leaned closer to the counter, but Havard placed itself on his shoulder and firmly pushed him away.

"Do you see this?" Vik said, pointing at it while it pushed against him.

"I wish you'd stop. It would be nice if you were allowed near the kitchen."

"It's not my fault…"

"It's completely your fault. Like that time with the knife. It wouldn't let us cut anything ourselves for a week after that."

"Oh yeah," Vik smirked, "that was a long time ago."

"I'm sure it remembers just fine."

"We've got the orange pills, it's not like I would've died."

"You keep torturing that poor thing."

"It's not a thing…" Vik started, looking at the auto-arm as it made a flicking 'shoo' motion at him. "Its name's Havard…remember? We came up with that when—"

54

"I wanted to talk to you about staying."

"Let's not do this again," Vik said, holding his hand up near his face.

"Vik," Marek searched for words, "...they're going to come back."

"Sure, when we've run out of working dispensers and starved to death. They'll probably come back." Vik pretended to be a Thesmekka, speaking with a heavy voice, puffing his chest out, and holding his sides with his hands, "I knew we forgot something!"

"I know it doesn't seem like it, but this is a test of faith. Don't take the stairway again. You should never have helped them build it."

"You should be taking it and getting Mira out of here before there's nothing left. Or worse..." Vik jabbed at the air between them, "I saw it up close, the Gate. It's just a metal ring, a portal latched onto the stone, hanging there."

"I know, you told me. I saw you and Savan pulling at it too, can't believe you did that."

"I had to. People weren't able to get out."

Marek glanced at him with a raised brow, "Yes, that would've been terrible."

"There's a Gate on the outside too, did you know that?"

"No," Marek said, blinking to suppress his curiosity.

"It's connected to this one. It lets us go through the solid wall, isn't that incredible? If it stopped working..."

"I don't know what you're worried about. It's not going to break," Marek snapped, looking away.

"You're right, everything else seems to be holding up so well around here. Besides, if the Gate stops working I guess it's not that big of a deal."

"Vik..."

"We'll just run out of water and air, in the dark—"

"Stop lecturing me," Marek snapped at him. "It's not an easy choice. But I choose to believe they didn't create this whole sanctuary for us and then *forget* we were here. I don't like sitting on my hands, but I have my family to think about."

"I'm thinking about my family too," Vik growled, "I worry about you guys every day out there."

"You are worrying about us?" Marek scoffed, "It must be paradise out there."

"It's getting to be. Please, come with me."

"I was being sarcastic," Marek stopped his outburst short, knowing what he wanted to say next was a delicate topic, "Dad sounded a lot like…I'm worried what happens if you can't make it out there. If things fall apart or it's too dangerous and you have to come back here, will it be enough anymore?"

"It's never been enough," Vik said, wishing they were his words and not their father's. He dropped his arms, "Why do you want to stay here?"

"I've always been happy here. I know that's not you, but I need you to understand that I want different things. I don't want a dangerous life," Marek motioned upward with his arm, "I want to see a Thesmekka, be here when they get back. But I know you don't and that's alright. Just promise me you won't stay out there when everything tells you to come back."

"Everything was telling me not to come back."

"Please, just promise you won't get yourself killed. That's all I'm asking."

"Yeah, I'll try," Marek glared at him and Vik sighed, "I promise."

Vik stood outside his old house for a long time. Since he'd left, Marek and Mira were going to make it theirs instead of moving in with her family. He was really leaving without them. Savan might not like it, but he'd stay for a couple more days. Mira was scheduled to go to the medical facility to have her babies brought into the confined, gray world they wouldn't be able to leave without a fight. He smiled at the thought of being the uncle who came to visit them from the outside, tan and covered in dirt, smelling like trees and grass and other things they wouldn't see until they were old enough to climb the stairway on their own. If they even wanted to leave. His smile faded as he realized they might turn out just like their father and look down on him for leaving the safety of Haven.

There were kids playing on the second level, below and across from his front door. Laughter and playful screaming bounced off the stone walls, coming from children on every level. He approached the edge and peered over at them. It was like a vacation, being back in his cool, clean cave of origins. He could finally appreciate the comforts of Haven after experiencing the discomforts of Agrona. There was a line of children chanting a little rhyme about the Gadling, what they called the children chosen by the Thesmekka. Vik amused himself with thoughts of how he made himself a Gadling, instead of waiting for the Thesmekka to take him as a child. He wondered if anyone in his family had ever been taken, back when they used to visit every decade. The Gadling tradition was one that came with bittersweet emotions, as the Thesmekka would take the small child, the Gadling, into the sky through the Gate and never return. The elders say it used to be an enormous honor, that Gadlings were chosen to roam the land with their saviors and serve them in their great war against the Brutes. That all sounded very heroic, but Vik knew what to think of eldertales. They were always so full of crap even the old codgers couldn't keep a straight face while they spoke. These children probably didn't know what a Gadling really was, but children do a lot of things without understanding what they really mean.

> Gate, Gate,
> Time to fly,
> Now we go up in the sky,
> Sun, Sun,
> All too bright,
> We are joining the great fight,
> Chosen, Chosen,
> Here's the vow,
> Britta is a Gadling now!

The line of children kept their hands joined and closed the circle around the girl named Britta who panicked before bursting into laughter with her friends. The point of the game was to say the rhyme and then try to all say the same name at the end of it. The game always started off sloppy, but they would end up flawlessly in sync by the third or fourth time, all of them guessing the same name no matter how many of them were playing. Guessing games were popular among youngsters, which most people attribute to why their intuitions are so honed as adults. Vik was of the opinion that there just wasn't a lot to guess about.

The children all had oversized clothes tied around them, but kids were rowdy and thick knots don't play well. Some of them even went without the overalls, the tunic easily reaching their ankles. When Vik was that young, he remembered a few kids with clothes that fit. There weren't many of those anymore. Clothes actually made in sizes for children were too tattered to be worn appropriately. He amused himself with thoughts of how much less stubborn the faithful might be about staying in Haven when they ran out of clothes to wear.

Three children screamed across the stone street, shrieking and chasing each other like tiny missiles on a crash course for the first solid object. An adult reached out too late to try and stop them from going down that particular part of the gray pathway on level three. Vik grimaced as he watched one of the children get snatched by the arm. An elderly man whipped him around and shook his finger in the child's bewildered face. The long row of idle elders on level three sat on the cold ground in front of a bland, gray house, a couple of them pacing around to catch passersby just as that one had. The other two children had stopped running and watched helplessly from a distance as their friend was reduced to tears by the cruel and bizarre things the old man was telling him about life and how everyone he loved was going to die. After he released his tight grip on the child's arm, they cackled as he ran to his friends and they disappeared under the part of Haven directly under Vik.

"Don't stand so close to the edge, Alistanik's son…"

Vik spun around. Three elders stood unnervingly close to him near the edge of the top level. They weren't the oldest, but at the stage of life just before reaching the level three, med-fac dependent age. Their wrinkled faces pulled up by the edges of their mouths with mischievous laugh lines on their old eyes squinting eagerly. They were the worst. A lifetime of boredom had made them unbearable to be around, so they surrounded themselves with other elders. Most children knew well enough to avoid them and everyone else who had to cross their paths scampered quick as they could, staring at the ground like it had something to say.

"Oh, don't pick on him, Shurik…he looks like he's been outside for a while."

"Have you?" asked Shurik.

"…Yes."

"Wonderful! Good for you!"

"Do you like it out there, heh, or did you come back to stay?"

"It's great," Vik answered stoically.

"No, no, don't be silly, he's lying to us. He's just wanting to outdo his father."

"That's the ambition of every young man, you know."

"You're right, so right. As usual."

"So, will you jump from the middle of the stairway or the top?"

They burst into cackles and their hunching grew worse as they bobbed up and down. Vik's face felt like fire and he balled up his fists, but quickly stretched out his fingers. There were those who did physically react to their prodding, but every single one of them just happened to turn jumper no more than three days later. They really knew how to dig into a person's soft spots and had no reason or desire to let go. They had lived their sixty to eighty years watching jumpers and realizing they could cause one of the two most exciting scandals in Haven. They could find a jumper behind every poorly drawn on mask. All they needed were the right words.

"Is that why you all came up here so far from the med-fac?"

Their smiles sank, but not from insult. Shifting their eyes and squirming in place, Shurik sighed loudly and moaned before he explained.

"My idiot grandson has convinced us to leave Haven. That abomination there," he motioned to the stairway, "In our old age, he wants us to climb it. And why not? We'll be dead soon."

"I did not say that," said Savan, who had come jogging up from a nearby doorway after spotting his grandfather near the edge.

"Of course not," Shurik rolled his eyes, "You'd never say that. Or anything like that. I don't know why I shouldn't call you my granddaughter instead, heh?"

The man behind Shurik was distracted by a woman passing by. He lecherously called to her and whistled, winking and making blatant, loud comments about her most attractive features. She turned bright red and skipped into a running jog, anxious to get out of direct eye and earshot.

"Too bad," the old man chuckled.

"You're leaving, too?" Vik sucked in a breath, "And it was gonna be so nice…"

One of the elderly women behind Shurik gasped and shook her head, mumbling about the lack of respect. Savan's grandfather smirked and gave Vik a quick slap on the chest with the back of his hand.

"You lot need us out there, heh, gotta remind you about your faithless ways. Can't wait to see the Thesmekka tear that stairway down, too. But…heh, until they do…"

"Might as well see what's out there," said the other old man.

"That's right."

"Well I'm not carrying your wrinkled carcass up there," said Vik.

"It looks like you're not carrying anything?" asked Savan, glancing at the empty sack still tied around his waist.

"Oh, I'm staying here just a couple of days. My brother's sieva's going to the med-fac tomorrow."

"That's great!"

"I'll be out with a full bag of bloodstones the day after that."

"Alright, no rush. We'll be more than fine with this one until you get there. Just be careful, it's tricky getting out with a full bag."

Shurik looked like he had an overload of things to heckle about, but he still took some pride in avoiding the low-hanging fruit.

"See you soon, Vik," said Shurik coyly.

Vik scowled, tense and unblinking, and then marched away. He set his sights on the diner on level four and tried to ease his anger along the way. That only served to rile him up even more.

The diner door quietly buzzed open. A waft of sitter smoke soothed his senses and invited him in with promises of good feelings, and pickles. Everyone was eating them and Vik trotted to the nearest table, waving his hand over at the idle waitress smoking at a table against the wall. She cocked her brow at him from across the room, glanced at her sitter, sighed, and set it carefully on the rim of a cup in front of her.

"What'll it be, Outsider?"

Vik paused, his eyes lighting up and a smile stretching across his face, "…Is that what we're called now?"

"Sure," she said blandly.

"Pickles, please. I'm dying for some."

An Upper couple got up from their table behind him and glared as they left, muttering under their breath. Vik was only half as aware of them as the waitress. He rubbed his hands together, salivating at the thought of his favorite treat. The young woman reached over to the table behind him and plopped the Upper couple's pickles in front of him. She crossed her arms and put on her best snobbish face, but didn't expect Vik to do what he did. He picked up the half-eaten pickle and ate the whole thing in one bite. His eyes watered and he drooled just a little bit, chuckling with his mouthful and leaning forward to catch any that might drip onto his stale, rank clothes, already dirt-colored and torn. Her nose scrunched up and she fled the area as quietly as possible, slinking back to her table and deeply sucking a puff of smoke from her sitter.

"Yes, clearly the outside is a better place. We should all go there so we can be like you."

Vik glanced up and rolled his eyes when he saw Vojak lording over him. When the giant man pulled out the chair across from him, Vik wished he hadn't packed his cheeks full so he could protest. Vojak set both elbows on the table and patiently waited for him to finish chewing, leaning forward and staring at him with a knowing smile the entire time.

"What do you want?" said Vik, finally able to speak again.

"Just wondering what you're doing here. This isn't how the bloodstone runners normally do things, they're usually in and out. No long walks, no stopping for pickles and a sitter."

"I'm not staying, if that's what you're getting at."

"Are you sure?"

Vik bit another piece of a pickle off, scowling at Vojak without reply.

"It isn't because of your father, is it?" asked the meddling Gray.

"Why wou' my fa'fer have any'fing to do wi'f my de'fisions?"

"Poor manners and completely oblivious…" Vojak said, sneering.

Vik gulped the bite down, "I may look like my father, have some of his mannerisms, whatever. But I am not going out into Agrona because he jumped. That doesn't even make sense."

"You're right. He wanted out so he jumped. I'm sure you've never thought about jumping and I'm sure if your father were still alive, he would never have thought about taking the stairway."

Vik threw the other half of his pickle down on the plate, "You didn't know my dad. He was lost without my mom. He messed up, but you can't take that one back. That's all it was."

"He was selfish," Vojak grumbled, "A selfish man who left his young boys all alone because he didn't think there was anything for him here."

"I see what's going on here. You're getting on in years, practicing your best annoying impression so you can fit right in with the elders?"

"...Do you disagree?"

"Of course I disagree," Vik tried to see the door around Vojak, but his shoulders were too broad. "There wasn't anything for him here. What could he possibly do that mattered?"

"Short-sighted, just like him. He decided there was nothing he could contribute to around him because he didn't think any of it was worth it."

"Why are you talking to me about this, Vojak? Why the hell do you care about my family?"

"He was my family, too," said Vojak, almost as if he didn't mean to.

"What are you, my grandfather?" Vik chuckled.

"No, I was his other-brother."

"Older?"

"Younger," said Vojak, nodding sarcastically. "Believe it or not."

"Not. That's not even a close enough connection. Why don't you follow your own kids and grandkids around?"

"Because for some reason, Vik, we keep jumping. My kids, their kids...all of my brothers, most their kids too, and so on. No other family has a record like this. You, Marek, Harlok, and Tayna. You're all that's left of my family."

Something about the news hit Vik deep in his gut. Turned his stomach, made him queasy and anxious. Suddenly, all he could think about was the Gate and his brother.

"That's why I'm telling you, he could have done more with his life before throwing it away. He could have united us, Grays and Uppers, even just a little. It wouldn't have been easy, but what else did he have to do? You and your brother could've been beacons of unity, but now you're just Uppers with dark eyes…loose pebbles in the pile. Don't make the same mistake twice."

Sitting back in his chair, Vojak sighed and shook his head. He pulled his arms off the table and crossed them, acting like he wanted to say something several times, but it never came out. Instead, he pushed his chair out, the Thesmekkian metal squealing and grinding against the stone, and left the diner. Vik curled his lips inward and stared down at his plate. There was nothing he could do inside greater than what he could do outside. The leak had already sprung.

He plucked up the last pickle from his plate and took a small bite. Every Gray and Upper in the room watched him without looking at him. They ate quietly, spoke softly, the ones with their backs to him would ask those across from them with their eyes if anything was happening to which they would receive a rapid, head-shaking "no". He knew in that moment, for whatever reason, that he was never going to be able to convince Marek to leave Haven for the outside world. He knew that over the years, they would slowly lose touch with each other, and that possibly none of Marek's children would want to live outside. Having children solidified his brother's resolve to stay in the safety of Haven. Vik had lost the battle on one of the few things he truly cared about. Swallowing his meager bite, he put the rest of his treat down and realized it didn't taste as great as he thought it did just moments ago, the aftertaste too acrid for the back of his throat.

Outside their house, a couple of levels down, several performers were in the middle of their play. It was about a siv and his sieva, waiting for the Thesmekka to return. The play would end with the doubting siv jumping to his death just before the Thesmekka arrived. Once, a man most people knew little about had volunteered to play the part and actually jumped at the end. Ever since then, the number of people with an unhealthy interest in seeing the play had increased. At a glance, Vik recognized it as one he'd seen enough times to quote. If he hadn't felt so ridiculous acting in front of people, he might've participated a time or two. He could never get passed knowing everyone watching was fully aware that their display wasn't real.

Sera was on stage, if the street could be called that. She was easy to spy even two levels away from the way she carried her tall, slender figure. The unofficial queen of Haven, in her own mind. It was possible the perpetual indignation she wore on her face had never allowed her to fully opened her eyes or look at anything directly. Vik snickered at the thought as he descended to join the audience.

Beside Sera was a man Vik hardly recognized. He kept fumbling with his lines every time he met Sera's gaze. Knowing from the way his performance was going, this was no jumper. He was still too excited about things like pretty girls and nervous about doing well. In fact, the gathered crowd shifted uncomfortably, the sounds of clearing throats and brief murmuring settled in as the young man struggled to deliver a line he'd forgotten.

"Don't miss me—" Vik called out from the back of the gathering.

"Don't miss me after today," the young man shoved the words out of his mouth over the sound of the crowd's laughter.

"You wouldn't," said Sera dramatically, "Think of our children."

"That is what hurts me most."

The weight of the scene had been shattered, but it was worth it to see the guy's face turn such a deep red. Vik was going to have to leave shortly. That somehow made it easier to cause the kind of ruckus he would have normally avoided.

After almost a day of absorbing Haven again, Vik stood at the base of the stairway, staring straight up at the climb. He'd only just arrived, but couldn't stop thinking it might be better if he just left before things got too complicated. Even though each step was a mishmash of anything they could spare and break loose from Haven, he was proud of it. Doors were split in half to make two steps, whole houses were broken up and taken piece by piece to the top level. As a result, every step varied greatly in size, but each one shared a similar perceived precariousness. It was supposed to have wound around in the space between the top level and the Gate, instead it ran about as straight up as it could. The space between each step was about the length of his feet to his waist.

"Excuse us," said a woman behind him, snapping him out of his daze. "Oh, heya Vikki, I didn't recognize you."

"Nikiva, hey," Vik said, surprised to see her and her more regal sister near the stairway, "Sera."

Sera pursed her lips and rolled her head to face away from him, as if that were just another way to acknowledge a person.

"We're going outside today," Nikiva beamed, rocking back and forth from the balls of her feet to her toes. "How is it? Do you have any pointers for us?"

"Sure," Vik held the back of his neck, buying himself some time to think, "It's hot, so stay out of the sun."

"Check. What else?"

"Are we going or not?" Sera snapped.

"Don't be such a rotty-rock," Nikiva sighed, "Do you mind if we go first?"

"I'm not in a hurry," said Vik, taking a step back from the stairway.

"See you on the other side, Vikki!"

Given the state of the stairway, not crowding climbers was the unspoken, polite thing to do. He watched the tomboyish Nikiva bounce up each step, turning to pull her daintier twin to the next stone slab. They did this until they got halfway up and then Sera demanded they take a break.

Someone slapped Vik's shoulder and it nearly threw him out of his skin. Kalan, Edik, and Ziven laughed and cheerfully pushed him away from the stairs. They were one of the few groups of triplets in Haven, although not identical. Even though Ziven showed tendencies toward becoming a scrimshander, they still took him everywhere with them, in part to try and dissuade him from the morbid hobby by keeping him around the living.

"Where've you been all this time, outside?" Edik said, pretending to be offended.

"I can't believe you guys are still here."

"Just wanted to make sure we were ready to leave it all behind," Kalan said, craning his neck to have a good look at the stairway. "Why didn't the Gate look this far away until now?"

The four of them followed the stairway up with their eyes.

"Got the feeling today was the day," Edik confessed, still staring upward. "So we can't back out now."

"You first," Kalan said to Edik, but it was Ziven who hopped up on the first step before them.

"Be careful," Edik said to him.

"I heard that outside, the sun will blind you if you look at it, even once," said Kalan.

"That can't be right," Edik said. "There would be blind animals all over the place if that were true."

"Maybe there are," said Kalan.

"I'd be blind too," Vik said.

"What kind of animals are out there?"

"Uh," Vik thought about the only things he'd seen, but he didn't want to scare them away from leaving. Agrona needed all the extra help they could get, "I haven't seen too many. Just some birds, but they're way too high up to even see us, I think."

"I bet they get to eat more than bloodstones every day."

"I hope so," Kalan said, glancing behind him at Haven.

"Hey, guys," Vik said, nodding his head toward the ramp leading up from the second level.

A large crowd of Grays had ascended the walkway and were gathering on the top level, not too far from the stairway. Leading them was the bald, stone pale Harlok. He had lost so much weight since the last time Vik had seen him, there wasn't enough of him to stretch out. He may have been the one who helped get the stairway started with his persuasive speeches, but Vik did not have fond memories of the man and shuddered at the sight of him. He and Vik's father never spoke again after Alistanik came to the top level. It was this madman who had predicted the death of his brother and did nothing to prevent what preceded it. It was his face, not his father's, that he saw in his nightmares of that day years ago, on level fourteen.

Harlok had more of a knack for predictions than most, so his words were zealously heeded by a large number of Grays. His fanatics grew more potent the closer to level fourteen they lived. The precision with which he predicted was eerie, but Vik didn't believe it was anything more than proper guesswork. He was certain Harlok was just a brilliant conman. A man so bored, he used his followers to stir up trouble. An elder before his time. Vik hated when someone acted like they were predicting the future by following "that feeling", "their gut", or "instincts". He wasn't the type to listen to his gut on anything more than what felt right or wrong, like choosing whether or not to throw a rock at someone's head or push someone off the edge. He'd been taught these things were wrong, despite his strong urge to do both when he met Harlok's glazed gaze. This gathering of over one hundred Grays with Harlok on the top level was also one of those wrong feelings. Even Kalan, Edik, and Ziven could sense something was happening and stopped climbing to watch.

"We have all been blessed by Thessa. It is through her gift that we rise above our enemies," Harlok began before he'd settled in the middle of the crowd. Hearing him say enemies confused even the feuding Grays and Uppers, as it didn't seem like he was talking about the two groups at all, "Seeing through the veil is automatic, it's what you do without thinking. But when you go looking, that's when you're blinded by it. Learn to look without sight, see without trusting your eyes. It's not in your heart and it's not in your mind, but somewhere in between. The way through the veil is seen when you are as small as a piece of grain on the rock."

"What do you mean?" A woman sincerely asked from the crowd.

"I speak of the sight. With it, I have learned a terrible truth. Today is the last day for many of us."

His voice scratched and clawed its way out of his throat, bouncing off every wall like a sack of nails. Once he stopped moving, he turned his back to the edge. The people were already silently waiting on his next words. The gallery of gray faces outlined in black hair hung motionless before the sickly herald. None of the guys had ever seen so many Grays on the top level before, not all at once. It's not that they weren't officially allowed, nothing was really official in Haven, but they hated being there and the Uppers hated it too.

"I have spent days searching and finally, after piercing the veil, I've come to tell you all of what I've seen. Our silent watchers have been wrestling with our fates for too long. They fear us and our stairway. Soon, very soon, we will taste the rain and see the sun no more."

The crowd murmured and grew uneasy. Vik looked at his house over the crowd and saw Marek standing at the doorway, staring at the gathering. Ziven had seen enough and started climbing again. Kalan slowly followed suit, turning to look at the crowd after every step. Vik and Edik hung back, listening to Harlok's mystic, raspy voice confuse the gathering. They thought they had trekked up from the bottom for good news. It was so quiet and the stone cold walls could reflect noise so clearly, even those down on level fourteen could hear his voice, even if the words weren't clear.

"To those of you who make it out, you may consider yourselves lucky." Harlok looked straight at Vik and shook his head, "but your road is the hardest I've seen. For the rest of us..." Harlok took a step backward and held out his arms as you would welcome an embrace. "Come, let us go home."

He wrapped his chest with his arms and stepped back until there was no more street to step on. He gave a light hop at the end, falling flat backward, down the middle of Haven. Several people screamed as they watched him disappear and several seconds later, crash against the stone of level fourteen.

As fear and unrest rippled through them, a great rumble erupted from every corner of Haven. The ground quaked and with nowhere to go everyone panicked, screaming and shouting, hunching over until it stopped. A crack shot up from near the bottom, around the tenth level. They couldn't see where it had started, but it splintered up the side of their walls, spewing caustic steam as if the mountain wheezed in pain. The fissure darted through the levels with alarming speed. It burst past the top level and on its way to the Gate, it spat out a single stair from high above them. The stair crashed into a house, but no one ran out of it. The Gate itself creaked and leaned so far off its anchors that part of

Haven no longer felt the sun. Those who had heard Harlok's final words could see their fates written like a short line in Haven's cold palm.

# CHAPTER FIVE

The mountain was an active volcano of anarchy. Every person turned to magma, their only concerns were getting out or finding their families, no matter who or what was in their way. The crowd slammed together before billowing out. Several of Harlok's most devoted acolytes dove after him, their arms cradling their chests, accepting the death he had predicted for them. Uppers burst from their houses, either attempting to stop the chaos or joining into it. Many people chose to rush the stairway. Ziven and Kalan achieved impressive speeds, hurdling up each stair like their lives depended on it. Vik knew his own life was in danger the more vicious and desperate the crowd grew. Edik and Vik had made it up two steps when one of the Grays hopped up beside them and growled out, "You had your chance, Outsider" before shoving Vik down. His thigh hit against the edge of the stair and he flipped, his head hitting the ground with a thump and hollow crack.

Vik groggily opened his eyes and like he was underwater, everyone else screamed and shouted in muffled tones. For a moment he was distant, safe, but everything quickly sped up. He blinked away his blurry vision and felt blood oozing from a very tender wound on his head. He wasn't to the side of the stairway anymore, but directly under it and just far enough out of the way to not be trampled. Beside him, lying flat on the stone street with his eyes open was Edik, staring straight at him. There was a gash so deep on the side of his head he could see a bit of his skull. Edik's blood flooded every crevice in the stone around them. Set on the ground beside them was a large, dislodged rock covered in dark red, a couple of bloody spots beside it from the stone bouncing after it had been dropped.

"I'll kill you!"

"Get out of here, get out, last chance," bellowed Vojak, shakily holding his fists up between them.

The blood-stained attacker yelled incoherently, his red face bursting with veins, then he took off for the stairway. Vojak dove to the ground beside Vik and checked his head.

"Let's go, we've got to get you out of here."

Vik's head spun, his own blood pumped so hard the wound on his scalp started throbbing even harder. He scrambled away from Edik, stumbled to his feet and looked up at the stairway. Both Grays and Uppers were fighting to get out and tumbling off the steps. The space between the top level and the Gate was about six levels high. Normally it only took two levels to fall from to die, three to be certain. Most of them were falling from three levels high and cracking open on the streets, if they were lucky. If they were around halfway up the stairway, they were already directly above the hole in the middle of Haven. The ones who plummeted from that height fell long enough to think about what was coming before they hit level fourteen. The sound of a body falling from so high was never what Vik expected. No matter how many times he'd heard jumpers and accidents before, it was always jarring. He couldn't imagine there was much of a difference between their bodies hitting the bottom and the sound of someone dropping a metal table from the top and it hitting with the legs straight up.

"I've got to get Marek," slurred Vik.

"You get back here," Vojak bellowed at him as he stumbled away.

"Fix that!" Vik shouted, pointing at the churning chaos at the base of the stairway.

Vojak growled and narrowed his eyes after the boy, but turned to the violence instead. Swinging his massive arms around, he started pulling people apart from each other, throwing them to the ground.

Vik wove around crying children, people shouting names with hands cupped around their mouths, and others kneeling beside the bodies of those who had perished in ways that made him think of Edik. Vik was certain he was only out for a few seconds, like a heavy blink, but he couldn't believe this much damage could be done in such a short amount of time. More and more Grays seemed to be appearing from all over Haven, cramming onto the already cramped top level. Vik pressed against the wound on his head despite the burning pain, trying to stop the blood from running down his face. He had finally stumbled and shoved his way close enough to see the lack of detail on his home's metal door. Just as it should have whirred open for him, it ejected two Grays who nearly trampled over him on their way out. They were frantic and in a hurry to get out of there.

"Marek!" Vik called out, barely able to wait for the automatic door to whir open again. Inside was a mess, there was blood everywhere and Marek was on the opposite end of the couch trying to shove it across the room, toward the door.

"Give me a hand," he shouted.

Vik bounded over to his side, put his hands on the couch, but stopped, "Where's Mira?"

"She's in the bedroom. Come on," Marek groaned, the couch barely scooting across the floor.

"Get her," Vik met Marek's eyes, "You know we can't stay here."

"We're not leaving!"

"Then you're going to die!" Vik's face was red and he took a step closer to Marek, "The mountain's breaking apart, the Gate is falling, you're going to get the both of you killed."

"We can't leave," Marek insisted, his voice quivering.

"You can't stay," Vik said more softly, "There are so many people trying to get out...we still might not make it before the stairway is ruined or the Gate is gone for good."

"I know," Marek confessed in a high-pitched voice, resting his weight against the couch, "I know, but Mira..."

Vik's stomach dropped. He hadn't considered her condition against the rioters in the streets. It'd be difficult to get her up the stairway on a normal day. A deafening crash shot through Haven, so loud they were shaken even inside the house.

"We have to leave," Mira said from the bedroom doorway, eyes bloodshot and holding her belly.

"Mira," Marek hurried to her, "I don't think that's a good idea."

"I don't want to leave either, but what choice do we have?"

The front door whirred open and an enormous Gray barged in, initially unaware of them. Vik dove for the bloody knife on the ground and snatched it up with both hands. The intruder had tried to do the same, but wasn't fast enough to beat him to it. Vik swung the knife at him, cutting the man along his forearm. As the red line started to drip across his skin, the gigantic intruder grabbed Vik's arm, twisting it until he dropped the knife. He swung his fist around and slammed it into Vik's face, sending him straight to the floor. Marek ran around the couch, ducked down, and swiped the blade off the floor. In one fluid motion, he rammed it into the man's side before shoving him down.

Marek pulled Vik up by his arm and held his face in one hand, "Are you alright?"

"Yeah," Vik nodded, slowly pushing Marek's hand away, "I think I'm fine."

Adrenaline spoke for him, but there was too much going on to realize the room was blurring in and out of focus.

The intruder put both feet under himself again and held one arm out for a better look at the knife jutting out from his side. He wrapped his hand around the hilt and ripped it from his body, growling the entire time. The brothers stepped back until they were pressed against the kitchen counter. Havard swiveled anxiously behind them, the whirring of his motors stopping and starting. Just as the man stomped toward the brothers with the knife held in his clenched fist, the auto-arm dropped a knife of its own on the countertop and rapidly spewed utensils, plates, and cups at the intruder's head. Vik plucked the knife up and lunged forward, swinging it around until it found the Gray's neck twice. It was a sickening feeling, ramming a blade into a man's flesh like that, his hot blood gushing over Vik's hand. The man was nearly drowned before he finally fell to the ground. They watched him choke and sputter to death, all of them tense and unmoving until he was completely dead.

"We need to go," said Vik, hands shaking and trying to wipe the blood off on his pant leg, but the material wasn't absorbent enough to do more than smear it around.

"Mira," Marek urged, holding his hand out for her.

She flung her hand into his and they rushed to the front door. Vik was about to follow when he heard Havard tapping frantically on the countertop. When it was sure it had their attentions, it dumped the remainder of its insides: plates, forks, knives, orange pills, and then shoved them all uncharacteristically aside in one rough sweep. In the cleared spot, with the same delicacy they were used to seeing from an auto-arm, a single pearly ball was plopped out of the chute. The entire kitchen drooped, lifeless, the orb rolling aimlessly around. Vik picked it up with two fingers, examining it carefully, but it was perfectly blank.

"Grab another knife," Marek said.

Vik slipped the pearl into his pocket, rolled several orange pills into his hand, snatched a second knife off the countertop. He popped an orange pill in his mouth and chased Marek and Mira out into the riotous street.

Outside, the street was still as full as it had been before going in the house, but the rioters were twice as dangerous. Slumped against the dark stone walls lay bodies scattered out as far as he could see, blood pouring from fresh craters in their skulls. All of their dead eyes stared upward at the brightly glowing Gate. The last thing they wanted to see before their unwaking moment. It was early in the evening, but everything was like a nightmare. Illuminated by the sun, even more grotesque in the revealing light, their dead faces ignored them, preoccupied with their newfound freedoms. And they all started to look like each other. Vik's wound began to mend itself and he could feel the pull and strain of new skin weaving and stretching over the still tender gash. With the orange pill working through him, he'd be able to be a bit more reckless than usual for a while.

Vojak had been trotting over to them when they came out of the house. He had given up on quelling the raging masses, sporting a new set of cuts and bruises, and was about to pull them out kicking and screaming if he had to. He was relieved when they emerged on their own.

"Why is this happening?" Marek cried, putting as much of Mira's weight on his shoulders as he could. "I knew things weren't great, but I had no idea they were this bad."

"That's not it," Vojak shouted over the general chaos. "They were expecting to go outside. They knew it'd be dangerous and took weapons with them…they weren't meant for Uppers."

"Tell them that," Vik snapped.

Vojak reached over and threw Mira into his arms. The two brothers split the knives between them and escorted Vojak to the stairway, clutching the blades in their hands like they were the only things keeping them alive. They very well may have been. Vik and Marek had to threaten more people than they could count in order to get the giant Gray to the stairway in one piece. Vojak had been pelted by rocks, his arms pulled and scratched at by all manner of people completely out of their minds, and Mira was even bleeding from her leg. Someone flew at the brothers, punching Marek in the face and stabbing Vik in the chest. He gasped, wheezed, and then stabbed the man back, shoving him away as hard as he could. He could feel the wound closing up, like a thousand huge needles prickling every muscle in the area. Vik groaned loudly and felt for the wound, but it was already gone.

The closer they got to the stairway, the sicker Vik became until he could feel the color draining from his face. The orange pill was breaking too rapidly through problems that had formed in his brain from all the trauma and it was making him woozy, among other things. To their surprise, Uppers had retaken the base of the stairway and managed to subdue most of the crowd though they would not disperse. Vik marched straight ahead, pushing the nausea aside, hooking his arm in front of him and brandishing the knife with loud promises of retaliation. Immediately both sides saw Mira and hesitated to stop them. The brothers used this to force their way mostly unhindered to the first step, pulling Vojak up as fast as they could without hurting Mira. Vik sucked in a deep breath and took a single step forward before someone jerked him around. Another Upper hit the man in the back of the head and started a fight between the two, distracting the Gray long enough for Vik to launch himself up another step. His entire body was shaking, he wasn't sure if he was even breathing and the wound on his head would

72

not stop pounding across his skull, but he pulled himself up from the next blood splattered stair. He concentrated on his physical pain, taking each step without thinking. Just the *woom, woom,* of his pulse to drive him forward.

Vojak had to take a break by the time they reached halfway up the stairway. Behind them the crowd was restless, growing louder and more riled. Each step was spaced out much more than normal stairs and after all the traffic they'd seen, gave just a little when Vik put his weight on them. He could feel his body freezing up. His hand touched the next step and it lurched more than any of the other steps had. His stomach sank into his feet and all he could think about was the clattering sound of bodies hitting level fourteen.

"We can't stop," Mira panted, "we're almost there."

Vik was rattled back to reality, but not only by Mira. The mob below had burst out of their lapse in violence. The remaining Uppers and Grays below were shouting, screaming, throwing fists, pulling hair, gouging eyes, and worst of all, climbing the stairs at an alarming rate. Vik's heart shoved blood through his veins, but his body wasn't getting the signal. He had to climb the stairs, they had to help get Mira up this rickety death trap, but all he could see was himself falling. That gut instinct he hated was screaming for him to listen. All he wanted to do was curl up on the stair and let the mob pass him. He took deep breaths.

"They won't pass you…they'll throw you off. Come on, you're already halfway there…"

Vik stopped muttering to himself and pulled his legs up to the next stair, turning with Marek to pull Vojak up with them. As he took a single step forward the entire thing wobbled like an uneven table and Vik lurched, slapping his hands onto the next step. He let his foot bounce and hopped up to the next stair with quick, awkward motions. Each step was reached on his belly before rolling over, sitting up and doing it again. Vik strained his neck back and looked up.

The Gate was so close, his hand couldn't shield the light of it from his eyes. He felt a renewed sense of motivation, a fresh surge of energy. He was going to make it. Not only was he going to survive this ordeal and get back out alive, but he was going to be outside with Marek, Mira, and Vojak. That's all he'd wanted for so long. He could smell the fresh air wafting in with every gust of wind from above the mountaintop. It was less chilled like cave air and earthier, muggy and despite the heaviness of it, he wanted to weigh his lungs down with the air from Agrona once again.

Peering down at them, panting and resting on his hands and knees was Savan. Over the month that Vik had been outside, Savan proved to be a selfless, unstoppable force of productivity and motivation. More than any of them, he was focused on the future of everyone living outside being the best it could be and voiced his hopes entirely too often. Vik desperately waved to him and Savan waved back before crawling through the Gate and back into Haven. The mob was moving like a flightless swarm of insects along the side of the mountain. Steps flew out of their crevices, cutting the riotous masses in half, but not stopping them. Vojak let Mira down on the step above him. He and Marek worked together to get her out of Haven. Vojak simply couldn't carry her weight anymore. The giant Gray's arms shook violently when they were still and he wheezed with tears in his eyes. Vik couldn't handle the sight.

As Vik reached out to touch the next step with the others, his foot slipped in a fresh pool of blood. His trackless shoe squealed and he lurched forward, hitting his belly on the edge of the next step, forcing the air from his chest. Slumped over, one hand still resting on the stair above him, he felt the step under him move. Unlike the teetering of the stairs before it, this one was gliding. Vojak and Marek felt it too and used all their strength to pull Mira up to the next step before they all fell. The stone sliding out of the socket scraped out a grainy, grinding warning. Still unable to breathe, Vik tightened his fingers on the stair and tried to shout or even gasp, but his insides were still rebooting. He threw one leg up onto the rocky step. With one foot still set on the unreliable slab, the stair slipped out of the chiseled hole. Vik's leg dangled and weighed him down, but he slapped his hand on the other side of the step he lay across and dragged himself fully onto it with Marek's help. His lungs finally started doing their job, working together with his diaphragm to suck in more warm air. He gasped loudly, as if the sounds he tried to make earlier finally caught up with him.

Savan reached out to them, having effortlessly bounded down the steps to get to them as fast as he could. With Marek pulling one arm and Savan on the other, Vik was able to catch his breath and watch them ascend a couple more steps before the mob got too close. The missing step that separated them from the masses wasn't enough to hold off the truly desperate ones. As Vik pulled himself to the next step, he saw an Upper leap the gap and manage to cling to the step while several others missed and fell screaming down the middle of Haven.

Savan, Marek, Vojak, and Vik worked together to lift themselves and Mira through the Gate and out of Haven. *We're almost there*, Vik chanted. Savan was already through the Gate, pulling Mira all the way out and helping her to stand just beside the metallic ring. He reached back in and helped grab Marek by the back of his shirt as he dangled from the creaking metal ring. Vik watched as the few successful rioters climbed even closer, just four steps away. Vojak leapt through, struggling to wriggle his body against the conflicting gravity of upright world and a sideways Gate. Vik took one step back and rocketed his body forward into the hardest run he could. Just three footsteps into it, the Gate groaned, lurched and the familiar click of the latch detaching rang out over everything else. Vik leapt forward, wrapped his arms around the curved metal just as it began to drop. Savan and Marek grabbed him, but his legs were pressed against the underside of the ring by the pressure of it falling. At most, they were only keeping him pressed against the ring instead of flying off into the depths of Haven. Marek yelled for Savan to pull harder, staring wide eyed at the view over his brother's shoulder. All of Haven was rushing passed him and each level spinning by like a whirlwind. With a violent lurch, Vik was ripped from the metal ring, spinning in and out of view, falling to his death while his brother watched him the whole way down.

"Hold my legs!" Vojak bellowed, throwing himself through the Gate.

Marek and Savan took one of his calves each and held on as tightly as they could. Vojak could barely open his eyes. It was like his upper body was in the middle of a tornado. Blindly reaching out, he shouted Vik's name, feeling his hands a second later. Instantly, Vojak hurled him over his shoulder, out onto the rocky mountaintop just as there was a static-sounding *thwip* and the bottom of level fourteen flickered out of view. Vik's heart hurt, it was pounding so hard. He yelled at the top of his lungs with his chest pressed against the hot black rocks, feeling everything setting itself right inside as he did. That is, until Mira erupted into a blood-curling scream and everyone scrambled back away from the Gate. Half of Vojak was gone, missing from the chest up. What remained of his body lay limp as blood spread over the rocks that now covered the middle of the Gate.

Vik tried to jump away, but fumbled on his hands and knees, his whole body quivering. He thought he was going to be sick. Everything spun, the heat beat down on him, the air filled his lungs like smoke, and all he could hear was a scream. Marek brought him to his feet and they embraced like Vik was still falling. Then Marek pulled himself to Mira and held her tightly from behind, repeatedly kissing the top of her head. Savan couldn't keep himself on his feet, his knees rocked and threw his legs around underneath him until he gave up, staying on his backside. He glanced over the Gate, unsuccessfully fighting the urge to be sick. The top of the mountain was reduced to dark scree and a useless ring of Thesmekkian metal with nothing but stone in the middle. In a flash, Haven had been sealed and buried under the impenetrable black rocks.

Trotting up the side of the mountain, several dozen Uppers and Grays scrambled to see what all the commotion was about. Tayna was among them. She was relieved to see Vik, Marek, and Mira all alive and out during the turmoil of the mass evacuation. It was only when someone shouted about the Gate that she stopped her approach and stared down at it. The purplish-gray metal looked just as it did when the portal was open. It was just as sleek, just as spotless, but it was a foreign object to her now. It was no longer an active part of either world. She let her eyes search every corner of the opening, refusing to understand what had clearly happened.

"My father, did he," she tried to speak but it came out in fractured pieces, "Did Harlok make it out, did he have anyone with him?"

"No, he didn't make it out," Marek said flatly, "He jumped just before everything happened."

Tayna grabbed the front of her hair and slumped down to her knees, franticly muttering to herself, "No, no, no. Why would he do that, that's not what we talked about, this isn't how it went…" Savan tried to help her to her feet, but she cried out at the empty space in the middle of the metal ring, "My boys! My boys are still in there, let me go," she yelled, wresting herself free from Savan's arms.

She dug her hands into the rocks, pulling up only bits and pieces until a solid layer prevented her from going any deeper. Vik was still shivering, but all he could think about was how that was almost him. He watched her, slumped in the middle of the ring while everyone else descended the dark mountainside, leaving her to her grief. Tayna started searching around, unable to see clearly, until she found a sharp rock. She flinched at the heat, but gritted her teeth and held onto it anyway. She cut at the palms of her hands and threw the rock down when she was finished. Bleeding onto the black rocks, Tayna felt enough relief to get her back down the mountain. Others who realized the Gate was closed for good followed suit. It was a common tradition after the death of a loved one, but usually done in private with the med-fac healing any scars that might be left behind.

Getting the full-term Mira safely down the outside of the mountain proved to be almost as difficult as getting her up from the inside. She blacked out twice. Only for a second each time, but it was enough to send Marek into hysterics. He took a few steps ahead of her, his legs and arms trembling from all the exertion. Someone could have told him he had rubber bones and he would've believed them. He stopped, held his arm out behind him, waiting for Mira to grab it. When she didn't, he turned to look at her and saw her mouth hanging open as she stared off in the distance. She was still holding her belly with one hand, but the other was stretched out, unmoving in mid-reach. Dizzy and soaked in sweat, she thought she was hallucinating.

"I think I'm going out again," she whispered just loud enough for Marek to hear her.

But when she spoke, the feel of her own voice solidified her reality. Marek followed her eyes and saw an oddly bulgy mountain on the horizon. Too far to see it clearly, but not so far it'd faded into a haze. When it shifted to the side, they both froze up. The head of the mountain lifted and easily brushed the underside of the clouds. The lumpy mountain bulged where the shoulders would be and several seconds later, a deep rumble rolled over the horizon, blowing over them.

"Don't worry," said Savan with a cracking voice, easily trotting up beside them. His large, twine-wrapped feet maneuvered the uneven terrain with little difficulty, "It doesn't bother us."

"It bothers me," Marek wheezed.

"What is it?" Mira asked.

"A Brute, if I had to guess," Savan said, shielding his reddened eyes from the sun for a better look, "I can see why the Thesmekka didn't like them, though."

"You think it's a Brute, but you're not worried about it?" asked Marek.

Savan forced a smile, "Not worried one bit."

Mira dusted off her pants and reached out to grab Marek's hand. They watched Savan bound along in front of them, treating the side of the mountain like a ramp in Haven. Mira could feel the tears welling up, but the heat dried them before they got too far down her face.

"Let's get off this mountain," she said, squeezing Marek's hand tight.

# CHAPTER SIX

Vik and Tayna caught up with Marek and Mira before they reached the bottom of the mountainside. They helped lift and guide her along as they bumbled down the rest of the mountain without any major incidents, trying not to stare at the blood trail they followed along the way. The encampment at the base of the mountain was nothing compared to Haven, but Vik and the rest of the earlier evacuees were proud of it. Their budding settlement had come a long way since Vik first left the mountain. Several structures dotted the clearing, many of them even looked reliable. People were clumped together in groups working on bizarre projects with twigs and mud and giant leaves stretched over sticks acting as personal canopies. There were two more buildings being set up, but even if those were finished by the end of the day, it wouldn't have been enough to house them all that night.

Everything that happened in Haven felt like a different time and place, like a vivid nightmare that was already fading from memory. Until they ended their descent from the peak and reached all the people below who were finally figuring out what happened. As most of the people who were going downhill with Vik and the others arrived on level ground, they spread word of the Gate closing. Many of those who heard clumped together to validate it multiple times from everyone who had just come down the mountain, hoping someone would shake their head and say that everything was actually fine. That it was a trick of the light.

"Britta?" A woman screamed, checking the few that had just descended the mountain. "Have you seen my daughter? Britta, where are you?!"

People started to wail and cling to others around them, holding their faces in pain. Others stared at the mountain, blinking only once every minute with their mouth hanging open while a minority of Grays simply continued working. They had no one to miss and already dedicated themselves to this new world.

Once they stepped down from the mountain, a Gray man ran up to them. Vik didn't recognize him and knew he was one of the recently escaped over the last hour. He had bloodstains on his hands and nothing to wash it off.

"Are you all the last ones out?" he barked.

"Yeah," Marek answered, gently steering Mira around him.

The Gray sidestepped into their path, "What did you do to the Gate?"

"We didn't do anything," Mira answered, disgusted by the thought. "How could you say that?"

The man shoved her and she fell on her back. Like a flash of lightning, everyone was pulling someone off someone else. Shouted insults about Uppers and Grays erupted throughout the clearing, along with their newfound violent tendencies. Marek and Vik had tackled the Gray man to the ground while Tayna and Savan were trying to move Mira out of the way. She continuously assured them that she was fine, unaware that she could've been trampled staying where she had been.

Vik and Marek pounded on the man's face until they were plucked off by bigger men. Marek quickly held up his hands, surrendering to them before running to Mira and making sure she was alright. Vik, on the other hand, had finally snapped.

He shouted profanities and threats at the bludgeoned man as another Gray tried to help him up, "We deserve to be out here! *What did you do?*" Vik repeated himself louder, nearly popping a vein, "***What did you do?***"

The Gray pushed his help away and jabbed his finger into Vik's chest, ignoring the others that held him back trying to separate them, "You think just because you're Uppers," he wiped the blood from his lips, "you have more right to be out here than the rest of us."

"I'm an Outsider, not an Upper, not a Gray. I worked on those stairs from the beginning," Vik shook loose from the two holding him and bowed up to the much larger Gray, "While you hid under the level until we were done, I was out here with other Outsiders. We burned so you could come out here when everything was a little easier. That blood on your hands," Vik thought about Edik and all the other dead Uppers he'd seen on the way out, how he was almost one of them, "They deserved to get out more than you."

The two erupted into fist throwing and grappling to the ground. Tayna rushed over to the both of them and motioned for others to come pull them apart. Vik was in a blind rage until she slapped him across the face.

"Go take a walk," she barked, ordering him more than suggesting.

Vik shrugged loose of the other tanner people who had been out there with them all those weeks and started walking toward the forest that surrounded them. The Outsiders that were no longer holding Vik back formed a wall behind Tayna as she confronted the enraged, bloodstained Gray.

"Whatever you did in there, whatever was done to you, it's done now."

"You have no idea what—"

"You don't interrupt me out here," she said, cutting him off.

There was a chilling still in the muggy air. All of them were frozen by her words and by those who made it obvious they were willing to enforce them. Everyone stayed silent. The Gray huffed, his shoulders heaving up and down. He knew who she was and even though her father was dead and buried with her sons in the mountain, Harlok's name still carried a great deal of weight with the Grays.

"We're all on the same level now, do you understand?"

The Gray clenched his jaw and tilted it to the side before he answered, "Yeah, sure."

"If I ever see you or hear of you starting anything again, I'm going to have you put to work in the forest. And trust me, you don't want that," she clinched her fists, feeling the sting of her wounds and the hot blood running down her fingers.

"Alright, yeah, I understand," he rattled off, glancing impatiently at the forest and all the other Grays watching him carefully.

Tayna called everyone's attention to her, "I was the first one out here. Sunskins like me, we get treated with respect until you've gone through enough burnt days to understand. We cannot hold on to the grudges of our past lives. It is hard enough out here and with the Haven Gate closed," she swallowed hard, waiting to speak until she felt the lump in her throat subside, "There's no food to fall back on. No med-fac, fresh water, or great shelter to fall back to. We only have each other now."

Her own words sunk into her heart like a slow blade. They only had one full sack of bloodstones left and more than triple the number of people than they had that morning. So many of them were already burning in the sun and there was nowhere for them to hide. She could see the pink turning to red on their once pale faces. Forcing herself to think only of the problems at hand, she turned her back to the mountain and carried herself well enough as she helped to organize the massive amount of new workers along with Savan. They told them how it was and what to expect. They left out that they didn't know how they were going to eat in a couple of days or what they'd do if someone needed the

80

med-fac. Tayna felt like with their numbers, they could stand to venture briefly into the forest. The ones covered in blood, those who still thought as Grays and Uppers and tried to start fights, they wanted shelter and water just a little bit more than they wanted to attack each other.

Tayna strolled toward Mira after everyone had been sorted and put to work. She needed to find out what to do with her. There was no med-fac to deliver her babies and the siv, her cousin Marek, was surely in need of some reassurance. The thought of Mira's impending motherly joy burned behind Tayna's eyes. She took in a deep breath, holding herself together with the shock of it all. None of it was real yet. Her life was still going on as it had for the past month, with only the flood of new people to deal with. There would be more people to manage, more of the same problems, but Haven couldn't be gone. Not her boys, not just like that.

Screaming erupted beside her as several children burst out laughing, playing games in the middle of the clearing. A Sunskin woman told them to keep quiet and they listened for a few minutes before they went back to their rowdy games. It was at the sight of the kids who had made it out that Tayna found her breaking point. Her baby boys would never see the sunlight. All the building she did, all the days she pushed herself passed her limits for them to have a safe place to join her…all of her purpose was gone.

She crumbled behind one of the shelters, out of sight from the bulk of the escapees. Covering her face with one of her hands, streaked with dried blood, she clenched her teeth together so hard they might've cracked. Thoughts of her father poured into her weakened mind. She remembered his promise to bring the boys out after a couple of months had passed. Harlok had assured her without breaking face that he would take care of them. She didn't know how they died, she didn't even know if they were still alive but forever out of reach. Alone in the darkness without her.

"Damn you," she growled under her breath through clamped teeth, thinking of her father. "I hope Thessa burns your soul."

She was glad there were no bones from her father to make his scrimshaw. She consoled herself with the hope that his soul was trapped at the bottom of Haven forever, weighted down by his sins.

It didn't take long for everyone to learn the only rule they needed to know about the dense woodland: stay away from it. The forest loomed like a wall, the trees towered high over them though not as high as the black mountain. The barrier of gnarled, loosely connected trunks and separate skinny trees gave the illusion of them being in a deep and wide pit with the mountain as the escape slope. The screeching that would burst out from the unknown wilderness filled them with such horror, the established rule was enforced by instinct. In the morning, the mountain's shadow engulfed them and it wasn't until close to midday that they could see the sun. When chattering erupted from the surrounding forest, everyone knew to hold their breath and hold still, even if they didn't know why.

Vik finished skimming the perimeter of the woods for resources after his first skirting around the border and found Tayna. She was working with some other women on braiding twine out of strips of fallen leaves. They would be wrapped around segments of a wall meant for the newest addition to their budding settlement, being built just a few steps away. Her eyes were glazed over, raw and puffy.

He sat down across from her and stared into the dirt, "I'm sorry, about yesterday."

"I might've done the same," she droned, not looking up from the twine.

"No, I meant...I'm sorry about the Gate and, everything else."

Tayna's face tensed up, "It seems both our fathers were too afraid to face their lives when we needed them most."

Vik nodded silently, watching her weaving grow more hectic and sloppy. He put one hand on her shoulder, but she waved him away, assuring him she just needs to work. He left her to it without another word, wandering around like too many others until he found Marek and Mira in one of the half-constructed shelters.

Mira was lying in a bough bed with Marek at her side. These bough beds were made of branches loosely fitted together to make a box, filled with leaves, grass and anything soft they could find. Savan spoke in hushed tones with two other helpful people nearby as they nodded along and listened intently to what he had to say. Mira gasped, surprising herself.

"What's wrong?" Marek asked Mira, leaning over the bed and taking her hand.

"Nothing. Sorry, it was nothing. I think one of them just kicked me," she forced a chuckle out to ease Marek's nerves, but her grip tightened on his hand.

Vik tapped Savan on the shoulder to get his attention. Savan's whole faced scrunched up into a smile even as he spoke to Vik. It was hard not to instinctively return the gesture, a kneejerk response to his overwhelming sincerity.

"Hey, will you come over here with us for a second?" Savan asked politely, motioning to Marek as well.

Vik thought about telling him no, that he didn't want to hear anything that couldn't be said in front of Mira, but he was sweating, his eyes were swimming and the other two weren't making eye contact with anyone. Marek joined them, taking a few steps away from the small shanty and out into the bright light. Marek looked up, but the sun was so intense he groaned and covered his face with his hand. A large blue circle dotted the center of everything, even as his eyes were shut.

"You'll go blind if you look right at it," Savan warned him.

"I think I have," Marek said, rubbing his eyes and trying to blink away the sun-sized spot covering everyone's faces.

"That'll go away, don't worry," he chuckled. "Isn't this great though? Out here, outside of Haven. For the first time in two hundred years."

"Yeah," Marek answered unconvincingly, looking around at all the people baking in the heat, trying to understand what they saw in this desperate way of life. For the first time in a couple of centuries, people were making their homes and involving themselves in the world around them. Faces were knotted in concentration and quick to break under the weight of a smile but there was no other option. Even the few children that made it out were working tirelessly. It was exactly how Vik always wanted it, but now it was exactly like it had been in Haven. There was no quitting and going back home for any of them.

"There's so much for us to learn without machines to show us everything," Savan looked back at Mira. "They did so much for us, but I believe we'll figure it all out in time."

"In time for what?" Marek asked.

"Just, in time. You know, over time, in due time," Savan rambled.

"What's wrong?" Vik asked.

"Nothing's wrong," he spouted. "I spoke with Miksi, she's seen the machines deliver babies before. There's nothing to worry about," he motioned to Miksi, "Isn't that right?"

Vik looked to the older woman who'd been eavesdropping and came over to stand with them. Her face was pressed into a scowl and though she would always consider herself to be an Upper, she'd burned most of that out in the few weeks she'd been outside. She assured them that Mira would be just fine, far more convincingly than Savan could manage.

"Why are you so nervous?" Vik asked, "You got us worried."

"I've just, never helped with something like this before. I mean, my sister has twins, still in Haven though, but she just went into the clinic and came back out with them. I never thought about how it happened, it just happens."

"Calm down," Miksi hissed, meaning that for all of them.

Savan had successfully made them worry about Mira when the two brothers hadn't even considered the dangers of what she was about to go through. In over two hundred years, she would be the first human that they knew of who would be giving birth naturally. Sure there were a couple of other pregnant women out there with them, but Mira was ahead by several months.

"If Miksi's seen it before, then she knows what to do," Marek assured Savan, "I'm sure it's easy, otherwise machines wouldn't be able to do it."

"You're right," Savan breathed. "I'm sorry about that, I didn't mean to worry you."

"Yeah well, keep it together. You're stressing me out," Vik grumbled.

"Right, sorry," Savan rambled, continuing to rattle off apologies.

"Can I help with anything out here?" Marek interrupted, glancing around.

"Sure," Savan exclaimed, "Well I don't have anything right now, but Vik, uh, do you need anymore people?"

"There's nothing more to do on my end. It's fine though. You stay with Mira, I'll take him around. Keep us updated on her," Vik said, pointing at Savan before taking Marek's shoulder and turning themselves away.

Once they had gone a few steps, Marek spoke to Vik in a hushed voice, "But I want to stay close to Mira. I don't think she's feeling well."

"Let her sleep," Vik assured him, "Don't let Savan make you nervous, he's like a one-man med-fac. Any time one of us gets hurt, he fixes us up. Besides…" Vik glanced around, "If everyone sees you sitting around, not helping, they're going to give you trouble. Tayna tries to keep it together out here, but until we all completely forget about Haven, there's still going to be Uppers and Grays."

"Yeah," Marek scoffed, "It sounds so great out here."

"It is, give it a chance," Vik tried to convince him.

"I don't have a choice now, do I?"

"That's not how I wanted it to be," said Vik.

"I'm sorry," Marek started uneasily, "You almost got stuck down there because of me. Hell, we all almost died because of me."

"I know."

Marek grunted, "I'm trying to be serious."

"I know."

"Come on, I hate when you do that."

Vik grinned, "Oh, I know."

84

After walking the perimeter with Marek, telling him about all that they'd done in the past month and seeing right through his feigned enthusiasm, Vik decided it was time to get his brother's hands dirty. Wandering over to the stout little Miksi with her short, thick black hair, he tapped her on the shoulder. She gasped, jerking herself out of her productive trance.

"Thess'above," she barked, "What?"

Just beside them, a few other people were slopping mud onto a matting of fat leaves and spindly twigs. After the mud was spread evenly across the top, they all took a step back and let the sun bake it.

"I was thinking you might need some help with…anything," said Vik.

"We need more supplies."

"There aren't any more."

"Then there's nothing for you to do here."

Marek chimed in, "The forest has to be full of—"

"*Do not* go in there. Do not go near there," Miksi started to coil a cord around her palm and elbow. "You'll get snatched up by those things, whatever's in there. Don't set a single toe passed that first wall of trees."

Vik deflated. He was finally outside with Marek and now they were being told they couldn't help with anything. He wanted to work together, show him what it felt like to accomplish something with his own two hands for once. The clearing was a smaller space by far than Haven and they'd used up everything that had been scattered around the safety of the open space.

There were kids playing with pebbles they'd dug up and some were racing across the settlement, bouncing right back up when they tripped. Outside was so much softer and more enchanting, but they were still captives. Several Grays and a few Sunskins worked to move in unison over to the mostly established structure as they lifted the wall of matted leaves. There were plenty of them to carry it and even more beside them just hovering eagerly nearby. Vik almost wanted to go around and ask who would rather take a break or be playing, but he laughed at the idea. The faces of the people with tasks were set, one hundred percent focused. He knew what he would say to himself if he'd been asked that. He saw a couple of people rolling and dicing bloodstone fronds with a pile of sitters stacked nicely behind them. They sat with their legs folded and when they finished a roll, pivoted quickly around and gently stacked another on the tiny pyramid. Just a few steps away from the sitter makers, three women worked feverishly to create a fire, gently blowing on the fragile, flickering light.

Vik carefully snatched a couple of sitters and nearly smothered the fire to light them, "All these extra Grays out here now, there's nothin' to do."

"Should we be worried?" Marek asked quietly, glancing around. "There are so many more Grays than us."

"We're part Gray," Vik said with a grin, slapping Marek's chest with the back of his hand. His brother was not amused.

"I don't think they're going to care about that."

"Just don't throw rocks and you'll be fine," Vik shrugged the worry off, but his lookalike wasn't calmed so easily.

"What happened in the forest?" Marek asked, taking the sitter from him.

"I don't know exactly. There's something out there and no one wants to go in," Vik took a puff, "But we need to. There's barely any food left already…"

"How did this happen?" asked Marek quietly.

"If we hadn't waited fifty years to figure out we've been abandoned, there'd be a place out here already set up for us. We'd be growing food, have plenty of shelters…"

After several minutes of quiet smoking, Marek finally cleared his throat, "It's not doing us any good to wish for a different now."

"Yeah, I guess not," Vik said, standing up with a groan.

They trudged over to Mira's side and flopped down, ignoring the burnt, moaning Upper beside them. Mira was unsettled in her sleep, her head halfway off the makeshift pillow and eyes moving wildly behind closed lids. Vik and Marek leaned their heads against the wall and shut their eyes, a sitter still resting between Vik's teeth. The three-walled hovel did nothing to block the noise outside, but it was a welcome sound. The kids were playing again, their small feet scraping against the graveled dirt, bouncing laughter chirping around like tiny, happy birds. It was the sound of safety they fell asleep to.

A lengthy nap later, some undried mud leaked down and splattered across Vik's face, waking him up. Someone had decided to let one of the new arrivals patch the cracks in the roof. Vik and Marek had been asleep while the light stretched into the opening of the lean-to hut, baking parts of them while they rested. The original constructors didn't know well enough to have it facing the other direction to avoid that problem. Half the buildings out there reflected this lesson learned. The sun was so ever-present outside of Haven and even cloud cover was more than their pale skin could handle. Marek was surprised how quickly he came to hate what had always brought light and warmth into his world. Vik found his love of it waning as well.

As the Sunskin lectured the new roofer outside on the correct way to patch holes, Vik and Marek felt the effects immediately after waking up. The harsh rays had stripped away the extra, exposed skin and their clothes stuck to every part of their bodies, but now the breeze actually cooled their sweat-caked skin instead of rolling right over it. The burnt Upper was still sleeping beside them, unaware of the sun's cruelty. He smelled like musty sweat and Vik could see it beaded up on his skin, parts of his clothes clinging fully wet against the man's body. Mira's bed was mostly covered, so she stayed protected for the most part. Her feet dangled over the end of the bed, the tops of them as red as the inside of a bloodstone.

Marek felt as though everything he'd eaten had rotted in his stomach. He leaned forward and took in a few slow, steady breaths.

"You feeling alright?" Vik asked, sitting up as well.

"No, not really," Marek groaned.

The blinding, burning, sweaty world outside had been easier on Vik when he had something to keep busy with, but this idleness only drew more attention to the oppressive climate. Marek was already dreaming of his room back in Haven with glazed over eyes.

"Marek," Mira said, voice cracking from disuse.

"Hey sunshine, are you doing alright?"

She was pale and her eyes were glassy, "Have you come up with another name yet?"

"Not yet, but I'm on it," he said, squeezing her hand. "You just relax and let me worry about everything."

"You always do," she said, both her smile and her words weaker than normal.

They told her about what it was like outside, since she was stuck in bed. Despite how animatedly Vik rambled on, there was nothing terribly exciting to regale her with. She put on a good face for them, but wasn't fooling anyone. Marek got to reminiscing about Haven and Vik shrunk back against the wall. He didn't miss it, not even a little bit. Hearing Marek and Mira swoon over the old days when the new ones had just began made him restless.

During the middle of a story involving her father, sister, and a malfunctioning automatic door, a horrible screeching squeal broke out from the woods. It shot along the edge until it filled every nook of the clearing. Vik and Marek huddled with Mira together until it was over, but when it all settled, no one could tell them what it was. Vik jumped up and badgered everyone he could, but all they could say was someone went past the edge of the trees and a few minutes later, the shrieking started. That Gray never came back out.

As the sun set, the trees and the mountainside became black silhouettes. They melted into a solid wall of darkness that leaked cries and shrieks from every shadowy place. The escapees of Haven were dotted around the clearing, clumped together in groups of those who knew each other before the Gate closed. Grays with Grays and Uppers with Uppers. Sitting alone, facing away from everyone, was Tayna. She had her legs flat out on the ground and stared into the forest. By that time, everyone had declared the wandering fool dead. No one goes into the forest. Tayna didn't look like she was going to go in, but she was very interested in something out there. Then, as if she knew he was staring at her, she turned her head and looked at Vik. Directly at him. She didn't need to scan the faces of the people sprawled out, she knew exactly where she was going to set her gaze.

After several uncomfortable seconds, Tayna lifted her hands and put them over her ears. Vik strained to hear, but there was nothing. The news of her sons, looming starvation, and a full day of being unprotected from the blazing sun had made her as mad as her father. The children that were supposed to be supporting the new wall broke into playful song, clapping their hands together in rhythm.

Gate, Gate,
Time to fly,
Now we go up in the sky,
Sun, Sun,
All too bright,
We are joining—

The forest erupted in shrieks and squeals, spreading like wildfire around the clearing. Vik slapped his own hands against his ears and even Mira did the same. He could see Marek shouting, but couldn't hear his voice. Each shriek would eventually rattle out into chattering, with other squeals still resonating around it. Vik thought it could be a massive swarm of something.

Several of the strange, skinny-legged creatures galloped back into the clearing, but they didn't stop. With their heads tucked down, they charged in a straight line through a stunned group of workers, most of whom didn't see them until they were trampled. Blinded by the shrieking, some of them didn't even know what hit them. The blueish herd stomped back into the forest on the other side they'd appeared from and weren't seen again.

88

The screeching finally trailed off into the distance and slowly Marek took his hands from his ears. As the sounds crackled far away, he realized whatever these things were, they were all over the forest. Not just a swarm of animal, but maybe even the trees themselves. They were so big, he had a hard time believing they survived on sun and dirt alone. Maybe they needed something more. As the canopies rustled in the wind, Marek pulled his legs up to his chest and held them tight.

The next morning, the sun peered over the treetops and spread a warm greeting over everything except their weary faces. The black mountain held the light back, keeping the earliest parts of the day the most pleasant. Groans rippled over the people who reluctantly pulled themselves up off the rocky soil and stretched out their sore arms. Many of those who were trampled the night before were still being cared for in the same shelter as Mira. Six total had been stomped over, four were resting in bough beds, and one was killed on the spot. She had been laying down in the dirt while she covered her ears and her head was stepped on directly by their rock-hard hooves. Ziven had spoken to anyone around, asking if she had family. When it was discovered that she had been the only one that made it out, he worked all through the night beside the tiny fire to avoid unsettling anyone else. His fingers trembled, but he managed to carve out a decent scrimshaw from the bones in her delicate hand. It was his first act as a scrimshander, so he made a necklace for himself. There was no one else to wear it.

Everyone stumbled over to the bags of bloodstones and groups of six or seven took one to share. Savan came over to Marek, Vik, and Mira with a bloodstone, but Mira wasn't hungry. The color had drained from her face and her lips were cracking. Over and over she chanted that she didn't want anything.

"Come on, you need to feed yourself."

"Yeah," Vik chimed in, nudging her with his elbow, "You gotta feed Garek...Gik and Gira, too."

"I'm not, Gira..." she said airily, trapped in a daze, eyes searching around like she wasn't really there.

"He knows that," Marek pretended to joke, but shot Vik a frightened look.

Vik stood up from beside her, his back and bones creaking from disuse, and darted over to where Savan was idling.

"What's wrong with her?" Vik asked, "She looks really bad."

"I'll get Miksi," Savan blurted, taking off to look for her.

Vik swiveled around, watching Marek comfort Mira, over to Savan winding through the clumps of people to find Miksi then back to

Marek again. Someone shouted his name from a different direction and he knew who it was before he saw him.

"You made it," Kalan shouted, genuinely surprised to see him. "I thought you were still in Haven for sure, if not dead. I heard from some of the other Uppers that things got pretty bad just before the Gate closed."

"Yeah," Vik said somberly, holding the back of his head. "I don't know how it happened so fast."

"What happened to Edik?" Ziven asked curtly, almost cutting him off.

He stood behind Kalan with his arms crossed and his eyes fixed on Vik's face. His fingers were stained red.

"Marek didn't make it...did he?" Kalan asked.

"No, he and Mira are right over there," Vik pointed over their shoulders.

"Edik," Ziven repeated, "what happened in there?"

"He didn't make it, Ziven, what do you want me to say?"

"He's not mad at you," Kalan clarified.

"What happened, who killed him?"

"I honestly couldn't tell you," Vik let his eyes wander anyway, just in case they saw the man to blame, "I fell and when I woke up, he was already dead."

"But was it a Gray?" Ziven pressed.

"Yeah," Vik crossed his arms and nodded, "Yeah it was."

"I can't believe this."

"Hey, calm down," Kalan put his hand on his brother's shoulder, but he shrugged it off.

"They get a free pass for killing people, just because we need the help out here. Edik gets murdered, and no one's going to do anything about it."

"No one will even talk to us about it," Kalan told Vik as Ziven marched off.

"I'm not surprised. Everyone's struggling with just being out here, they couldn't handle having to deal with something like that right now."

Kalan scoffed, "Yeah..."

"Hey, I'm not saying I agree with it," Vik quickly added, "I'm just saying, give it time."

"If you see the guy again, let us know."

"Of course," Vik assured him.

Kalan started to walk away, but turned back and gave him a hard pat on the shoulder, "We're glad you made it out, Vik."

90

*****

Deep in the woods, not too far from the escapees of Haven, a group of people from the far black mountain slowed to a stop among the lofty trees. The constant earthy smell was gently swept aside by a breeze that managed to weave through the tangle of trunks and roots. It carried with it the sweet aroma of freshly tapped sap. Zaruko and Gamba exchanged a glance when the fragrant scent reached their senses.

"Drass," Gamba whispered with a nod before they all scanned the trees for signs of movement.

The group moved over and under obstacles like a gentle stream, ready to melt into the ground at the first sign of danger. Zaruko gathered his warriors in silence. The men and women loyal to him huddled close together in order to hear the orders whispered by their leader. Their soft, leather-soled shoes barely crackled against the mulch under their feet, sounding more like rustling leaves than numerous footsteps. They were dressed in skins and cloth not given to them by machines but made by human hands from the creatures living in Agrona. Drass attacked Threshold with enough frequency to make use of their scaly hides. White jackets were grateful for the shearing, and so most of their clothes were made from these two sources. They blended with the dangerous forest and further hid themselves with mud rubbed over any place their skin was exposed. All except one.

Jahzara had been sent to accompany Zaruko on his journey to the other black mountain. Taking that hot-headed, warmonger of a woman along was the only way Lord Durako would allow him to travel outside of Threshold to retrieve more Sinovians. He would've gladly let Zaruko aimlessly wander the forest, but he didn't trust the fire in his son's eyes. When Zaruko brought the existence of more Sinovians to the high society's attention, he did so while his father was indisposed so they might have time to think on it before Lord Durako burned it down. By the time Durako arrived at the casual meeting in his throne room, the other prominent Impery were prepared to persuade Lord Durako that there was value in adding to the number of Sinovians producing food and goods for them. Seeing the Sinovians as more of a harnessed force than a growing force, Durako was unable to persuade them to treat the non-Impery threat with the kind of fear he knew they should. Lord Durako knew it would only take finding one more powerful group to ruin them. Still, he wanted to keep his people happy with his rule and sent Jahzara to ensure his son kept his treacherous ways to a minimum.

She was Durako's prospective sieva, but also the only one he knew he could trust with absolute certainty.

Zaruko glared at his father's harlot, standing in the middle of the dense forest like a pillar of flickering flames. She adamantly refused to cover herself in filth.

"Hiding is not the Impery way," she had said, in the most condescending tone he had ever heard.

All of them were aware of what to do when they encountered the Sinovians from the black mountain across the green waves, but their obstinate tagalong had other plans. She sighed aloud, letting out an irritable groan and rolling her eyes at yet another thought of why they were out there in the first place.

"How much longer is this going to take?"

"*Jahzara*," Zaruko barked as quietly as he could, "lower your voice."

"Don't burn my ears," she snapped at full volume. She sneered at the skittering scratches of unseen fodderbugs and the massive trees like they were all creatures too beneath her to exist in the same space. "What do *we* have to be afraid of out here?"

Jahzara strutted around the narrow clearing, taking her first time out of Imperyo about as seriously as a stroll through the outer streets of Threshold. Truthfully though, no one was safer. Anything happened to her and the rest of them would be burned alive the moment they returned home. Despite his extreme disdain toward begging, especially to his father, Zaruko had pleaded in vain to leave her behind. But Lord Durako was adamant. They gave unconvincing reasons for it, but Zaruko knew she wasn't just there to keep an eye on them. She wasn't a warrior like the other women in his company, but a wispy creature with devious, slender eyes that judged everything they gazed over. Her fire did burn more fiercely than anyone Zaruko knew, but out in the wild most things were drawn to the flames.

"Tallbugs, Jahzara. They aren't afraid of our fire."

"Then you burn too weak," she hissed.

Jahzara peered into the darkness of the woods before them, trying to see what had disturbed the hanging branches. Zaruko and his warriors crammed into the tight clearing and rested close together. Experts in delving through the forest, they were good at ignoring the suffocating humidity and their body's reaction to it, the beads of sweat rolling from every porous escape hatch. They were quieter than usual on this expedition. They'd taken longer journeys but the one to this other black mountain was different. So much more was at stake. If they were strong like the Brutemen, that could be a great stroke of luck, but if they

92

were aggressive toward his warriors, Threshold's growing resistance could be over for good. He had no idea what these new people would be capable of and while that made him uneasy, it was in part due to his anticipation.

Zaruko had his back to Jahzara, securing one of many provision bags meant for the new Sinovians. If all went well, this would be Zaruko's second group of outsiders to bring back to Imperyo. His first group was given the name Brutemen, as even their women were taller than Impery men. Zaruko had been prepared to offer them a place around Imperyo for safety, but found it hard to speak boldly in their presence, unsure of what he'd do if they refused the invitation. To everyone's relief, the Brutemen turned out to be a peaceful and reasonable people. He squeezed his eyes shut, ridding himself of unnerving worries and forced up better ones from the more secure places of his mind. These Sinovians would bring him tied with his grandfather. Two brought to Imperyo by him, the Shinies and the Jawnies, and two brought by Zaruko, the Brutemen and whoever these new Sinovians were going to turn out to be. Were he still alive, he would have burst with pride at the sight of Zaruko's success with yet another group of people being brought to the warmth and protection of their mountain. Zaruko imagined the old man's face grinning and for a moment felt like a child again, unaware of a smile slowly dragging his own mouth to the side.

Fire ripped him from his nostalgia.

Jahzara spat flames into the foliage through the tree trunks, lighting up the underbrush with dangerous attention. Zaruko shouted for her to stop, but it was too late. Screeches erupted and spread all around them, the heavy trunks bowing and creaking under the weight of things hidden above them.

"Tallbugs!" shouted Zaruko, motioning for everyone to take the positions they'd practiced.

Jahzara was pulled back from the edge of the forest by a rusty haired man and thrown to the ground before a vine snapped out and struck him in the back. He hit the ground without bracing, but was soon stretching out his face and blinking away the spots in his vision. Jahzara slapped her hands over her ears and watched unmoving as the black, barbed vine patted over the mulch like a blind man with a stick. Following the unusual strand up into the canopy, Jahzara saw a carapace flashing reflections of sunlight as the leaves rustled, letting out flickering rays of light. It was composed of glistening, mucus-covered plates and many tendrils that hung down from the underbelly, one of which finally found the stunned warrior. It stuck its barbs in, wrapped itself around his leg and with no effort at all ripped him from the ground.

Jahzara burned up at the treetops, but the screeching only grew louder and closer. The canopies rocked so violently that black shells could be seen from within the clearing at regular intervals. Zaruko snatched the back of Jahzara's hair and gave a swift jerk. The two chemicals that launched in a jet stream from under her tongue splashed together too close to her face. Heat stifled her vision and fire splashed on the dry mulch at her feet. She coughed and gasped until he slapped his hand over her mouth and held her firmly still while the screaming insects raged on, calmly and carefully sidestepping a barbed tendril as it wildly searched the area.

The cries spread throughout the woods until they reached the ears of the people from Haven. A frantic search began among the ex-Haven dwellers for their children and loved ones, confirming that the screeches were not from a meal at their expense. Vik and Marek slapped their hands over their ears and took a step back from the edge of the forest.

When the screeching finally died down, Marek turned to Vik and shook his head.

"I don't wanna do this, Vik. Let's go back and find something less stupid to do."

"Like what?"

Marek examined the tree in front of them, "Like eating rocks. Doesn't that seem better than this?"

"No one's making you come with me," Vik grumbled. "Whatever's getting everyone is going to be on the ground. So we go up."

Part of the tree in front of him faced the clearing with its rotund back to the forest. Vik placed his hand on a gnarled lump in the bark and began to climb. Marek cursed under his breath, turned and looked around for something, anything, but no one was stopping them or even concerned about what they were doing. The patchwork bag of bloodstones sat in the middle of everything, slumped with countable lumps like bones pushing through an emaciated body.

Marek put his hand on the bark where Vik's own had just been and followed him up into the trees to look for whatever they could find.

# CHAPTER SEVEN

Trees weren't how Vik imagined them to be from the holograms in Haven's library. The trunks weren't smooth with a flourishing tuft of leaves above like a neatly packed bouquet of green petals. Sunlight didn't bounce around with dim shadows on the grassy, mushroom-laden floor. Trees from his preconceptions would have been eaten alive by the real ones. Maybe they had been. They were enormous in size, both around the trunk and from exposed roots to treetops. They stretched upward at least six or seven levels high. It wasn't until recently that the Sunskins discovered that the skinnier trees weren't trees at all, but aerial roots that shot straight up out of the ground. The branches twisted around each other even from other trees, all aware of one another like a chain of nerves covered in gnarly lumps. Vik used these natural handles to easily climb up to a level where the branches became a walkable surface of their own, like a sturdy net of heavy rope. The top level of the forest. Each branch swayed under their weight the higher up they climbed. For the first time since Vik grabbed hold at the base of the tree, he felt uncertain of his actions. He looked down and saw Marek climbing up after him, but with his face angled toward the ground.

There were sounds up there that had not been as audible from below and many smaller creatures skittered around the woven tree tops. Agitated, furless creatures with long, pointed tails and chattering teeth clicked and chirped among themselves, letting each other know that they had a strange new visitor. An insect the size of Vik's foot scuttled by, dark blue or bright green depending on how the light hit its smooth carapace. The steady tapping of its six, hooked legs against the bark remained consistent. Either it was unaware or unconcerned by their presence.

One of the furless creatures leapt forward with surprising accuracy and snatched up the busy bug with both its tiny, human-like hands. The creature slammed it multiple times onto the tree branch in front of him. Vik stumbled back, tripped, and was barely caught in a loose netting of weak branches creaking precariously under his weight. He reached up for the sturdier branch he'd been using and pulled himself to safety, swearing through clenched teeth. The jittery creature carefully watched him with its bulbous black eyes, pulling the shelling off the dead insect as if it could do that in its sleep and tossed the shells down below. Deeming Vik a secondary concern, it reached into the soft part of the bug and pulled out bits to devour. Several of the other creatures effortlessly leapt over and started to fight over the carcass, their chirps rolling into hair-raising, repetitive howls.

Vik was just under the breach of the canopy. He scanned around the oddly cleared area, but saw no hopeful options. As he looked back down, contemplating how much effort it would take to descend, he realized he was no longer at the edge of the forest. The spindly branches had carried them into the dense woods and he could only see in a peculiarly shaped radius of cracked and crumpled branches around him. He wanted to assume the furless creatures had eaten out an area of leaves and made a makeshift home up there, but their teeth were too sharp. They weren't eating any leaves. Vik was relieved they were only half his size, but there were at least twenty of them. All of them had been idly watching him while acting out their strange, busy lives, but now they were focused on something below him.

"Vik?"

Around the corner of a winding set of branches, Marek finally emerged. He climbed with relative ease, hauling his matching weight awkwardly but without too much care. Heights weren't so much the problem as all greenery was foreign to them. Marek had a headache from all the non-gray colors.

"There you are," he said, heaving out a sigh. He lurched back at the sight of the small creatures all around, "Whoa, what are those things?"

"I don't know. Don't worry, they don't seem interested."

"They're not what's grabbing people…"

"I don't think so," Vik assure him.

"Good," Marek kept his arms crossed and his eyes alert, "So have you found anything up here yet?"

"We just got here," Vik said through a sigh, "And you already want to leave."

"Yeah," Marek said, as if that should be obvious.

"There's these bugs, those guys seem to like eating them. See, over there," Vik pointed to three of them digging into the carcass.

Marek groaned, turning away from the sight of slop being shoved into saliva drenched jowls and smacked around in their openly chomping mouths. Vik stood and hopped carefully, reaching for one of the fat leaves above his head. He grabbed the end of it, but when he pulled down on it, water splashed over his face.

"Is that water?" Marek asked eagerly.

Vik licked his lips, "Well, it doesn't taste like anything else. Smells normal..."

"Normal? What's it smell like?"

"Nothing, it's water."

"Why didn't you just say, *it doesn't smell?*"

"Because that's normal," Vik snapped, warily glancing over at the jittery creatures.

Marek gave a light hop next, snatching the end of the leaf with his mouth wide open. He got most of it in and wiped his face with the back of his sleeve. He swung under one of the nearby limbs and plopped onto a swaying tangle of branches. The chattering creatures kept their eyes on Marek much more deliberately than they had on Vik.

"I wanted to try to look around, but I can't get up there," Vik said.

"What, we're not high enough for you?"

"That's not—"

"Just climb to the top of the mountain, you can see over the trees better from there anyway," Marek leaned his head against a vertical branch and tried to relax.

Vik grumbled, throwing himself more carelessly down near his brother. He wanted to go back by that point, too. The furless things creeped him out, staying too still and too quiet. They'd lost interest in the half-eaten carcass and had fanned out to watch them, unblinking and leaning forward. But he didn't want Marek to be right so he kept it to himself.

"How do you think Mira's doing?"

"I think everything's going to be fine," said Vik, rubbing the back of his neck.

"Do you want to come up with names?" Marek asked, still not looking around.

"No," Vik snorted, "I really don't."

"Come on," he finally looked at him, "It's bad luck not to have a name ready for them."

"You just made that up."

"Yeah," he tilted his head side to side, "but it feels true."

Hissing erupted from the small beasts around them. The furless creatures backed up, teeth bared, all staring straight at them. Vik and Marek leapt to their feet, holding their arms out defensively.

"What are they doing?" Vik shouted.

"Why are you asking me?"

The brothers heard a shifting shuffle from behind. Vik and Marek craned their necks, peering around the branches.

A single, beady black eye honed in on them and an enormous pair of glossy pincers broke through the solid branches. They jerked hard enough to scare the furless creatures into darting away. The giant insect squirmed at them, legs searching out everywhere, pincers snapping at the air. The two brothers scrambled away, sprinting and stumbling across the woven branches as they bobbed under the weight of their pursuer. The exoskeletal flaps blew open on either side of its head and the air whistling out was so loud it deafened them. Vik shouted to Marek, his palms pushed into his ears, but he couldn't even feel himself yelling. He dove back from the giant insect, getting out of the way of its clamping maw.

Long, harmless antennae felt around and settled on Marek's back. The pincers snapped around, feeling for what it could smell right in front of it. He shook off the feelers and launched in the other direction, crawling on all fours across the woven sticks. Marek's footing gave as he blindly put his hand through a wide gap, sending him falling headfirst to the branches below.

Vik was completely surrounded by the squealing sirens. The giant insects were hidden behind every clump of leaves and he wished he were anywhere but mouth-level with them. The sun would occasionally burst through an opening canopy to blind him. As he neared a thicker branch, he smelled something vile, like days old death baking in humid heat. Clamping out blindly from the leaves near his head, Vik dodged a set of pincers and threw himself around, closer to the putrid odor. Wedged into a tightly tangled set of limbs was a revolting pellet of remains. Vik leaned forward and realized too late that he was looking at a rotted human skull peering out of the rounded muck that held it. Unable to stop himself, he shouted and backed away until there was nothing left to back up on. His next step fell on air. The top of the forest had many layers of aerial roots and branches, but they grew less forgiving the further down he went. Each layer of branches he hit barely gave at all. When he finally stopped falling and bouncing off stone-like stems, he writhed in pain on the fat layer of solid wood. Havard's orb was pressed between him and a branch, pushing into his bones. It was intact and the only thing he was still certain of being in one piece. The wind had left him and he lay gasping for it, like a man willing to beg but with nothing to say. He wanted to move, to get far away from the snapping jaws and dangling feelers, but he also wanted to curl up until he could breathe again.

The forest was darker where he was. More menacing and complex. The density of the roots had become even more obstructing

98

than the leaves. Overhead, the large insect scuttled passed, having a rough time of it. They seemed to be more accustomed to sitting still and waiting for their wandering prey. Beneath its glistening black carapace was a much softer underbelly and from there hung tendrils too numerous and in constant motion for Vik to count. Not that he was planning to sit still long enough to do any counting. There was a small patch of well-fortified branches under the ones he was on, but they wouldn't be easy to get to. The root-like tendrils were closing in, the scraping sounds of the giant bug wedging its body through the treetops was loud enough to be heard between the screeches. The branches he rested on were starting to rock and snap worse with every passing second.

Vik's whole body was shaking and his arms felt as reliable as wet mud. He dropped under the branches and held on to the offshoots, swinging his legs for momentum. He reached out for the next branch just as the one he was holding snapped in half. He dangled by one hand for a few seconds before flinging his other one up to join it. As he hung there, he felt something warm brush the side of his face. One of the many legs had found him and the creature above stopped wriggling through the treetops. Vik twitched, shrugged, and kicked at it to try and get it off. He gained enough momentum to get to the next branch, but the creature swung a barbed feeler directly into his thigh, catching his leg in the backward swing. Before the feeler could coil up around his leg, Vik chose falling to his death over being eaten alive. The force of his sudden drop yanked the barbs out of his flesh and the force of his sudden stop knocked the lights out in his head.

*****

The clouds rolled in over the budding settlement, fast enough to catch them off guard. Only minutes passed midday but as dark as late evening, the Uppers and Grays of Haven distracted themselves from their bickering just long enough to grow concerned together. A dark rumbling rattled through the clearing, from the opposite direction of the mountain-sized giant they'd seen from atop Haven.

"Do you think there's another one?"

"You better pray to Thessa there isn't more than one Brute out there, big as Haven and all."

More whispers spread out, full of the fear that there may be two Brutes that could squish them all in one step. They worried they could be surrounded. Every rumble could be death's footstep in disguise.

Many of the Uppers and Grays rushed to collect large leaves that had remained intact on the ground, cursing their lack of resources and progress on making enough cover for all of them to huddle under. The newly evacuated knew what the clouds meant, but the rumbling was new to them. The Gate had always filtered any and all noise from going in or out of Haven. Doing as the Sunskins did, the Uppers and Grays buckled down as best they could, preparing to ride out the approaching torrential downpour. Tayna sprinted across the clearing toward Miksi who had taken over for a man in charge of overseeing the roofing project. That man was so worn down, the thunder hadn't stirred him from his rest in the slightest.

"Excuse me," Tayna panted, swaying behind Miksi.

"Sorry, running out of daylight," she responded, waving her hand at Tayna dismissively, keeping her focus on the project.

Even though they'd been out there for a month together, Miksi was still an Upper and Tayna was still a Gray. The older woman ensured a sloppy rooftop made it to the walls about ten steps away.

"There are people in the woods."

"Well tell them to get their feet outta there," she growled impatiently, "Stupidity's got to cure itself out here. Thessa knows I don't have time for it."

"No, I mean, other people. People not from Haven."

The hasty workers slapped the roof onto the top of the supports, scrambling to stop it from spilling through the gaps. Miksi, satisfied with their efforts, turned her attention to Tayna.

"So, Harlok's daughter..." Miksi barked, "You're going to feed me a story, is that it?"

"I've seen them."

"Sure, you saw them, like your father saw things. I've not got time for fortune telling or wild daydreaming. Don't bother us hard working people with your schemes."

Miksi marched away, leaving Tayna confused and irritated. Just hearing her father's name made her face flush a bright red. She had seen these people with her own eyes, not through visions. Tayna was so accustomed to Harlok's name holding such clout that she didn't consider how Uppers felt differently about him, especially after the Gate had closed. She looked up at the distant storm rolling in, considering she may have had the lightning flashes play tricks on her with simple foliage between the trees.

"Tayna!" A Gray called to her from one of the makeshift structures before trotting over to her, glancing at the sky like it might drop at any time. "Please, come tell this woman, what's going to happen to her."

"Who?" Tayna asked, following the woman's eyes to Mira, "No."

"We all need to hear it, please. Are we going to be successful? Are any of them going to make it?"

Tayna wriggled her arm free of the woman's hand, "You shouldn't base whether or not you help on what's going to happen to her."

"We don't want to cause her unnecessary pain."

"I am not my father."

"Please..."

Tayna glanced over her shoulder even though she was trying not to look at Mira.

"I'm just guessing, but she doesn't look like she's doing well. I'd say she probably won't make it."

"She's been saying as much herself, but we need someone to tell her, well, are the infants going to die?"

"If they were going to die, do you really think I'd tell her that as one of the last things she's going to hear?"

"So...they don't make it then?"

"Get away from me," Tayna hissed.

The night rumbled and crackled. It split open and dumped heavy sheets of water on them in alternating ripples of intensity. Rain pelted the waxy leaf over Tayna's head hard enough that her skull ached. Lightning flashed and immediately thunder cracked over their heads, rattling her like she was held together with loose pieces. If it weren't for the rocky soil of the clearing, they would have sank into the mud within the first hour. She dug her feet into the soggy earth as deep as she could. It was warmer than having them out in the storm and getting sick without the medical facility was not an experience she wanted. Tayna's cavernous stomach shook with every rumble from the sky. The only luxuries for the ones under shelter were the constant streams of rain rather than the drenching deluge. The sloppy tarps they'd made held together for a few solid minutes before splitting at the weakest points.

One section of the crude roof sunk down low enough to break apart. Mud and water poured down into Mira's already soaked bough bed. Tayna jumped up, tripping when her feet didn't immediately dislodge from the mud. She slogged toward Mira, trying to avoid stepping on limbs as she entered the remains of the structure. The leaf she'd been using was splattered with sludge after her tumble, but she slapped the muck off before setting it over Mira's head. The bough bed wasn't so secure that it held all the water, but the leaves and other soft

101

fillings had been thoroughly drenched. Mira stopped blinking so fervently and weakly lifted the leaf up just enough to see Tayna.

"Where's Marek?"

"He's going to be fine. He got lost, but he'll be back."

"So everyone's going to lie about everything…"

"It's the truth," Tayna's eyes widened and she leaned forward, "I'm certain of it."

"Then tell me, am I hanging on for nothing?" Her voice cracked. "Are they already gone?"

"I don't," Tayna just shook her head, stunned at the confrontation, "I don't know. Please, don't ask me that."

"Find someone to kill me," Mira deliriously begged, moving her head side to side. "If they didn't make it, I don't want to be here anymore."

Tayna wanted to set the leaf down and run, but there was nowhere to go.

"Uh, I can't, this won't be the most accurate, so I could be completely wrong."

Tayna fidgeted, trying to get herself under the leaf as well. She put her hands together, her thumbs resting against her forehead. She wasn't sure how long this would take or if anything would come to her at all. Most visions only played out if they were directly related to Tayna's life in some way. Usually, she was more prepared as well, having an entire set up ready with a full stomach and plenty of water beforehand. It might be a vision she would see or it could be a full trance she would enter. She hoped it wouldn't be the latter. Those were difficult to come out of and time could whittle her away if she wasn't prepared or if no one pulled her out of it.

Harlok's ramblings rattled around like loose change in a metal purse. She could hear his voice, going on and on about the first veil. He would say it was the veil Thessa wore to protect her truth from prying eyes.

"You won't know it's there until you see passed it," he would say. "You can only see through the first veil when you stop looking."

She pushed these nonsensical old phrases and distractions from her mind, focusing on the spot her thumbs were resting. She had gotten used to the rain, but the booming thunder rattling them all to the bone was a major hindrance to her meditation. Since Tayna had trained to use visions from a young age, she was always aware of them even if she didn't listen. After coming outside, the thunderstorms had stirred up deeply unsettling visions, manifesting as fears instead of certainties or even possibilities. She had foreseen such horrifically unnatural images

102

during the last storm that she prayed to Thessa for sleep so they would stop.

Crackling sparks shredded through the dark sky and vivid images of monstrous beasts dove at her in the illumination followed immediately by the mountain-sized giant pushing Haven down on top of all of them. It was so real to her, she clutched her chest and gasped wide-eyed at nothing. Mira put her hand on Tayna's arm and shut her eyes with her. Her warm touch soothed her enough that Tayna found herself slipping away, into a waking dream. The rain grew quieter, the thunder that rolled turned to a constant buzzing hum and everything slowly became brighter, until it was glowing. The moment was freezing, time was stilling and although Tayna knew she was in a trance, it was nothing like knowing when you're in a dream. She would be released when it was done with her, not when she chose to wake from it.

Tayna looked down at her bright hands as everything came to a stop. People all around her were illuminated, huddled together under the raindrops waiting to fall. Some people were brighter than others. She was surprised to see an old man beside Savan with a light shining as bright as some of the children suspended in play. Mira's hands were a dark gray, more than anyone else in the area. They were on an unchangeable path at that point. Tayna focused on Mira, knowing she was not going to make it through the night. Absorbing her face, pitying how she would spend her final hours, Tayna wished there was more she could do for people than tell them what was going to happen. As her chest grew heavy, she saw a dim light beginning to shine through the middle of Mira's belly. The side of Tayna's face began to tingle and she put her hand over it, amused at the feeling. All physical feelings were absent in a trance. This had never happened to her before.

As if a cup of frigid water had been splashed on her face, Tayna was jerked out of her trance. It was still dark, raining, and she didn't feel any more or less hungry than she had before, although the returning sensations were unpleasant. The guy that had begged her to speak to Mira earlier was holding her up on her feet and had just slapped her across the face. The burning was starting to tingle across her cheek.

"Hey! Hey, wow, there you are, I'm sorry…it's just," he stopped and nodded toward a gathering at the edge of the clearing.

Tayna pushed him away and stumbled over to the group of people. There were Grays, Uppers, Sunskins, and then some she didn't recognize. The ones that had emerged from the forest were armed with primitive weapons and their leader was clothed in layered green and patchy-blue scale armor with buckles down the middle. They set bags of food down between the two very different groups of people. Everyone was tense and although the storm had not yet died down, it was at the back of their minds. Tayna saw Miksi speaking with their leader. He called himself Zaruko and was so tall, he had to bend over to be close enough to hear her over the cascading storm.

The people from Haven all hovered too close, craning their necks and tilting their heads to better hear the exchange in the deluge. So many of these new people had just emerged from the forest all at once, as if they'd been casually walking through it. They held improvised torches and showed no fear of the flickering flames that erratically danced in the downpour, as if trying to avoid every raindrop. Even though their leader was drenched from head to heel, his inner framework was constructed like someone of nobility and superiority. Even bent at the waist with his head cocked to one side, listening to an old woman shout in his ear, it was easy to see who he was by the way his people acted around him. The warrior's eyes darted from movement to movement and even though they kept their weapons down and didn't move, they were ready to attack at a moment's notice.

Miksi and Zaruko politely shouted at each other over the rain.

"We're not going with you, Zaruko, and that's that. I'll not ask these people to set one toe in that forest."

"We understand your hesitation, but you aren't safe out here. You must come with us to Imperyo."

"Must?"

"Please," Zaruko lowered his head even further, "we are offering you a safe haven. We have homes, a city, walls for protection. We have food and water."

Jahzara lurked beside Zaruko giving him irritated glares and sighs, triggered by his groveling. Tayna thought she had a cruel look to her, but wrote it off as an effect of her reaction to the foul weather. Her hair was soaked and matted against her forehead and she was holding her arms very tightly. Her nostrils flared every time Miksi refused Zaruko, who was offering his best arguments for why they should go.

The rain began to ease up and Tayna could finally hear the words they were shouting to each other.

"Lord Durako is offering you all his protection," Zaruko said, his tone dropping.

"You may stay until morning, but then I must ask you all to leave us. I gave you my answer, stranger. You cannot convince me to set a single toe in those woods."

Zaruko stood up straight, sighed, and looked around at the pitiful camp. They would have to stay there in the clearing, exposed to the elements all night. It would be the best way to garner trust with these people and get many of them to follow him back to the mountain city.

Jahzara moved like a bolt of lightning sent straight from the storm. She ripped a small, misshaped dagger downward from the belt strap between her breasts and jammed it into Miksi's throat. Screams popped out above the lessening rain and everyone started to stumble back, avoiding the blood and putting more space between themselves and the new strangers. Jahzara tore the dagger away from Miksi's throat and a pressurized jettison of red sprayed out, drenching Jahzara's arm, but the rain worked fast to rinse it away. She shoved the Upper back and she fell flat, too stunned to brace herself. The terrified crowd jumped away from her, cowering into themselves. No one attempted to catch her or come any closer to help the woman many of them had claimed to be so close with.

"Jahzara!" Zaruko barked, coming back around the people to reach her.

Jahzara ignored him, bent down, and pulled Miksi's shoe off, beginning to saw at her big toe. Miksi coughed and blood shot straight up, coming back down across her face, but no other sound was heard. When the toe was freed, Jahzara tossed it into the woods. The toe rolled to a stop just a little further from where it landed. A smile trickled across her face, lingering even as she spoke.

"We are the Impery and an Impery doesn't grovel. Especially not to Sinovians. You'll do what's commanded," she shouted, glaring down at Miksi.

Jahzara jammed her dagger into the sheathe just as Zaruko grabbed her shoulder and roughly spun her around.

"You were to be silent during negotiations!"

"I was just hurrying things along," Jahzara scoffed, pushing his hand away. "I know, you were almost to the part where you put your face in the mud, but I'm tired of standing out in the rain and I am not staying out here all night. I want to get back home and be done with this."

Zaruko tightened his knuckles around the hilt of his sword. He spoke each word through clenched teeth. "Do not interfere again."

Jahzara gave a mocking bow.

"Everyone, please," Zaruko ordered loudly, trying not to look down at Miksi's body, "follow us. I assure you, we will all make it safely through the forest to Imperyo if we stay together."

Jahzara scoffed, rolled her eyes, and trudged toward the middle of the bewildered bystanders. They were all watching her, afraid to be the first to move around her. Tayna fled to the half-standing structure where

Mira still rested. The remainder of the people started to hesitantly follow their new captors into the woods they had so adamantly avoided those past few days.

Savan followed Tayna to the injured, as well as Mira.

"They're just going to leave them?"

"Mira," Tayna said, taking her hand. "I think we're going to have to move you."

"You never told me what you saw," Mira whispered.

"What's this?" Jahzara said, standing behind Tayna. She was looking at a man with an injured leg and sniffing the air. "Oh, my, burn me...what is that smell? Is he dead?" There was a long pause, but Tayna was too afraid to turn around. "No...he's just rotting. Leave him. And what is this?"

Tayna tried to use her tiny body to cover Mira, but Jahzara kicked her out of the way. Mira drew a quick breath and her pale, broken lips parted at the sight of Jahzara hovering above her. The violent Impery dropped to her knees beside Mira and began asking rapid questions, but all Mira could do was slowly blink. Jahzara turned to Tayna and grabbed her by the sleeve.

"What is this?" She asked, every word over-annunciated.

"She's...pregnant," Tayna answered.

Jahzara slapped her, "*I can see that.* Why is she not prepared? Why is she lying like this?" When Tayna didn't immediately answer, Jahzara slapped her again.

"I don't know!"

Tayna's face was burning on one side and her eyes started welling up. Jahzara roughly guided her by the arm to the other side of the bough bed. She took the knife out of the sheathe and Tayna's heart slammed to a stop. As Jahzara bent over and spoke to Mira, mouth to ear, Tayna wished she had more thorough visions. She could've prevented Miksi from being murdered. They could've been prepared for these invaders if she hadn't given up so easily earlier. As Jahzara drew back and slid the knife across Mira's throat, Tayna gripped the side of the bed and squeezed her eyes shut. She couldn't breathe. She couldn't see Savan's face draining of color. There had never been violence like this, even on level fourteen. The jumpers did it of their own accord and it was over as soon as it happened. She hadn't been there during the evacuation of Haven, brought on by her own father. Hearing Mira choking, she ignored her gut, opened her eyes and watched everything happen.

Mira was startled, but unafraid and looked as though she was simply struggling to count very high very slowly. From the corner of her eye, Tayna saw Jahzara taking a knife to Mira's belly. Mira reached her hand out and Tayna took it. She knew she was squeezing as hard as she could, but it was just a loose grip. Mira had nothing left in her. Nothing but that single glowing light.

# CHAPTER EIGHT

Rain collected in the man-sized leaves making them sag like cupped hands. They poured water down the skyward-reaching roots when they grew too heavy. Above the forest floor, a webbed tangle of braches held Vik captive. He had dropped down into a rounded bundle and fallen too far to climb back out the way he came. The tallbugs were gone and he had no idea how long he'd been in the forest, hanging in its net. The sunlight could barely squeak through the cracks in the canopy. He couldn't see Marek anywhere.

Vik kicked at the smallest branch directly under him. The worn, thin soles on his slick shoes absorbed none of the shock from the solid wood smashing against the soft middle of his foot. When that didn't work, he stood straight up, held the branches around him like a prison cell and stomped his foot down over and over. He used both feet after a few tries, jumping up and down, using the sway of the tree limbs to gain momentum behind his weight. The branches swung upward as he stomped down, turning his ankle sideways. Vik fell against the wood and heard a snap. He expected to feel the surging pain just before his ankle swelled, but it never did. The sound was of a branch finally breaking loose. Hearing another crack from above, the stubborn cage lost another crucial branch and the single split turned into several more snaps and splinters before the cage fell, hitting waves of branch layers on the way down.

The forest floor was mostly made of mulch and shredded leaves. Leathery flowers bigger than a man budded out from the base of the trees, not bothering to angle their white and yellow centers toward the light. Thin with wide petals and bright orange, they were too cheerful to blend in with the quieted woods. Every assortment of flying insect took turns to rub its pollen on their bodies. Amidst the twisting branches and tremendous trunks all shaded in the half-light, the soft orbs of color were like faint stars just above the dirt.

As Vik wriggled out of the bent cage, he heard a strange warbling ring out. He only heard it once, but the hush that followed it was unnatural, like a subtle signal for everything in the know to abruptly shut up and duck down. Glancing over the lush scenery around him, the roots that he had been climbing on up in the tree tops, drooped down all over the area around the main segments of the tree. He had mistaken them for thinner, straighter trees standing around a mighty one on wavy, stilted legs. The bulky trunk of the tree started much further above the ground, standing on its curly, coiled roots underneath. It was still raining, but his only real clue was the meek tapping far above and the trickling streams flowing down every skinny root. There was no wind that deep in the forest and nothing else around. Nothing he could see.

Leaning against the wall of gnarly bark, Vik noticed a puncture in its skin. Oozing from the wound was a transparent, reddish-colored sap. He poked at it and his finger stuck fast, creating a drippy string to bridge the displacement. The sweet, tart aroma tempted him to stick out his tongue like a curious toddler, but he hesitated. Recalling the younger children that went around Haven licking rocks, their mothers exasperated and disgusted. Vik remembered when he had been in the kitchen, waiting for Havard to finish helping his mother prepare bloodstones into slices. He pushed his tongue against the wall he was leaning against and heard his mother's bouncing laughter. She was holding up a bloodstone slice and shaking her head.

"Do these taste that bad? I guess too many of my taste buds have died."

Vik licked the goop on his hand and although none of it actually came off, the taste was smooth and sent tingles down his neck. He didn't dare try to bite off a bit or his teeth might never come apart. It didn't have the punch of a bloodstone, but a sweetness that flowed into every corner of his entire body. The edges of his mouth turned up and he closed his eyes. The first thing he'd ever tasted not made from bloodstones, rocks, metal, blood, skin, smoke, and water. It was nothing like any of that. His chest tightened and the whole forest became a little less dark and strange.

It didn't help with how lost he was though. Unable to see the sky, the mountain, or anything but trees and parts of trees, Vik considered his options. He stood perfectly still and listened for the bustle of the settlement, but even standing in the middle of it, they didn't make much noise. Taking a few steps to one side and leaning to see around a trunk, then spinning around to look directly behind him, he licked another bit of sap off his hand and murmured under his breath.

"Tayna would love this…"

Vik closed his eyes and sighed, opening them again and scanning around him with as blank a mind as he could manage. With a foolishly wide grin plastered across his face, he walked in the direction he felt most compelled by, continuing to lick his sappy hand and feeling good about going with his gut for once.

Just a few minutes into his journey Vik heard another warble and stopped, mid-stride, sucking in a deep gulp of muggy air. His smile melted like the sap in his mouth. There in front of him, hanging effortlessly from the side of the giant tree, were three perfectly motionless creatures. Each of them six-legged and from head to tail each was as long as two grown men. Their tails were half their body length and they were covered in tiny, glossy scales. They were a sickly green color with dark blue patches all over, like they were supposed to be spots but they got smudged. These creatures also had the strangest heads. Stunted, round and wrinkled with no eyes to speak of, they used their two sets of nostrils stationed near the top of their heads to breathe in and absorb their surroundings. Two separate inhales and one long exhale through both sets.

The one closest to Vik let out a warble like the sound from earlier, the one he'd ignored but a little bit louder. Several more unseen creatures returned the call. They began descending from the trees and hanging roots, using their larger pairs of legs and arms to crawl vertically while their smaller set of arms were held safely tucked against their chests. The smaller hands had claws that were black as the night and straight as they could grow. They could have easily cut through a man Vik's size. The warbling was a great contrast to their appearance. It was sweet and bouncy, curious bubbly as they chirped at each other from tree to tree. There were so many of them and they were all facing him and sniffing at the air, only moving in short bursts and then becoming like statues as they waited. When the one closest to him hissed it was a light sound, like dragging your finger across sandpaper. Vik didn't need a loud sound to convince him to step away. The creatures filled the area with the hissing, but it never evolved into anything louder than that.

The hollow echo of a snapping crack directed their heads away from him. Muffled thumps rained down as they started leaping from the trees. Vik turned toward the resonated sound, dug his slippery shoes into the mulch and started running as hard and fast as he could, tripping over everything along the way. And there was a lot to trip over. The forest felt more like an obstacle course when he started running through it. The mulch made the ground deceptively even, but coiled roots were constantly popping out and grabbing at his feet along with the ones he had to duck under and weave himself through. The creatures hissing grew louder as they dropped down or ran up too close to him, the frequent reminder of their proximity adding to his frenzy. As he misplaced his next step, his foot fell through the mulch and his body launched him forward, down a short, steep hill. The beasts did not follow, instead responding to the playful rallying cry of their leader.

*****

Marek slowly blinked the woods into focus from inside his tiny, wooden cave. Rock solid under-roots curled above to cover him while he hid beneath the base of a colossal tree, balanced on its woven foundation like a dancer suspended mid-swirl. The muggy, earthy smell made his thoughts dizzily float during every inhale like a first-time swimmer over deep water. Blood matted in his hair, coating the pulsing pain on the side of his head in coagulated warmth. Still in a daze from the fall and the dense air, he reached up to feel it, his fingers massaging into his clumped black hair until he found the wound. The searing stab made him lurch and hiss through his teeth.

Carefully sticking his head out of the woven shelter under the enormous tree, he squinted through the shadowy areas beyond the roots.

"Vik?" he called out hoarsely, his hands cupped on either side of his mouth.

The forest was the only one to respond. Bouncing, bubbling cackles echoed between every tree, going from maybe three creatures to dozens as their eerie chortles multiplied. Marek ducked down and slid back, scanning the area as best he could until the curious sounds faded back into the trees. Something heavy and wet slithered down his shoulder, spreading across his back. Reflexively slapping at it, he drew back his hand covered in reddish goop and tried to rub it off on his shirt. The fabric clung to his hand and the longer he took to wipe it off, the harder it got to move his hand.

"Dammit, Vik," Marek grumbled, steeling himself to step outside. "I follow him and something bad always happens…"

Not ten steps away from the tree, a scratching sound could be heard from above. He narrowed his eyes, peering hard into the tangled treetops, but he couldn't see anything. Stomping over the crunching mulch, he continued trying to rub the transparent, sticky substance off his fingers but it had formed a firm layer over his skin. Once again there was a scratching over his head, but this time it was followed by a thumping, and louder more frequent scraping. Not just from above but from the sides, behind him, and every direction except for one.

Marek chose the less ominous path and bolted in that direction, pumping his arms and legs as fast as they could go, trying his best to hurdle over roots and branches in his way. His head started to throb once again and his vision would shift around, disorienting him. Tripping over a hidden root curving out of the ground, Marek threw mulch every which way with his face. Rolling over on his back, he groaned and blinked hard, tensing up his whole body. Another set of eyes met his, attached to a creature twisting around the corner of the wooden, gnarled tower, nestled in the crevice of a protruding branch. It was so perfectly still, Marek had been staring at it for too long before realizing that wasn't a part of the tree. He jerked back, falling twice on his way to his feet and let out a cut off, pitch-flailing shout he would've been embarrassed of if anyone else had been around to hear it. The creature responded to his movements with the only movement being the vibration of its throat releasing a playful, trilling chirp.

Marek didn't wait to find out what might answer its call. He kicked up dirt and clawed his way over the terrain. Pushing passed the next tangle of hanging roots, he stumbled forward and slammed directly into an Impery warrior. Marek and the stunned man hit the ground gracelessly, slapping up wood chips in every direction. Shouting broke out around him, but his head was buzzing, muddling what they were saying. The Impery rolled him off and held him on the ground, his knee against his chest. He held a crude spear choked up to the sharp end just in front of Marek's face. He appeared to be too surprised to form words.

"Gamba, I'll handle it. Get them up and closer together," Zaruko ordered, pointing toward the startled Sinovians.

Gamba's eyes were still wide and fixed, but Marek was the one who couldn't believe what he was seeing. This man was not from Haven. His eyes were thinner, his skin was much darker than he'd ever seen a man's skin get before. Bronzed, like a child of the sun should be. Even comparing the Haven Sunskins to them would've been like night and day. His hair was not black like theirs, but a reddish brown, just like his eyes. Gamba lifted his knee off of Marek then offered his hand to help him up. He took it and was roughly jerked to his feet.

While Gamba herded the Sinovians together, Marek saw two undeniably different groups of people. Those from Haven stood out like unpainted black and white splotches in the woods, but the new men looked to be made from pieces the forest.

"Who are you...?" Marek barely managed to get the words out.

"What did I say to everyone when we started out? Don't separate."

"What?"

"Stay with the group. Do you understand?" Zaruko glanced at Marek's hands, "Did anything follow you?"

"Uh, yeah," Marek turned and pointed behind him, "these things, they were chasing me. Big, crawling things. Same color as your shirt."

"It's armor," Zaruko corrected, snatching Marek's arm and inspecting the goop on his fingers. "You saw a drass?"

Marek was surprised they hadn't come barreling after him. It was eerily quiet in the woods again and the Impery knew they were still nearby. Following the scent Marek carried with him. Zaruko held his hand straight up above him in the air with his thumb tucked in and many of his warriors mirrored him. The Sinovians from Haven settled into an uneasy silence, huddled together like cattle. Their eyes darted around while they hunched, except for Tayna. She adamantly stared at Marek, trying to catch his attention so he would know she had to speak to him. She was holding a newborn baby boy in her arms.

"Were they drass?" Zaruko whispered.

"I don't know what that is," Marek whispered back.

"Next time, pay attention. I don't like repeating myself."

"Who are you?" Marek asked, glancing around at his people and taking note of their numbers, "Is that everyone? Are we going somewhere?"

Zaruko studied him, screwing up his face. Although the Sinovians from Haven were not the cleanest they'd ever been, Marek was by far the most filthy.

"Have you been out in the wilds this whole time?"

"Yeah…"

"Alone?"

"No, I think my brother's still—"

A warbling coo broke into their conversation. They whipped their heads around and saw the face of a drass leering down at them, its nostrils frantically flaring while the rest of it held perfectly still. Deeming the size of the group too large to be worth the trouble alone, it disappeared with a simple flick of its neck. Zaruko seemed to ease up just a little, but his motions were still carefully guided. One of the lady warriors lifted the back of Marek's shirt and roughly turned him around.

"Off," Zaruko barked, pointing at his shirt. "Get this off, we'll get you another," he snapped his fingers at someone else while he said this to Marek.

"But this is my grandfather's, why do I—"

"They're just clothes. Hurry up."

Marek reluctantly pulled it over his head, the sticky sap peeling away from his skin. Zaruko balled it up and hurled it as hard as he could into the forest. They all heard the familiar thumping of drass bodies throwing themselves around where the clothes had fallen.

"Do they, uh, do they hate sweaty clothes?"

"They eat the sap. They especially love when some stupid animal gets trapped in it." Zaruko turned his attention back to Marek, "Now go over to the vein, there."

He pointed to an aerial root nearby, thick enough around to be mistaken for a tree like the holograms he'd seen of normal ones in Haven. Marek stood by it as he was told and Zaruko twirled the air with his finger while the same lady warrior stayed by them. She licked her lips like she was about to start a speech and spit on the ground off to the side. Several small chunks of mulch caught fire.

"What are you doing?"

"We've got to get the sap off or you're going to attract more of them," Zaruko told him, "Do not move, hold the tree if you need to keep still."

"Is this going to hurt?" Marek asked, his voice going up high at the end.

Zaruko appeared amused, but shook his head, "No. Not if you hold perfectly still."

Marek found little comfort in his words, especially since the Impery man took several steps back. The young woman gave him an assuring pat on the back and Marek shut his eyes tight, sucking in a deep breath. The Impery spit into her hand and smeared in on the sap stuck to his back, then took several steps back, drew in a heavy breath and blew a jet of flames out from her mouth. Marek could hear some of the Sinovians gasping and screaming, but Gamba tried to calm them down. Zaruko jogged over to the group and held out his hands, but Marek couldn't hear what he was saying over the abrupt fiery blast. The heat against his back reminded him of pressing his bare back against the cold, stone walls back home. He could feel the woman searching his back with her hands for any more sap, catching here and there but not deeming it enough to concern herself with.

"Alright, hold out your hands," she ordered.

Zaruko shoved a loosely woven shirt the color of a bruise into Marek's arms and motioned for him to join the rest of his people. He stumbled forward, pulling the garment over his head and tying the twine on the right side, over his shoulder, as tightly as he could. Marek approached the ex-Haven dwellers, noticing that some fearfully watched their captors while others let their wide-eyes wander around above them. He saw Tayna, but her back was turned. An Impery woman was lecturing her and he didn't see Mira anywhere. The woman finished with Tayna and started shouting at Zaruko.

"Why are we cooling our heels? Let's go! I want to get back with my little Garek here…" Jahzara cradled a newborn baby in her arms, rocking him back and forth. Marek was overcome with desperation and panic.

"Garek!? That's my son, that's my son!" He shouted, attempting to snatch his child from the stranger's arms. "Where's Mira? Where's his mother?"

Jahzara had turned her whole body and Garek to the side, aiming her shoulder at him. She was filled to the brim with indignation. The warriors froze. Every single person in the woods watched them without speaking a word, but Marek didn't notice anything besides his son in the stranger's arms.

Jaw set and eyes nearly popping out of their narrow slots, she snapped at him, "She's dead. And this is the only one."

Not even the trees rustled. Zaruko watched Jahzara out of the corner of his eyes, as if direct contact would send her into a raging blaze.

"Give me…my son," Marek said slowly, teeth bared.

Jahzara's gaze did not break. She kept her shoulder pointed at him, her stillness growing more unnerving with every passing second, but on this he refused to budge. Gamba held his arm out to the warriors and they eased their aggressive stances. They couldn't risk hurting the infant. Marek was keeping himself numb to everything but what was right in front of him. During their silent standoff, the woman's words began to register. Mira was dead. No goodbyes…

Garek stirred in Jahzara's arms and her grip tightened before her whole demeanor sharply morphed before them. She loosened her stance, raised her chin and forced a very stiff, unconvincing smile.

"Be careful with him," she said, gently transferring Garek into Marek's arms.

Zaruko wasn't breathing and his brows were crammed together. Marek carefully cradled Garek's head in the crook of his elbow and breathed down at the tiny baby boy.

"Hi Garek, hey…" he whispered, his eyes and nose burned furiously, "I'm your daddy. I've got you now."

"He can't understand you," Jahzara snapped.

Even though the situation looked to be diffused, none of the warriors were settled by what they'd seen. Many of them took turns trudging over to Zaruko to whisper suspicions in his ear. Most of them he was already aware of, but some he had tried not to consider. As Gamba talked quietly beside him to one of the other warriors, Zaruko watched Marek wiping his tears off with one hand, smiling down at the baby's scrunched up face. Zaruko shifted his eyes to the dirt, his brows creased together, wringing his own hands as he felt without thinking about the way it all should have been.

Jahzara marched over to Tayna and grabbed her tightly by the arm. Her nails dug deep into her skin, easily piercing it and striking blood. Once she had led Tayna far enough away, she unhinged her talons.

"When we get to Imperyo, I'm giving you my mark so people know not to touch you or to hurt you in any way."

"Th…Thank y—"

"Don't," she hissed, rolling her eyes and sneering, "In the meantime, even before we get there, I need you to do what I say. Without question."

"Jahzara," Zaruko said after waving his arm in a circle at her, "We're leaving."

Jahzara gave the girl one last tight squeeze before pushing her back to the Sinovian group, but Tayna couldn't take her eyes off Zaruko. Every time he made a quick motion such as jutting his arm out to point or moving too fast, she saw a flicker of something not there. A piece of her trance, left over. This had never happened to her before. Harlok might've said something about it, but she stopped listening a long time ago. She wanted to say something to Zaruko, but there was nothing to say that he would understand. All she saw was broken images of fire, a woman with a burned face, and two children, boys. As soon as she found a quiet moment, if they lived through the woods and made it to the Imperyo they kept telling them about, she was going to prepare and meditate on these visions. Knowing the significance of this Impery man could be the only way she could see her boys again.

Once Tayna was herded in with the rest of the Sinovians, Zaruko began repeating his instructions on what not to do from there on out. Marek was in the very back and having trouble hearing his deep, subdued voice.

"What'd he say?" he whispered to a woman beside him, but she was a Gray and turned her head from him as soon as she saw his face.

Despite the gash on his head, various cuts and bruises, grime from the forest and their unfamiliar predicament, she still only saw the Upper in him. She could have been one of the Grays that got out during all the chaos. The thought crossed his mind that she could even have thrown Uppers from the stairway herself. A heat rose up into his cheeks. He sneered when she wasn't looking and searched around for someone less appalling to speak to, but found he was surrounded by Grays.

"He said don't touch anything," she finally mumbled, facing the other way.

116

"Don't touch anything?" Marek scoffed, "Why not?"

The Gray woman just rolled her eyes at him and that was the last bit of attention she paid him. She wasn't the only one to be giving him the cold shoulder. Marek cradled Garek tight to his chest, gazing over the crowd for Vik, but he didn't see his brother anywhere. He was all Garek had left. Tayna was there, but he didn't believe she could protect his son from anything. Besides, his cousin was Harlok's daughter. That's not how he wanted Garek raised. These thoughts were wrecking him, raising his paranoia and anxiety levels as high as they'd ever been. The baby's neck suddenly seemed even more fragile and his head was so loose, every time he took a rough step he snapped his eyes down to ensure his son hadn't suffered from it. Exhausted and untrusting of his legs, he took it nice and slow. All it would take was for him to trip one time…

"Marek," Tayna said, strolling up beside him. "Do you need me to feed him?"

"What? Oh, yes, please take him," Marek rambled, awkwardly transferring him to Tayna's arms.

As she pulled the overall loop over her head and ran it up one arm, she raised her tunic up one side and cradled Garek in front of her breast. Marek shifted his eyes away toward the branches creating a woven roof above them. He started thinking about how Mira didn't want strangers raising her child and how they were going to be living in his house, since Vik was living outside. It didn't feel real yet, them being trapped out there, cut off from Haven, her really being gone. There was no closure. Again he started to think about the worst of it. No final words, no goodbye…

Tayna tried not to think of her own children as she looked down at the baby, but Garek's pudgy face was just like theirs. Her boys were a couple of years older, but time flew by as they grew. Stroking his silky-soft head with the back of her fingers, she looked up and watched the path they took more carefully. After coming over a large root jutting out of the ground, her eyes met with one of the Impery warriors, a woman with only a few years more than Tayna. She smiled at her instinctively before looking away, blinking profusely with her lips curled inward and pressed together. Many of the other warriors were watching her with upturned brows or smiling, tearful eyes. Some of them were men as well, watching her not with lust but mournful longing.

"Marek," Tayna whispered. He leaned closer without looking at her. "I don't know if you've noticed…but these people seem strange about children."

"No, I hadn't noticed."

Tayna took a deep breath and marched ahead, toward Zaruko, Gamba, and Jahzara. She was looking at the back of Jahzara's head and trying not to imagine her face. When Tayna cleared her throat, Jahzara whipped around with those same sharp features she wore like a warning label, but at the sight of Garek they softened into a tolerable scowl.

"What?"

"I was...wondering, um, what are we, uh...when we get to Imperyo, or afterward...whenever, um..."

Jahzara sighed very loudly, "Lucky for you, it's a long walk."

"What are we going to be doing at Imperyo?" Tayna spat out the words just to get rid of them.

"Working."

"On what?"

Jahzara shot her a glare that chilled her straight through. Tayna apologized before she could stop the words from leaving her mouth. Jahzara marched ahead of her, snapping at anyone who dared to look at her, warrior or Sinovian.

"You'll mostly be farming," Zaruko started speaking without looking at her. His face was bright red and his hands were fidgeting to keep themselves busy. "But there are many other things to keep you occupied. Many other things that need doing."

"Farming?" Tayna said airily.

Zaruko smirked at her, but quickly turned his head away again, "It's not as fun as it sounds. There's a lot of work to surviving out in Agrona. We don't have dispensaries or any other machines to speak of..."

"So the Thesmekka haven't come back to your people either?"

"Do not," Zaruko tilted his head toward her, "mention the Thesmekka again. That can get you in a lot of trouble."

"Why?"

"It's a long story I don't feel like telling right now."

"So you do know about them then. They saved your people, too."

Zaruko dared to sneak a peek at her face, scowling but turning quickly away before his eyes could wander, "No. They tried to kill us."

Tayna's brain couldn't process what he had said. It tried to rework the words, then it tried to imagine all the possible ways his people could have misunderstood what the Thesmekka were really trying to do for them.

Jahzara sauntered up behind Marek, biting her bottom lip to keep from grinning, "So you're the father?"

118

Marek whipped around, stumbling on the uneven terrain, "Y, yes."

"I need to talk to you about the mother," Jahzara said solemnly. "I should tell you what happened."

"Yeah," Marek was hit with a cold sweat, "Yeah, please."

Marek didn't want to hear it, not yet, and not from her. If anyone was going to tell him how his sieva died, he would rather it have been someone he knew. Someone he was certain wasn't trying to steal his son.

"Let's talk right over there, it won't take long, we can catch right back up. It's not proper to talk about in front of other people."

Marek steered off with her, following her behind a series of obstructing roots, hurdling over a twisted, arched protrusion. Jahzara peered around the corner and saw that Zaruko was plenty distracted with the Sinovian girl and the baby. She ripped the knife from her sheathe and pointed the blade at him.

Marek held up his hands and backed away, "What are you doing?"

"Don't be afraid yet," she assured him with a wild grin, "I'm just going to tell you what happened."

"You can do that without the knife…"

"It's a very important part of the story. Your sieva, you do have sivs and sievas, right? You don't just go around making more of your kind with whoever…"

"She was my sieva," Marek snapped.

"That's so…civilized," she blinked slowly, "Your sieva wasn't going to make it and she was killing the babies inside her, so I cut her throat, then I cut little Garek out of her." She made a slicing motion in the air at Marek, "So you see, I brought that baby into the world. I saved him from the mother that tried to kill him. He's mine."

"I would die before I let you touch him again," Marek promised, leaning toward the knife without fear.

"The only thing holding me back is the mess. And the tantrum your Lord of the Mud People throws when one of you gets a scratch," she sneered in Zaruko's direction, "It's disgusting. But you're in luck. Not many people get a warning from me."

"I guess I'm just not very grateful."

Jahzara scoffed, shaking the knife in his face, "Are you turning down my offer?"

"You are a complete roller," he sneered, "And if I ever see you near us again after we get to wherever we're going, I'll kill you."

Jahzara burst out laughing, breaking entirely away from her fortified stance until Marek tried to return to the group by going around her. She took a swing at him with the knife and cut him across his face. He swung out, knocking the knife out of her grip with the back of his hand and taking a wild swing at her, missing entirely. She pushed him as hard as she could when he stumbled at her, knocking him onto his side. While he struggled to get up, she plucked the knife off the ground and sucked in a deep breath. She lifted her tongue, preparing to spew fire over his body and watch him turn to ash. A few flecks of combustive chemicals flew off her lips as Vik's fist slammed into the side of her face. His momentum and element of surprise was enough to snuff her light and she toppled backward, flipping over the exposed root they'd hurdled on the way over there, the knife flying out of her hand. Vik scooped it up and stomped toward her, but Marek called out to him.

"Give it to me," he growled, holding his hand out.

Vik offered it eagerly and Marek slid over the root, holding the knife just above her belly. He heard the shouting in the distance and hesitated just long enough for Jahzara to become aware of the situation. She prepared to breathe fire at him, but he slapped his hand over her mouth.

"Stop!" Zaruko bellowed, nearly at them, "Don't, please wait."

He trotted to a stop beside them, not even a little out of breath. Giving the twins a double take, he hesitated while his brain sorted out the overwhelming similarities between them. Gamba appeared at his side not an instant later and held his hand out to Marek, "Give it to me, now."

"Please surrender the weapon," Zaruko negotiated, "I'm sure she deserves it, but if she dies then we all die."

Marek ground his teeth, squeezed the hilt tight enough to flex the tendons in his hand, shaking the knife in her face, "I will kill you if I see you again."

Blood ran from Jahzara's broken nose, spilling down her cheek into her hair and over her lips, smearing across her teeth. She cracked a crimson-stained grin and cackled on her back.

Marek and Vik plodded on in silence, unable to find the words for their relief, anger, and grief. But most of all, the confusion. Agrona was supposed to be a fresh start, to make a life for their people outside the confines of the mountain with only the fear of Brutes and the hope of seeing the Thesmekka again. There weren't supposed to be other people outside. No one was supposed to die. Mira was supposed to be there with them.

"Here, you should take some of these," said Vik, putting several orange pills in Marek's open hand.

120

"Thanks, keep those out of sight," said Marek, in a hushed voice.

"Marek," Vik cleared his throat, "I'm sorry I took us away."

Marek trudged along quietly for a while before he spoke to Vik, "You couldn't have known this would happen."

They didn't speak about it again during their journey through the woods, but Marek filled Vik in on what he understood to be going on, letting him know what he needed in order to stay out of trouble.

Gamba handed Zaruko a small chunk of bloodstone the other warriors had carved up, but he politely refused.

"You have to keep up your strength," Gamba insisted as they plodded along.

"I just need something to drink," Zaruko said, shaking his head.

"Don't worry about Jahzara. We're bringing her back alive. No one's getting punished for that. None of us, anyway."

"My father's already on edge knowing I'm bringing in new Sinovians. He sent his whore with us for a reason. I just don't think getting her nose cracked was part of their plan, that's all."

"What are you thinking?" Gamba asked, eating the piece of bloodstone, freeing his hands so he could give Zaruko his water.

"I think she's in too good a mood. I think, if she can, she's going to try and snuff us all before we make it back."

Zaruko's eyes darted around, but they couldn't find anything unusual. The trees were quiet, the foliage was inactive and there wasn't a chirp or a whistle to be heard. The group of Sinovians moved like a clumsy herd, but around them there was only silence. Zaruko's foot kicked something soft and he bent down to pick it up. It was an open leather bag, full of sap. There was another hanging from a tree and two more spilt out over exposed roots.

Tayna's pace slowed, her eyes glazed over and she stared unfocused into the forest. She held the sleepy baby and squeezed him a little tighter into her covered chest. Her posture turned rigid and she grew even paler than usual.

"Something's coming," she whispered. No one paid any attention to her so she shouted, "Something's coming!"

Several people were startled by her, Zaruko and Gamba included. Vik and Marek were right in front of her and jerked so hard when she yelled that they shouted angrily in return. A single, resonating warble rang out across the woods around them. Everyone became a statue, some mid-step, others holding a quickly drawn hunch. Even Jahzara dropped her demeanor and gazed fearfully into the woods. Warbles and chirps continued, ringing out over them like playful banter. Zaruko started shouting orders, no longer afraid of drawing attention from the forest.

"Circle up! Get together! As close as you can!"

One drass plopped down from a great tree nearby, directly in the middle of a group of Grays. Its scales brushed some of them and it clumsily slammed into a couple more. Everyone should have been able to easily obey Zaruko's orders, but they weren't in a clearing. There were nooks and crevices everywhere and many of them were scattered far enough away with too many obstacles between them to clear in a panic. No one wanted to be on the outside of the huddle either. The outer shell of the circle broke and they scattered around, pushing themselves between the curly roots that held up the giant trees and huddling together in their cave-like bellies. They forgot what Zaruko had told them, everything he'd said had been pushed aside to make way for their frantic search for safety.

The drass nested in the cave-like bellies of the trees and those who dove into their homes tried to scramble out before being shredded by the blind creatures. Most were too slow or realized their mistake too late. Others forgot to keep away from the vines, roots, and flowers. Some were swiftly coiled up by false vines into the maws of tallbugs which set off the familiar screeching wave across the forest canopy. Drass dove at the frantic Sinovians from around every corner of every tree and root. Zaruko and his warriors had passed through this exact part of the woods on their way to Haven and despite drass normally avoiding the scent of other creatures, they had since swarmed the area.

"Stay together!" Zaruko shouted in vain.

"Come back!" Gamba yelled, ducking and glancing upward to find the source of the whipping vines.

Other warriors tried to call for the Sinovians to return until they were confronting drass themselves. Zaruko threw the leather pouch down and blew fire into the face of a pursuing drass, causing it to give a shrill shriek and turn away on its heels. Tayna squeezed Garek tight, watching the Impery as they appeared to breathe fire. She felt safer and more helpless all at once.

Zaruko swung his sword around, stabbing one of the beasts in the neck and ripped it downward, hitting the ground hard enough to leave a dent in an exposed root. Tayna had never seen such violence and fled from it like a frightened animal. She had Garek held firmly in her arms and was spinning around, searching desperately for a safe place to hide that was still close to the Impery warriors. Each time she started running toward a crevice, people would flee from it as a drass pursued them, its elongated body swaying from the head to the tip of the tail.

122

When an Upper slammed into her, she almost knocked her down but Tayna caught herself on one knee. The woman was hit in the chest with a barbed tendril and yanked up into the air in a flash. Tayna put her other knee down and hunched over Garek, her face nearly touching the dirt. She tried to foresee this catastrophe more clearly, decide whether she should lay Garek down in the dirt or be prepared to run with him. She looked down at his face but his newly opening eyes were unfocused. His tongue was sticking out and his fingers stretched aimlessly out, but he did not seem to care about the screaming. Someone slammed into the ground beside her and she jerked hard enough to scare herself. A woman was shredded by a drass close enough to fleck blood on her clothes and Tayna screamed from her gut. She'd never felt that deep a fear. She'd never screamed that way in her entire life.

Trembling and whimpering, she wobbled up to one foot and immediately fell back on her knees before making herself get back up again. Garek was squirming in her arms and she cradled him tighter. Just as she neared a place to hide, someone grabbed her arm and jerked her around.

"Stay beside me," Jahzara hissed.

Jahzara guided her into the middle where several Sinovians were crouched down on the ground, covering their heads and keeping their eyes squeezed shut. Most of the Impery warriors were formed into a circle to surround them, blowing fire from their mouths and swinging their swords and axes at vines that came too close. Jahzara crouched down and yanked Tayna down with her. She kept a painfully tight grip on her arm, but Tayna didn't dare flinch away. She stared down at Garek and tried to focus on him. He was lucky he didn't know what was going on. Jahzara jerked her arm and held a long, slender finger in front of her face before hopping up and running into the fray. Tayna scuttled around on her knees until her back was pressed against someone else. It was Marek. He had followed the fire-breather's instructions like the few others around them.

"Is Garek alright?" he shouted.

"I think so," she struggled to say.

"Where's Vik?"

"I didn't see him," Tayna said, flinching from the heat of the Impery warrior in front of them.

Vik was lying flat on the ground, having just had a drass tail slam into his back as it made a sharp turn to slaughter someone. While he lay there, hands over the back of his head, all he could think about was Marek. He searched the area, still lying on his chest, but couldn't see him

123

anywhere. He cursed and shouted Marek's name with his hands cupped around his mouth. Several Impery were hurling pointed sticks straight up into the treetops. After Vik scrambled to his feet, a barbed tendril dropped right in front of him. The skewered body of a tallbug was falling through the weak branches and tumbling off the hovering roots. It broke loose from a thin tangle of branches and began its freefall down on Vik. He dove forward, barely escaping being crushed. The underbelly of the insect was lined with spear-ends and several warriors flew past him, ripping their weapons and pointed sticks out of the carcass and running back out toward the drass.

Vik saw on the ground in front of him a trail of orange pills, scattered out of his worn down pocket from the fall. As he reached out to try and grab them, someone hurried up beside him and started trying to pull a spear out, but was having trouble dislodging it. When he looked up at her face, he saw that it was Jahzara tugging on the spear, teeth bared and glaring right at him. He jumped up just as she managed to tear it out of the tallbug's carapace. She swung it wildly around as she staggered at him, barely missing each time. She managed to catch him on the top of his arm and opened up a gash across his skin. Vik yelled out, but it blended right in with everything else. The wound burned and bled, unhealing. The pill had worn off sometime after the forest, after all the many repairs to his body that adventure had required.

Jahzara took a deep breath, her chest puffed out and her eyes wide open. When she exhaled, she curled her tongue up to the top of her mouth and two chemicals jetted out from the space underneath. When the liquids met they ignited fiercely, billowing out at once, a roaring inferno rushing toward his face. Vik lunged to the side, but some of the chemical got on his clothing. He slapped his leg trying to get the quick spreading fire out. It felt like a chilled rock from the bottom levels was being held against his skin. Jahzara sucked in another breath and Vik scrambled out of the way. He sprinted around the bodies and the drass, panting, screaming, and tripping over every uneven piece of terrain in his path.

His foot fell through a hidden space between roots, bringing his attention to a good hiding place while Jahzara briefly lost sight of him. He slipped onto his side, rolled himself over on the soft mulch and wedged under some horizontal, low-growing roots. Jahzara stalked closer, coming to a stop just in front of where Vik was hiding and slammed the end of the spear into the ground. There was a pause where he could see her legs straining to keep her balance as she looked around more. She roared and rammed the end of the spear into the ground again and again. She stopped short and held the spear in the middle.

124

"No, this is good," she assured herself, "he's dead out here."

As she spoke, the roots above Vik creaked and he could hear a drass slowly approaching Jahzara. He got his hopes up, but in a single jet of flames she drove the curious creature back into the tree it had crawled out of. She let out one last furious shout and then marched away shortly after, leaving Vik alone under the mossy tree. He let his head hit the cool ground and shut his eyes so he could finally breathe.

In the distance, the screaming, screeching, and warbling calls eventually died down. The small space he'd inhabited under the root smelled too much like musty rot to stay any longer. Trembling, he slowly pulled himself out of cover and stood on weak legs. They were as sturdy as vines, ready to collapse if he came face to face with anything. He stumbled back to the clearing, rolling himself over a fuzzy green root, gnarled into a strange sort of one-way staircase and dropping over the other side. Landing on his hands, he buckled and hit his chin on the ground. Groaning, he rolled onto his side and looked across the forest floor. His eyes searched over every tree, every root, and between every branch for a living person.

He saw no one.

# CHAPTER NINE

Above the weary travelers, the intertwined branches and roots creaked and moaned. A giant bird landed and jabbed into a tallbug's shell, sounding like someone knocking on metal with a hammer. When the shell finally cracked the tallbug shrieked and squealed. The remaining survivors slapped their hands over their ears and ducked down, but their guides pushed them to their feet. Gamba waved his hand over his head in a circular motion. They couldn't afford to stop every time the forest made a sound. There weren't enough of them left.

In the thick of it, far from any clearing or mountain, beasts were not accustomed to eating people or even the scent of them. Another reason Zaruko came to the decision he had made. Drass nested that deeply in the woods would not gather on their trail and wait to ambush them like they did. They lived in small packs covering modest territories, which they rarely ventured out of. People were a foreign scent, something to be observed or avoided, and he had been sure to leave a minimal trace behind. The aroma of sap from the giant trees was what drove the drass to aggression and curiosity, nothing else interested them so much as that.

"Vik!" Marek shouted repeatedly, both hands cupped around his mouth.

He had just finished searching the survivors and couldn't find his brother anywhere. The Impery warrior nearest him threw his spear into his other hand and grabbed Marek by the back of the neck, leaning in close to growl warnings in his ear. Marek held his hands up at chest level in a surrendering gesture and the warrior let him go, shaking his head as he stomped ahead, irritably swinging his spear around every obstacle. Tayna saw the exchange and hurried to his side, offering Garek to distract him from his worries.

Zaruko threw a sloppy leather bag into Jahzara's face and sap splattered everywhere. He felt like he was like pulling on a drass' tail, but it was worth it to see the look on her face: jaw dropped, sap stuck in her hair, dripping onto her well-made clothes. The thinned herd came to a trickling stop as all eyes settled on the two of them.

"You...you, **slag!**"

"Jahzara, if you question me, speak to me without being asked, if you do *anything* other than follow along quietly for the remainder of this expedition then I am going to break your arms and your legs and then I'm going to leave you out here for the drass."

"Your father—"

"Will do nothing to me unless he has another heir," Zaruko bluffed.

Cheeks and ears blazing, Jahzara was struck silent in her humiliation. The sap was impossible to wipe away but she kept trying. Jahzara ran her hands over it, tried to use the leather bag to wipe it away, and even looked around for something more effective, but there was only the shallow stream they were about to come up on.

"When I am your father's sieva, we'll have this conversation again."

"You better hurry and wash that off before we have to burn it."

Jahzara marched away like a vicious storm, kicking up mulch and rocks, screaming and shoving anyone who got too close to her. She approached the stream and bent down to dip her hands in it, but that wasn't enough. She growled to a roar, lowered her face even farther, and dipped it into the cool stream.

"Don't worry about her, she's as barren as the mountainside. Some other woman will take her place and we'll be rid of that witch," said Gamba.

"One way or another."

"...What's happening?" Tayna asked.

They both turned to look at her. She was holding Garek while he slept and covering his face with her free hand. They towered over her like the trees. Their walk and talk would've put any Upper to shame, and Tayna couldn't help feeling like they had just been a warmup all her life for these new people. But it was they who had a hard time speaking to the tiny captive.

"How did you know? Earlier, with the drass."

"I just, I don't know..." Tayna started, "...I guess I heard something in the forest..."

They both knew it was a lie. Both of their bodies reacted, but neither of them acted on it.

She stopped talking and cradled Garek, "What's going to happen to us?"

"I told you what's waiting for you at Imperyo."

"Then why did she lure the drass to us?"

"You just need to stay away from her. It shouldn't be hard."

Zaruko urged her to remain closer to the main group as they traveled through the brightening thicket. Tayna knew it was going to be impossible to avoid Jahzara once they got to Imperyo. She had plans for Tayna and the baby and Jahzara wasn't the forgetful type. She prayed to Thessa in secret, just thinking the words as hard as she could. She begged for a sign that things would be alright. She hoped they would make it out of the forest without another incident and she prayed that Garek wouldn't be without his father as soon as they arrived in the fire-breather's city.

*****

The woods crackled with skittering and mysterious calls. Not the threatening kind, but the calls that filled the quiet spaces when creatures felt safe to make them. Vik nervously wandered back to where the main group would be, following the increasing number of bodies. They weren't just dead, he'd seen that before. What he'd never seen, what distressed every fiber of his being, was the sight of half-eaten, dismembered, and unrecognizable corpses splayed out in unnatural poses. Images of Haven's streets on that final day had been exaggerated and replicated in color on the forest floor. The odor of feces and damp rot hung in the air, making it as breathable as a pool of bog water. The stifling humidity had taken all the smells and completely saturated the forest with the rancid combination. Vik thought he could breathe through his sleeve, but everything was permeated with it, pressing his sleeve against his face just held the smell closer. He heaved at the base of a great tree towering over him. The wide, gnarled giant watched Vik carry on as he did, unresentful of all his busy motions. There wasn't much to expel from his system so he was able to suppress the heaving after a while.

No one was moving. He was completely alone in the middle of the forest.

The woods chattered to remind him he wasn't without any company and he struggled to plant his feet, dragging them along in the direction he thought might be right. The mulch seemed to be carved into a path and he hoped his people were the ones who'd made it. Every muscle ached to lie down. Each soft patch of mulch or secluded space between the roots he passed by whispered false promises of a safe rest. He wanted to lie down more than anything. He wondered if death would really be so bad. Floating around as a soul sounded a lot less painful than carrying on as he was.

128

"I can't lie down," he chanted quietly, "I have to move. I have to keep going."

He thought about the orange pills, scattered across the forest floor. Lost to him forever. He had managed to save one and felt for it in his pocket to be sure it was still there beside the orb. He pulled out Havard's parting gift and examined it for cracks. It looked so much more delicate than it was. Not a scratch.

Something rustled in the leafy foliage nearby. He could've sworn he saw someone jumping out and run in another direction. Vik looked at the path under his feet, stared ahead at the trees just in front of him and then listened to the occasional patter he would hear on the mulch. There was definitely someone over there. He left the path and tried to step as quickly over all the debris as he could. After the drass fracas, there were more tree-sized branches than normal littering the forest floor, each one curled like tumbleweeds.

Vik chased after the rustling shrubs and occasional human-shaped shadow in a zigzag all around until he was exhausted, all the while harshly whispering after them to stop running. He just needed them to see him and then they'd realize he wasn't one of the monsters. After Vik chased the sporadic footsteps for far too long, he flopped down next to the base of one of the grandest trees he'd come across in the forest. The skyward roots actually pierced the canopy and brought down on it a shining ray from the sun. The wavy, loopy roots it stood on formed a perfect chair. His body may have ached no matter how gently he'd lowered himself down, but the wood of that tree was harder than stone. As he reclined back, he started thinking about what he was doing. He didn't care about the rest of them, but Marek needed him. They were each other's only real family and if he didn't get back to him, there was no one else. He certainly couldn't count on his own people to keep Marek or his new son safe. They were all too concerned with themselves.

Footsteps thumped nearby and he sat up straight, watching in their direction. They ran about five steps before stopping. Vik narrowed his eyes, trying to see past the roots and leaves, but there was nothing. Another thumping of footsteps went off right behind him and he whipped around, expecting to see someone running straight at him. What he actually saw were several chunks of blackish green shells rolling around, having been dropped by the tiny, furless creatures up in the highest levels of the forest. He remembered them, eating the smaller insects that scuttled around slowly up there and peeling their shells off before tossing them away. He put both his hands over his face and shook his head, groaning quietly.

"Idiot," he mumbled at himself.

Hoping he'd be able to go back and follow the trail he had been on before, he rose to his feet, wallowing in his own disappointment.

Vik's stomach roared from his diaphragm, tired of being ignored. Around him there were many of the orange, puffy flowers lining the trees, but also slender strands of leaves spiraling upward like gentle spikes ready to skewer anything that might fall from above. They grew straight up and so weren't horribly out of place with the cascading roots all around. Pushing his near-useless body along, he walked right up to one of the blades. He held his middle finger back with his thumb and lazily flicked the leafy stalk. It wobbled just as he thought it might, but then the leaves peeled open on their own. Vik cocked his head to the side as they revealed a column of bright yellow and blue flowers with black spots and stripes inside the petals. It looked like the yellow and blue had been spilled over them and the black had been squiggled on by a child. They were all shaped like tubes that curled out a little at the end. There were four columns of them lined up with their backs to each other. Vik reached out and gently patted the silky top of one flower and it bobbed wildly despite such a light touch. Then, as if allergic to him, the flower spewed out a fine mist of dust with a great puff of air.

Vik staggered back, waving his hand in front of his face. As he breathed in, his lungs rejected the air and his whole body started to spasm. He began waving his arms in a frenzy around him, trying to rid himself of what he was breathing in but that only stirred it around. The mist clung to him, following him like it was drawn to his skin. The burning intensified in his nose, spreading under his face like wildfire until he couldn't open his eyes. Tripping over a root, Vik hit the ground hard but it didn't distract him from the powder. He tried to shout or groan or whimper, but his throat and his lungs worked against each other to make unrecognizable, sputtering sounds. He couldn't smell anything and wasn't sure he'd recognize the sense in action even if it had been working, but the putridly sulphurous taste seeped into every nook of his mouth. Vik writhed around on the ground for several minutes, leaking mucus and tears, taking in the sharp air until he was hit with something that broke apart as soon as it touched him. He started to feel cool and his clothes clung to him.

Water.

He couldn't believe how hard it was to recognize. Someone tugged roughly on the neck of his tattered shirt so Vik eagerly held his face up. He hoped they would throw another wave straight at him, douse his face in sweet relief and that's exactly what they did. The suffocation was alleviated, but the burning would linger on for hours. A leather pouch was shoved into his hand and he felt blindly for the top of it,

130

ramming the spigot to his lips as soon as he found it. The water rushed in and was greedily absorbed by every soft organ and tissue that had been touched by the dust. The liquid felt thick and tasted sweet, but he attributed that to desperation. Vik wanted to open his eyes, but he was afraid they had shriveled up. Everything had leaked so profusely that the bottom half of his face was soaked even before the water was thrown in it. He held the leather flask up to his eyes and pried them open one by one, pouring water into each of them until he was able to open them. His vision was still recovering but he could make out a small figure in front of him standing with both hands on their hips.

"That was the dumbest thing I've ever seen," the child said.

*****

On the positive side of having lost so many of the Sinovians, at least they were easier to manage. With just over two hundred left, Zaruko knew this group would hardly warrant a cautious well done from his father. He would've loved to have seen his father squirm on his throne, knowing his son was becoming harder to threaten. Instead, Zaruko was fully expecting hearty congratulations through side smiles and overly celebratory cheers, all devoid of underlining worry. Completely lacking in respect. Especially since most of the new Sinovians were either sickly looking or charred from sun exposure and disturbingly similar in appearance. There were slight variations in facial features here and there, but all of them with dark black hair of the same exact tone, all with light grey eyes. Except for the twin brothers with the baby Jahzara had her charcoal heart set on, their eyes were almost as black as a Rider's would be.

Zaruko glanced over at Tayna who was unencumbered, kicking up mulch as she marched along with the others. She had a different enough look about her to pick out of the crowd right away. A short young woman, not crying, not bloodied up, but taking each step one at a time with a distant fire in her eyes.

Jahzara watched Marek as he held his baby. The smug look on her face grew more irritating as they drew nearer to Imperyo. Zaruko continuously consoled himself with the image of her face when he threw that bag of sap in her face. He would have that for the rest of his life. Jahzara noticed him distractedly smirking at her and spit a small bit of combustible chemicals through her teeth at the ground between them. The already wide berth the Sinovians had been giving her grew even more spacious.

The Sinovian had been very intuitive earlier. Or possibly her senses, like all of her kind, were heightened such that they could hear the drass in the trees. Although only Tayna had seemed aware of them. *No,* Zaruko thought, that wasn't it. They didn't know the sounds of the forest, she couldn't have been so sure from a noise she didn't recognize.

"What's your name?" Zaruko asked, handing her a scaly fruit the size of her hand.

"Tayna," she answered, taking it suspiciously. "What's this?"

"It's a drass toe."

She cringed and held it away from her with two fingers and he flinched to catch it. Taking it from her, forcing himself not to smile, he started to peel back the tough skin. Within the dark greenish brown shell were three glossy strips of fruit attached to the indented stem from the inside. He plucked one out and gave it to her with an encouraging nod.

"It's not really a *drass toe,* that's just what they're called."

"Whoa," she said, covering her mouth when her first bite shot out a bit of juice. "This is so…"

"It's sweet," Zaruko said when she couldn't find the word. "Not quite a bloodstone."

"No," she breathed out a small chuckle. "Thank you."

"I wanted to ask you something," he said, glancing around.

"How long," Tayna swallowed hard, then tried to shake her brain into gear, "How long have you all been living outside your mountain?"

"Usually when someone says they want to ask a question, they're the ones doing the asking."

"You said the Thes," Zaruko shot her a wary glance, "You said they tried to kill you. I just want to know how long you've been out here."

"That doesn't sound related…but alright, uh," Zaruko stared upward, blinking repeatedly while biting his lip, "Maybe fifty years."

Tayna gasped and choked on a splash of juice that went down at the wrong time. Her eyes watered and she held up her hand to assure Zaruko she wasn't dying. The answer he gave was exactly the one she feared, but hearing it somehow added evidence to the contrary. Even though the Thesmekka had tried to kill these people, even though they'd been outside for just as long as the Thesmekka had been absent, even though Jahzara was such a violent warmonger, she couldn't believe these were the same Brutes they'd been warned about for centuries. They couldn't be. It was just too absurd. The mountain-sized giant in the distance, that was the kind of thing to rival their valiant saviors, not people similar to themselves.

132

Brows still furrowed and brain still racking itself over the purpose of her question, he managed to stutter out the question he originally wanted to ask during their pause.

"I wanted to ask you, how did you really know about the drass?"

"Tayna, is everything alright?" Marek asked, trotting over to join them.

"Try this," Tayna said to him, holding out the rest of her piece.

"Are you trying to hurt me?" he asked, raising his brows.

"Don't breathe it in and you'll be fine," she said sarcastically, watching him hesitantly take a bite.

Catching sight of his palms, she pulled one of his hands back just a bit from Garek and examined it before glaring at him. He jerked away, opening one of the fresh scabs in the process. It only bled a little, but it stung plenty. Tayna knew why, but she wished he would wait until they were somewhere safe. A self-inflicted injury like that was an unnecessary risk to take, especially when he had Garek to watch out for.

"That *is* good!"

"He wants to know how I knew about the attack back there before it happened."

Marek started to choke on the juices and Tayna gave him a couple of hard pats on the back.

"You can't know about something before it happens," said Marek, as sternly as he could with his squeaking voice.

"See, I think you might be misremembering wh—"

"Because if you could know about something before it happened," Marek interrupted her, "then you would've done something about it, right? You're not the kind of person who just lets terrible things happen."

Tayna and Zaruko continued to march alongside him, confused by his strange remark. Realization started to dawn on Tayna's face and she redirected her gaze to the ground.

"There's no such thing as real fortune telling. Thanks for the snack," he said, then peeled off from the two of them with Garek nestled snuggly in his arms, snoozing as soundly as if Marek were sitting on his couch in Haven, rocking him to sleep.

"What was that about?" asked Zaruko, plucking out the last piece of fruit and lazily tossing the shell on the ground.

"Nothing…family history."

"Hm," Zaruko chewed a small bite, noting their relation. His head twitched to the side when he noticed her stifled tears, "I suppose you wouldn't have been able to stop the drass in that situation, regardless of any early awareness of the attack."

"Why do you call them drass?" Tayna struggled to change subjects without appearing too distraught.

"That's, just what they've always been called. I'm not sure," said Zaruko, thinking about it for the first time.

"What else do you have names for?"

"Everything," he breathed, glancing around, "There's the drass, the tallbugs, the babblers, then the fodderbugs. Everything eats the fodderbugs. Laughing dogs, I don't think we'll see a crawler, but that's a blessing."

"They don't sound like something I'd want to see," she chuckled. "What else?"

"Uh, the flowers, the ones you're not supposed to touch, we call them mace flowers."

"Mace?"

"It's a word the Riders gave us for the, the," Zaruko made a flicking hand motion with all his fingers, "They spray out a mist. It's terrible."

"Do you have a name for the trees?"

"The really big ones, they're called Arsinia trees."

"That's different, and pretty. Where'd Arsinia come from?" Zaruko glanced sideways at her and she grimaced, "I'm sorry, I sound like a child."

"No, it's all new. We all wanted to know at one time," Zaruko scratched his chin, trying to remember the tale, "There was a Rider, a woman called Arsinia, who, well, she tried to talk to the trees."

"The heat must've pushed her over the edge," said Tayna.

"No, she was a Rider," Zaruko said, as if that explained anything, "They say she would stand in front of them and shout for hours, but then always end the day being pulled off of them by one of her family. One day, they caught her with an axe, digging her way into one of the trees until she was covered in sap. she managed to kill two people before they took the axe away, but she suffocated before they could burn the sap off."

Tayna squinted at him, "That...is not true."

"Yes, it is. You can ask anyone."

"That sounds like an eldertale to me," Tayna scoffed.

The world was full of tales already. They had theirs, but it was hard to imagine them being as interesting as the ones out there. After all, they didn't have tree huggers and sap-eating monsters. Their entire world had all been stone and gray and bloodstones for over two centuries.

The foliage underfoot grew more dense as they neared Imperyo. The monstrous trees became more sparse and dwindled down to the wispy, less gargantuan roots jutting up in tangled clusters. Many of the roots started to stay underground and the sunlight was able to pierce through the canopy more often. The mulch they trampled over was thinning out and their footsteps went from crunchy to muffled and soft. It was more obvious that it had rained recently as the underbrush gave off a fresher, earthier smell. The air breezed over them for the first time in a long while. It stole away some of their burdens, whisking back into the woods behind them.

The lateness of the afternoon crept up on them, but the Impery were at ease. The ruddy guides had begun to traipse rather than stalk through the woods and some of them were even chatting quietly amongst themselves as they traversed the less taxing terrain. Everyone could feel the mood had lightened and spirits were lifting. They were getting close.

Despite her worries, Tayna was eager to see this great city and even more keen on getting out of the woods.

"Hey Marek," a young woman spoke up from behind them.

Marek immediately recognized her as one of Mira's good friends. The thought made it hard for him to speak, so he nodded to her instead. She asked the baby's name and he told her, but when she offered her remorse for Mira's death, he pretended something was caught in his shoes and waved her on ahead.

"Are you Tayna?" she asked, switching away from Marek as soon as she understood.

"Yes," she answered quickly, looking at the Upper's face.

"I'm Nikiva," she said, holding both hands out, palms facing upward before tucking them back into her folded arms. This was an overly polite greeting, as was especially expected of strangers from different parts of Haven. Her show of familiar traditions out in such a foreign place made everything and everyone else far away. She was taller than most young women, two whole heads taller than Tayna. Her skin was burnt from the sun and her black hair frayed every which way, but she seemed steady, unshaken. She wore that confidence in every expression she made. Her equally tall sister, Sera, glared at them as she plodded along behind them. An identical twin pair, but very easy to tell apart. Sera jerked her chin up every time Tayna glanced back at her and stumbled over the slightest faults on the unmarked trail. Sera wore her hair tightly braided in a circular bun on the back of her head and her skin remained unblemished by the harsh sunlight.

Nikiva spoke with Marek and Tayna for a good portion of the hike, asking what they thought Imperyo would look like and how many people they'd see there. Most of all, they wondered how they'd be received when they arrived. Would they be ignored and left to fend for themselves, to figure out on their own how to mix with these strange people who had lived outside of their Havens all this time?

"We don't know anything about Agrona except how difficult it is to be out here," Nikiva said, her brows furrowed as she imagined the worst scenarios. "That's been made painfully clear. How are they going to handle having to hold our hands?"

"Maybe they'll be glad for the help?" Marek suggested.

"...Maybe."

"There she is!" an Impery called from up ahead.

Marek briefly rested his hand on Tayna's shoulder before he broke into a sprint, passing all the ex-Haven dwellers, Jahzara, and Zaruko, as well as all the other Impery warriors. He cautiously slowed to a trot as he neared the man who'd made the announcement, warily observing him until he came up to the edge of the ridge he stood by. They would need to change their course, to avoid walking off the edge of the short, but abrupt drop. Marek's heart rushed with excitement and fear, fluttering hard enough to make him dizzy as he gazed out over the sight before him.

The second black mountain jutted up from the densely entwined, tropical forest coating the land. Its jet black rocks gleamed in the sunlight, like a dark diamond. Smoke billowed from the hole at the top where the Gate once was, replaced by a blasted out opening. The Impery no longer relied on the Thesmekka's gift of solitude. Threshold, the heavily established settlement surrounding Imperyo, was where all those not native to the black mountain lived and worked the land. These people were not the same as those who lived inside the mountain. To the Impery, they could never be equals.

Out in the fields of Threshold, outside the protection of the town's gray wall, workers toiled in the fruits and flowers. Nine types of crop grew as far out from the town as they could, stopping just short of the woods. Fellenwort trees swayed heavy in the breeze, their branches weighed down by bulbous, brown fruit hanging in pairs. Young teenagers took turns sitting on each other's shoulders to pry the fuzzy produce loose while the smallest ran back and forth to bring baskets of food into Threshold. Little girls and gentle young women worked in the sweet-smelling sunbloom field. These sunbloom berries required a delicate touch. Each flower contained a berry nestled within its pink petals, ready to be harvested when they turned a golden yellow. These berries were like egg yolks and were covered in a thin membrane almost as fragile. If the blossom was jostled too roughly, the stem would inject poisonous chemicals into the berry. It wasn't enough to kill, but it was enough to learn from.

A long shadow soared over the fields, but the workers were already out of sight. They had been warned by the lookout of a skyward predator heading their way. Whistlers are what they called the giant birds, from the high and slow trill they emitted while gliding overhead on their sun-blocking wings. The savage whistlers avoided the smoky mountaintop and so it made an angular turn away from Threshold and Imperyo. The deceptively serene chirping filled the air as it lazily flapped toward the horizon far above the treetops. Breathing sighs of relief and shielding their eyes from the sun, workers emerged from under the fellenwort and jabulian trees, others crawled out of the twirly bushes, all of them getting straight back to work so they could feed their families that night and still have enough to give their Impery proprietors.

On the outskirts of Threshold, butting up against the fragmented metal wall that contained and protected the large town, a string of simple homes stood in a sloppy row. They were made from a few sturdy branches the size of logs, but mostly of mud and clay like most homes in Threshold. Despite being made of the same materials and style, it was easy to spot the difference in this row of homes from all the others in the town. Not only were they new, but they were built by hands more used to gripping axes and spears than slapping clay together to bake under the sun. These warriors were no more familiar with building than the ex-residents of Haven.

"I can see my house from here," said Gamba jokingly.

"I can see the house I made, too," said Zaruko, thinking idly about his old home in Imperyo.

"They seem eager enough," Gamba motioned to the gawking Sinovians.

Zaruko mumbled to Gamba, "It does look peaceful from up here, doesn't it?"

"One day it will be," said Gamba.

"I'd like to believe that."

Gamba nodded solemnly, surveying his homeland with the tyrant's errant son.

*****

The refugees and the returning residents approached the gateway to the city. It was made from a gaping hole in the metal wall, formed with tall, uneven stakes of wood that reached high enough to block the mountain from view when they stood near enough to it. Shorter wooden spikes stabbed out of the ground in front. The space between the spikes and enormous stakes was piled with small stones all the way around and there was only one entrance. Covering the opening was a long leather curtain. One of the residents of Threshold, a yellow-haired woman with bright, curious eyes moved it to the side using a long stick and latched the hide tarp into a dull hook protruding from the wooden post. The smell of the leather drape broke loose as it was moved and everyone cringed, pulled the corners of their lips down hard and pinching their noses.

At the exact moment that the curtain was pulled back, a couple of chatty women were revealed having been about to cross through the gateway. They had dark burgundy hair braided in spirals around their heads and rosy, olive skin painted various colors with dimples in their cheeks. Their features were loose and overly-expressive, as showcased by their wide, startled eyes and fully dropped jaws. They were holding a bucket of off-white water and sloshed some of it on the ground. They hunched over and quickly shuffled away from the gate, set the bucket down and took off running back into the city. Marek, Tayna, and Nikiva shared a troubled glance. Jahzara marched up to Tayna, moved her hand away from her broken nose, and motioned to Garek in Marek's arms.

"Take care of this like your life depends on it," she smiled at Marek, who couldn't believe her audacity.

"Everyone!" Zaruko shouted, comfortably using his voice for the first time since leaving Imperyo three days before. "When we go inside, you'll follow me to end of Threshold where you will be officially accepted into the city by Lord Durako."

Marek was surprised to hear that the outlying city had a different name than the mountain, but was too distracted by the acrid odor wafting from the wall. They followed one by one through the gateway, thickening up the line as they filed through the streets behind Zaruko. Residents of Threshold came out of doorways from all over to watch them. They could hear them chattering on how few of them there were, about how strange they looked, but it was all neutral. Purely observations, not irritated or anxious about the newcomers, but assessing them at face value, as if considering their current worth. The entire city had a musty funk about it that seemed to waft from every which way when a breeze fluttered through.

Fires crackled in the homes made of mud and weak black stone. They were set shoulder to shoulder with enough space between every other home for two people to uncomfortably walk through. Many were decorated with painted lines and dots of various colors and patterns

138

around the doorways and windows that were too similar to mean nothing. Shurik, the most elderly to escape Haven and survive the forest, stopped when he noticed the patterns and stared, his mouth agape, before being gently pulled along by Savan.

Everything was still soggy from the rain and people were putting emptied water buckets back on their rooftops in preparation for the night that was ready to drop down on them as soon as the sun let go. The buckets were made of shaped mud and etched with images of people reaching up to meet the rain or pouring water from the buckets over crops. Round baubles suspended by twine from the overhang of rooftops rustled with the sound of shifting sand when the wind touched them.

After the long walk from the entrance of Threshold to the elevated entrance of Imperyo, the sun had fallen past the horizon and left them wandering up to the cave by the firelight carried by Zaruko and his warriors. A young boy ran straight for them, screaming something unintelligible with his arms extended in front of him. Gamba reached out and swiped at the air, coming back with a fluffy, white creature fluttering in his hand. The boy was relieved, thanking Gamba. He gazed wide-eyed around the group of newcomers as he took his flapping pet back in his arms, quietly chastising it for trying to escape. Its big eyes were fixed on the torches.

They stood quietly before the entrance, feeling curious eyes on their backs, waiting for something to happen. A whistle rang out from the sky. All the warriors scanned the darkness above them, but as a reflex rather than fear. The ex-Haven dwellers had gone from a loosely single-file line to a huddled mass on their way through the streets. Jahzara abandoned them as soon as she could, flying into the tunnelway and disappearing out of sight. Finally, after a long time of waiting, the mutterings of anticipation and anxiety humming within their numbers, a light could be seen bobbing inside the tunnel entrance. It slowly grew brighter, footsteps could be heard stomping in unison along with the distant clanking of metal. Marching and lights filled the opening, backlighting a statuesque figure with Jahzara strutting by his side, looking like a child's doll compared to the burly men around her. Behind Lord Durako and Jahzara stood four soldiers wearing simple metal plating and holding spears with the points straight up in the air. As the light bearers passed them on both sides, the metal armor Lord Durako wore caught the flames and flashed its noble grandeur into the crowd. As if he emitted his own holy light in blinks. In the chest of the armor was engraved a six-legged drass with flames billowing around it. His crown was made of metal shards and pointed teeth. Durako's beard was thick and covered his neck while his hair grew passed his shoulders, worn out like a mane that settled on the fur-lined shoulders of his armor. Zaruko greatly resembled the Lord of Imperyo, but with scruff for a beard and shorter hair. When Lord Durako spoke his voice bellowed pure and deep. Tayna would not have been surprised if they could hear him on the other side of Threshold.

"Welcome, all of you, to my land. I am Lord Durako of the Impery, the holders of fire and direct descendants of the goddess. Whatever hole you came crawling out of, this is not that place. Here, in the safety of Threshold, you will work to live. As long as you do this, you will live a peaceful life and have no troubles. Behind me is Imperyo, where the Impery live and where the eternal flame burns. Do not enter the mountain. Do not look at Impery women and do not touch them. All of these are crimes punishable by death, but these are the only ones. I am a fair judge.

"Do not tremble at the sight of the fire-breather, but fear us. Respect us, and we will have no troubles between our people. Pay your dues on time and without complaint, and we will have no troubles. You are our guests, we saved you from your helplessness. Never forget our benevolence, never forget our mercy, or we will remind you of our power. May the glare of the goddess keep you dutiful."

With a knowing nod to Zaruko, Lord Durako turned and marched back into the tunnel without a second glance, with Jahzara's arm locked in his. His light bearers and guards followed in the same formation they arrived, silent and staring straight ahead. Zaruko muttered something under his breath and turned to the speechless, bewildered crowd.

"That cave there," he called over them, pointing up and over his shoulder, "As he said, never go through it. If you keep out of there, you'll be just fine. Now follow me."

They filed around in a semi-circle after that, plopping tired feet into mud puddles and tripping in the dark. Threshold's residents weren't following them anymore. Seeing Lord Durako may have been more appealing than seeing the new Sinovians, a word they were starting to understand encompassed all non-Impery, or people without fire. As they left the tunnel, Marek noticed none of the Impery warriors that had guided them from Haven going into the mountain through the tunnel. Not even Gamba or Zaruko went inside. The warriors that had taken them through the forest dispersed out into Threshold, heading for their own homes outside the black mountain, near the Thesmekkian metal wall.

140

They passed the dark houses made of mud, sticks, and smelling sweet up close. Above the doorways and windows unfurled hides gently rippled, hanging down over the openings for protection and privacy. People's hushed voices could be heard as they passed, but not what they were saying. After leading the Sinovians for several minutes at a leisurely pace, Zaruko came to a halt in front of multiple rows of slapdash structures. They were flush against the sleek, grayish wall and the mud bricks were still wet. There were no curtains, no hides, no decorations, and nothing inside, just a doorway and a single, imperfect window on the face of each one. They were far more impressive than their attempts at building outside of Haven, but that was a low bar.

"Make yourselves at home, get plenty of rest. In the morning, wait for me here. We'll work out what is available for each of you," Zaruko droned.

Tayna watched as the Sinovians filled the houses. There were enough just like he'd said, but they were still dividing Grays with Grays and Uppers with Uppers. She was certain other Sinovians in Threshold wouldn't be able to tell the difference. Tayna walked toward a house that looked empty, but as she passed Zaruko he called to her.

"...Tayna," he said.

At the sound of her name, her heart fluttered, her mind raced, and all the rest of what he said was lost. She could feel herself drifting into the space between the present and the future, but nothing was connecting. He had triggered something, but she was still unable to grasp it.

"Do you hear me?" he asked, waving his hand slowly in front of her face.

"No."

"No? You didn't hear anything I just said?" He turned his head away before looking back at her, "I know you're tired, but this is important. This is for any burns. You need to keep it on you at all times."

Tayna looked down at Garek, sleeping soundly in her arms and then over at Marek, signaling him to take it for her. He reached out to take it, but Zaruko drew back.

"She needs to keep it on her."

Tayna angled her hip toward Zaruko, wanting him to drop it into the pouch hanging off her side. Zaruko hesitated, carefully pulled the flap out with one finger and dropped the small ointment pouch in, withdrawing quickly. He looked between the two of them, held his mouth open but then promptly closed it, turning away without another word.

"Do you feel like something bad's going to happen?" Tayna asked Marek softly.

"Don't start that."

"Yeah, you're right," Tayna breathed, forcing a smile.

Tayna looked over the houses, heard people shuffling around in them, desperate for a safe respite. Eager to lay their bodies down on the bare ground. Overwhelmed by the desire to join them, Tayna forgot her concerns and squeezed into a hovel beside a few others she couldn't see clearly in the dark. The ground felt like clay, cool and smooth. Some of it was sticking to her clothes and skin, but she exhaled and gave her cares to the wind.

It wasn't more than two hours later that she heard a commotion outside. Someone was calling into each house, wanting to know where she was. Tayna slapped Marek's chest until he woke up, shushing him when he spoke. Not wanting them to find the baby, she put her hands firmly on both Garek and his father, then scrambled up and stood outside the doorway. Jahzara paced outside the houses as a couple of women backed out of it. They were all robed in dark material, with their hoods off. Jahzara sneered at the mud hut before seeing Tayna shivering with her arms wrapped across herself.

"Get the baby," she hissed in the dark. When Tayna just stood her ground, Jahzara whispered again. "Where is he? What have you done?" Tayna just shook her head.

"Someone took him, I don't know who they were."

"We're too close to the Watching hour, Jahzara," one of the women complained.

"Are we going to miss it tonight?"

"No, we're not," Jahzara growled fiercely, frightening one woman into silence.

"But we don't have time to search for this one."

"Look through the rest of them," Jahzara barked, "And when you find it, join me. They have to have him somewhere nearby."

Jahzara charged passed the two Impery women, grabbed Tayna's arm and jerked her along in front of them, swinging her torch dangerously close to her face. Tayna jumped along, hopping forward to keep up the pace and ease the pressure on her squeezed arm.

Marek slipped out of the hut, behind the two robed women lingering too far behind Jahzara. He was almost around the corner and out of sight when Garek cried out in protest of the cold. All of them whipped around and Jahzara pointed, barking at the two women to chase him down and grab the baby. They sprinted after him, their robes billowing behind their backs. The cold air poured over Garek and he howled furiously, preventing Marek from hiding anywhere. He tried to lose them through a series of narrow alleys, but came across one he almost couldn't fit through without having to set Garek down and reach back through for him. After almost getting wedged, he chose to stick to the main streets out in the open. The only problem was that the chilly night air sent Garek into screams that woke the entire neighborhood.

Passing by a raucous building, Marek doubled back and dove inside, nearly sliding down the entryway stairs. Garek's screaming was completely drowned out by the shouting, laughing, and constant hum of voices inside the long structure. He stepped slowly inside, staring around at all the different people sitting around together. There were giant people, painted people, and ones that looked like Marek's people, but with yellow hair instead. Warmed by alcohol and exhaustion at the end of a hard day's work, the people inside heated the room enough to remind him of the deep, humid woods.

"Hey there, daddy," a young, painted woman with intricately braided hair teased at Marek from behind the counter, "What can I…hey, you one of the New Ones?"

Marek could only nod in response, still out of breath from his escape.

"You can't have a drink if you can't pay," she said with her mouth pushed to the side, "I'm sorry, new one, but you can stay around as long as you'd like. I'm surprised though. I would've thought you all would be too tired to venture out tonight."

She smiled at him encouragingly, but he couldn't fully process anything she was saying. The room had no others attached to it, no places to dart into and hide except around the counter where the woman stood. The door to the tavern creaked open and despite their quiet entry, the entire room fell silent within seconds. Everyone stared at the two robed women in the doorway while they slowly descended the steps.

"Give him here," one of them ordered, holding her hand out nervously.

Marek stepped back, ramming his thigh into the nearest table. He turned to brace himself and those sitting saw the tiny infant in his arm. The two Impery women repeated themselves, but Marek set his jaw and stood against the table. One of them marched forward and stood just in front of him.

"Give us that child, or Jahzara will have you killed."

"This is my son," Marek said quietly, the room hushed enough around them to clearly hear the break in his voice. "I'm not giving him to that murdering whore."

Several people in the room stood abruptly, their chairs flying out from under them. Marek flinched, his heart sinking. He hadn't intended to anger the drunken patrons behind him, but was surprised when the Impery woman held up both her hands and back up submissively. Approaching either side of him were three strangers, all of them towering above him. Their leader was a strong-jawed, muscular woman with her arms crossed and a resting expression of contempt. She was two heads taller than Marek and the two men that accompanied her were a head taller than her. Each of the men had arms as wide as Marek's torso.

"Stay back!" said one of the Impery women, in an attempt to be threatening. "I don't want to have to use force, but I will."

"What does Jahzara want with someone's newborn baby?" The woman asked in the flattest tone he'd ever heard.

"She—" the Impery was interrupted by the other one slapping her arm and eying the door.

"If you two are a part of that vile ritual, you remember, the one we were assured was just a rumor…"

"Of course not," the Impery woman said quickly.

"Why couldn't you find anyone to escort you tonight?"

"I don't know what you're trying to insinuate," the bolder Impery woman sneered.

"Then let me be clear," said the bulky Sinovian, "I find you guilty of thinking we wouldn't understand what's going on here. Stupidity's a serious crime out here."

"How dare—"

"It can get you killed."

The door to the tavern opened and a couple of Sinovians the size of the woman's companions idled behind the two Impery. Their eyes darted between the groups in front of and behind them.

"Kismet," the giant woman muttered, smiling with narrowed eyes.

She motioned at the two behind the women and they grabbed them in a choke hold, covering their mouths with their free hands. The two men on either side of the Sinovian woman charged forward and assisted them in subduing the two Impery. One of the robed women's neck snapped during her struggle and the other was turning a bright red, scratching and clawing at the hand and arm of her captor. Marek trembled, blinking slow and covering Garek's face in case a fight erupted, but the woman finished issuing silent orders to her men and faced the rest of the tavern.

"I know some of you don't agree with everything I've done in the past, but does anyone have a problem with this here tonight?"

144

Not a single hand shot up. No one stood, and for several heavy seconds, silence balanced over their heads. Then at once, the sound of the tavern resumed, louder and more enthusiastically than when he'd first entered.

"Don't be afraid. They deserved more than that for what they've done. Everyone in here knows it. They've been sacrificing children, although they'd deny it even if we caught them with blood on their hands." She smiled down at Garek, "What's your name?"

"Marek," he breathed, "This is Garek."

"Lucky you came in here when you did," She smirked, "You New Ones are bold. But you can't talk to the Impery like that. They'll take you to the middle of town and roast you as an example to us all, do you understand?"

"Yeah…"

She held her hand out, "I'm Nattina, leader of the Brutemen."

Marek put his hand in hers and she raised it to her forehead and waited for him expectantly. He quickly mirrored her and she smiled, then followed her men outside.

*****

Jahzara jerked Tayna around the corner, growling at her to hurry up. She had overheard enough of Jahzara's frantic rambling to understand what was going on. The crazed Impery woman was going to sacrifice Garek during the Watching hour, though she wasn't clear on what that was. Tayna struggled with the concept, wondering if there was another definition of sacrifice or if it was a non-lethal practice, but Jahzara's nature and the unlikelihood of a partial or safe sacrifice became obvious the more she thought about it.

They eventually came to a wider house, still only one solid door but three front-facing, fully covered windows. Jahzara swung the door open and startled some of the inhabitants into waking. She threw Tayna inside and barked at her to stay put until she got back, and then was gone. Tayna turned around, hearing the rustling of other people in their beds. There were only four of them in the sprawling house, three were girls around her age and one of them much older. One of the girls got out of bed and gently guided Tayna over to an empty bed in the corner. Tayna was suddenly aware of the movement in the middle of the room and tried to peer into the darkness, but the torchlight was still burned into her vision, leaving a blueish image everywhere she looked. As she sat down on the bed, she realized they were the closest things to solid beds she'd felt since leaving Haven. They were short, barely off the ground, but far better than bough beds. Grass, leaves and other such things were tied together with twine and covered tightly in a thick, wooly cloth that pulled apart if you picked at it.

"We just watch the infants," the girl whispered softly. "If we just do this, we don't have to work in the fields or bring waste to the wall…you're very lucky."

"What?" Tayna whispered, not sure what the girl was saying at first. It finally occurred to her what it was she had seen moving in the middle of the room. There were cribs lined up, and infants squirming, distressed by the noise. Two cribs were empty.

"I used to have to bring waste to the—"

"You know what she does with them?"

"It's best not to think about that…there's nothing we can do."

Tayna stared into the darkness, wishing she could see her face. Everyone in the room was still and silent. She couldn't believe how completely they'd resigned themselves.

"They've all been abandoned or orphaned," she continued, donning a tone of reason, "They wouldn't have made it…and some of them will make it under our care, if she doesn't choose them. They'll be fine."

"How can you make that excuse?"

"You don't understand yet. Let's talk about it later. I don't want to get caught when she comes back."

Tayna settled her eyes on the faint highlight of a doorway and windows and thought about the twin moon eclipse and about the Thesmekka. It was far more likely that they would've saved them back in Haven, but here is where she found herself wishing for their return. She didn't want to hear any more of what the girl was saying. The reasoning that girl had given buzzed irritably around her brain while she stewed. If she'd been paying attention, if she'd listening to the girl and accepted what she had said then she might've gotten out of there. She would have felt more clearly the danger that could not pierce the veil of her outrage.

Just when she thought she was going to nod off sitting straight up, the door burst to the side. It was so dark out with the eclipse that light barely trickled into the room. Several of the infants started to make a fuss and the older woman flew out of bed to settle them down. The dim light hit her face oddly and gave her the illusion of a marked strip of skin. Tayna glanced at the girl beside her and jerked away. Her skin was horribly mangled and one of her eyes was gone, covered in skin like there was never a place for it. They were all burned and disfigured. They were all given the same mark Jahzara had promised her.

# CHAPTER TEN

"Where. Is. He."

Tayna quaked, shaking her head and pleading unintelligibly over and over. Jahzara ripped her from her bed and held her by the throat without choking her, tilting her chin up and examining both sides of her face. Tayna threw her arms around, tried her best to get away, but there were two new women with Jahzara and they grabbed her, holding her as still as they could. She screamed and pleaded until Jahzara slapped her and growled in her face.

"If you don't shut your mouth I'll be the one who stomps the last flame out on your ashes."

Tayna still struggled against her captors, but the only sounds she made were suppressed and came out as whimpers. She couldn't see the other girls in the room, but she knew they were there.

"You made me miss my contribution to the ceremony," Jahzara said, stifling a toothy sneer. "Others offered their exchange to the goddess while I stood by and thought only of this moment."

Jahzara snatched her face by the cheeks and flicked her wrist from one side to the other.

"It's hard to tell, but I think this is your good side."

Then, on the good side, she spat a vile smelling liquid from under her tongue onto the top of Tayna's face, letting it run down the left side until it dribbled off her chin. Tayna tried to wriggle free, but the two Impery tightened their grip and all she could do was hang off her arms. Jahzara reached up with her free hand and wiped the fluid from her eye so hard it left tiny stars.

"Don't want to mess that up again," she said, winking at the one-eyed girl behind them.

Jahzara took a shallow breath and spit a second chemical into her face. The sound Tayna made woke all the infants and even those who lived nearby. Fire roared for Tayna like a burst of thunder, overshadowing her own screams. For Tayna it seemed to go on forever, but was over in seconds. The two women dropped the Sinovian while Jahzara took a step back to admire her work. She reached for a pouch strapped to her side as she yelled for her marked women to quiet the noise. They scrambled to obey her, but Tayna just fell back onto her bed with her back pressed against the wall, holding a hand out in front of her face. She was too afraid to touch it. Jahzara almost handed the pouch to Tayna but withdrew it at the last second.

"This is for the burns, but I think I'll keep it. Unless you know where he is…"

Tayna sat wordlessly whimpering and refusing to acknowledge her presence. Jahzara kicked her legs and asked again, repeating the question a few more times before sighing and reattaching the pouch to a buckle on her side. Jahzara scanned the room, gazing over each infant as she passed them.

"If you don't tell me where he is, I will take them all next time."

Jahzara's teeth clenched harder and her fists balled tighter. She shouted for her to answer, but Tayna just curled up and turned her face away. One of the infants was wailing throughout the encounter. The other girls were too terrified to move.

"Why is that baby still crying?" Jahzara shouted over it.

Two of the younger ones jumped up, knocking into each other but the oldest woman was already at the crib. She scooped the infant up and bounced it gently, disappearing into the shadows on the other side of the room. She had been startled by the scene between Jahzara and the newest girl, but the old woman had experience serving Jahzara. She knew to disappear, she knew not to thank or apologize. She knew her place.

"You have until the next eclipse to bring him to me," Jahzara bent down closer to her ear and Tayna flinched away, but the wall stopped her from going far. "I brought him into the world. *He is mine.* I want him back."

After Jahzara left, the one-eyed girl hurried over to comfort her, but Tayna pushed her away.

"You shouldn't upset her like that."

"She never forgets."

"Just stop talking," Tayna whispered at them, the smell of her own burnt flesh and hair overwhelming her senses. They obliged her and spent almost an hour consoling the infants before tiptoeing back to their beds for the night. Tayna sat with her back against the wall, trying to control her moans and whimpers but nothing could distract her from the pain. She struggled to pull out the ointment pouch Zaruko had given her, fingers shaking as they dipped down and came up with a dollop of off-white cream. She gasped aloud as she tried to touch it to her face, trembling harder each time she tried. After a few attempts, she smeared the ointment back into the pouch and gave up, deciding to try again when the shock and pain subsided. Images of the fire started to feel like visions that sizzled and charred all her thoughts through the long, sleepless night.

*****

The forest was giddy in the early mornings, rambling on with chittering and whooping. A lazy stream drifted along, revealing windblown breaks in the canopies with sparkling winks. Creatures too gentle for the harsher times of day cautiously drank from it, always one with its head up, watching for danger in turns. Vik's own head was planted in the dirt. He kept it there when he woke, letting the ground floor of the forest come fully into focus. The earth was damp and cool, but the detritus was rough and uneven. All the roots were filled with the furless creatures running up and down them, squeaking and squealing playfully. Pushing himself up from the mulchy dirt, he sat and wiped the drool from his cheek, stretched his arms high above and let the back of his head rest on the draped root behind him.

"Good morning," the child said.

Unsettled by speaking to anyone that was capable of speaking back, the anxious boy consoled himself from the shock of his words. Not in his head or quietly to himself, but out loud and thoroughly while he smashed up a familiar grey food the size of his head with a rock.

"Got to accustom myself to it again...not a tarlillyque...don't miss the solitude...just finifugaling, like last time..."

"Where are we?" Vik carefully interrupted.

"Uh, well," the boy momentarily stopped smashing the bloodstone to point in three different directions, "between places."

They sat across from each other, encircled by the lofty roots, comfortably secluded from the bulk of the forest. This was not a young boy from Haven, but a different Sinovian, as an Impery might call him. He looked to be no more than twelve years old with sloppy, bright blond hair and large black eyes, the iris and pupil almost indistinguishable and the whites of the eye barely visible from straight ahead. He had some hi-tech eyewear hanging around his neck that he kept habitually checking for with the side of his hand. The child had just finished smashing the bloodstone open on one side. He greedily picked up the dislodged pieces and shoved several into his mouth before tossing the rest to Vik. It landed in front of him and rolled unevenly between his splayed legs. Flecking the bits of leaves and dirt off the meaty center, Vik held it up to his mouth and as he took a bite straight into it, the child watched him

150

suspiciously, his mouth agape. His mouth full of food, Vik sputtered out a conversation.

"So what's your name?"

"Radeki Luken Athapéle," the boy acted busy with his hands as he asked, "so...what's yours? Name?"

"It's Vik. Is there something else you go by? Something shorter?"

"Uther calls me Zaki."

"Uther? Who's that?" Vik looked around, but they were alone.

"He's...my...friend..." Zaki answered slowly, watching Vik carefully with every overly annunciated word.

"O...kay..." Vik said, mimicking him. He took another bite and decided not to ask any more questions about Uther. "Where did you get the bloodstone?" Zaki stopped chewing mid-bite and stared at him so Vik tried again, "Never heard of a bloodstone? No? This...uh, I guess it's a vegetable?"

"Everywhere," Zaki quipped, replicating the attitude of all Haven teens.

Vik shot him a sour look, but started looking around for any obvious signs of bloodstones he might've missed. Zaki immediately slammed his mouth shut and looked like he just forgotten something important. After Vik finished their potent breakfast, he stood up, stretched again and peered out from behind the root wall. Something large rustled the foliage and he jerked back.

"That's Uther, probably..." Zaki said. "He likes to keep an eye on me. I think. Sometimes it's not him, but I think it is this time."

"Is Uther a person," Vik couldn't contain his curiosity about 'Uther', "or an animal? A friendly one I hope."

"We're going to Imperyo, but not past the forest."

"So, Uther?"

"We can't go up to the gate, they don't like us there. Someone's meeting us for...something."

"Okay," Vik gave up on Uther, "Do you know what that something is?"

"Yes," he answered with the familiar teenatude again.

Zaki picked up a stitched together bag made of skins and threw the strap over his shoulder. He set off into the forest passed Vik, sauntering over and around obstacles, using true vines to swing over disguised holes until he was gone. Vik struggled to keep up, but he just couldn't move like Zaki. He felt like he might as well be walking on stilts with a blindfold.

"What are you doing?" Zaki asked, sitting impatiently on a log-like root. "We need to get there before sunset."

Smoke billowed from the gaping hole at the top of Imperyo's black mountain, reminding the Sinovians of the ever-present Impery power. Inside, laid out exactly like Haven and every other Thesmekkian-built refuge, each stone house sat in the same place and each curved street went the same way. Lord Durako's modified manor rose above as the only exception. The splendid manor assimilated stone, wood, hides and a plethora of Jawny-crafted décor all pieced patiently together into a multilevel masterpiece reaching for the hole where their Gate once hung. The Gate was replaced by an actual hole of roughly the same circumference.

A short pace outside Durako's extravagant abode, the eternal flame burned strong, outshining the midday sun. Five Impery formed the flame, facing each other on the edge of the top level, blowing fire at an angle to meet in the very center. The five stagger their chemical jettison so that the flame never goes out, being replaced by five more and so on throughout the day. An ever-blazing symbol of their superiority. Lord Durako started the tradition twenty years ago, when his father was still the reigning Lord. Proof of Impery unity and strength of spirit. There was always a flood of volunteers and the flame never faltered.

"Isn't it beautiful?"

"Yes," Durako said, brushing Jahzara's long hair from her shoulder.

"You know what I'm talking about," she grinned.

"The five of them together don't burn half as brightly as you do."

"You know you don't have to stoke my fire. We could leave them to it and get to work," she teased him suggestively, but then a thought crossed her mind that she couldn't keep to herself. "You know, these new Sinovians," her eyes started burning, "they have three children at once. I saw it myself. And they remain so capable of caring for their young…"

"Don't douse yourself, we will make it will happen. Our child will be born healthy and their fire will be stronger than anyone's has ever been."

"Yes, it will be," Jahzara's eyes stung and she dabbed them with the sides of her fingers.

"Come here."

She sat on his lap and wrapped her arms around his neck. They closed their eyes, leaned in and pressed their lips together. She could feel the heat on his mouth and her own desire growing in her chest, pounding hard and loud, tingling in her fingertips. She pressed her lips deeper into his and he pulled her closer, his hand wrapping around her waist.

They were so caught up in one another that neither noticed Josanna approaching the manor. She was masquerading as a servant of Durako and had a debt to settle with the Lord of Imperyo. Setting her eyes on the eternal flame, she could feel it fueling her resolve to do what needed to be done. It was time for her father's plan to finally be carried out, but better than he had originally arranged. This time, she had a Gadling Rider waiting. All she needed was what was in Durako's room. Zaruko's patience be damned.

Josanna wore a scant disguise, as did most young ladies who served around Lord Durako. Unlike the Sinovian women, Impery ladies did not shy away from displaying their bodies, attractive or not. With the fire ever blazing in its center, Imperyo boasted a rarity of conservative attire from either gender. Josanna's hair reached the middle of her back, longer than most Impery ladies kept it. She tied it up in such a way that it messily hung in front of her eyes. With so much of her exposed, she didn't need to try hard to hide her face.

Two other working girls paraded by, giving her no more than passing glances. Josanna took a quick breath, steadied herself and snatched a rag from one of them as they passed. Prancing up the tight, spiraling stairs, she was able to peer across at floor level before revealing herself. There were a few guards in chairs at the middle of the room, sharing a conversation over nearly burnt-out sitters. Josanna's bare feet patted the wooden stairs and they lethargically nodded at her, smiling with lazy eyes. The staircase continued and she again peered over the next floor before going all the way up. This floor was empty except for all of Durako's comforts and treasures. He had plenty of prizes once unknown to the Impery: trophy skulls from drass and an infamous Rider, as well as armors, weapons and jewels. But the real treasure lay on the top floor, the next one up. Josanna crept quickly, looking beneath her to ensure no one was watching. Slower than with the other floors, she peered up. She allowed her eyes to dart over the smoothly sanded floorboards covered in rugs and pillows, gazing across the walls covered in a mural of paint normally worn by the Jawnies, its meaning lost on all but the craftsman who made it.

After feeling safe enough to step up, on the pads of her feet she daintily crept over to a door in the middle of the dimly lit room. She reached into her tight top and pulled out a key. Her hands were overexcited, jittering and making more noise than she wanted with the key against the door. The lock turned easily enough and the door clicked open. The nearby balcony erupted with laughter and she jerked, threw herself through the door, and tried to gently close it behind her. She cringed as it clicked shut and held her breath, closed her eyes and listened for the sound of them finding her out.

The two continued their conversation completely unaware of the intrusion. Josanna turned from the door and took a step toward the disfigured lump in the middle of the room covered in a patchy, ragged tarp. She felt the fabric bend stiffly beneath her fingers and hovered over it. Her heart skipped around like a little girl, elated by what she was about to see...what she was about to do. She could hardly believe it when her father had told her and there she was, about to see it for herself. It was all such a long time coming. But she was getting ahead of herself. This was only the beginning. There was still so much to be done.

The tarp pulled away without a hitch and revealed a heap of gleaming metal, untouched by rust in all those forty-something years it sat idle, locked away. Josanna could see where the torso was intended to be, the two pairs of arms, two hefty legs, many delicate extensions branching from the shoulders and chest with tiny gadgets on the ends of each one, all laying limp from the main body. The entirety of the being looked to be made of gold and pearl and Josanna couldn't stop herself. She ran her hand over its chest and caught her breath. It felt as though her fingers were being met by an invisible force, there was no friction at all and it was as cold as it was dead. She let her hand run up to the head, thinking how delicate it felt as she brushed by its neck, traced the deeply set lines outlining the jaw and eye line, up and around the top of the head. The lines were like heavy sleep marks and she withdrew her hand nervously when she thought of it waking. The eyes were set open, not made for blinking, powered off, and translucent. The whole of the face was disturbingly similar to a man...or a woman, it was difficult to discern. She bent close to the face and saw inside its head through the eyes, but it was an incomprehensible mesh of smooth circuits and wires. In the middle of its forehead, directly centered between its eyes was set a pearl so large it fit perfectly in the palm of her hand.

A Thesmekka, a real one, right in front of her.

Long dead, of course, but there it was. She carefully pried at the plates on the forehead, but it wouldn't budge. She looked around the room for a tool and saw a small pile of junk pulled from the carcass of this metallic servant of Thessa.

"Chadrik's going to be so jealous," she whispered, sifting through the junk until she found a wedge to use.

Josanna rammed it into a plate on the forehead and then cracked it open easier than she'd expected. The sound carried into the next room, but Durako was already giving his speech to the people. Far below, in the middle of the remnants of the fallen Gate on the fourteenth level, a hastily constructed platform held two oversized prisoners. Bound and kneeling, they were drenched from the top of their heads down in a clear liquid that smelled like vinegar and sulfur.

"From the murder of two Impery women, Neema and Dalia, let our sacrifice of justice shine bright for the goddess and her watchful eye to see. And let the eye of the one who should be watching her people not be so blinded again by drink and foolish neglect."

Among the spectators stood Nattina, escorted into Imperyo by Zaruko and Gamba. As a leader of Sinovians, it was especially dangerous for her to set foot inside the mountain, even with the son of Durako protecting her. But she would not be dissuaded. She had commanded the murders and knew neither man doused in chemicals would speak against her in their defense. As the executioners spewed fire down on their statuesque bodies, Nattina's jaw clenched, her fists balled into solid stone. Zaruko glanced over at her face, but there were no tears or expressions of sadness. Nothing he could comfort or offer a kind gesture to. Nearby onlookers spat at her, some even spraying tiny embers like flyaway ashes from a collapsing fire. He held his breath and hoped with every fiber of his being that she would remain stoic. The Bruteman leader had not earned her rank from strength alone, but he knew she would cause too much damage to their cause if she went off. It wasn't the time yet. She knew that.

"It's done," she finally spoke, only loud enough for Zaruko, Gamba, and a few others nearby to hear.

The bodies of the two Brutemen fell forward and they were dead. There had been no shameful amount of weakness shown while they burned, save the roaring bellows afforded a warrior in great physical pain. Nattina glared up at the top level. Although unable to see Durako and Jahzara's faces, she imagined a scenario involving much disgrace and a great deal of screaming.

Back in Durako's manor, Josanna finally pried the pearl loose from the Thesmekkian carcass. She blew out a sigh and crept over to the door. There was no place to put the pearl in her disguise, so she kept a firm grip around it with her offhand. Softly spoken sweet talk could be heard from the other side of the door. The execution was over. Despite her revulsion, she knew waiting only a few more moments would be the perfect time to sneak out. If they were distracted enough, she could ease right by and down the stairs without drawing their attention.

"The big ones burn the longest, but they aren't as repentant as I'd like," Jahzara moaned.

"They got death whether they were sorry or not, it doesn't matter now," Durako threw down his lordly decorum beside the bed onto a finely crafted, wooden end table.

"Sunshine…what's that?"

"What?"

"Over there, in the door…"

Josanna snapped her hand back, away from the handle and searched the room for somewhere to hide. There was nothing but the uncovered Thesmekka lying slumped in the middle of the room. She could hide behind it, but they could easily flank her. She thought about hiding underneath with it, but she wouldn't be able to see them. They could set her on fire before she knew what was coming.

"That's the key…what's it doing in the door?" Durako stomped away from the bed, stopping in front of the door.

It burst open and swayed in Durako's hand as he hovered in the entryway. In the center of the room was the metal corpse covered by an off centered tarp. He lurched forward and ripped the tarp away. Josanna flung herself around the back of the door, slamming it shut behind her. She turned the key and threw it to the balcony while Jahzara screamed for help, scrambling to cloth herself in what was minimally respectable. The key stuttered across the floorboards and slipped off the balcony, clanking onto the stone street below. Josanna threw herself at the stairs, her heart racing in circles around its tightly confined space. When her face was level with the floor, she blew a wave of flames across it, igniting the décor more than the wood. She descended past the level beneath, but the one with the guards caused her trouble. They were both at the stairway and one snatched her by the arm, jerking her back up to their level.

"What's going on?!"

"An accident, getting help," Josanna stuttered.

They were high enough on their sitters for her to pry herself free and flee downward as they ambled up, joining Jahzara in her attempt to stifle the flames. As Josanna reached the bottom floor, she heard a series of crashes and knew that Durako had finally broken free of the room. Shaking all over, she knew she'd be killed for what was seen in that room. A grin sprung across her face as she leapt from the manor's doorway and barreled into the street. From the smoking balcony above, Jahzara screamed out for all of Imperyo to hear.

156

"Thief! Stop her!"

But as the execution had only just been resolved, most Impery residents were at the bottom level, unable to clearly see the accused. Josanna flew passed homes with no opposition until she got farther down. She bolted through small groups and hurdled around last-second attempts at stopping her. She even darted by her old home on level ten, but it was on the ramp leading down from level thirteen where her luck finally fell behind. Four men brought her to a violent halt, hanging their arms out and catching her in the chest. She whiplashed, hitting her back on the ground so hard she didn't even have the air to wheeze. They grabbed her by her corset straps and jerked her to her feet. She could hear her pursuers, but the man's hand slapped over her mouth to stop her fire from spilling out. Struggling against four stronger captors, Josanna could feel her defeat crashing against the rising fear. Zaruko had told her to be patient. She wasn't sure whether to kick herself for ignoring him, or for her own failure to escape. She realized in her fall that the pearl had bounced out of her hand and was rolling down the ramp.

Nattina, Zaruko, and Gamba slowly passed by as her escape attempt was thwarted. They continued walking, Nattina speedily scooping the pearl up as it rolled across her path. In all the commotion, no one seemed to notice the tiny orb fleeing the fray. Zaruko glared at Josanna, balled his fists, but didn't say a word. They casually left through the cave entrance and exhaled deeply once the sun's light touched their faces.

A muzzle strapped over her mouth, Josanna was dragged to the middle of the bottom level and thrown onto the platform beside the two charred remains, still heavily smoking. The smell of their corpses was so intense, she heaved but resisted, motivated by fear of choking. Impery had gathered around the edges of the fallen Gate surrounding the platform, many of them shouting and spitting fire at her while her hands were being bound behind her back.

"Punishment!" Some in the crowd called out.

"Cut off her hand," another yelled.

"No, kill her!"

"Kill her!" The crowd began to shout as one.

Josanna closed her eyes, imagining her father's face. She'd seen Nattina take the pearl, she knew that much had gone according to plan, but she wanted to oversee the remainder of the mission personally. That Sinovian man-child she was supposed to meet up with was going to mess everything up on his own. Not only would he never find the Gadling guide out in the forest, but putting down his sitter would have to come first.

"Everyone," Lord Durako bellowed from the top level, Jahzara clinging to his side, "I will not execute an Impery woman on the same day as Sinovians, let alone on the same platform. No matter how much she wants to be one of them."

Josanna was jerked to her feet by the two men on either side. The crowd deflated and dispersed, satisfied with the Brutemen burning and the reasoning for Josanna being spared.

Outside, Zaruko stormed down the ramp and toward the market, radiating rage. Gamba tried to come up with something to say, but Josanna's actions had stunned both of them.

"She couldn't wait," Zaruko growled.

"We'll speak to your father, try to get him to—"

"She saw it, she's dead. That's it. Stupid girl…"

Nattina split up from Zaruko and Gamba, heading over to a secluded bundle of houses near the side of the metal wall filled in with clustered wooden pillars. Sitting with his mother, Reeta, and a full travel pack was Chadrik, puffing on his sitter and staring up at the sky. Nattina had almost stepped on his feet before he noticed her. She slipped the pearl into his hand and glanced around.

"Reeta, this wasn't what we all agreed on."

"Did something happen?" Chadrik asked.

"I saw an opportunity and Josanna was willing to jump on it, no offense to your men's sacrifice," said Reeta. "I didn't have time to organize a meeting."

"Zaruko won't appreciate this."

"I don't think I care," Reeta snapped.

"Disappear," she grumbled, nodding once to Chadrik before turning on her heels and marching away without another word.

"What did we expect," Reeta scoffed, "Leave it to an Impery to muck things up. Get in, get out. It's not that difficult."

"None of us could've done it," the Chadrik sighed, flicking his sitter into the gravel and spitting at it before grinding it underfoot.

Reeta lifted the pack off the ground and held it out to her son, "I want you to be careful out there, Chadrik."

"What are you, insane?"

"Don't talk to your mother that way," she snapped.

"I'm not going out there alone."

"You'll be fine."

"It doesn't matter if I'm a Shiny or a Bruteman, I can't go without Josanna. She's the only one who knew the guide. I don't even know where he's at or even if it is a he."

"Any person wandering around out there, you're safe to assume is the Gadling guide," she said irritably.

"If they show themselves," Chadrik said, throwing the pack over his shoulder and walking away from the wall, "Face it, she had her bases covered. We have to wait for her."

"Why would we wait for her? They'll kill her."

"She's an Impery woman, they won't kill her. She just needs to take me to the guide, we've already got what we needed."

"But I don't th—"

"Would you relax and stop spitting at the wind? We'll go when we're ready."

Reeta jogged in front of him and put her hand on his shoulder, "If you were to come back with the Thesmekka, just you, triumphant for all the Sinovians to see…"

"I know, mother. They could not deny our right to rule," Chadrik recited, bobbing his head side to side, "But I need to get there first, alive."

Chadrik carefully strapped the pearly orb into a leather pouch hanging from his belt. It may have only been the size of a sunbloom berry, but it was twenty times as heavy.

*****

Zaki fidgeted impatiently, sitting on a root rolled right out of the ground like it was just a bench. Vik wheezed, pushing aside the foliage that had grown thicker as the day went on.

"Can you breathe?"

"Barely," Vik gasped, holding his hand over his chest.

The air was so thick and full of water, he felt like a set of gills might actually be useful. Vik slumped down on his knees beside Zaki, using the root bench as a headrest instead.

"You'll get used to it," Zaki patronized.

Vik thought of about twenty sarcastic remarks, but none of them were worth the extra effort to say out loud.

The clearing they'd arrived in was peaceful, beautiful and filled with just enough noise to make them comfortable. The trees were getting thinner, the foliage more dense around their feet and the light regularly made it through the treetops. They had made it into a section of the forest that was mainly aerial roots reaching up as high as they could and curling off at the top. It was like a textbook forest until looking up.

Something clumped along behind them, sprinting passed them on the left before Vik could clearly make it out.

"Don't worry about that," Zaki said.

Vik blinked slow and heavy, shaking his head and not really wanting to make this next decision.

"I have to keep going."

"You have to get to Imperyo that badly?"

"Yeah, I do. My brother's there, he needs me," Vik pulled himself up on the root and stretched his back as he stood up straighter.

"Why?" Zaki asked in a weak voice, his big, black eyes locked on Vik with only a sliver of white showing.

"He's not safe," he responded quickly. "You really should come with me. It's going to be safer there than it is out here."

"For you, maybe."

Vik threw his hands up, "Alright, stay here then."

He didn't look back and he wasn't followed, but it ate at him for an hour. In the end, he knew he shouldn't have left that kid alone even if he had to drag him along. That child had been so afraid of Imperyo he couldn't help but wonder what had happened to frighten him away. The possibilities he created as he walked made him unsure whether or not to turn back and apologize or continue on as he'd intended. Before he could make up his mind, he looked up from the ground and squinted against the direct sunlight. The trees had ended. The forest parted to reveal a black mountain decades ahead of where his own had been when he left it. Buzzing voices carried by the breeze through the tended fields swept over him and his lips parted into a smile. It was home at first sight.

# CHAPTER ELEVEN

Arriving at the edge of the forest, Vik surveyed the fiery horizon glowing over the formidable wall surrounding Threshold. Stainless but fractured, the sleek grayish barrier nestled into the ground was so out of place among its mortal surroundings. The fields encircling it were arranged in specific plots, though Vik didn't recognize any of what was being grown, even the bloodstones in their natural state. Sunblooms drooped like yellowish droplets knee high off the ground, their bulbous berries still encased and maturing. Beside them grew the bloodstone stalks, their familiar fronds much longer than Vik was used to seeing.

Coming out of the woods, Vik glanced back and forth but most workers were back in Threshold for the day. Only a small group of dedicated farmers lingered in the spitfires and drass toes, both growing just in front of the entrance to the city. Vik reached into his pocket and touched the top of Havard's pearly orb, its weight a reminder of the comfort he left behind. One young man, younger than Vik by at least a couple of years, tossed his basket down and bounded toward him, carefully avoiding the plants.

"Did I see you coming out of the forest?" he asked Vik.

"Yes, I just, I got separated from the others...there was a group of us."

"Of course there was," the young man chuckled, "They arrived just the other day, you're one of the New Ones." He waved over his shoulder to beckon his friends to him, "I've never met a Gadling before."

"Neither have I," said Vik, fidgeting from all the sudden attention from these painted, wildly expressive people.

These men had darkly-tanned skin, as a people who worked under the sun would have, almost purplish red hair that was braided in two rows going back from the front of their heads like soft horns. The youngest among them, possibly ten years old, had his duel braids rolling forward, stopping just above his eyes. All of them were painted with various colors and patterns with dark streaks smeared under their eyes. Their visages were enhanced by their enlarged features. Big eyes, wide smiles and every part of their face seemed to join in to magnify every expression, no matter how small.

"A Gadling, you know, someone who survives in the woods alone. I didn't believe it could be done." Saying he had a contagious smile would've been an understatement, "I'm Haku," he grabbed his hand and raised it to his forehead, then waited for Vik to return the gesture.

Vik widened his eyes and mirrored the motion, glancing between them all to ensure he was doing it correctly, "I'm Vik."

Haku grabbed Vik's hand again, this time with both of his hands and held it tightly before trying to pull him along. He smiled even wider.

"Come!" he encouraged.

Vik put one foot in front of the other and the men scooped up their bounties to follow them. There was an odd smell wafting with the breeze, but they didn't seem to notice it. Vik craned his neck to see the top of the smooth Gate wall as they approached a split in it, covered by a hide tarp pinned to one side. They passed through and Vik registered what the acrid odor reminded him of.

"Is that piss?"

The painted men laughed hard and encouraged him onward, through the second curtain. As soon as Vik stepped through, his eyes watered up and he gagged though there was nothing to throw up. The odor of pungent urine hit him like a curtain of bitter air. On either side of the entrance, buckets of liquid waste sat idly waiting to be distributed along the sleek, Thesmekkian wall.

"Why?" Vik managed to gasp.

"It scares away the drass, most of the time. If we don't cover the walls they would never leave us alone."

They steered him along the main road leading passed vibrant houses of colors Vik had never seen outside of holograms. As his giddy guide skipped along, he called out to everyone who looked at them.

"A Gadling," he would say with an overly-excited grin, pointing back to Vik.

And people started following them. They were curious, but he couldn't figure out why. They arrived in the middle of the market circle and took a left, veering off between several stalls being packed up for the day by their owners. Coming up to a heavily built structure, the clattering, cackling cacophony of a good time poured out through every crack like a dam about to break.

"We'll go inside now, if you want?"

"Sure," Vik mumbled, his brain fried from the overload of new information.

162

Everything and everyone was made of colors. Even in the fading light, they just shifted into an entirely new set of hues to look at. Standing at the doorway of the tavern like a gray stone statue, dressed in dirty white clothes and shaggy black hair, he felt like a blank page.

Haku opened the door and pulled Vik inside, relinquishing his grip only to shove the lost New One in front of him. He raised both his hands and shouted from behind Vik.

"Everyone, look this way!"

The entire room shifted its gaze and Vik felt himself shrinking. Haku put one hand back on his shoulder to keep him from running out the door.

"A Gadling," he called out over the quieter room.

Murmurs broke out in a ripple over the tables and it only took a few seconds for someone else to respond with questions.

"I saw him myself," Haku announced, turning to his friends who had followed them all the way in.

They were just as animated as Haku, retelling the story with slight embellishments each time. By the end of the fourth retelling in just a few short minutes, Vik had swung out of the forest on the leg of a tallbug, narrowly avoiding a hoard of drass that were right on his heels.

"That didn't happen," Vik mumbled, feeling horribly embarrassed.

The room filled with warm laughter and a woman twice his age marched over and put her arm around Haku. She pulled at Vik's face once to get a better look at a scrap under his eye.

"You look drop job and under a tree."

"...What?"

The room filled with laughter again, but no one explained what she meant. In the corner of the room, at a table full of blonds and booze, Chadrik watched the New One bumble through the concept of payments with the barkeep at the counter. He flicked the ash off the end of his sitter and sucked in a deep cloud of smoke, squinting at Vik as he walked out of the tavern.

"You should talk to that one," his friend, Ridiak, suggested.

"Bring him here," Chadrik slurred.

"I can't," Ridiak sighed, "He's left..."

"Well go find him."

"All those New Ones look the same."

*****

The sun had risen well into the next day. As it grew warmer, a sweet and musty odor filled the room, as if that were just the smell of baby Sinovians. But no amount of pleasing fragrance could soften Tayna's mood. No one else spoke to her that morning. Jahzara's marked girls just stood as far on the other side of the hut as they could and whispered too loudly about her. Apparently, everyone's first night is the worst. Tayna couldn't shake her anger toward them though. All they had to do was tell everyone what Jahzara was doing.

There was a rapping at the door and all the girls stopped their gossiping to watch it. No one moved or breathed, especially Tayna. After a long pause, the door slowly opened. When Tayna saw who it was she wobbled to her feet, powering through the spots that danced across the room.

"You!?"

"There you are," Zaruko said warily.

He was holding a bowl that fit perfectly in the palm of his hand. There was a pale paste in it that was both grainy and glistened in the light. The odor was so strong, it punched her senses before he got to her. It smelled like muggy armpits and an overripe bloodstone.

"What, ugh, what is that?"

"It's an ointment, for your burns," Zaruko held the bowl carefully and came closer. "Didn't you use some of what I gave you before?"

She leapt from her spot and when she reached him, slapped him so hard across his face that the others gasped and flinched. Zaruko clenched his jaw and held the ointment out for her.

"You knew this would happen! You knew?" she screamed at him but it cracked and cut out some words.

"Would you rather have let her take that child? I came here to make sure you didn't do anything stupid."

"It's not stupid to try and save them."

"In the way you might be thinking, it is. There were others who made this mistake before you, who tried to warn everyone about all this here. Don't anger Jahzara."

Tayna could feel more than her face burning. She glanced at the ointment bowl in his hand and slapped it out, letting it spill across the floor. Her body ached for it, but she was trembling for another reason. Ordering him away with a hoarse, shaky whisper, Zaruko raised his chin and tossed a sealed pouch to her anyway.

164

"Around here, being there after the damage is done means more than trying to prevent it."

Zaruko gave no recognition to the others, but begrudgingly nodded once to Tayna before leaving in a huff. Someone was waiting for him outside and their voices trailed off as they walked farther away. One of the marked girls, the one with only one eye, carefully made her way to the bowl on the floor and started trying to scoop the remnants into it.

"You can have this, I don't want it," Tayna offered her the pouch.

"This is for you too," the girl said quietly and sheepishly. "It's very difficult to make. You have to put it on early or it won't make as much of a difference. Just rub it gently over your burns."

Once she got enough in the bowl, she set it next to Tayna and backed away from her without another word. Unable to explain it, that slap had changed her more than it had the man she unleashed it on. She had never done anything like that before in her life. Violence against others was less of a taboo for the Grays on the bottom levels, but still, it wasn't common. Especially not for a small girl, the daughter of a revered...fortune teller. Tayna thought about Vik and Marek for the first time in a while. Jahzara killed her cousin's sieva and now wanted to kill her nephew. The Gate closed, separating her from her boys and her drugged out father's corpse. She was running out of family. All these thoughts rushed to her like they had been running all night to get there and smashed through the door.

She squeezed the tough leather pouch and some of the ointment oozed out, stinking up the immediate area so badly she cringed as she rubbed it between her fingers. Putting it on her face was the last thing she would've done, but as soon as she did the pain pulled back. The ointment sunk into her skin, made it feel like there was nothing wrong. Just a dull, noticeable burn like the sun had given her before the Impery came to Haven. Tayna dried her eyes with the backs of her wrists and made her way to the door.

The one-eyed girl called out to her, "What are you doing?"

"I've got to find my family."

"You can't leave. Not during the day."

"Why not?"

"These burns aren't like you'd get from a fire. Jahzara says it's because their fire is sacred. It won't be that way forever, but it does last a long time."

Tayna scoffed and walked through the door, stepping outside and feeling the sun warming her whole body. Her face took a few seconds, but even with the freshly applied ointment a new burn like that was too sensitive to the sun's light. She covered her face, but it did no good. The burn alone wasn't going to stop her from searching, even if her eyes were welling up and her chest fluttered with each wave of pain. What was going to stop her was the blindness as her eyes refused to open.

She backed back into the nursery and shut the door, slinking to her bed and waiting for a less harsh time of day to walk about. In the meantime, she planned to gather what she needed for a solid meditation. She swallowed her pride and glanced at the other marked girls. They were watching her over the cribs from the other side of the room.

"Tayna, are you in there?" someone shouted from outside the nursery.

She could hear a baby wailing outside. Tayna jumped up from her bed, dizzily scrambling for the door. She flung it open and cringed back when the sunlight hit her face. Marek charged through the cracked door, pushing passed Tayna on the other side.

"I need you to take care of him," Marek begged, holding the squirming newborn in his arms, "He's hungry, it's too hot, I can't..."

"Marek," Tayna breathed, "You know what that woman wants—"

"What happened to you?" Marek gasped.

Tayna turned her face away, covering it as best she could with her hood, "She thinks I belong to her now."

One of the other girls approached Marek and sheepishly offered to take care of Garek.

"No thank you," Marek blurted out, gawking at her deformed face.

"It's alright," Tayna assured him, "Besides, I need to talk to you about this."

Marek allowed the scarred girl to take Garek out of his arms, watching her anxiously as she wandered off into the corner of the room. She sat down on her bed with Garek still furiously fussing, cradling and shushing him gently.

"Why did you bring him here? After everything we did to try and keep him safe?"

"There are people out there who want to help us, Tayna. I can't talk too much about it here," he glanced around at the other girls, "but you should know Garek and all these other infants are safe here, safer than anywhere else in Threshold. At least for now."

"How can they be safe?" she hissed.

166

"They told me all about what's going on with this place. That woman, Jahzara, she keeps these children here to sacrifice them so she can have her own children."

"Yeah, I know. You're a roller for bringing him here," Tayna scoffed.

"But she can only do this once a month, when the moons align to look like an eye. They call it the Watching hour, like it's Thessa's darker eye."

"They don't like hearing about the Thesmekka either," Tayna whispered, facing away from the others. "Apparently that'll get you into a lot of trouble around here."

"It's different out there," Marek muttered excitedly. "If you can ever get away from here for a time, there's some people I'd like you to meet."

Tayna stared at him without speaking or breathing for so long his smile faded and he asked what was wrong in his defense.

"Why do you want me to meet these people?"

"I just," Marek stuttered through a few more attempts, "I thought you'd want to be a part of things. After what she did to you. You're family…"

"Don't," she snapped, squeezing her eyes shut and jutting out her chin, "Don't pretend there's no Grays and Uppers anymore. Tell me the truth."

"I thought you might help us," Marek slowly confessed. "You're Harlok's daughter, a lot of Grays would listen to you. These people want to get to know our leaders, but we don't have any. Not yet."

"I'm not a leader. Look at me."

"Tayna, you're a far better choice than any Gray I know."

"I'm the only Gray you know," she grumbled. "I'll think about it, but I need something from you."

"Anything," he insisted.

She scoffed, "A new face."

"Tayna…"

"I need some supplies."

"What for?"

"I'll be meditating. I'm not sure for how long and I won't start unprepared."

"…Meditating?" Marek sighed. "Are you really going down that road?"

"I am Harlok's daughter," she mocked, throwing her hands out to her side. "And you want a Gray leader. How do you think he got so popular?"

*****

After leaving the troubling nursery, Marek trotted out into the market circle in the very center of Threshold. Along the way, he passed by several Jawnies sitting outside their homes or just inside, near the windows. They were applying their unusual, clay paintings to each other's faces. Every pattern meant something to each person and every person who used their fingers to smear the colorful clay onto their loved one's faces knew exactly where to put them.

Market stalls covered in multicolored fabrics and a wide assortment of goods dotted the opening, intending to get in the way of a straight path from one end to the other. Several pure white, fluffy bugs with splotchy-patterned, black and white wings gathered around the top of posts spread out and stuck around various locations. The posts had cut open bloodstones and overripe hairy berries tied in bushels as treats to keep the child-sized moths occupied. A man who had been tending a stall with pretty necklaces and bracelets bolted out from behind the stand to chase a thieving babbler as it chattered hysterically, fleeing on three hands with its prize clutched against its furless chest.

Marek jogged by a stand with jewelry, one with toys made of fellenwort husks, and another with soft shirts made from the wool off white jackets instead of rough scales or leather. After weaving passed four more stalls, he spied the one he was looking for. It was littered with roasted twirlies, shelled hairy berries, marinated drass toes, and even strands of bloodstone being peeled by the merchant with a simple, rotating device. He had one hand supporting his chin and the other slowly spinning the tiny handle on the bloodstone peeler.

"Excuse me," Marek started.

"No," the shopkeeper blurted out.

"Can I have some bloodstone strands?" Marek pressed on anyway.

"Do you have anything to pay with? No, I didn't think so, New One. If you want a handout, go down the Bruteman street there and stop at the first large building, they've got the stew pot. Or go work and earn some credits."

Marek groaned, but hurried away from the grumpy merchant's stand toward the road he mentioned. A lot of merchants were irritable

168

with their people lately as the concept of payment for what you need was still foreign to them and there were plenty of mistakes being made. Before he fled the market circle, Marek heard a familiar voice and stopped fast in his tracks.

"So I swung its leg around a tree branch, tied it in a knot, and then ran deeper into the forest. It tried to follow me, but the stupid beast was stuck. It fell right out of the treetops and onto its back and I wrestled it with my bare hands until it died. And that's how I saved the New Ones, but also got separated. They ran to safety and I stayed behind."

"Vik!" Marek shouted, jogging around the group of children gathered in front of him.

"Marek, you made it," Vik said, throwing his arms around him.

"Whoa, they're exactly the same!"

"Not exactly…" one of the more skeptical kids said, squinting between the brothers.

"Is this your brother?" One of the kids asked excitedly.

"Oh, the one that you saved by grabbing the drass tail and swinging him around?"

Marek rolled his eyes toward Vik, "Grabbing a drass tail…"

"That's enough stories for now," Vik apologized when they all acted sad, "I know, but maybe later I'll tell you about the mysterious child with no eyes and a giant shadow."

They screamed playfully with each other, pretending to be scared and ran off, scattering into the field of flapping fabrics and people with money.

"I'm glad you made it out of the woods, again," Marek chuckled. "It sounds like you had a real time of it."

Vik glared at him sarcastically, "They keep calling me a Gadling and they think I've done something really incredible by just, I dunno, being in the forest by myself and making it back alive."

"Well I have to agree, I'm surprised to see you again."

"Did you mourn my tragic passing?" Vik teased, faking a crying face.

"I've been busy."

"You didn't even mourn me?" Vik shouted.

"I was getting around to it," Marek spotted Savan and called out to him.

"Don't change the su—"

"Hey guys!" Savan said, trotting to a stop in front of them, cheery as ever. "Vik, I'm glad to see you."

"You too," Vik said sourly.

"Uh, Marek, I wanted to let you know that Kalan's mentor is really pleased and he'll even get a credit today."

"That's great," Marek said, resting his hand on Savan's shoulder, "What about Ziven?"

"Uh, farming isn't really something he seems to want to do," Savan struggled to be polite, "He's still pretty upset I think. About his brother."

Vik couldn't help but remember Edik's face, the memory in all black and white except the blood.

"I'll try to find him something else, but if he's still like that in a couple of days let me know, will ya?"

"Of course," Savan nodded.

"Well, aren't you busy?" Vik teased.

"Our people can't just hide in those mud piles until we starve to death. Have you even seen those things we live in?"

Vik shook his head, "Nah, I slept in the tavern last night."

Marek pursed his lips and prepared to tell him how horrible their living conditions were when a blond stranger strolled up to them and silently joined their conversation.

"Uh, hello," Vik said warily.

"Is one of you the Gadling?"

"That'd be him," Marek smirked, pointing at Vik.

"Finally," Ridiak sighed, blinking heavily, "You all look so alike...I asked someone earlier, turned out to be a woman," he chuckled.

"What do you want?" Vik didn't appreciate the implication.

"Why don't you guys come with me?"

He started to walk away, but Marek called out to him, "Why *should* we go with you?"

"Quiet," he hissed, glancing around.

The market circle was still bustling and brimming with shoppers, and no one took any notice of the three of them at all. Ridiak waved his arm in a circle, begging them to follow. Marek and Vik gave each other suspicious glances and followed him carefully. He was going away from the Bruteman street, in the opposite direction Marek needed to go. The houses along the road they were on had no painted shapes, no flashy banners, coverings, or any type of bright craft hanging outside. They all had drass skin curtains for doors, open windows and modestly painted pots outside their front doorways. To the north, over their rooftops, the two stilted water towers lumbered overhead. All around it smelled like sweet honey, but that was anywhere far enough from the urine-stained wall.

"Is Garek with Tayna?" Vik asked quietly, trying to break apart some of the uncomfortable silence.

Every person they passed was blond with golden tans and bright blue eyes, but otherwise very similar to themselves. Not much difference in hairstyles, height, or mannerisms.

"Yeah, he is," Marek answered quickly.

"This is Shiny street," Ridiak finally spoke, the first time since leaving the market circle.

"Shiny street?"

"They're called Shinies," Marek said, then whispered under his breath to Vik, "Everyone seems to be a little uncomfortable about them."

"That's just because we look like Riders," Ridiak scoffed, "So I've heard."

"Riders?" Marek asked.

"Yeah, Sinovians with all-black eyes. They used to be a part of Threshold back when Durako's father, Lord Vosko, was in charge. Brought us the wall, lot of good it does," he added sarcastically. "There was a big fight and they left to find the Thesmekka. Killed a lot of people, it's best not to bring them up." Ridiak stopped walking and faced them.

"Why've we stopped?" Vik asked.

"We're here," Ridiak motioned to the door, "After you."

The house they stopped in front of was the largest in the small cluster just a short walk off the main Shiny street. The two brothers cautiously walked inside, using their arms to move the stiff, scaly curtain out of the way. The inside and outside of the house was like night and day. Everything from the ceiling to the corners of the floor was well manicured and as clean as it could get. There were paintings of landscapes on the walls, wooden statues of laborers on several of the shelves and rough pillows stuffed with fibers strewn across the floor. Two of them were occupied.

"Marek," Reeta stood as quickly as her aching bones would let her, "I wasn't expecting to see you here."

"That's my brother, Vik," Marek corrected, "I'm Marek."

"My goodness," Reeta chuckled, "The resemblance is unbelievable."

Chadrik cracked a smile from the pillow on the floor and took another puff of his sitter before stamping it out in the tray on the table slab in the middle of the sloppy circle of seats. He motioned to Ridiak and their escort took himself outside through the bumpy curtain door.

"Sit, please," Chadrik ushered them with wide swings of his arms.

Reeta plopped her stout body down on the pillow she'd been occupying before they came in, but Marek and Vik sat across from them, using the table as a separator.

"I've been hearing stories about the Gadling's adventures in the forest," Chadrik began, smiling through half opened eyes, "I almost thought you were a Jawny."

"I may have had some fun with things," Vik confessed, shrugging.

"We want to know something very specific," Reeta interrupted, "You said there was someone else out in the woods, was there any truth to that?"

Vik thought about Zaki and how stubborn he was about going too close to Imperyo.

"You didn't invite us here to listen to his Gadling stories," Marek said, crossing his arms.

"Tell us why we're really here and I'll tell you what I really saw," Vik said.

"You wouldn't understand the significance even if we told you," Reeta stated.

"We know how to get to the Riders," Chadrik interrupted, continuing despite his mother's silent outrage, "At least, we think we do. But we needed the Impery woman who got caught and is being kept in the mountain."

"Why can't you go in and get her?" Vik asked.

"You can't go in the mountain unless you can spit fire," Reeta told him, then turned to Chadrik, "Besides, we don't need her. Not if he knows what the guide in the forest looks like and how to find them."

"I do," Vik answered curtly.

"But you're not going to tell us," Chadrik smiled with his sitter twitching between his teeth.

"He didn't seem like he wanted to be found by anyone from here. He saved my life, I won't betray that without knowing exactly what's going on. Why do you all need an Impery woman and a guide out in the forest?"

"That Impery woman's got a piece of the Thesmekka Durako keeps in his manor..."

"Chadrik," Reeta hissed.

"There's a Thesmekka in Imperyo?" Marek asked, exchanging a glance with Vik, both of them stunned.

"A dead one," Chadrik corrected, "We're going to take this piece of it to the Riders, bring them and the Thesmekka back here, if they really found them..."

172

"They had to have found them," Reeta grumbled.

"And use the information of a new safe place, the place the Riders are at right now, to sway more favorable treatment of the Sinovians. We'll leave if there's somewhere else to go."

"When were you planning on telling the others about this?" Marek snapped at Reeta, "I thought the leaders were supposed to work together?"

"Nattina knows. Taolani knows too and so do I. Even Zaruko knows," she sneered before composing herself again, "You don't know because you're new, we don't know you, but most importantly, the way I hear it your people are divided. On top of that, they don't consider anyone their leader. The Gadling is the most qualified to be your people's leader."

"I don't know about you, but I'm feeling so cooperative right now," Vik mocked, pretending to be flattered.

"There's way more Sinovians than Impery, right?" Marek started asking, "Why hasn't there been a revolt or anything like that?"

"Not only do they breathe fire," Reeta said, "But they've got us rigged to burn at the first sign of trouble. You know that sweet smell in the air? That's the sap used to hold our homes together. It doesn't just lure drass here to keep us afraid and dependent, but it's extremely flammable."

"Will you come with me to meet with the guide and find where the Riders are?" Chadrik asked, tired of explaining. "It's either you guys or Josanna, the Impery girl. We have no other choice."

"I can't," Marek blurted out, "I've got my son here, I can't leave."

"I'll have to think about it," Vik said, "I just got here. I almost died so many times, I just, I'm not convinced it's worth going back out there."

Reeta's face burned red and she squared her shoulders at him, but Chadrik stopped her rant before it could come bursting out, "Alright, that's fair. But when you're convinced, come see us again."

"Sure," Vik scoffed.

"Oh," Chadrik lazily waved his hand out in front of them, summoning them back as he remembered a detail he left out, "if you say anything about the Thesmekka to anyone, even each other," he shrugged and looked genuinely regretful, "we'll have to kill you. No hesitation or excuses."

"We won't say anything," said Marek when Vik wouldn't speak.

"Good," snapped Reeta.

With a flick of her wrist, Reeta pushed Marek and Vik with a strong gust of air out through the curtained door as it was whipped around by the stirred up breeze. They stumbled forward, but kept on their feet. Exchanging looks, they knew the puffed up threat they'd received might not have been all fluff. First the fire-breathing Impery, then the air pushing Shinies. Vik and Marek felt more vulnerable than they should have after that shove.

Ridiak was lounging on the front steps with a sitter in his mouth. He hopped up and smiled at them, going inside and leaving them to wander off on their own.

"There goes our only other chance," Reeta complained.

"They just got here, the Gadling just got here last night," Chadrik lazily rose to his feet and stood in the hallway entrance, "They don't know what it's like yet. I have a feeling when they see how things are for themselves, they'll be back."

# CHAPTER TWELVE

The sun stretched out over Threshold, spilling warm orange over the part of the sleeping city not covered by the black mountain. Each poorly covered window and doorway became a beacon of light, filling every crevice in the rooms it touched. Vik and Marek struggled to pull their stiff bodies out of their indentations on the dirt floor. They were the first in the room to show signs of life, but they didn't feel good about it. Most of the muscles and joints in their bodies were either pulled, unusably sore, or completely asleep from being smashed into the hard dirt all night. Marek felt like his hand was twice its size and kept squeezing it despite how weird it felt to touch his own skin without being able to feel it. He yearned for the soft beds in Haven. Vik shook his head and flicked out a pebble from his ear.

"You had rocks in your ears," Marek laughed through a yawn at the real-life idiom.

"I think I'm dead," Vik groaned, slouching over his knees.

"Me too," Kalan mumbled, facing the wall nearby.

"Be quiet," Ziven whined, his voice muffled by his own arm.

"I can't do this again," a middle-aged Upper sobbed on the opposite corner of the room.

Marek crawled over to him and shifted his weight to sit on the less sore side of his posterior, patting the man on the shoulder, "Don't say that. Just take it easy today."

"But not too easy," Kalan said, finally rolling over to face the others in the room. "I heard if you rest for too long when you're sore like this, it only gets worse."

"See there, looks like you don't have a choice," Marek joked with him.

"Stop talking," Ziven grumbled again, moving his head just enough to speak around his arm.

"We used to have a choice, we used to have homes. Cool rooms and clean clothes," the man said airily, "If I wanted to, I could walk out into the forest right now."

Everyone was quiet again, glancing around at each other, not wanting to be the first one to break the uncomfortable silence. Vik remembered his own dazed marched out of the house before there was a stairway, snapping out of it right in front of the edge of the top level with Marek dragging him away.

"Why did you leave Haven then?"

"Vik…" Marek started, but he ignored his brother's discouragement.

"I left to live. Being inside Haven wasn't living and it nearly killed me. Out here it's hard, yeah, but we're alive. I feel so much pain and hunger, but when I rest and when I eat, I've earned it. We weren't alive before. I think life, it's supposed to hurt. The stairway was the easy part, the forest was the hardest part so far, and you made it. You made it through that, but you're still not happy. So if you don't want life, if you're gonna walk out into the forest because this is too hard for you, then go. Don't try to bring us down with you."

There was a long pause where Vik's words were chewed, but not everyone in the hovel enjoyed the taste. The homesick man jumped up and Marek hopped after him. He tried to reason with him just inside the muddy doorway.

"He's not a morning person," Marek chuckled awkwardly, "We're all having a hard time. You'll be fine."

"If I kill myself then you're to blame, Vik."

"Please, not that," Vik yawned.

Ziven rolled over and yelled with his eyes shut, "I'm going to kill all of you if you don't—"

"Shut up," Kalan interrupted, scrambling to his feet.

The older man sneered at them, "You guys are a bunch of—"

"Quiet!" Kalan hissed, hunching over as a loud thump blew dirt under their tattered window curtain.

They all turned and watched an enormous shadow blot out the light slipping in through the cracks. A rapid tradeoff of snorting and snuffling grew louder, accompanied by a few more heavy, shuffling footsteps. The miniscule, scaled tarp over the window flapped twice before a blunt, eyeless head crammed itself into the hole. The seven guys in the room pushed back against the wall farthest from the intruding drass, but it had already sniffed them out. It pushed itself against the window frame and the whole wall crackled in response.

"He's gonna break the wall down," Kalan whispered through his teeth.

A piercing shriek rang out from outside. It was like a whistle and jarred everyone in the area awake. The drass flailed against the window, its large tail thumping twice against the wall as it tried to squirm its way out. Everything shook and small crumbs broke off from the dry walls. Once it was free, it dug its talons into the dirt and shot across the clearing, keeping low to the ground as if something were going to scoop it up from the sky. There was a section of the metal wall that was filled in with wooden pillars where it'd snuck in. It used that same entry point to scramble up and out.

The seven of them emptied out of the hut and looked around for what had saved them. Nikiva stood with her mouth agape, her arms supporting Sera who looked as though she'd just recovered from nearly fainting. She had screamed until there was no air left, but at the sight of the giant lizards, she couldn't think straight enough to inhale. Nikiva saw the guys staring at them and grinned, giving Sera a single, firm shake.

"Look at that, you're their hero."

Sera was dazed. She blinked profusely before she finally supported her own weight, pushed her chuckling sister away, and stormed back into the hut, tears in her eyes. They could all hear her sobbing and cursing their newfound poverty. Ziven pushed passed the others and ran into the hut after her. He held her in his arms and consoled her with comforting words that were too gentle to hear through the curtains.

"It wasn't meant to be like this," he whispered to her as she wept into his shoulder, "People like us aren't supposed to be digging in the dirt."

None of them could hear, but he didn't want them to. Nikiva raised a brow at Kalan who just shrugged with a smile.

"I can't believe that just happened," Vik breathed, trying to get a better look at where the drass had come in from.

"We have got to fix these," Marek said, examining the damage done to their miserable hut, "Any earlier and we could've been asleep. Nikiva, get Savan. Vik, come with me."

"Yes sir," Vik joked, but jogged along to keep up with his brother. "Where're we going?"

"It came in from over there, right?"

"It looks that way," Vik said, eying the tall, wooden pillars nestled in the metal crevice.

"I bet the other side's got those hole all in it too, from its claws," Marek made the motions of the drass climbing.

"We could," Vik grabbed the back of his neck, "Okay, we could put spikes facing down, all up the outside, spikes facing up on the inside."

"Forget the inside ones. We'll need to pull those stakes down to put spikes in…but wow…"

"Yeah…it smells so bad," Vik said through his dirty sleeve.

"I'm glad you're here, Vik," Marek said, giving him a half smile while rubbing the scabs on his palms, "We're going to build a life for ourselves out here."

"I can't believe I'm actually hearing you say this," said Vik.

"But you gotta keep your motivational speeches to a minimum."

"I was just trying to help…"

"You told him to go kill himself," Marek chuckled. "You're insane."

More than half of the New Ones divided off toward the quarry, far away from the fields. The past couple of days revealed how lucky Vik was to get out of that job. They were often covered from head to toe in mud, smelling like baked sweat, and ripe, wet dirt. Many had broken limbs set by Brutemen with much bigger, stronger hands, not accustomed to tending to smaller people who required a fraction of the physical force as their own people. If they weren't breaking limbs, it was fingers and toes. Scrapes and inhaling dust were too normal to complain about. Those New Ones returned with the life beaten out of them by their work. The giants unintentionally crushed their spirits even more with their minimal effort and vastly superior productivity, but continued to be surprised by the New One's disproportionate endurance. The pale little lookalikes worked like a colony of ants: small load portions, long work days, few complaints.

Almost slamming into a couple of stunning young Jawny girls at the gateway, Sera jumped back and teetered out of their way. Their skin was smooth and clear, their eyes were striking in shape and color, and their lithe bodies were alluring even as they worked. They slipped her polite smiles with perfect teeth and strolled by with a bucket in each hand. Sera sucked in a deep breath and cheerfully called after them, scurrying to catch up.

"What's she doing?" Kalan asked.

"I think she's trying to find another job," Nikiva said, watching her with mild curiosity.

The two girls nodded, smiling wide and putting their arms around her. Sera glanced back at Nikiva and threw her a haughty wave, dismissing her concern.

Vik arrived in the fields just little after Haku, who was ecstatic as usual to see him. It was almost too much that early in the morning, but a breeze blew the sweet smells of the fresh, dewy air over his face like a

178

splash of cool water. This was his third day working in the spitfire field and he still didn't know what one tasted like. A spitfire grew underground and marked its spot with a bushel of fluffy green leaves. The leaves were used for ointments and ground up for spices, but would teach a nasty lesson if eaten by themselves. The actual spitfire root wasn't quite as hot as its leafy top, but it couldn't be called mild by a longshot.

A couple of hours had drifted by and Haku jogged over to Vik with a mangled, off-white lump in his hands.

"It's a spitfire, go ahead, try a bite," he coaxed, smiling wide, his eyes lit and narrowed. It was really too easy to read a Jawny's face.

"Just bite into it?" Vik asked, taking it in his hands with two fingers each.

"Yes," Haku sniggered, "You'll love it."

"I know you're lying to me," Vik grinned, "But I'm gonna try it anyway."

Haku laughed and agreed with his friends as they called Vik a true Gadling indeed. Vik chomped down on the end and despite its tough-looking skin, was surprised by how easy it was to crunch into. His tongue was met with a disarming sweetness that filled his mouth that made him close his eyes in pleasure until only seconds later he found he couldn't open them. His entire skull burned and everything clenched shut. He could hear Haku and the others cackling and tried to call them names, but wasn't going to spit out his challenge. He knew it was going to be hot, he just had to power through it. Besides, it wasn't quite as bad as when he touched the mace flower in the woods. But it was close.

He chewed like a madman and swallowed chunks so big he could feel them sliding down his throat. His eyes and nose were leaking and he wiped the drool from his numb lips. Haku and his friends laughed so hard they were crying too, but they started clapping for him when he opened his eyes.

"Gadling!" He shouted, spurring his friends into echoing him.

"Rollers," Vik gasped, playfully shoving Haku away when he tried to put his arm around him.

Kalan could hear them from the hairy berry field and shook his head, calling over to Marek, "Sounds like someone's having too much fun too early in the day."

"It's probably Vik," Marek sighed.

"I'd like to have some early morning fun, if you know what I mean," Kalan muttered, motioning toward the edge of the sunbloom field.

A busty, blonde Shiny was wiping sweat from her brow and leaning back with her face toward the sun. Marek noticed the beauty, but went back to plucking ripe hairy berries from bushels.

"You don't think she's a gem?"

"I think I'm busy," Marek grumbled sourly.

Vik learned to resist the urge to touch his face right after shredding spitfire leaves on the first day, so by the third he had mastered using the back of his arm to scratch any itch. The midday sun had finally climbed to the top of the sky, beaming down on them like it meant to hurt them. Vik remembered when he used to long for it, dream about seeing it from the outside instead of through a hole in the mountain. He thought back on his undead lifestyle, roaming the cold tomb and wishing for an accident to free him. Drenched in sweat, Vik finished shredding a bushel of leaves and stood up a little too fast. Everything went black and he heard a couple of people yelling before everything cut out and quickly switched back on, except he was on the ground and the back of his head was throbbing.

Haku dropped what he was doing and helped him sit up while one of his friends gave them his water and sprinted toward the city to get more. Vik hadn't realized how thirsty he was until the warm water touched his tongue and then he couldn't stop himself. He chugged the whole flask and gasped for air when he finished.

"You look drop job and under a tree," Haku sighed.

"I have no idea what that means…"

"I know," Haku smiled, "Take care of yourself, Gadling."

"Yeah, I didn't mean to," Vik mumbled.

In the sunbloom fields, Nikiva worked with the other women and careful young men to caress the knee-high flowers until they drifted open, revealing their yolk-like fruit inside. They were then plucked and put carefully into a covered basket that was taken into town twice as often as any of the other fields.

"How are you doing?" one of the Shiny girls asked her.

"It's so hot," she gasped. "But I think I'll make it."

The Shiny girl smiled politely, but seemed too drained to react any more than that.

"I kind of like it though," Nikiva thought out loud, "It's beautiful out here."

Vik was too far away to see or hear anyone other than those in his section of the spitfire field. He glanced over his shoulder at the colossal, metal wall and then just before it, at the hairy berry fields where he knew Marek was weeding and toiling. His dizziness hadn't faded enough for him to feel safe standing up. Even as he swiveled his head around, his vision just barely couldn't keep up. He shoved his palms against his eyes and rubbed them until he felt some level of mental stabilization, a stronger connection with the world around him. That action worked against him, burning his eyes with the spitfire dust from his hands instead. He groaned and blinked repeatedly, sheltering his eyes from the sun and trying to get the stinging to subside. A bizarre buzzing started ringing in his ears and he shook his head to be rid of it. When he saw everyone glance up at the forest, he realized he was hearing a distant tallbug screeching through the trees. Haku and the others casually went back to work. Tallbugs never left the forest, they were scared of the open space, unable to hover above their meals without the treetops.

A fluttering series of gigantic, flapping wings launched out of the canopies in response, taking red-feathered whistlers to the sky with them. Haku and the others shouted, pointing up at the sky, letting everyone know what was happening. Vik had been warned that if anything came flying at them, they were to run to the fellenwort fields adjacent to their own. It would be a decent sprint and he might just barely make it before the whistlers got to them.

Vik jumped up and started running, stumbling over his limp legs until he fell face first into a thankfully empty basket.

"Get up!" Haku shouted over his shoulder, turning around to get back to Vik.

He struggled to his feet with Haku's help and the two of them ran as fast as they could, trailing far behind everyone else. Vik felt the adrenaline putting power back into every step and he pumped his arms and legs furiously, glancing up at the sky every time one of the airborne beasts cried out overhead. It felt wrong to be running toward them, but the fellenwort trees were just a little taller than a Bruteman and covered anything under themselves like an umbrella. A couple of the silhouetted birds dove down, tripling their speed and revealing the bright red feathers on their back along with the faded brown and white feathers facing the ground. Easy to spot by other whistlers, but not by prey underneath.

The first two birds missed their targets, but the gust from their passing was enough to throw both Haku, Vik, and their intended targets in front of them. They could hear the high-pitched, single-note cry behind them and knew at least one of the birds had already turned around in midair. Vik kept shooting glances over his shoulder. Each time the bird was closer, like a terrifying slideshow. The sun was blotted out behind Vik when Haku dove over and shoved him to the ground with his whole body. The whistler caught Haku with one clawed foot before

181

he hit the ground and swiftly raised a talon, piercing through his chest. Haku's body went limp and the bird fluttered off with the others, crying and trilling like they were fighting over the prize.

Vik kept his face in the dirt, tightly wrenching a tuft of his own hair. Havard's orb left a circular pain on his thigh, sure to bruise but the bauble was still intact. He hadn't made it to the fellenworts, but they were already far enough away that people started dispersing once again. He heard a young girl wailing and screaming while others tried to quiet her down. Her anguish seared into his brain like a branding. The contorted face of a Jawny in pain was a sight Vik would never forget.

The rest of the day was unbearably quiet after that. Vik was beaten, subdued. Shaken to his core. Haku's friends worked tirelessly, staring down at the dirt, the paint on their faces smeared every which way. It was so quiet, Vik could hear the shredding of spitfire leaves all around him. Finished with pulling the greens apart, he gripped the stem and dug around it, yanking the root right out of the ground. He rubbed it with his raw, blistered hands until most of the dirt was gone and then tossed it into the basket with the other eight. He rubbed his eyes with the back of his arm, clutched the basket, and rose to his feet, making his way back into the city.

The sky was not fully dark when the bonfire rose up into the sky from the middle of the market circle, far away from the houses. Haku's family sat together, completely devoid of paint. Everyone who knew him had washed themselves clean and stood plainly around the fire. Where their regularly painted patterns once were, they had paler skin underneath in the same shapes.

A man approached Haku's mother and spoke so softly to her that only those in the immediately area could hear them. Vik noticed Chadrik watching nearby and wandered over to him.

"What's going on?"

"There's no body, so she's going to give her own bones for the scrimshander to use."

"What?" Vik gasped, whipping his head around to see them nodding like a deal had been struck. "Where's the father?"

Chadrik pushed his jaw out before he answered, "Haku was twenty two years old."

"What does that mean?"

"There's only a few out here the same age who aren't one of the fireless children. Impery came out of the mountain after a particularly barren year for them. They seduced or raped as many women as they could get their hands on. When the children were old enough, they took

182

them to Imperyo, but a year went by and none of them had the fire. So they didn't keep them. His father is some purist bastard sitting in his safe house. He has no idea what happened today and I'm sure he wouldn't lose sleep over it either."

Vik watched them tie a ribbon tightly around Haku's mother's left arm, cutting off the blood flow to her hand as much as they could. The scrimshander stepped aside and cleaned a cleaver with water he poured from a bowl.

"Wait," Vik muttered before gaining momentum. "Wait!"

Everyone turned and stared at him, indignant at first but unwilling to stop him. No one wanted to see a mother lose not only her oldest son, but her hand as well.

"He sacrificed himself," The scrimshander narrowed his eyes at him, but the mother's meek, trembling voice was what he heard next.

"He did?" she asked, afraid to believe him.

"Yes, he pushed me out of the way. That would be me up there, instead of him," Vik's voice cracked, but he quickly recovered.

Vik hoped their beliefs were the same as his, even if their rituals were more elaborate and less matter-of-fact than he was used to. Haven had been just as bored with death as it was with life.

The mother put her hand on the side of Vik's face and looked him in the eyes before untying the ribbon and letting it fall to the ground. The rest of the family passes by him and mirrored her staring gesture without touching him as they filed away in a line behind her. The crowd dispersed quietly behind him and several people started snuffing out the fire with dirt. Vik breathed a sigh of relief. He had been right. Across the cultures, a sacrifice has the power to make someone more than they were.

The next morning, the sunlight pierced in through the tattered curtains and woke them like it was just another day. That's how it was for the sun, nothing new but endless possibilities. Yesterday felt like things were going up and then suddenly Haku was dead, for no reason. Vik still felt like he had been hit by a flying rock. His hands were sore, the skin on his palms feeling tight over the fresh scabs when he balled his fists. A bruise outlined the cut on his left hand.

"My body," Marek groaned, grabbing his lower back and wincing in pain. "Are you alright?"

"I'm just gonna stay in today," Vik mumbled, his cheek pressed against the dirt.

Marek thought about dissuading him, but he was too tired. No one slept well enough that night. Marek scooped his complaining body up off the ground, pulled his shirt over his head and laced the strings on his shoulder. Vik stayed on the ground the entire time, so his brother left without bothering him. It was hard for Marek to get used to, waking up without the harmony of choirs. No one sang out in the forbidden world.

As soon as Marek stepped outside the hovel, he saw Chadrik idling not too far away, puffing on a sitter. He jogged over to him and mocked his morning choices.

"Some days need a little help to get going," Chadrik smirked. "Where's your brother?"

"Oh, you can tell us apart now?"

"Not at all, I just guessed he wouldn't be up as bright and early."

"Whatever you're planning, I'm not going with you."

"I know that."

"If Vik changes his mind, please, be careful taking him back out there. I don't have much family left."

Chadrik gave one slow nod and looked toward the hut Marek pointed toward before he left.

Kalan, Ziven and the other occupants of the dented, lopsided hovel passed Chadrik with curiosity. No one other than ex-Haven dwellers and a few Impery guides had been seen in their rundown neighborhood since Zaruko dropped them off.

Chadrik called through the hanging tarp, "Can I come in?"

"I'm sleeping," Vik grumbled.

"Yeah, me too," Chadrik said, ducking into the tiny abode.

Vik grumbled irritably when the Shiny lazily kicked the backs of his legs, "Leave. Me. Alone."

"That was real heroic yesterday, what you did for that mother."

Vik rolled over and glared, "I want you to leave."

"When you saved that woman's hand, made her day a little less horrible. And I heard what actually happened out there. You think you're responsible. That's selfish twospit talk. He made the choice himself, you even said it. Don't belittle his sacrifice with your guilt."

"Fine," Vik lied, hoping he would go away.

"So what are you doing? You gonna dry clay on a cloudy day?"

"Do we even speak the same language..." asked Vik, squinting at the bright window behind the pushy intruder.

"You'll get used to it," Chadrik said, briefly leaning against the wall until it creaked under his weight. He shoved off it quickly, looking up to judge the shanty's stability.

"Don't you need to find your mother?"

"She doesn't follow me everywhere," Chadrik scoffed, "It sure feels like it though. This is one of those occasions where she's better off
184

at home. I need to get Josanna out of there and we're running out of time for her. Enough days have been wasted keeping these people in danger, don't you think?"

Vik sat up, angry at first. Maybe it was the soreness in every muscle or the despair he'd been wallowing in, but he couldn't find the strength to swing his fist into the Shiny's face.

"If we can get her out, get to the guide and just," he held his hand flat out and pushed it forward like it was gliding along an invisible path, "get to the Riders, we can save all these people."

"Save them from what, all the whistlers and drass or just the dirt floors we sleep on every night?" Vik quipped.

"All of it," Chadrik boasted. "We only need to get the orb to the Riders…"

"Orb?" Vik asked quickly, furrowing his brows.

"Yeah, an orb. It's like a ball, only—"

"I know what an orb is. What does it look like?"

Chadrik stared at him for a long time before giving in, "I want you to know, I'm trusting you here. A lot. This would be enough to get me killed if you told anyone. You too, but I'm mainly worried about me."

"I understand," Vik assured him, watching Chadrik unlatch the strap on a satchel hanging from his waist.

"This is it," Chadrik beamed, holding the smooth, pearly Thesmekkian orb out between them.

Vik's stomach dropped and his heart gave one heavy thump before it stopped. Chadrik noticed and withdrew his hand.

"That's," Vik spun around and dug through his own pile of the few items he owned, pulling an oblong pouch out of the mix, "Just like mine."

When Vik pulled out Havard's orb and showed it to Chadrik, he sobered instantly. Chadrik cursed and laughed and cursed again, completing the full cycle of madness in front of Vik.

"If we'd only met a few days earlier."

"Let me see that one," Vik said, holding both orbs in each hand, "I have an idea."

*****

Everyone who was anyone was gathered in the tiny hut, huddled in a close circle, sitting on blankets Chadrik had brought from his own home. Gamba stood watch outside while Zaruko, Reeta, Nattina, and her protector, Benne, sat around the tight circle. New to Marek and Vik was

185

the Jawny leader, Harash and her granddaughter Taolani as well as their guard, Makai, the most straight-faced Jawny any of them had ever seen. Although he was an age between Taolani and her grandmother, he had copious excess skin, wrinkles under and around every feature, but they remained stoic, chiseled into place as if his face belonged to a statue. Vik delicately placed the Thesmekkian orb alongside Havard's identical pearl in the middle of the circle.

"Two of them?" Nattina asked, looking to Reeta for an answer.

"I'm just as surprised as you," she responded, sitting up straighter.

"One of them is a fake," Vik announced, "It's from the auto-arm in the place where we came from."

Harash didn't say anything, but she chuckled weakly, wheezing just a little as she did. By far the oldest one there, she made Marek and Vik a little nervous, but she was nothing like the elders they were used to. Her hair was braided the most ornately of any Jawny in Threshold and her face was riddled with painted symbols rippling over her crinkled skin.

"I'm going to make a trade with Durako for Josanna back," Vik stated, "With the fake, of course."

The floodgate of opinions burst apart and outside, Gamba flinched, glancing irritably over his shoulder at the ruckus the hovel was making. After letting them argue for a minute, Zaruko held up his hands and voiced his own concerns.

"That's not going to work for so many reasons, but we can try to figure this out. You'll need witnesses to the trade to go with you into Imperyo. They might not be easy to find."

"On top of that," Nattina added, "he'd arrest you or more likely just kill you on the spot, saying you helped steal it to justify his actions."

"He wouldn't let the witnesses out of the room either. Can't have all those people knowing about a Thesmekkian piece," Reeta said.

"What if we don't know what it is?" Marek suggested, "What if we pitch it back to him as a valuable trinket she stole that we're willing to return?"

"That might help, but he would still never trade an Impery female to a bunch of Sinovians," Zaruko said, noticing the sideways glances.

"Couldn't you send Gamba in to get her while we're having the meeting?" Marek asked.

"They'd recognize him," said Zaruko.

There was a long pause, a lull so deep in the conversation that nothing could be thought of to fill the void. They avoided looking at each other for too long. Makai stared contemplatively at the pearly orbs, but he had no intentions of speaking his mind. A hand peeked through the tattered hide over the doorway, parting it to one side. Tayna glanced around at the nine figures crammed into the tiny space afforded to them.

"What is she doing here?" barked Nattina's guardsman, Benne.

"She is one of Jahzara's girls," Harash said with her harsh, wispy voice.

"I belong to Jahzara as much as someone belongs to the fire that burned them," Tayna said carefully, pulling away her hood with no reason to hide her face once out of the sunlight. "I'm the leader of the Grays, one half of the New Ones."

Her body trembled and her lips were cracked, but she refused to sit. The burn that marred her face was even more gnarly in the illuminating, natural light. She had been in meditation for three and a half days, surviving without food or water through the power of the trance. Zaruko had come by twice daily to deliver ointment only to see her lying in bed each time, her eyes rolled to the back of her head.

"Three leaders for the New Ones?" asked Harash, skeptically.

"You're not counting me, are you?" asked Vik, glancing back and forth.

"I'm here to tell you exactly how you'll get Josanna out," said Tayna.

"How do you know that name?" Nattina asked, looking around for someone else who might've told her.

Zaruko slowly shook his head, his eyes widened and his lips unwittingly parted. Vik and Marek were familiar with Harlok's speeches enough to know how the rest was going to play out.

"Zaruko will go into the prison house on level ten," she ignored Zaruko's flinching back in astonishment at her familiarity with Imperyo, "let them know we're doing a tradeoff with Josanna and Lord Durako wants her present. You must not hesitate or act unsure of yourself in any way. As soon as you walk out the door with her, immediately walk, don't run or even hurry, down the ramps and to the entrance of Imperyo."

Nattina scoffed, "This is ridiculous."

"They will be so distracted by the hoard of Sinovians ascending their sacred home that they won't notice two of their own," Tayna continued telling them, "Once Josanna is safely out of Imperyo, Zaruko needs to run up and meet with the ascending group as fast as he can. You must get to them before they reach his manor."

"It's too simple," Harash chuckled.

"And yet so much could go wrong," said Nattina.

"I have seen it," said Tayna, catching herself in mid-tremble.

"Do you have visions?" Harash asked.

"It'll work," Marek insisted, much to everyone's surprised. "I don't care for calling them visions, but that's the best plan we've got and I feel good about it."

"Same here," Vik said, "count me in."

Everyone looked to Zaruko. He had the biggest part to play and the most to lose.

"I'll do it," he said, still staring at Tayna, surprised by the words coming out of his mouth.

"Let's gather some witnesses," Vik said, snatching the orbs from the middle circle and handing one back to Chadrik. "Keep that safe," he ordered.

Chadrik raised his brows, "Of course."

After the meeting dispersed, each leader trickled away to avoid attention. Marek and Vik spoke in hushed tones with Chadrik while Reeta hovered anxiously nearby, straining to overhear their conversation. Gamba and the Jawny guard gave each other respectful nods as Makai led Harash and her granddaughter back to their part of Threshold, through the marketplace and down the dusty path lined with painted houses. The only ones left inside the hovel were Zaruko and Tayna.

"Do you need more medicine?" he asked after a long silence.

"I think you've given me enough," snapped Tayna.

"I had nothing to do with any of Jahzara's plans."

"That's hard to believe. She's been a part of everything you've done since our people met."

"She did not have permission to attack that wom—"

"Stop making excuses," Tayna hissed, throwing her hands down to her sides, "I didn't know, I wasn't involved, she wasn't supposed to...Excuses don't stop people from getting killed or burned and they don't change anything. Being there to console victims after is for sivs, sievas, and the cutting knife. Not for leaders."

Zaruko's mouth had parted, but he clenched it shut along with his jaw when she stopped lecturing him. The side of her face that could still do so flushed red and her eyes started searching the tiny hut for some resolve.

"You knew what she might do, and you didn't warn me."

"I am so sorry," said Zaruko, lowering his voice along with his head. "I have never had anything go so wrong as our retrieval of your people. I handled everything in the worst possible way and it seems I can't stop doing so."

"I...well, thank you. I accept your apology," she said, absorbing a forming tear with the knuckle of her thumb.

188

"You gave me that tanning without expecting an apology?"

"...I thought we were just Sinovians," she whispered to avoid using her cracking voice.

"You're not a prisoner, you're a leader. The leader of the Grays, half of the New Ones. Isn't that what you said?"

"It is," she answered fast, blinking repeatedly. "I'm not feeling well."

"You look tired," he said, "Let me walk you back."

He swiftly, gently pulled her hood up until it rested over her head. He then reached out to pull the tarp aside and waited for her to pass through it. The sun slapped her burns and she jerked the hood over them, but the pain lessened when Zaruko used his own body to block the rays from her face. With one hand on her back and Gamba trailing behind, they marched around the edge of the marketplace and anxiously stopped in front of the cursed nursery. By the time they reached the door, Zaruko had lost himself in thought. He brought himself back to the present over and over, but clearly couldn't stay there.

"Don't worry," Tayna said to him, "Everything's going to work out as it should."

"Right," he said, looking around and exhaling.

"Thank you for taking care of me," Zaruko turned into a dumbfounded statue, but she quickly followed up with, "And for trusting me with this. You're taking a big risk on faith alone."

"If you can really see the future..." Zaruko asked quietly. "I have nothing to fear, right?"

"This will work," said Tayna, flashing a comforting smile.

They parted ways and she waited quietly behind the closed door, leaning her weight against it. Once she was certain he was far enough away, she sunk to her knees, covered her eyes, and found it hard to breathe under the weight of all her new deceptions. She reassured herself with thoughts of the visions and of accomplishing a greater good in the end.

*****

Standing at the entrance to the black mountain with a herd of witnesses in tow, Vik steeled himself for what was to come. Marek wished him luck, but stayed behind. The temptation for Jahzara to kill the both of them at once would've been too great a risk to take. Vik hated the idea of going back inside another mountain, knowing full well that again he might not come back out. He knew there could be no living out there for him as things were though. It was too much like Haven. He didn't want to learn to tolerate his new life, he wanted a better one than before. The part of him he couldn't name but always listened to was shouting that where they were going was the right path toward the right reward.

Benne stood beside the twin New Ones and gave both Marek and Vik a hard pat on the shoulder. He was glaring straight into Imperyo's dark maw.

"If we do die in there, it'll be with ten fingers."

Marek tilted his head to the side, but Vik had resigned himself to being lost in translation. Never one to think too hard on a good gut feeling, he clutched the pearly orb tight in his hand. Moving his eyes down from the top of the mountain until they settled on the cave entrance, he took his first step toward Imperyo.

# CHAPTER THIRTEEN

Charred wooden floors creaked unsafely under their footsteps. Jahzara pointed to a place in the middle of the floor and two young Impery girls carrying a long rug scampered in and dragged it over the manor's wound. Repairs were ongoing, but she refused to have to look at it every time she went into that room. She shooed them out, flicking her wrists and slammed the door behind them. The other door in the room was gone and replaced with a decorative blanket. Throwing herself onto the bed, glaring at the smoky stains above her. Durako knocked once and slowly opened the door, smiling down at the new addition.

"I like it," he said.

"Don't step on it, I can still see the room underneath."

Durako came up to the bed and put the back of his hand delicately against her face, "What's the matter, sunshine?"

"One of our own people broken in here, into the manor of the Impery Lord, to steal a bit of the Thesmekka...*for Sinovians*. That's what's wrong," she ranted.

"Josanna is hardly one of our own people," Durako chuckled. "Sometimes fire spreads where it shouldn't and just needs to be put out."

Jahzara sat up and sighed, looking around at all the fire damage she couldn't cover up. She took Durako's hand in hers and leaned in close.

"What if this is the first step?"

"The first step...You mean to a Sinovian takeover?" Durako swept some of her hair off her shoulder, "I think you're overestimating them, sunshine."

"I can't help feeling they were involved. How did she know exactly where it was? Where was she going with it?" Jahzara whispered, "Where is it now?"

"Josanna was acting alone. She always does. Even Zaruko won't claim her actions. She went too far this time, that's all. This was just the vengeful action of an angry little girl. It's exactly what her father threatened to do, you remember this? You think she would've shared such sacred information with Sinovians and the Impery that won't claim her as their own?"

"I guess not," Jahzara sighed.

"The true nature of this breach will die with her. Without knowing what she took, the Sinovians are probably breaking it up and making baubles out of it as we speak."

"I hope so."

"If it wasn't for all the sympathy my father gathered on the Sinovians behalf, I would rid you of your worries," he kissed her on the lips and finished with, "But they're not entirely without benefit to us. They make us an extra layer of safety, provide us with food. And if the Sinovians ever did attack us, we could be rid of them without any major complaints."

"They need to make the first move...I hate waiting."

"I know you do," Durako said, kissing her again.

Someone knocked at the door and called Lord Durako's name through the solid wood. He left Jahzara to see what was needed, while she strolled over to her new rug. She pulled the corners back and glared down at the workers through the hole in the floor.

"What's taking so long?"

"We're just trying to make it right," one of them called up to her.

"The Sinovians built this manor in a week. If they can do that, what's taking you so long to fix a few holes?"

"Looks like there's some things they can do better," the disgruntled, sweaty carpenter said up to her with an overly-fake smile.

Jahzara burned with rage, but wordlessly threw the covering down over them and tossed herself in bed again. Once she had Durako's child, once she was his sieva, people were going to stop talking to her like that.

"Lord Durako," Jahzara heard on the other side of the wall, "There are Sinovians heading into Imperyo."

"How many?"

"More than ten of them, including your son and Gamba."

"Zaruko is leading them up here?"

Durako threw himself through the door back into the room where Jahzara sat, her ear pressed against the wall. She flinched and jumped up to comfort him. He towered over Imperyo on the balcony with Jahzara clinging on his arm and watching the ascending offenders around his shoulder. Her nostrils flared and she pressed the side of her head into his arm.

"As soon as I'm with child," she grabbed his face with both her hands, "We can be rid of him."

192

*****

Vik felt as though he'd walked into an old memory. It didn't quite look right, but he remembered where everything was supposed to be. Fourteen levels, a hole at the top and the Gate at the bottom, right where he'd left it. There were decorations not at all like the ones outside. These were all Impery made crafts. The pottery was shaped differently and with carvings instead of paint, thickly woven mats were hung from the edges of rooves to give each home a sort of banner and fire burned in every corner. There were no cold steps taken on the way up to Lord Durako's manor. But behind every decorated rug, every clay pot and stick of fire was a grey stone wall on a dull grey house. There was even a crack that ran up the side of the mountain, just like in Haven on that final day.

At level ten, Zaruko veered to the left and strolled purposefully into a house. Only a couple of Sinovians had looked at him before quickly remembering not to do so. He charged through the door and headed directly to where he knew Josanna would be held. A lounging Impery sprang up from his chair beside the door and put his hand on Zaruko's chest to stop him. The son of Lord Durako summoned indignant outrage from the depths of his being, channeling them out through his face without a word. The Impery pulled his hand away, but stood his ground.

"I'm sorry, you're not allowed in here."

"Did you forget who I am?"

"No, no sir, of course not," he glanced around, "But Lord Durako doesn't want anyone visiting while Josanna is here. She speaks lies about him."

"Why would you be worried about that with me?" asked Zaruko coyly.

The Impery's face burned and he fumbled for words, but Zaruko continued with his front. He felt like he was freefalling underwater, not afraid of hitting bottom but unsure of how he'd ever get back to breathable air.

"There are Sinovians here wishing to speak with my father, I'm supposed to take her to him."

"Why?"

Zaruko tilted his head to the side and smiled, "Because he commanded it."

"Of course," the Impery bumbled out of the way, flustered and clumsy in his embarrassment.

He approached the door and waited for the Impery man to unlock it. Zaruko grabbed Josanna by the arm and jerked her out of the cell, masking his concern for her condition. Escorting her out the front door, he whispered to her and she remained quiet the rest of the way out of Imperyo, strolling along as casually as if they lived there. Josanna glanced over her shoulder and saw the small huddle of Sinovians on the sixth level.

Vik lead the Sinovians higher and higher. He knew none of their names, but they were all willing to follow him into the fiery lair to trick the dragon itself. All of them were in support of change, of turning over the Impery throne and spreading the Thesmekkian knowledge they hoarded from the Sinovian people. The same educational cubes Vik remembered using to learn reading, math, and the basic ways of the world, like what a tree might look like and how the sun worked, were bound to be in Imperyo as well.

Ember-filled spitting, crude name-calling, and crass shouting accompanied the Sinovians with increasing intensity the higher they climbed. People came out of their houses on level four and higher to throw whatever they could find at them. Gamba wasn't immune from the ridicule. Traitor and fireless were just a couple of the many insults hurled at him, but he did not retaliate. His glassy eyes stared off like they could see through the walls of the mountain he had once been a child in and away into the distant horizon. A place where no man dared go, so no other man would be.

Feeling his pulse quicken as he approached the ramp to the top level, Vik's eyes swiveled around, moving his head as little as possible. Zaruko wasn't there. Gamba was unreadable. The rest of the Sinovians were worn out from the climb, some of them with tears in their eyes, but all of them determined to make it to Durako's manor. Vik's calves throbbed, begging him to turn back and he was drenched in sweat, but he breached the topmost level despite the nagging discomfort. The fear that Zaruko was not going to make it in time started sending sparks through his nerves. He slowed down and approached the manor cautiously, but several of the Sinovians urged him onward until someone paraded out of the front door, stopping just a few steps out. Lord Durako didn't greet them. He was scanning their mundane faces for his arrogant son. When he couldn't find them, his eyes lit up like an explosion.

194

"You know the penalty for coming here unsupported."

Lord Durako saw Gamba and knew who he was, but he did not have the authority to do something like this. Only Zaruko could bring a group of Sinovians in to meet with his father. Someone pushed Vik to the side from behind him.

"I'm here," Zaruko grumbled loudly, "They came with me."

He was panting and covered in sweat, but doing his best to compose himself. His father sneered at him, mocking how he fell back with the group.

"You're supposed to lead them here," he said.

Vik glanced up and saw Jahzara watching him, gripping the railing with white-knuckles, her face contorted and eyes wicked with fury, reflecting the fire from the eternal flame behind the crowd. She might not have known which brother he was, but her intentions would've remained the same. An unexpected rage boiled up inside when he saw her again, but he pushed it down as best he could, trying not to think of her chasing him away in the forest. The more he tried not to think of that, the more the thought of everything else she'd done to him and his family. Tayna's face, trying to sacrifice baby Garek, murdering Mira…a burning chill went down his spine. Jahzara balked in disgust at the sight of so many Sinovians. She spit embers down at them before pushing away from the balcony railing and disappearing into the room.

*****

Outside Imperyo, a shrouded Impery woman marched into the evening light. She stomped passed the three armed guards without looking up, but they weren't going to stop her from going to the market like most Impery women liked to do. She was still shivering from the rush of the escape and her desire to brag about it to anyone who would listen. She had been told Chadrik was waiting for her out in the fellenwort grove and she planned to tell him all about it. Marek and Reeta idled in the market circle with Nattina and her imposing men. They saw Josanna passing by and all acknowledge each other.

"It worked," Reeta whispered, still disbelieving.

"So she tells the future?" Nattina asked.

"She would say it's not that simple. You'll have to ask her about it."

"Can you all do this?" asked Nattina.

"I don't know," Marek said with a hint of exasperation, "I guess we could."

Josanna slapped the hide tarps out of the way, flying through the gateway and cringing through the acrid, urine aroma wafting in the air. She broke into a full on sprint, passed the drass toes and spitfire fields until she trotted to a stop in front of the fellenwort trees, hardly out of breath.

"You actually showed," Chadrik chuckled, taking another puff of his sitter.

"You are the laziest..." she continued grumbling under her breath. "Come on already."

She kicked his legs and picked up one of the two packs on either side of him. Chadrik took his sitter out with two fingers and peered up at her, her face perfectly illuminated in the sun's setting light.

"We have to wait for Vik, this Sinovian. He's a Gadling and he—"

"We can't wait here," Josanna snapped, "Do you really think we're going to get that lucky twice? That they'll just be able to walk me right out and then leave? Besides, our guide might not be able to wait for us much longer."

Chadrik hesitated, "But this guy, he'll be totally blown if we leave without him."

"I feel bad about that, I really do," she said, throwing both straps of the pack over each shoulder, "But we can't afford to get caught. They could come running out that gate at any second."

Chadrik blew out a cloud of smoke and stared at the metal wall protecting Threshold for a couple of seconds before swearing under his breath and rolling himself onto his feet. He churned his sitter out on the tree bark and let it fall to the naked ground underfoot.

"Let's follow the wind then," he said.

*****

Back in town, down the middle of the main street and just off from the market circle sat the tavern where most Sinovians had gathered for the night. It was a long building, half buried with a short stairway leading down to the door obstructed from passing view by the ground. Savan and Tayna wandered nearby, neither wanting to explore the city alone.

"I just think you should take better care of your face," Savan suggested plainly.

"What does it matter?"

196

"Oh, well because, since your face is, well the scarring could get better and, I mean your face is still pretty, and, uh…"

"Thank you Savan," Tayna teased, feeling all too aware of the marred side of her face.

Savan rubbed his hands through his hair and blinked until he remembered to speak, "I came to get you because I thought you'd enjoy this place. And Nikiva was asking about you."

A door swung open across the dirt street and the sounds of rowdy people erupted from it.

"What's going on in there?" Tayna wondered aloud.

"That's where Nikiva wanted us to meet her."

"Let's go then," Tayna said with a half smile.

Tayna grabbed his hand and dragged him through the doorway where they lingered, gazing with their mouths half open. There was a short stairway from the door and the long room was half underground, its walls being made of hastily crafted clay bricks and stuck together with a substance that filled the room with a sweet aroma. The top half was wood, tethered together by twine and lined along the ceiling with enormous wicker fans that spun lethargically, powered by a half dozen patrons pedaling in place on tall stools along the walls of the room who in turn were powered by the free tart wine for their service. The fans spread the sweet aroma in with the heavy musk of sweat, but combined they were not at all unpleasant. Wooden cups slamming and tight ropes creaking, chairs scraping across the floor, and loud waves of laughter filled the lengthy room until the door opened again.

Nikiva and Sera tiptoed in, Sera the more obviously reluctant of the two. The room became quiet, the groaning twine of the fans filling in the absence where conversation used to be. Tayna scanned their faces. They were mostly Jawnies, but Shinies and Brutemen were easy to spy as well. A large Bruteman by the name of Larle stood up slowly, swaying like his legs weren't strong enough for the job, using all his focus to keep his cup upright in one hand. His features were made to intimidate, even with a permanent smile held in place. His eyes pierced through them, his enormous jaw opened, and he raised his cup over his head.

"New Ones!"

His bellow was followed by laughter and mimicking and the rest of the enormous occupants of his table smiled the same smile, each with daunting faces made in their own abrasive ways. Larle stumbled away from his chair, slamming into a Jawny who apologized profusely for being in the way.

"He's coming this way," Sera hissed.

Larle came up to the four and chuckled, wobbling slightly.

"You can't get drinks from the door," he slurred. "Come!"

They followed him about ten steps away to the Jawny man standing beside the barrels with a slender counter to his side. The man had colored clay painted on his face, lining under and over his eyes with an unintended smudge on the bridge of his nose. The room had filled with sound again, just like before. Tayna felt less noticed, but still pulled her hood over the side of her face.

"One big one!"

The barman ducked down and scrambled around behind the counter before emerging with a large cup the size of Larle's. He didn't fill it quite full and when he tried to place in on the counter, Larle held up his hand to the barman.

"I paid you with a perfect drass tooth, one of the big ones, didn't I?"

The barman immediately spun around and topped it off, being careful not to spill any as he placed in on the counter. Larle snatched it up, splashing a bit on the counter, and held it out to Savan.

"New Ones!" Larle growled in a friendly way.

Savan carefully took the cup and they watched Larle weave gracelessly back to his table. The four of them looked between each other.

"We share I guess," Nikiva suggested.

Sera sneered and leaned away, crossing her arms and glaring over the crowd. Nikiva ignored her and egged Savan on.

"Go on, take the first drink. Tell us what it tastes like."

"It smells really good, but off."

"Well, take a drink already," Nikiva said.

Savan nervously looked to Tayna, but she was just as curious as Nikiva. When he glanced to Sera, one side of her face was squinted in disgust, but she wasn't about to help him with anything. Savan put the warm liquid to his lips and sipped a burning swallow, his eyes watering and his body trying to reject it.

"That tastes awful," he sputtered, "Here, try it."

*****

At the top of Imperyo, inside the manor, there was no cause for celebration. The Sinovians gathered inside the largest room in Lord Durako's manor, the original one made of stone. Much to Vik's disorientation, it looked exactly like his own home. The kitchen's auto-arm hung limp over the counter, just like Havard after he relinquished his source of life, entrusting it to Vik. He still wasn't sure why the machine did this. It made his heart ache to know his silent, lifelong friend would never be anything more than a shiny rock.

There were several armed Impery warriors lining the walls around their leader who sat on a wide, leather throne not intended for comfort. Tallbug pincers acted as armrests and a drass skull in perfect condition was mounted over his head, the mouth opened wide to show off all its teeth and a set of swords on either side. The rest of the room was filled with baubles and décor meant to show off their prowess in battle, though Durako's fighting days were behind him.

"We want to discuss some terms fo—"

Vik was interrupted when an Impery guard spun his spear around and clubbed his chest with the blunt end. Lord Durako held up his hand and the man backed down.

"He's one of the new Sinovians, isn't that right?"

"Yes, father."

"So, don't speak in my presence unless asked to speak," Durako said, still staring at his son, "Present the terms."

Zaruko stepped forward and cleared his throat, putting his hands behind his back and standing at attention, "The Sinovians would like to negotiate for better protection."

"In exchange for what?" Durako seemed bored, "Don't tell me you all come up here in mass to intimidate us…"

The room filled with light chuckling and Durako seemed pleased with himself.

"In exchange for what was stolen," Zaruko said, motioning for Vik to reveal the orb.

Clutching the pearl tight, he raised his hand and peeled his fingers apart, showing them all the orb Lord Durako had sent his men to scour all of Imperyo for over the last three days. He almost jumped out of his oversized chair, but pulled himself back into it at the last second.

"Too many of their people are getting killed lately," Zaruko started to explain, but Durako interrupted him.

"You brought in so many the other day, this could be Agrona's way of keeping the balance."

"You don't really believe that," Zaruko breathed, disbelieving the level his father was stooping to.

"The Watcher's Eye saw them the night they arrived, it could all be as it should be," Durako paused and leaned back, glancing at the orb again, "But I will see what can be done. I don't want anyone to suffer needlessly."

Jahzara's tip-tapping footsteps carried her down to the bottom floor. She had her mouth as small as it could be and was glaring at Vik the entire time. Gliding gracefully to his side, she put her arm on Durako's shoulder and he briefly touched the top of her hand.

"Is that all?"

"That's it," Zaruko confessed.

Durako motioned for Vik to come forward, holding his hand out for the orb. He took two wavering steps forward, sucking in a deep breath. The orb reflected some of the light off the fire and he feared for one long, lingering moment that he was making the wrong decision. Standing in front of Lord Durako, he met his narrowed eyes before turning them to Jahzara. His audacity was raising the temperature of the room and stilling the air around them. He opened his hand to the Impery leader, then closed it around the pearl once again. Durako's eyes snapped up at him.

"I forgive you for trying to kill me," he said to Jahzara, before reaching down with his other hand and unsheathing the knife he'd been given by Nattina, "But you're trying to kill my nephew…"

Vik ripped the knife up and at Jahzara's neck, but his hand was stopped short. Durako caught him with an unbreakable grip a solid second before Jahzara even flinched. Vik struggle to be released and when he couldn't break free, he threw the orb down on the ground and it shattered into countless pieces across the stone floor. While Durako remained too shocked to respond, most of the Sinovians attempted to flee from the room and Zaruko tried in vain to stop the escalation of violence.

Dropping the knife out of his captive hand and catching it with his other, Vik swiped at Lord Durako's arm, cutting him deeply. One of the Impery guards swung the pointed end of the spear at him, but he dove out of the way, bolting for the door. A volunteer witness was skewered through his chest before the spear was ripped back out and his body fell dead to the floor. Several others met their end this way before they were able to flee the room.

"Zaruko!" Lord Durako shouted over all the yelling and screaming inside his house. His face was fire-red and he spit embers with every other word, "You are banished from this house. If I ever see you in Imperyo again, you or your men, I'll kill you myself."

The Impery wouldn't breathe fire on the Sinovians inside, but out of the manor they weren't so lucky. Many of them ran straight into the flames. In their blind panic, they stumbled off the end of the top level like meteors crashing down to the ground, remaining on fire even after they hit the bottom.

200

Vik ducked and pushed his way through the chaos, Gamba doing his best to guide him without getting burned himself. Someone swung around and punched Gamba in the jaw and he stumbled toward the edge. Vik managed to reach out and with Benne's help, pull him back before it was too late. Zaruko stormed out of the manor, furious and breathing fire to deter his own people away. They ran down the ramps in a great, descending spiral until they could see the cave entrance just ahead. Two of the Sinovians that were following them were pulled to the ground and beaten relentlessly until their attackers were satisfied, then set on fire. Zaruko jerked Vik forward by his arm, shoving another potential Impery attacker aside so hard he fell back and tumbled off the edge. They heard him hit the ground with a crack and his cries of pain afterward gave no one any comfort.

Sprinting through the cave, Vik doubled over and panted with his hands resting on his knees, but Zaruko shouted for him to follow them. By the tone he was using, Vik didn't hesitation for questions. Gamba was even acting wary of him. They kept running down the main street, passed the market circle and all the empty stalls. Jogging right by the many Jawny homes, they resembled a kaleidoscope of colors in the evening glow. His legs hurt so bad, he thought the muscles in his calves were going to break and the ones in his thighs might split apart. They flew through the tarps over the entry to Threshold so fast they flicked out of the way with a thwap and swung restless long after they'd gone by.

Zaruko stopped abruptly just before the fellenwort field and jerked Vik around by his collar, "You just got all those people killed," he shouted, close enough to his face for Vik to feel his hot breath, "I can't go into Imperyo anymore, you've crippled our plans and now, it looks like you're on your own."

Vik glanced passed him, but there was no one waiting for him under the trees.

"She deserves to die," Vik growled, shoving his hand off his shirt.

"And so do you!" Zaruko roared, heaving between each breath, "So go, *Gadling*, get out of here before I decide to bury your ashes."

*****

The two moons were both high in the night sky when Gamba found Tayna, still in the pub with Savan, Nikiva, and Sera. They had managed to find ways to keep getting drinks for hours. Savan was on one of the stools, his fan rotating a little faster than all the others. Sera sat in the corner, as far away from the others as she could get, pouting with all her might. Not a drop had passed her puffed out lips and not from a lack of anyone trying. Nikiva leaned in close to Savan's ear as he pedaled on the stool and whispered something to him that made his whole face turn bright red. He looked dazed and when she playfully bit his ear he flipped the stool out from under him. The barman shouted at him to be careful.

"I see...two men in your future," Tayna said, her palm pressed against the hand of a voluptuous Jawny woman with loosely woven braids tied up to the top and back of her head. The woman's eyes grew wide and a grin stretched across her face, easily showing all of her teeth.

"Two?!"

"Yes, two. The choice will be difficult. One is already in your life and the other...you will meet after...after..."

Tayna's smile faded and those who had formed a line behind the woman leaned in closer to listen. Her mind was muddled, but she couldn't stop seeing two mountains falling on top of each other. She'd seen it earlier with a man's palm on her own and had dismissed it as an effect of the strong drink.

"After?"

"After the great disaster," she finished in a hasty, excessively ominous tone.

The woman, thoroughly shaken by the news, thanked her absentmindedly and left the pub entirely. Tayna reached for her drink and let it pour down her throat, her head already floating and her eyes warm and pleasant to close. When she lowered the cup from her mouth, she met Gamba's eyes and grimaced. As though everyone else was on the same note, the room once again grew quiet, but this time no one was looking at him. He swung his hand around in a beckoning motion, but Tayna just mocked it with her own impression. Gamba cut to the front of her line and sat across from her. Those who had been eagerly awaiting their fortunes scattered around the pub. Tayna pursed her lips at the dispersed business and slouched back in her chair.

"Thanks."

"I brought you this," Gamba held out more ointment.

"This," Tayna held up her cup, "seems to be working better."

Gamba placed the ointment in front of her and hesitated before speaking, "You shouldn't drink so much."

Tayna scoffed at him.

"Why aren't you in the nursery?" Gamba asked calmly.

"Are you here for Jahzara or Zaruko?"

"If she finds you out here, it could be trouble for you."

"I'd like her to find me right now."

Several of the eavesdroppers nearby chuckled and Tayna smirked at their backing. She balled up her fist and pretended to punch something in the air between them.

"Be careful how you speak of her in public," Gamba warned her.

"I'll speak of her however I like. She may think she owns me, but she doesn't. This," she pointed to her marred face, "isn't a leash."

"Things didn't go exactly as planned," said Gamba quietly.

"Sure they did," said Tayna.

"People died. Sinovians."

"It didn't go perfectly, but did we not get the Impery out with what she needed?"

Gamba sighed and shook his head, looking around to ensure there was nothing to worry about. He noticed Sera glaring from a ways away, but the rest seemed safe enough. He nodded to Tayna and just as he was about to stand, Nikiva put her hand on his shoulder and leaned down close to his ear. She stared at it as she whispered the same thing to him that she had to Savan. While she waited for his reaction, she bounced her weigh around on one leg and grinned at Tayna. Gamba stood up and put his arm around her waist.

"Where are they going?" Savan asked, fumbling into the chair Gamba had just been sitting in.

"Hey, you have to pay for a future telling too."

"I don't think I want to pay to hear what you're going to tell me."

Savan leaned forward and put his chin on his forearms. A few seconds later he was snoring. Tayna thought that sounded like a great idea and hopped up, heading back to the nursery for the night with the ointment in her hands and a pocketful of jingly trinkets rewarding her for her careless showmanship.

# CHAPTER FOURTEEN

Chadrik and Josanna crept through the crackling flora, hunched and unspeaking. The mulch snapped under their footsteps, but the forest remained unconcerned. Unknown chirps and howls rose up and echoed all over, though they always started from the other side of the trees. The two from Threshold crept to a stop in the middle of a place where a single ray of sunshine as wide as a narrow pole had broken through the canopy. There were familiar markings etched into the trees, similar to the ones they'd been following on their way to that spot.

"Zaki," Josanna whispered as loudly as she could, "We're here. Where are you?"

"Were you followed?" another whisper called out from behind a winding root.

"No," she said, relieved to hear his voice, "We're safe."

They all revealed themselves, standing up straight but slowly. When they tried to get familiarized with each other, Zaki quickly stopped them. It wasn't safe to talk too much. Despite his youthful appearance, they weren't about to refute a fact like that. He motioned over his shoulder for them to follow and they started in on the trail only the young boy could see.

"You were followed?" Zaki groaned, after they'd been hiking for a short while.

"No, I said I did not think we were followed," Josanna over-annunciated.

"We thought we heard something following us, but it turned out to be nothing."

"It was probably just Uther," Zaki sighed.

Josanna and Chadrik exchanged glances, but when they asked about it, Zaki wouldn't explain. They picked up their packs and their feet, weaving their way south through the forest. The trees had not reached even a decent amount of tangling before they heard shouting around them.

"What was that?" Zaki hissed.

"Wow," Chadrik breathed, "I guess we were followed."

They bolted as fast as they could through the obstacle course, but the vaguely distant sound of the Impery search party was not getting any farther away. Zaki abruptly swung to the right, going over and under a complicated weaving of branches, nearly losing the both of them until he emerged in front of a blunt cave. It went deep enough to obscure anything inside of it.

"We'll stay in here until they're gone," Zaki ordered, dropping his small pack on the cave floor.

"We should keep moving," Josanna protested.

Zaki ignored her, taking a few steps deeper in and throwing himself down just as recklessly, moving with ease in the darkness. His big, black eyes like hollow points on his face when they could see him. Chadrik threw his own oversized pack against the cave wall beside the smaller one. She watched him flop down across from Zaki and offer him a sitter.

"Sure," Zaki said.

They both held their sitters and expectantly looked at Josanna. She set her jaw and narrowed her eyes at them. Chadrik reached into the pack and pulled out another sitter, wiggling it at her.

"You need one."

"We don't have time for this. We aren't even half a day's walk from the fields."

"Then you really need one."

She clenched her teeth and tried to think of something to say short of roasting them both, but nothing came to her mind. When she gave in and took the sitter, a smile spread over Zaki's face. Josanna sat beside him and spit fire on the cave floor between them. After quickly lighting their sitters before the fire ate itself up, Josanna was the only one who didn't immediately take in a puff.

"What do you need that for, you're too young to need it..."

Zaki didn't answer her, he just breathed in the smoke and let it soothe him from the inside.

"How old are you?" Chadrik asked between puffs. Zaki just shrugged. "I bet you aren't older than twelve...maybe thirteen."

"How do you know what a Rider looks like at twelve or thirteen?" Josanna asked.

"I don't, most kids look the same until they get older. But I guess you could be an old man and we wouldn't know it."

Zaki giggled and Chadrik grinned in response.

"Don't encourage him," Josanna grumbled, finally taking a puff of her sitter. After hastily inhaling one breath of smoke and exhaling, she flicked the sitter away.

"Hey!" Chadrik leaned forward, "don't waste 'em!"

"One of us has to be ready if they find us here."

"She's right," Zaki said.

"You know what else I'm right about? Not staying here."

"If you hadn't gotten yourself caught, our guide wouldn't need to hide us."

"Your delay was carceral?" asked Zaki, but they ignored him when he used nonsensical words.

"I didn't see you doing anything to help!" shouted Josanna.

"Please, no objurguns..." Zaki whimpered, rambling quietly under his breath, "No, don't get lakimoose, we don't need Uther yet, if he's even verid, veridical...another figment."

"I don't think you would've let me help if I'd tried," said Chadrik, resting his hand on top of Zaki's head until he stopped rambling.

"Can you blame me? I've seen the unwaking get more done, and with better reflexes."

"What's unwaking?" asked Zaki.

"A dead person," answered Josanna briefly, not breaking her glare with Chadrik.

For half a second Chadrik hesitated, but then looked away and puffed on his sitter, his eyes narrowed at the cave wall. Josanna hopped up, standing impatiently at the entrance to the cave and peering out into the tangled mess of green and brown. The leaves flicked every so often while the sounds of things scurrying nearby gave her chills. She held her arms but refused to slouch or leave the entryway. She could hear so much movement, but there was nothing she could see. The Impery hunting them could walk right up to the cave and take her by surprise. She called over her shoulder to Zaki.

"Why do you think they won't find us here?"

Zaki shrugged, "Everybody's dunkycow out here. Except Uther. And me."

Josanna blinked hard and slow, then exhaled, "There's the Uther thing again. And I wish you would stop that nonsense."

"What nonsense?"

"Using words that don't mean anything."

"They do!"

"We're in a serious way here, Zaki. This cave will only protect us if they don't see it. We're sap in an open bag," Josanna pointed outside, "They want to kill us."

"They won't find us," Zaki pleaded.

He grabbed the back of his head and pulled it down to his knees, tucking into as much of a ball as he could. Muttering the last few words he said over and over, Chadrik and Josanna exchanged a worried glance.

"Alright, they won't find us," she tried to console him. "I believe you."

"Hey, come on," Chadrik tried after he didn't respond to her apology, "You don't need to be afraid. If they find us, they won't do anything to you. Everybody loves kids."

Zaki stopped chanting and peeked at him from under his elbow.

"Except Josanna."

"Chadrik," she hissed, but was surprised to hear Zaki giggle and sniffle from the floor.

She exhaled and turned to face the woods again, trying her best to ignore how they were coming together at her expense. Something rustled in the low shrubs and a pair of eyes met hers so briefly, it left a series of imaginary guesses behind. She was left wondering if that had been a person or a creature, if she had even seen eyes at all, or if she was starting to hallucinate from the lack of easy air. Either way, she kept close to the wall of the entrance and let her eyes scan the forest thoroughly, darting them onto anything that dared to rustle or twitch.

\*\*\*\*\*

Vik stumbled across roots and branches, sifted himself through foliage and flinched away from every sound he could hear until his body demanded rest. He crawled on all fours under a root that had made an archway before dipping back into the earth. Rolling over onto his back, he stared up at the bark and traced the lines with his fingers before letting his arm flop to his side. There had been no sign of them anywhere. Not that he knew what to look for. There could be no footsteps to follow through the mulch and he couldn't call out to them for fear of drawing unwanted attention. He was one tiny speck trying to find pebbles on a mountain. He shut his eyes and shook his head. Something in the canopies above bellowed a long moan and shifted across the groaning branches. Vik's eyes shot open and he drew in a sharp breath. The more it moved overhead, the quicker his heart pumped and the more he pulled into himself. It stopped as suddenly as it started, but Vik refused to budge. He wanted to peer out from around the root to get a better look, but he didn't want to meet something eye to eye.

After several minutes, there was a swift pop and an unlucky creature shrieked from the ground up to the treetops before a loud crack silenced it for good. Vik bolted out of under the tree root, joining the rest of the fleeing herd of blueish creatures galloping away from the whipping crack. He aimlessly darted as low as he could while the screeching erupted all around the forest. They were calling out to each other and scattering the food around to share. Vik felt a vine crack near enough to flick his hair into his face. He dropped to the ground and crawled forward with his elbows, frantically searching for a place to hide.

Just ahead, an enormous tree cave sat empty and sheltered. In one fluid motion, Vik pushed up from his elbows and stumbled forward, preparing to dive into the cave. A barbed tendril slammed into the ground just before him and he tripped over it, scraping his leg along the spines meant to snare him. The tallbug felt him scampering around and sent another limb down to snatch him up when something bellowed deep and low from the not-so-empty tree cave. The vine wrapped around Vik's flailing arm and despite him pulling away with all his might, he felt his feet lifting off the ground. Instead of jerking upward, he lurched back down and forward as the tendril was clutched in the hands of a man at least twice the size of any Bruteman in Threshold. He wrapped the tendril around his own wrist and pulled hard. He took a step back when the branches above creaked and used his new positioning to rip the tallbug right out of the treetops. The oversized beast fell through the branches and landed on its back. Its many shorter legs thrashed wildly above it, clicking against themselves. The screeching was deafening from so close, but the giant man lunged forward with his axe and struck the monster in its embedded head. One hit was all it took to silence the beast.

The rest of the shrieking in the forest slowly faded away as nothing else caught their interest. Vik waited on the ground, his arms protecting his head, his body folded over his knees. The stranger dislodged his axe, most of him obscured from Vik by the tree roots around them. As he approached, Vik shakily rose to his feet, sighing loud and shakily, and examining his scuffed up leg. The man dropped his axe with a weighty thud and started walking toward Vik. His approach crunched the mulch, easily cracking most of the barky shredding under the girth of each step. Then he stopped and waited on the other side of a root.

"Hello?"

Vik could see part of the man's leg even though he was trying to hide. There was just too much of him to fit behind a skyward root. Vik approached the faux-tree carefully, taking care not to make a clumsy step.

"Thank you," Vik began slowly, "for helping me."

208

The leg disappeared behind the root, but he knew the giant was still there. His breathing was heavy and labored, rasping with each exhale.

"Are you from Imperyo?"

Vik rounded the tree root, coming face to face with the one who saved him. It was not a man at all. Not completely. He barely had any neck, his head resting on his torso with his back rising almost above it. His nose was smashed so closely to his face that it was only two bulging nostrils set just under the middle of his beady, green eyes. His jaw took up the remainder of his enormous head. He had no upper lip, but a protruding bottom one and a round, dented chin lightly covered in hair. He was bald except for the sparse layer of hair that covered his entire body. His tiny ears jutted straight out and one twitched while they stared at one another.

Vik's words caught in his throat and he stumbled backward before managing out a weak cry as the giant reached for him. It flinched when Vik made a sound and used the tip of its fingers to pat its mouth over and over until Vik slowly nodded at him. The beast man motioned for him to follow and approached the dead tallbug.

They stood near the body, Vik keeping one eye on it and the other on this deformed man, or intelligent creature. He still hadn't made up his mind, but his mind had switched off. The giant leaned forward, clutched a short leg, and ripped it off with minimal effort. Yellowish goo came gushing out of the fresh wound and the beast eagerly pointed Vik to it. When Vik just stared at him, the giant reached his own hand in, scooped up some of the dripping goop and slurped it out of his hand. He gave a pleased grunt afterward and then slapped the remainder of it into Vik's hands. It was almost too warm to hold, dripping off between his fingers. The main portion of it felt like a mass of jelly being held together by a thin membrane. At least it didn't smell like anything. Vik held his breath and planted his face against it, squeezing it into a point so he could take a bite out of the side. His teeth sunk in and the goop poured into his mouth, sloshing around between the bits still a little too solid to swallow quickly. Vik lurched forward, some of the liquid splashing out of his mouth. He fought back the oncoming nausea and gulped down the chunks with a pained, green face.

The giant had set down the pack he was wearing made of leather and bundled rolls of furs. The bag was the size of Vik. He could've easily fit into it were it empty, but it was completely full. He pulled out a glossy black container with twines wrapped around it to hold it closed and began unwinding it. There was another in the bag that Vik could see as he peered down into it. Once the creature finished with the twine he opened it and revealed a slight grime coating the interior. Vik recognized the container as being made from the smaller bugs he'd seen before. The giant drew a deep breath, spit into the interior of the shells and began rubbing with his elbow. He then reached into the tallbug and loaded both halves of each shell up with goop and abruptly slammed the two shells together, held them closed with his feet and started tying the twine around them as tightly as he could without bursting them apart. When he finished, he jammed a cork-like chunk of wood into a perfectly sized hole on one end, set the full one aside and pulled out the other one to repeat the process. The full one leaked a little, but not as badly as Vik's hand.

Hunger drove him to take another bite of the goop between his fingers. He wasn't sure when he'd get to eat again. He didn't want to risk angering the giant either. The yellow guts were less horrifying when he knew what to expect. A third bite and he was done. Whether it be from feeling queasy, his stomach shrinking, or the goop just being filling, he was unable to take another bite. Vik's face contorted with each mouthful and by the third the giant had noticed him. Startling Vik, he bellowed out a rumbling chuckle that caused his whole body to bounce starting at the shoulders. It was a deep and loud laugh, but it didn't carry far at all.

The strange beast loaded up his pack, slung it over his shoulder, and began walking away. Vik hesitated for a second, but only for a second.

"Wait," he called out, trotting to keep up.

The giant turned around and examined him, looked around, up at the canopies and then at the grimier side of the tree roots. He spun around before pointing north, a direction Vik had no concept of. Cardinal directions weren't something he found himself interested in learning about back at the Haven library, nor was it something he considered important. He did however, remember which way he'd come from before the tallbug attack this time.

"No, I can't go back."

The giant shook his finger in the direction of Imperyo, hunching forward and narrowing his face.

"No," he repeated.

The giant took a step forward and gave Vik a good shove. He landed hard on his backside and stared up at the brutish beast as he marched away. He felt like a child making a nuisance of himself and he hated it, but he could think of nothing else to do. This his best chance at surviving long enough to find the others. If he could somehow communicate with this beast, maybe they could work together.

Vik hopped up and gave the giant plenty of space, but still followed him all the same. Although he didn't turn around, the massive beast gave a deep sigh and plodded onward, regretting the price of his

210

kindness. They marched on for hours, not stopping to rest or eat or even drink. The only thing that drove Vik was his fear of being left behind. Wave after wave of fatigue begged him to give it up, but death's certainty promised to be there if he did. This creature made surprisingly little noise when he walked, but he rarely stepped into the mulch if he could help it. His pack was padded so that nothing clattered together and he moved so swift and nimble, Vik briefly lost sight of him multiple times.

They finally slowed to a stop in front of a massive tree, but it wasn't the giant's destination. Vik slumped to the ground a short way away, not wanting to crowd him again and risk being pushed away. He watched the beast man approach a root in front of it and trace a strange marking with his chubby fingers. Abruptly he spun around and began plodding along in a slightly altered direction. Vik's body protested and despite great effort, remained uncooperative.

"Wait," he weakly called out.

The giant was already gone, disappeared into the foliage without another sound. Vik slumped over even more and groaned out all the feebleness left in him, taking several motivating breaths and pushing himself off the ground. His legs felt like the goop he'd eaten earlier, his pants stuck firmly against his legs like his sweat was sap. Taking one step forward drained him of light and thoughts. He just watched his body move like a jerky machine about to break down. After just four more steps, his knee buckled and he collapsed to the ground. There was nothing left in him and he laid his head down to rest.

*****

Tayna lay on her back on the bed. She traced the grooves on her deformed face while watching the fan spin slowly over the full length of the ceiling. Each blade was as tall as a man and made of a single strip of bark fastened to the middle and powered by one of the burned girls lazily turning a crank in the corner of the room. If she listened, Tayna could hear the gears turning behind the wall. The girls were interested in her after her scrying, even if they didn't understand what she had done.

She'd nearly starved herself to death, but she'd seen everything highlighted in the glow until it started speeding along a path, slowing when it reached a time when she should pay attention. It was hard knowing she had to keep her mouth shut on things she wanted to scream about. She'd have to continue on like normal around the ones doomed to die, burdened to carry on, fated to suffer. Those thoughts had been at the forefront of her mind during the meeting, but the most haunting realizations came after she returned to the nursery. As she lay on her bed, she remembered seeing far into the future but nowhere did it show her sons. Deep down, she'd known it ever since the Gate first closed, but her heart weighed too heavy with the thought of never seeing them again. She'd moved passed being confused and angry with her dead father, Harlok. The great oracle. A charlatan, even with the sight. He couldn't have missed that day, but why would he do that to her on purpose? Why would he do that to himself?

"You'll get used to it," one of the younger girls said, watching her trace her burned face.

This girl sounded about Tayna's age, maybe younger, and had a small spot on her cheek that wasn't burned. Only one of her eyes opened and the other was completely sealed shut. She smiled with the corner of her mouth that was intact, the rest of her face remained motionless. "I hardly notice anymore."

"Good," Tayna whispered, sitting up so the girl could join her on the bed.

"I'm Beka," she said, setting herself carefully beside her.

"Tayna."

One of the other girls came over, holding a snoozing infant in one arm. This girl was larger than the others, her burgundy hair was braided to the middle of her back and half her face was burnt almost perfectly down the middle. She introduced herself as Gerta.

"Is that your child there?" Gerta asked, motioning toward Garek.

"No, of course not," Tayna answered. The two girls grew uncomfortable and she wondered if she should have said it in that way. "He is my cousin's son though. So he's family."

That thought unsettled her. She was appalled at the thought of Jahzara sacrificing her own child, but this one was still family and she'd done very little to prevent his fate. She had not even seen anything of him when she was scrying earlier. Maybe he was in no danger at all or that his death was necessary. Possibly he mattered so little to her desired future that she simply did not see his fate. Squeezing her eyes shut, she cast the thought from her mind. She was not going to let the fates of others become events without meaning. She was not going to turn into her father.

"I'm sorry," Beka said softly, touching Tayna's arm.

"I'm not going to allow it."

"What?" Both girls leaned back from Tayna.

"You don't want to upset Jahzara," said Gerta

"She is much more cruel than this," Beka pointed to her face.

"All the more reason to stop this. She's killing our babies…"

"Stop, please. That's enough, just stop," Beka whispered.

"Well, looks like we've got another troublemaker," said the oldest woman, Oksana. She didn't approach them and didn't lower her voice. She had learned to speak in a way that didn't disturb the infants. Her burn ran down from above her hairline, over her eye and just past her chin, like a mangled stripe. She didn't use her hair to hide the burns like Gerta or even part her hair to lessen the bald strip, but had her hair braided tightly in a spiral against the back of her head.

"Your burn is minimal," she began, "ointment is being delivered to you daily. And you don't even have to nurse your own child until the day she comes to take him away."

"That hardly qualifies me as fortunate."

"Give it time. For now it simply makes you ignorant. Don't think for one second that the four of us have sat on our hands here, some of us for the full three years this nursery has existed, and never tried to stop her from taking them."

"You'll forgive me for not quitting because the four of you weren't successful."

"There were ten of us," Gerta said.

"That's right, but now there's only us four," Oksana said.

"They just disappeared. We never even saw them leave the room," Beka said, leaning forward, giving Tayna's arm a light squeeze.

"Illa's asleep over there, but you can hear it from her when she wakes, I promise you it'll be the same story."

"All the same," Tayna began, "I won't quit on Garek because it seems hopeless now. Things are always changing."

"Then we won't be burned with you. Girls," Oksana ushered them away from Tayna, "you don't want to be pulled into her schemes."

Tayna approached where Garek was resting and he woke, whimpered, and then wriggled himself back into a deep sleep.

"You sure like your sleep."

Tayna smiled down at him and stayed by his side while the others scrambled about the room. She was going to stop Jahzara, even if it meant she was going to disappear. That didn't scare her half as much as becoming like one of the undead girls in that room. The idea of living out the rest of her life in a space even smaller than Haven, serving a monster healthy children every month, it sent chills down her spine.

*****

Agrona's lush forest pulsed mossy life through the brown veins running up and down and sideways along the dirt, pushing the mulch aside as it rippled along. The giant set his pack down against some roots near an under-tree cave. He used the back of his forearm to wipe the sweat from his brow and exhaled with a snort. In all his fifty long years out in the wilderness, he still yearned for the comforts of home. For his hovel with the centralized cooling unit and even the obnoxious neighbors that used to keep him up at night with their percussive music. He didn't regret the events that led him there though. In fact, the memory of that day stretched a smirk across his wide face.

Remembering his other cargo, the giant leaned down and pulled a pouch out of his pack. He walked just a few steps back and uncorked it, pouring just enough of the contents onto Vik's face. The frail tagalong sputtered to life, flailing just enough to shield his face. The giant handed the pouch to him and watched him greedily drink what was left. Vik set his head back, sweating and dazed. He looked up at the giant and thanked him for returning for him.

"My name's Vik," he said.

The giant just gave a solid nod and went back to his pack. Vik's shoulders slumped and he shakily stood, leaning against the root for balance until everything stopped spinning. The giant had pulled out one of the glossy black cases and was shaking it with his ear angled toward it, peering irritably into his bag and feeling for the leak underneath the dark shells. When it still sloshed inside, he gave a slight grunt and uncorked the end, pouring the yellowish goop into his mouth. He finished and held it out for Vik who ruefully took a swig himself. Twisting his face to the side, Vik tried one more time to communicate with the giant.

"Vik," he announced clearly, holding his hand against his chest.

The giant glanced at him and gave another nod, this time more slowly and with wider eyes. Vik repeated himself a couple more times. The giant could take no more.

"Vik, yes," he grumbled irritably.

"You can speak!"

The giant gently patted his own lips with his fingertips before scooping up his readied pack and slinging the strap over his shoulders. He started walking away and Vik hurried to follow him.

"Right, sorry, quiet. I'll stay quiet."

Vik was giddy with the idea that he could eventually speak with this giant being, but the beast was much less excited with his new traveling companion.

*****

A craggy cropping of rocks bulged out of the dirt, highlighting the top rim of the shelter just beneath the short ridge. The cave was cooling off significantly as the sun went down. Josanna hovered around the entrance as she had been doing most of the day.

"Alright guide, how do we know when the Impery are gone?"

"I don't know, I'm sure Uther will."

"Who is Uther?" Chadrik asked carefully, for the umpteenth time.

"It'll be soon, don't worry."

"Hey, Zaki," Chadrik said, leaning toward him, "you need to tell us who Uther is. Is he like you?"

"No," Zaki giggled to himself.

"Is he real?"

Zaki stopped tracing in the dirt and looked up at him. His big, black eyes grew wide and his mouth hung open. Josanna came in from the entryway, prepared to explode. They may have just wasted an entire day, possibly even allowed their enemies to surround them. She could feel her rage boiling.

"I'd thought about that before, but you think so too?"

"No, I was just curious," Chadrik tried to back out, but it was too late.

"I haven't seen him in so long, he doesn't like to be stared at or looked at. I can't remember his face very well anymore. Is he real...I've talked to this one before, I'm pretty sure. He feels less real than some of the others, but does that mean anything?"

"Zaki," Josanna snapped her fingers near his face, "cut it out. Are we waiting on someone real or not?"

"Quiet," Chadrik hissed, shuffling to his feet and pointing to the entrance of the cave.

Josanna and Zaki backed up as far as they could, but it wasn't a deep crevice. More noises and this time rustling, stomping, the occasional voice carried out just enough to be heard. Zaki wove around the two and crept toward the front of the cave, but Josanna snatched his arm. She quietly shook her head at him and tried to pull him back, but he shrugged her off.

"It's probably Uther," Zaki said. "It's safe to go now."

Zaki tiptoed to the entrance, looked back and forth, up, and then straight ahead. He slipped out into the dim forest light and disappeared around the corner. Josanna and Chadrik glanced at each other before deciding to creep closer to the opening. They couldn't hear anything. The forest was quieter, either in between times of the day or bracing itself, they weren't certain. Josanna slunk out first, squinting into the faint lighting at the foot of the cave. She could only see as far as a few steps away.

"Where is he?" Chadrik whispered.

"I don't see him," Josanna said, then called Zaki's name as loudly as she could without breaking a whisper.

She threw her arms up and grumbled about him taking off. She took a short breath and lit up the immediate area with a modest flame. She gasped aloud, choking on the hot air she sucked in. Pushing against Chadrik, she shoved them both back into the cave.

"What? What is it?"

"They've got him, they're right out there."

But it was too late. They'd seen her flames and followed them into the cave with Zaki in tow.

# CHAPTER FIFTEEN

The Impery easily gripped the boy's small arm tight enough to keep him in place with minimal effort. Asking him where the others were, it wasn't until the firelight blossomed from nearby that they saw his face. They realized their quarry had given themselves away, but also that the child they held hostage was no Shiny. When the Impery trackers saw Josanna and Chadrik, they pulled the boy to the front, using him as a shield. Three of the Impery had found them.

"Josanna, you're coming back with us," said the Impery with the burned splotch on his chin.

"I would rather die," she growled through her teeth.

"We'd prefer it that way, less trouble for us."

"Yeah, we could bring the Shiny back and blame him for it," said the shortest Impery.

"Shinies aren't burned enough. They're too arrogant," added the one holding Zaki.

"I'm not going back," Chadrik stated plainly. "So we can make trouble now, or you can let that kid go and be on your way."

"Or we could roast you right in that cave."

"You know what'll happen if you try," said Chadrik, steady as he could.

"Where is the dark-haired one, the pale Sinovian?"

"Tallbugs got him," said Josanna.

"So you want us to just walk away?" asked the scarred Impery sarcastically.

"That's right."

"If I had the chance to kill one, why would I leave a Shiny alive? Even if you are a fireless half breed, I would have to be a complete idiot. Is that what you think? You think I'm that stupid?"

Zaki whimpered when they pushed a knife against his chest. The Impery jerked the boy's shoulder to quiet him.

"No," Chadrik assured him, leaning forward, "We're out of Imperyo, out of Threshold even. Why are you chasing us?"

"She's a thief," one of the Impery snarled at Josanna.

"So? Why are you still trying to find us? No one survives long out here and what could we do even if we did? Nothing."

"Is that your explanation, for killing the three others with us?"

"We've been in this cave all day," grumbled Josanna, "It's the vines, they—"

"Vines don't crush people, or bash their heads in with rocks either. But a Shiny could."

"I didn't kill anyone," said Chadrik, raising both of his hands at chest level.

The Impery with the chin burn slowly descended into the cave and the shorter one followed him. The one with Zaki remained in place, keeping his leverage secure. The shorter Impery punched Chadrik hard in the jaw, hurting his own hand and limply shaking it out right after. Chadrik hit the dirt floor, blindly holding his arm out to shield him from another attack while the bells still rung in his ears.

"Josanna, we have a message from Lord Durako," the burned Impery began, "I am acknowledging your improper company and relinquish you of all the benefits you once held. Your property is forfeit and will be given to those loyal to the flame."

He ripped out a knife from a short sheath on his belt. Josanna spit embers in his face and it seared him under his eye. He flailed and hit her with his elbow, shouting at her and wiping the splattered chemicals away. The short Impery used the distraction to turn to Chadrik and suck in a short breath, standing over the Shiny half-breed. Chadrik ducked down, covering his head.

"Uther!" Zaki screamed joyously.

Both Impery turned to the cave entrance in response to the rumbling, gurgling growl. The one holding Zaki jumped away from the child, backing farther into the cave. In the entryway stood an enormous figure, silhouetted and nearly blocking out all moonlight from the outside. The sound it was making was low and ominous, its shoulders heaving up and down as it panted.

"What is that?" the scarred Impery uttered.

"It's a Brute," Zaki said, turning to the Impery, "A real one."

It turns out that even though they claimed not to believe in the Thesmekka and their ways, they still knew about the terrible Brutes. Uther roared and lunged forward, but the Impery man threw fire in his face. Illuminating the giant only frightened them more. The Impery man slapped against the cave wall and slipped passed Uther, disappearing into the forest. The other two trembled, but held out their tiny weapons. One of them blew fire at Uther, ignoring that Zaki was in the way. Uther snatched him, turned his back and roared as the fire scorched him.

218

A sudden burst of air lifted both Impery off their feet and slammed them against the cave wall. Uther stumbled forward from the force of the gust while Josanna remained on the ground, curled up, protecting her head, and pressed as close to the wall as she could make herself. The dazed Impery wobbled to their feet, feeling the wounds on their heads and staring blankly at the blood on their fingertips. It blasted them again and this time broke the nose of an Impery against the stone. Chadrik rose to his feet and lurched as if being pushed back, sending another wild burst of air at them, this time breaking their skulls against the rocks with sickening crunches. They fell limp to the cave floor, blood pooling around them. Josanna scrambled up and examined the scene around her.

"Chad, are you alright?"

"No, I'm gonna be sick, go over there," he winced.

"Who is this, Zaki? Uther? Is this who you were talking about?" Josanna asked.

"I knew you were real Uther, I'd almost forgotten, but I knew! I thought I was going fey…"

Uther set Zaki down outside, examining him for any wounds with only incoherent grunts rather than words. His hands were half the size of the young boy, each finger as big around as Zaki's leg.

"Vik," he growled.

"It can talk?" Josanna said, emerging from the cave.

"Of course he can. And he's not a Brute."

"You're the one who said he was," she grumbled.

"His name's Uther, he lives out here. He used to live with my people, but that didn't work out for a lot of us."

Vik came into view, dragging an enormous pack along the ground beside him. Each step was a struggle. He saw Zaki and dropped the strap, jogging over to them.

"Is the orb alright?" Vik asked Chadrik when he saw him.

"It's right here," he assured him. "Sorry we left you behind."

Josanna crossed her arms, "We did what we had to do."

"That's funny. I was thinking the same thing while I was in Durako's place, nearly getting a spear through my chest."

"They tried to kill you?" Chadrik asked, "I guess I shouldn't be surprised. You did have the orb."

"Yeah, they just…attacked, as soon as they saw it."

"How'd you get out?" asked Josanna, arms crossed.

Zaki interrupted them with his disturbing level of excitement over the way the two Impery warriors had been killed. He reenacted them being smashed into the cave wall with sound effects and exaggerated facial expressions, making raspberries with his tongue.

"Alright, that's enough of that," Chadrik said, holding Zaki's wildly flailing arms down. "Vik, look, we didn't want to leave you behind and I'm sorry we did. We're glad you caught up to us."

"Stop speaking for me," Josanna snapped.

"So you don't want him here?" Chadrik scoffed.

"I do, but you're not in charge so quit with the "we're this" and "we're that", you didn't know what my opinion was until I said it."

"Guys, if I say I don't care, will you stop…"

"You're not leading us. After all that talk, you couldn't even get out of Imperyo."

"You couldn't have got half as far," she gloated.

"That's not my fault," Chadrik asserted.

Uther grumbled and flopped his bulky body on the hard cave floor. He had enough excess skin that he sounded like a leather sack full of mud being tossed on the flat stone. He couldn't understand what they were saying, but their tone was wearing him out.

"I'm the leader," Zaki stated, idly searching through Uther's pack with both hands. He looked away from the bag and they were all staring at him like he was out of his mind. He raised his brow and gave a snarky reply, "I'm leading us, so technically, that makes me the leader…obviously."

"What's our next move, leader?" Josanna asked, crossing her arms.

"It's too dark to go out. We need to cover the entrance as much as we can and," he pointed to the two dead Impery, "we should put them outside."

"I don't think we should stay here," said Josanna.

"How many times have you stayed out in the forest?" Chadrik asked. "I think we should do what the guide says."

"He's a child," Josanna motioned at him, "No offense, Zaki. We're just risking a lot here."

Chadrik and Josanna continued to bicker as they unraveled the tarps on their bags and put them over the cave entrance using heavy rocks. Uther carried the bodies out one at a time, disappearing into the woods for several minutes before returning for the second one. Vik and Zaki divided up a pile of rations without speaking to each other for most of the time. Blood stained the wall beside the child and Vik found himself staring blankly at it while his hands worked unsupervised. He'd seen so much death since he left Haven. Seeing a jumper used to be a spectacle, something everyone gossiped about for months. An event

220

picked apart by nosy neighbors and loudmouthed family members, but that seemed so trivial to him now. Haku's death played out like a lightning storm of flickering images until he blinked them away and cleared his cloudy mind.

*****

The sunlight struggled to filter through the thickening clouds and a cool breeze blew in through the windows, making the fragile curtains wave and tap the walls. It was quiet enough that Marek and the others would've slept on regardless, but the sound of bugling horns filled the air. His eyes shot open before he understood why. They sat up and stared wide-eyed at each other for several seconds before Kalan finally spoke.

"What is that?"

"I don't think it's an animal," Marek said, scrambling up and stumbling outside on weak legs.

It was impossible to tell where the sound came from, but the fire caught his eye. Near the top of the black mountain, a stunted balcony jutted out over Threshold. Two Impery warriors stood on either side of Lord Durako with two enormous sticks of fire held in both hands. The Impery blew the horn again, its ethereal call gliding smoothly over the city.

Many of the people had emptied out of their homes and gathered beneath the balcony, surrounding a wooden platform directly below it. Marek wandered into the back of the crowd, finding himself tightly packed in quicker than he liked. Kalan, Ziven, and the others were spread out from each other, pulled apart by the flow of the crowd compacting together, squeezing it to get as close as they could. Lord Durako put his hands on the railing and leaned forward to look at his Sinovian supporters.

"I'm sure you're all wondering why I've called you here so early on such a dreary morning. There's been an attack on my manor, just last night. Several Sinovians were killed," the crowd erupted into mumbling questions among themselves, all checking if the person next to them knew who was responsible. "And I come before you today to tell you this will not be tolerated. We risk our lives to protect you when our own numbers are so difficult to replenish. Now some of these newcomers have decided they don't like the way of life we've established here, the way of life that we've had for almost fifty years. They don't yet understand how dangerous it truly is to live in Agrona. But you all understand, don't you?"

The crowd answered in waves of fervent agreement and Marek flinched. He glanced side to side, but everyone was staring straight up at the man between the lights near the top of the mountain. It occurred to him as his eyes flitted from face to face, he didn't recognize a single person. They jumped at the chance to agree aloud with him and many of them had their fists balled, throwing them over their own heads from time to time.

"We're all here just trying to protect our way of life. We don't want to drown out your culture and we don't want our fire to go out. I believed the troubles from our past to be behind us, but with this new wave of Sinovians comes new strife. A strife that I would ask you all to resolve without the need for our interference. If you are appreciative of our protection, of the wall we brought you into, the homes my father built for you, then stop these rebellious outbursts.

Despite the incident yesterday, one that took the lives of many Sinovians and injured some of your guardians, I don't stand here today to punish you all. I am offering greater protection, just as was requested before one rogue troublemaker attempted to take the life of my beloved Jahzara. All I ask in return is that every weapon in Threshold be turned in to the Impery. They will be coming around for the next few days to collect them. Fighting the drass is futile without our fire, therefore these tools of violence are unnecessary. All I ask is that we take this step to disarm those that would cause further tragedies and damage the fragile balance of survival we have managed to maintain in Agrona."

Many of the crowd members applauded him, but Marek couldn't escape no matter how forcefully he tried to writhe free. It was only after Lord Durako disappeared back into Imperyo that the gathering began to loosen enough for him to wriggle out of it. He jogged away from them and saw Zaruko standing against a building with Gamba and the rest of his supporters. Nattina was there as well, with more Brutemen surrounding her than usual. They watched the crowd dispersing and the Durako supporters watched them back.

"They're not really going to take all the weapons, are they?" Marek asked Zaruko.

"Every weapon they can find."

"Even yours?"

"Especially mine," Zaruko stated, his eyes locked on a particularly rough looking Jawny as he approached.

"Why don't you just stay in the mountain?" the man spat.

Zaruko lifted his chin and looked down at the man, but nothing peaceful came to his mind.

"Nothing to say?" said the man's Shiny companion. "You brought these New Ones without asking the rest of us. You've got your own agendas, everyone knows it."

A small group of people broke off from the dispersing mass and cornered Zaruko and his companions.

"Were you part of the attack?" one of them said, pushing Marek's shoulder so he'd spin around to face him.

"That's enough," Nattina stated calmly.

"We're not afraid of you, Brute."

"Walk away," said Benne, taking a step forward.

Nattina put her hand on his arm and shook her head, but the people had already started walking away.

"What are we supposed to do without weapons?" Marek hissed, glancing to ensure the harassers were far enough away by then.

"Bury as many as we can before they come around of course."

"We should hurry then," Marek said, prepared to do what needed to be done.

Zaruko smiled at him, "It's already been done. We thought this might happen and hid them last night."

"What, where?"

"Don't worry about it," said Benne.

"Your brother caused me a lot of trouble," Zaruko sighed heavily, "And it's not that I don't trust you, but I don't know you. His actions yesterday helped remind me of the dangers of acting on instincts alone."

"They want to murder my son," Marek growled, "I'm not on their side."

"I know that. We know that," Zaruko said, giving the rest of them meaningful glances, "But this isn't the place to talk."

Nattina uncrossed her arms and started walking away. Her men followed her, but Benne leaned close to Marek, put his gigantic hand on his shoulder, and said quietly that he would find him next time they're going to meet. Even the casual weight of Benne's hand was absurdly heavy. Marek couldn't help but lean under the burden of it. He nodded to quickly convey that the message was received and understood, hoping he'd remove his hand before his legs gave out in front of everyone. Zaruko started to leave but he called out to him.

"Wait, where's my brother? He never came back last night."

"He's gone, I sent him away from Threshold."

"What?" Marek shouted, "He was supposed to meet with the Shiny. Why would you do that?"

"Your brother attempted to kill Jahzara right in the middle of our meeting. He attacked Durako, smashed the fake, ruined the entire plan. People got killed because of what he did," Zaruko snapped back in his loudest hushed voice, a speck of ember hitting the ground between them. They both noticed it and he took a deep breath to calm himself before speaking again, "I'm sorry. I can't talk about this right now. I'll try to cool down before we meet with the others."

Marek tried to stop him again, but Gamba just held up his hand as they walked away. Several Jawnies and Shinies were watching them from a market stall nearby, dispersing when Marek noticed them. He turned in a wide circle before deciding to walk toward the nursery. It was between the platform beneath the balcony and the cave entrance to Imperyo, but most of the crowd was far away by then. He started thinking about what Zaruko said, how Vik had attacked Jahzara, attacked Durako, gotten people killed. He couldn't stop shaking his head in disbelief.

"How could he do that?" he muttered to himself, "Has he completely rolled off the edge?"

Beside the nursery, hovering around in a circle was a couple of Impery women and a New One he couldn't quite make out until he got closer. The women surrounding her darted off when they saw him coming up behind them.

"Just think about it," they said as they left.

"Hey," Marek said, jogging up to the New One he could finally see now that they were out of the way, "Are you alright? What did they want?"

Sera wouldn't look up from the ground, "Nothing, they were just talking to me."

"I thought they didn't like talking to us Sinovians…"

Sera's head snapped up and she barked at him with her petite voice and haughty attitude, "Some people can tell who's worth speaking to and who isn't."

"And they think you're one of those people?"

"Of course they do."

"They don't want anything from you?"

Sera accidentally glanced at the nursery, then her face burned red and she hissed at him, "I don't need a half-Gray bastard trying to clean the pebbles out of my shoe."

"My mistake then," Marek said, bouncing out of her way as she stormed off.

224

Inside the nursery, Tayna was cradling Garek in her arms and strolling around the room, talking to him in soft whispers. He watched her turn about the room, her burnt side facing him. The skin was mangled and gnarled like a shrunken picture of the forest merged with her face. When she saw Marek, she headed straight for him and delicately handed his son over.

"He's the quietest, sweetest one in here," Tayna said with a chuckle.

"He gets that from his, uh…" Marek trailed off.

"It's alright," Tayna assured him, "This is a safe place to think out loud. Who're they gonna talk to?" She snickered, motioning to the marked hermits idling around the cribs.

"Yeah, I guess, it's just…I miss her, but that's not the worst part…it should be, but I don't know," Marek's voice cracked, "She never got to see him. That was the only thing she ever wanted. That woman murdered her and I…I heard that Vik had the chance to kill her, but he wasn't able to. I can't stop wishing I had been there. I let him go instead of me. Honestly, I was afraid. I keep replaying it differently in my head, each time it goes my way. Each time I kill her in some violent way." Marek clenched his teeth, "I want to rip her heart out."

"Don't worry," Tayna said with an unwavering calm, "It's going to be alright."

She wrapped her arms around him, roughly rubbing his back, and squeezing him tight. He let his head fall on her shoulder and sighed, shuddering when he inhaled. Beka and the other burnt girls were trying to eavesdrop as casually as possible, but looked away then. They knew it was only a matter of time before that man lost his son and there was nothing he could do about it. To them, Tayna's offer of solace was too bittersweet to watch so shamelessly.

"But you can't carry this around. Our people are going to need us in the coming days and we need to be as the solid rock."

"Right," Marek breathed, nodding his head, "You're right. I wish Vojak were here. And Miksi."

"I don't," Tayna sighed, raising a brow, "They'd be doing nothing to help us. Thessa is looking out for us now. Marek, I want you to come to this place whenever things get too heavy. I'll listen and I promise, you and I, we'll get Garek through this."

Marek kept nodding and suddenly laughed, "My cousin…the next oracle."

She pushed her mouth to the side, "I'm trying to help and you're gonna tease me like that."

*****

In Durako's manor high above the residents of Imperyo, the lord of his people paced so furiously, the floor trembled beneath his feet. The servant girls and personal guards glanced above from the floors under Lord Durako with every booming thud, hoping the ceiling wouldn't cave in on their heads. He hurled a Jawny vase off his balcony and it smashed against the ninth level street. Jahzara attempted to calm him, but he just held his hand out to keep her at a distance.

"They can't do anything to us."

"They are still going to the Riders," he growled at her.

"With nothing to offer them. My source tells me they just banished the boy out into the forest for smashing the orb. Without it, they have no way to get inside the ruins. Even if they survive out there, they have only a group of our old enemies that may or may not even let them live."

"One of the men I sent after them just returned. A Rider is guiding them and they have one of those monsters protecting them. They could bring a Brute so terrible—"

"That what? We couldn't handle it?" Jahzara smiled, ignoring his caged stance.

"This cannot be willed away!" Jahzara flinched back and he continued his ranting, "The Sinovians are planning to overthrow us with my son at the helm. My son!"

"He's just a traitor," she hissed. "No Impery will support him."

"There are a few," he corrected her.

"Once we have an heir," Jahzara cooed, swaying toward him, "Our supporters will grow more willed. And so will we," she ran her hands through his hair and kissed his cheek. "These are difficult times, sunshine, but you're protecting our people. Keeping the eternal flame lit. If it were simple, it wouldn't be worth fighting for."

*****

The treetops groaned and a heavy gust of wind rustled the canopy, swishing the leaves above the forest floor. Furless babblers bickered among themselves, spurred into feisty brawls by the startling, cool air. Several shells of their disemboweled fodderbug lunches plopped down onto the shreds of bark around the small group's feet. Vik's eyes shot upward in time to see the small creatures leaping around from branch to branch.

"What is this?" Vik grumbled, pulling each step along through the thickening mud.

"I call it, the Black Marsh," Zaki announced, quite proud of himself. "See, the ground gets blacker as we go deeper in."

"Yeah, that's great," Vik continued groaning.

The trees had turned a darker shade of brown over the last hour and the upward shooting roots were farther in between. The humidity had turned to a steaming funk, the source of it coming from under their feet.

"I'm going to smell like this for days," said Chadrik, slogging along behind them.

Uther had no trouble traipsing through the ankle high muck, his colossal bare feet were made for it. Zaki sat atop his back and kept watch, his head darting around like every rustling leaf was a potential threat. He clung to Uther's twitchy ears with both hands but the giant didn't seem to mind.

"Over there," Zaki shouted, tugging on Uther's ears in the direction he wanted to go.

"No," the giant said, swatting at him, but veering off to the side.

Zaki stretched out his arm until he was close enough to snatch a crumpled leaf off the side of an aerial root. He looked like one of the babblers as he examined it, using quick motions and tilting his head from side to side for a better look.

"Finally, something different to eat," he said, biting into it.

To their surprise, the leaf squirmed for a second after he bit out a chunk of it. Zaki crunched and smacked his disguised treat on top of Uther's head. The giant could not have looked more irritated.

"Through this black marsh is the meadow, right?" Josanna called up to him.

"Quiet!" Zaki shouted at them.

Josanna clicked her teeth at him, but they could hear something ripping and slobbering somewhere nearby. A drass had caught one of the small, hairless creatures from the treetops. It had gotten stuck in the sap and drawn the drass too it like a magnet.

"They love when stuff gets caught in the sticky goop," Zaki explained in a loud whisper. "But they're not the worst thing around here."

After they'd warily trekked plenty far away, he suddenly jumped down from Uther's back. The giant flinched, reaching out to try and catch the boy but Zaki had already slapped into the muck. He jumped up, his side and face covered in bog water, then took off toward a matting of leaves.

"What are you doing?" she whispered loudly.

"I've gotta pee!"

Chadrik and Vik chuckled, but Josanna just shook her head, "I can't believe we are out here with this kid."

"Uther's got him covered," Vik motioned toward him.

Zaki came leaping and bounding back, stopping in front of the three. Uther kept his distance, waiting for Zaki to come back to him and lead the way.

"What is he?" Vik asked as quietly as he could.

"He can understand us, right?" asked Chadrik.

"Yes, he can understand us but he hates talking. He's bad at it. He's been alone for a long time, too. Like me."

"You said he's not a Brute," Josanna said, arms crossed and not bothering to lower her voice, "So what is he then? He can't be human..."

"Why not?" Zaki asked, looking at him with his head tilted.

"Because he's just not," she argued. "Look at him, where did he come from?"

Zaki started squirming and she asked him again, but he wouldn't look up from the ground.

"It doesn't matter," Vik said quickly, nodding discretely at Josanna. "We were just thinking about it."

"Oh, okay," Zaki said, hurrying over to Uther without saying anything else to them.

Uther helped him climb up on his back, giving the others a nasty scowl.

"What was that?"

"You were making him nervous," Vik said.

"I don't make him nervous," she snapped.

"How could you make anyone nervous?" Chadrik jabbed, "You're as sweet as a sunbloom blossom."

Vik snickered and Josanna hit him.

"I didn't say it!"

"Quiet," Uther grunted from in front of them.

They all jerked upright, glancing at one another with wide eyes. His voice was a deep rumble and it startled them with its easy power. Zaki was too distracted to react the same as the others. In fact, he hadn't heard Uther at all.

"Over there," Zaki whispered, leaning close to the giant's ear.

Uther looked where he was pointing and saw a single, cocooned carcass dangling from the branches by a fine, white thread. It was far above their heads, but what put it there might not be. Zaki stayed bent in half, resting his chest on the top of Uther's head, listening for any signs of trouble.

They plodded through the marsh all day, taking a couple of breaks just long enough to get the feeling back in their feet. The muck was cold and clammy, pulling at their every step and seeping so thoroughly through their flimsy shoes that Josanna wasn't all that surprised to learn she'd lost one at some point during the day.

"Here," Vik said, pulling off his own shoe and offering it to her, "It's going to be a little big, but you can just pull the straps tight and it should work."

Josanna raised her brows, "Thank you."

"Are we stopping here?" Chadrik called up to Zaki, but Uther turned around with one finger over his mouth. Zaki was snoring quietly on top of the giant's head. "Oh excuse me," Chadrik joked, "His majesty is napping, I'll keep it down."

"I get a ride next marsh we pass through," Vik announced.

Uther just snorted while he carefully plucked Zaki off his back and laid on him on the drier ground. Vik watched with his mouth agape as Josanna lit a pile of brush with a quick spit and they warmed themselves in front of the fire.

"What?" she snapped.

"I just can't get used to it," Vik said, "And what do you do, move things without touching them?"

"No, just push them I guess. I'm not very good at it," he admitted.

"Well, I can't do anything like that. I've just got myself to keep me safe out here," Vik looked at Uther, already asleep against a tree with Zaki under his arm. "Zaki's got a giant, you guys have your thing. How did we end up so different anyway?"

"What do you mean?" Chadrik asked.

"When the Thesmekka put us in Haven, I always assumed it was just us. We were the only ones left. But that's obviously not the case," he motioned to them, "So why'd they put us in separate mountains?"

"Isn't that obvious?" Josanna answered.

"You think things would be like they are even if we all started out together?"

"We're all too different. People would've had a hard time accepting that some could breathe fire and some could just paint on themselves. It would've been so much worse if we were stuck in a mountain together."

"That's why you Impery shouldn't be in charge," Chadrik said, pulling a sitter out of a canteen from his bag.

"Why, because I know people are different?"

"Because you can't see a future where the worth of a person isn't determined by whether or not they can breathe fire," Chadrik lit his sitter in the timid flames.

"Sure I can," she argued sarcastically, "When all the fire's been bred out and everyone's forced into the mountain by the drass..."

"Is that why you're out here, to keep the Impery in power?" Vik asked.

"No, she's out here for herself," Chadrik said, taking in a deep smoke.

"So what if I am? I don't care about the Sinovians or the Impery and all their politics. I know what I want, unlike you and Reeta and all the rest of them. I just want one man dead."

"There are easier ways to kill someone," said Vik.

"This'll make Threshold and Imperyo better places. Why do I have to care about politics to help everyone?"

"She's doing this for her daddy," Chadrik mocked.

"What's your point?" She growled at him.

"Okay guys, stop it," Vik said.

"That there's a reason he got killed and it probably had something to do with this plan."

"He never got that far, Durako got to him first," Josanna said.

"It's still ridiculous, he could never have pulled it off himself."

"You're just jealous."

"Why would I be jealous of him?" Chadrik snapped, surprising Vik.

"Maybe you're jealous of me?" said Josanna coyly. "I did get dad for more than just a couple of years..."

Chadrik pushed the fire away in one violent blast. Josanna and Vik slid a short way along the ground and rolled to a stop in time to see Chadrik stand up if a huff and start stomping away. He inhaled a deep breath of smoke from his sitter and blew it out in a quick burst.

"I'm going to take a walk."

"That's not a good idea," Josanna said, struggling to sit up straight.

Chadrik didn't respond to her, he just kept going passed the foliage and disappeared behind some tree-sized roots.

"Were you two ever…" Vik motioned between them with two fingers, pushing out his lips and raising his brows.

"He's my half-brother," said Josanna flatly. "We were raised together."

"Oh," Vik looked to the side and narrowed his eyes, dusting himself off, "But I thought only fire-breathers could live in Imperyo."

"We left Imperyo about, I don't know, ten years ago. When I was old enough to protect myself. My dad found Reeta again and they stayed together for a while."

"What happened?"

Josanna glared at him, "Why are we talking about this?"

"I'm sorry. I was just asking," Vik said quickly.

"Well I don't like talking about personal things with people I don't know. We're out here to get things done, so let's focus on that."

"Fine."

"Good."


As they carried on, slogging through the bog, they were unusually quiet. Zaki was, as usual, blissfully unaware, but the language barrier wasn't impeding Uther's ability to pick up on their mood. He was frequently turning his head to ensure they were all still there. It wasn't until Zaki started slapping the top of Uther's head that he noticed how bad of a situation they'd just wandered into.

"Go back. Back, back, back," Zaki whispered frantically.

Dangling from the high branches, several carcasses wrapped in thread gently swayed, as if they had been ruffled not long ago. More kept appearing the longer he counted. Uther marched backward, surprising the three following closely behind.

"What are you doing?" asked Vik.

"Yeah, don't step on us," said Chadrik.

Zaki shushed them so hard, he thought the hissing sound around the giant tree beside them was an echo of his own. A colossal scraping and skittering sound preluded to a danger none of them were too familiar with.

"It's a crawler," Zaki whispered, hunkered down over Uther's head.

Six, long scythes jabbed into the tough bark of the tree at even intervals with a constant rhythm until there would be a short break for the creature to drag its cumbersome, overweight body along. They heard another six taps and then the slow, sandpaper grind before they saw what a crawler was. Its head was armored with dark plates, though there was nothing to protect the light tan flesh underneath that except for the jittering pincers rippling incessantly. It's tiny, black eyes darted around. They didn't focus on them, but it definitely knew they were there. Behind the six scythe-like arms was the fatty, scaled torso that went on so far, they never saw the end of it. They didn't stick around that long.

Without verbal prodding, the group scattered, dispersing in every direction to get away from the beast. They dove behind trees and scurried under roots, all of them in different parts of the swamp. The hissing gargle the creature emitted was worse to them than any screeching tallbug. It was impossible to tell how close it was with that sound, without looking. Chadrik and Vik were close enough to see each other. Vik motioned wildly to him when he saw the beast winding around the tree to investigate the smell, stabbing into the trunk above the Shiny's head. Chadrik panicked, trying to push the creature with his blasts, but it did nothing but launch Vik back off his feet. He splattered in the bog water and made enough noise to catch the creature's eye. Without ever having seen Chadrik who dove out of the enormous torso's way, it jabbed and slithered its way toward Vik. In a poor choice of instinctual reaction, he clenched his teeth and braced himself for the impact.

A fire blazed out over his head. Bits of ember trickled onto his clothes, with that being enough to spur his body into motion. He scrambled up away from the chemicals and slapped his body against the tree he'd been hiding behind, watching Josanna spew hot vitriol at the gargantuan monster. It hissed, swiping at the air, trying to overcome its confusion.

Chadrik's footsteps splashed over from the other side of the tree and he grabbed on to Josanna's arms from behind. He glanced at Vik and told him to hold on to something. Josanna stopped breathing fire long enough to take a deeper breath and when she exhaled again, Chadrik let loose a force that pushed the chemicals farther, spread them out wider, and billowed the flames to four times their previous size. Vik hit his head on the tree bark. He threw his hand over the spot and braced himself harder into his shelter.

The crawler was fed up with the heat. It started flicking muck up at them with all six of its scythes as it backed away until it was completely out of sight, disappearing through the winding trees. Once Vik felt it was safe, he pried himself away from the straight-standing roots. Chadrik and Josanna were covered in chunky, smelly bog mud. They flicked their arms down at the ground, sneering and disgusted. Vik felt delirious in his relief and laughed openly at them. Josanna flung her arm at him, splattering his face with some of the grainy muck.

"My goggles," Zaki shouted from somewhere nearby. "I can't find them!"

The three wound around the trees and roots, seeing the two digging through the swampy water in search of Zaki's eyewear.

"We really need to get out of here," Josanna urged them.

"But we can't leave without them," Zaki pleaded.

"I think we're going to have to," said Vik.

Zaki's eyes watered and his face pulled into a pout, but he agreed with them. He laid his head down on top of Uther's head for the remainder of the sloshing trek through the crawler-infested bog.

# CHAPTER SIXTEEN

The second day came for the residents of Threshold to be harassed by Impery confiscators taking more than their weapons. They were shameless in their thievery, but no one would stop them. All it would take was one loose fire to set an entire neighborhood ablaze. Food, trinkets, clothes, and anything else that caught their eye they took back with them into the mountain. Those who supported Lord Durako offered their prized possessions willingly, eager to appease and repay their protectors. The Sinovians were promised one more day of the Impery thoroughly sweeping their homes before they'd let them be with what little they had left.

Zaruko's home had been viciously ransacked. He had to stand by as they searched every room, breaking pottery and tearing apart blankets in search of weapons he might be hiding. They took knives to his chairs, his bed, and busted out his windows. They seared his rugs and hanging décor, and dropped two untied leather satchels of sap on his bedroom floor. Sap splattered out of them and oozed over the edges onto the rugs and flooring. The only thing he could see that was still intact was the door they slammed on the way out. He picked up a shard of pottery off the floor and threw it against the wall as hard as he could.

Half an hour later, there was a knock at his door.

"Come in," he called out.

Gamba opened the door, recoiled at the damage inside and then said, "Mine looks about the same. Don't bother with anything, they'll just be back tomorrow."

"I'm sure they will be."

"What was that kid thinking…?" Gamba sighed, shaking his head.

"They would've found a way to do this sooner or later. My father's been getting more and more paranoid lately."

"You bringing in a new wave of Sinovians didn't help," Gamba added.

"You're right about that," Zaruko groaned, rubbing his eyes with his palms, "I thought it'd do more good than this."

"It still might."

"You think that girl might actually...see the future?"

"I don't know about that, but she knew how to get Josanna out of there and...though it disturbs me, she seemed to know there would be trouble. I just wish she'd have told us."

"The mountains are all laid out the same. And with a plan like that, it wouldn't take seeing the future to know there'd be trouble. Maybe she just has great intuition."

"That's something then, isn't it?" Gamba said with a shrug. "You should go see her. Keep her interested in what's going on. Make sure Reeta's wildfire doesn't spread to her."

"I don't know," Zaruko said, looking around his ruined home, "I'm not in the mood to go out today."

"You can't mope in here, it's harvest day. It'll raise your spirits enough to deal with tomorrow," Gamba encouraged.

"Why do you want me to go so much?"

"So I won't feel bad for going."

Zaruko breathed through his teeth, "It would be a slap in everyone's face if we celebrated after all this."

"That's right, it would be," said Gamba triumphantly.

*****

"Don't talk, don't touch anything, don't look at anyone. Understand?"

"Yes," Sera answered the Impery woman obediently.

"Stay close, but not so close I can smell you."

"Yes," Sera snapped with forced politeness.

The two women darted into the cave leading into Imperyo. It was a dark tunnel with a warm, red glow on the other end. Sera's heart was racing her, impatiently jumping up and down ahead of them but she had to keep pace with Jahzara's subordinate or she could be severely punished. No one was more willing to face that consequence than Sera. No one wanted to be in Imperyo more than she did.

"This way," the Impery barked.

Sera abruptly changed her direction and then snapped her eyes to the ground. She wasn't tempted to look around, she knew what the inside of a mountain looked like. That's why she was there.

Once they reached the top, they deftly passed through the doorway of Durako's mansion. The layout of the room was exactly like every other room in Haven. The familiarity didn't help ease Sera's yearning for the safety and shelter of home.

Lord Durako sat on a leather throne with Jahzara leaning against its side. She noticed her woman with Sera and that was all it took for them to have their place in line. There were two men brought in before they arrived being questioned about the previous day's attack against them and more importantly, against the Lord of Imperyo. Durako was in the middle of a trial and no one dared to disturb him.

"I will not ask again," he said, his white-knuckled grip tightening around the handle of a mangled cudgel resting its weight on the floor between them.

"We know nothing. Just kill us," one of the men growled though clenched teeth.

He was a Shiny and that alone was enough of a reason for some Impery to want him dead. Their arrogance infuriated Jahzara and by extension, Lord Durako. The defiant captive's companion was a Jawny man, trembling on his knees. His clay was smeared horribly and his body was so covered in sweat, he looked like a ruined, wet painting.

"Please, no. I know who was involved, please, I can tell you every name," the Jawny whimpered.

"Die with ten fingers, coward," the Shiny hissed at him.

Lord Durako rose from his throne, the enormous club in his hand. With two quick steps forward, he swung up from underneath the Shiny and broke his skull against the gnarled bludgeon before he could issue a blast of air in the confined space. On contact, the Shiny released a gust but it was only a fraction the strength they were capable of, pushing everyone with the force of a small child. A chunk of his skull came loose and flrew across the room, accompanied by bits of brain and blood, most of which landed just short of Sera's feet. When she jerked back, the Impery woman dug her elbow into her side and Sera tried her best to compose her terror. She couldn't get any father from the scene, her back pressed firmly against the cold, stone wall.

Durako let the blood-splattered cudgel hit the ground in front of the cowering Jawny. He snapped repeatedly at an attendant behind the throne until Jahzara turned to glare at them and they sprung into action, bringing him a cloth to wipe his hands and chin off with.

"Do you?"

"Y, yes, yes Lord Durako! I know every name, every single one," said the Jawny, looking and sounding like he were being electrocuted as he spoke.

"If you help us find all of these people, I will pardon your sentence. Do you accept?"

236

"Yes! I accept, I accept…" he pleaded.

Durako wearily tapped the table beside his throne, glancing up at the ceiling as the frightened Sinovian scrambled through the remains of the Shiny and put his smallest finger flat on the surface, bowed his head and squeezed his eyes shut. Jahzara pulled out her knife and eagerly handed it to Durako smiling knowingly at him, but he remained dutiful.

"Your punishment was death, but by your cooperation, repentance, and my mercy I let you live with this reminder of your crime."

Lord Durako brought the knife down on the Jawny's finger. He screamed and wailed in pain, but then gasped out his appreciation and gratitude repeatedly. Lord Durako ordered another more assertive attendant to take the man to another house and interrogate him fully.

After Lord Durako cleaned the knife and delicately returned it to the sheath on Jahzara's breast, they kissed and parted ways. Durako went with other important Impery men to discuss the Sinovian treason while Jahzara motioned for Sera and her guide to follow her up the spiral stairs, speckled with charred spots. Sera tripped twice on her way up, her legs sick from fear. Once they reached a room full of trophies and décor, Jahzara sat in a chair and shooed a couple of guards away with a flick of her wrist. They jumped up and evacuated the room, clattering loudly down the stairway. Once they were certain it was only the three of them in earshot, Jahzara tilted her head to the side and narrowed her eyes at the delicate little New One.

"So, you think you can keep a secret?"

*****

The neighborhood for the New Ones was filled with the curmudgeonly complaints of one of the oldest survivors in Threshold. His grandson was trying to drag him out of the hovel for a day of unconvincing festivities out in the blistering sun. He was determined to resist with all his might.

"I will not enjoy myself, I refuse."

"Now you're just trying to make things hard for me," said Savan.

"Now?" scoffed Shurik, "I've been doing my best all morning."

"Well I won't be stopped."

"Not until I'm dead, is that it?"

"Grandpa…" Savan groaned, "Stop being so dramatic."

"Stop being so damned helpful. I don't want it. I want to be left to die," Savan pulled his arm and successfully got the old man out the doorway without injury, "Curse you, boy!"

Savan nodded politely to the other Sinovians passing by, curious about the scene Shurik was causing. They chuckled when he gave them a reassuring gesture and continued on by without worry.

On the other side of the market circle, the building full of infants deflected the harsh heat, fanning itself on the inside. Tayna left the nursery, pulling the hood over her face to shield her unaccustomed eyes from the late morning sun. It wasn't fully midday, but it was getting close. That's why it was easy for her to see who was leaving the mountain under a hood of her own.

"Sera?"

She was too far away to hear her, but Tayna didn't like the looks of it. Nothing good could come of Sera being so close to the entrance of Imperyo. Tayna grabbed the corner of her hood and was about to jog after her when she nearly slammed right into Zaruko.

"Oh," was all she said.

"Sorry, I didn't expect you to turn around so fast."

"What are you doing here?" She asked, trying to find Sera but she'd lost her around the stalls in the market center.

"I was, I mean, I brought you this," he stuttered, holding out the ointment for her, one hand still behind his back. "And I uh, here's this for you," he said, regaining his confidence.

"What is this?"

"It's a, sweet twirly," he struggled to say those words without feeling too stupid.

Tayna laughed despite his efforts, "Thank you."

"The harvest festival is going on today, would you like me to show you around?"

Tayna repressed a grin, "How could I say no when you ask so properly?"

The market circle was packed with people. No one seemed to be working that day. Many of the people were having a good time, playing the various games strewn about and laughing with each other, but there were pockets of clashing conversations between the stalls. Some of them even erupted into shouting matches, only to be resolved when nearby friends pulled them apart.

Tayna noticed Shurik sitting up higher than a crowd of children. They were all eagerly listening, enthralled by the tale the old man was telling. Shurik was getting just as excited as his audience: leaning forward, waving his hands around, forgetting to blink.

238

"And then, while they were all watching, the Gadling walked right up to the edge, held out his arms and jumped from the very top level."

Tayna's mouth dropped open and Zaruko winced, both of them glancing around for whoever was supposed to be taking care of the old man. Tayna knew it should be Savan, but he was always busy and there was never a good way to find him. She knew Shurik probably snuck out when his grandson thought he was taking a nap.

"Did the Thesmekka come?"

"Did they catch him before he fell?"

"Of course not," Shurik scoffed, watching the disappointed and worried faces of the children grow more intense, "but he did sprout wings and flew right out of the Gate at the very top of our Haven. That's right, the very first Gadling just flew right out of there. He didn't wait for nobody to carry him away."

The children were satisfied with this ending. Shurik saw Tayna watching him tell his tale and winked at her with a smug smirk. She shook her head and leaned toward Zaruko.

"Please tell me elders around here aren't as ridiculous."

"I've never seen anyone as old as him. Except, maybe when my grandfather was alive," Zaruko confessed. "It's hard to remember just how old he looked when I was so young."

Zaruko strolled up to one of the games where they handed people a rock and they had to knock a drass toe off the pedestal. If they could accomplish the task they got to keep the strange fruit, only the rock they were given was entirely too small to accomplish such a feat.

"No," the game owner said, waving his hand back and forth, "You, go somewhere else."

"Why can't we play?" Tayna demanded.

"Not you, him."

Tayna sneered in disgust, but Zaruko just nodded to the man and strolled away with her, "It's not worth causing trouble."

They were turned away from a couple more games and even a food stand with glazed spitfires and jabulian sticks.

"I like the sweet twirlies anyway," she smiled. But when they got to the stand they were turned away again. "Why is everyone being so ridiculous?"

"It's not him," the stall keeper said, "I won't serve you. Jahzara's whores aren't welcome at my stand."

"You are mistaken," Zaruko said through his teeth, poorly feigning composure, "No one here belongs to Jahzara."

"I face like hers doesn't lie."

Tayna put her hand on his arm, but it was like stone, "They look like they've rotted anyway," she said to ease his temper.

The tension between the two men was causing the air to chill and Tayna didn't want to be the cause of a fight in the middle of the festival. Much to their surprise, she got her wish. Another scuffle erupted behind them between a Bruteman and three Jawnies. The outnumbered man sent one of them soaring over a stand, spilling its contents everywhere while two others half his size hung from his arm and back with little effect. The fray spread out from there like an outdoor pub brawl. The stand owner who had just been so rude ran out from behind his counter and stood between a scuffle and his stall, protecting it from their fight by shouting and pointing away. Tayna turned around and plucked a sweet twirly off the stand and smiled up at Zaruko.

"You can't do that," he said unnecessarily quiet.

"I know, I feel terrible about it already," she said, biting off the end of the twirly before offering some to him.

He blinked several times, looked at the distracted stall keeper and snatched one of his own. They both scurried off through the bustling street until they were far enough from the fray to enjoy their deserved treats.

The two settled in a tight alleyway, tiptoeing over pots and scraps of discarded materials. They leaned against the walls opposite each other and smiled, biting into their prizes. It was a different kind of rush than what he was used to. Zaruko had been defiant most of his life, but that felt different from what they were doing. The rewards were so much more obvious.

"You don't steal much, do ya?"

"Not at all. My grandpa taught me to never sacrifice my dignity like this," he said, unable to keep up his serious façade.

They both laughed and she shook her head, telling him off lightly for almost making her feel bad.

"He was a great man, but he didn't pay enough attention to his family."

"How so?"

"He and I traveled together a lot, we were usually gone with a large group of Impery to protect us. It left our home vulnerable most of the time. I don't know, I guess my father never forgave us for not being there when the drass made it all the way into the mountain."

"I'm sorry," said Tayna.

They were interrupted by a couple of people shouting and weaving through the alleyways close by.

240

"We have to see if she's over there," Tayna heard someone familiar shouting out.

Ziven and Kalan came darting through the alley they were hiding out in and ran straight passed them without a long look, heading toward the market circle center.

"You're so serious about her lately," Kalan said, panting as they jogged.

"She wants to be my sieva," Ziven said.

Kalan was speechless, but only for a few seconds. He started demanding to know if it was a joke and then insisted to know how it was even possible, suggesting her brain might be damaged from the heat.

Zaruko and Tayna eavesdropped on the two and she glanced up at him to share in the sweet humor of the moment. It was only after a few seconds of smiling at one another that Tayna realized the implications and turned quickly away. She took a large bite out of her sweet twirly and waited out the unintended moment. Zaruko cleared his throat uncomfortably, searching around for something to distract them.

"I don't believe it," Zaruko said after a long pause.

Gamba strolled toward the festival center with a young woman on his arm, a New One from the look of her. She was beautiful, but a bit unkempt. Both of them were smiling like they had no idea what was going on around them.

"That's Nikiva," Tayna said with her mouth half full.

The two were on the same footsteps and Nikiva let her head fall on his arm playfully. Zaruko couldn't believe his eyes, watching Gamba smiling and flirting with a woman.

"I bet I know when that happened," said Tayna with a coy grin. "They met while we were drinking that night."

"I didn't know you liked to drink," Zaruko said.

"Neither did I, until a few days ago."

"Would you like to meet with me for drinks sometime then?"

"Are you just trying to keep the fortune-teller close to you?"

"Not just, I'm also hoping we can take things down a more intimate route," said Zaruko casually, pointing toward Gamba and Nikiva.

"You can't just say things like that!" gasped Tayna, trapped between embarrassment and outrage.

"What?"

"I can't believe you said that…"

"You're overreacting," Zaruko chuckled.

"I don't know how your people do things, but we don't announce our intentions before anything's been established."

241

Tayna's face felt as hot as the day it was burned. She took a step away from him and leaned against the cool, clay wall of a house nearby. Zaruko watched her steam, facing away from him but not storming away.

"That was almost as exciting as stealing," he said, taking a bite of sweet twirly right after.

She caved a little, laughing but still facing away from him, "You're not the overly-proper man I th—"

He waited for her to finish, but she was frozen against the building. Tilting his head up, he strolled around her to see what she was getting at, but dropped his chin down when he saw her face.

"What's the matter?"

"No one's in the fields," she droned, "They're coming. It's too late to drive them out."

Zaruko put his hands on her arms and tried to gently shake her out of it, but a terrible sight blurred into focus over her shoulder. A drass was dragging a dead body out of a house farther down the street. It began feasting on it and two others climbed over the rooftops, licking at the walls and chewing on the overhang above the doorway. A man screamed, not a high enough pitch to frighten them away by any means. It was in fact, the perfect tone to intrigue them. Five more shuffled over the houses and more started pouring into the street.

"No," Zaruko whispered, his head whipping back and forth between the drass and the festival behind him.

Tayna snapped out of it and followed his gaze, gasping hard when she saw the horde of reptiles spilling into homes and streets. Despite being surrounded in screams, the sounds of the market circle appealed to their curiosity and the beasts began shuffling their way, feverishly sniffing the air and clawing at house walls as they went. Zaruko grabbed her hand and they bolted for the festival, yelling at anyone they saw along the way. The drass quickly caught up and by the time they were close enough to shout a warning, it was too late. Tayna screamed when a drass warbled not three steps behind her. All eyes in the market circle whipped toward the notorious sound.

The festival erupted into screaming. People threw down their baubles and trinkets, sweets and treats, littering the ground with everything they valued less than their own lives. The crowd fled in chaos and the drass scattered in predatory pursuit, steered by their playful whims. The warbling drass dove forward, chomping at Tayna but Zaruko flung her passed him, breathing fire on the beast as she stumbled to the ground. Scrambling to her feet just in time to see another drass galloping toward Zaruko from behind, she screamed at him but the beast plowed into his chest, knocking the wind right out of him. It hadn't seen him,

242

but was blindly running toward a particular scent that had caught its attention. Snapping at the air, the drass missed Zaruko but didn't stop to search for him, instead it shot straight for a stand of bloodstones lightly coated in sweet sap.

The horror played out in front of Tayna like a vision of the past, only they weren't in the woods. They were supposed to be safe. Their protectors were supposed to keep this from happening. Men, women, and children were being clawed up, eaten or running in circles, unable to get away. Drass came out of everywhere.

Fire burst out from the middle of the circle and for a moment Tayna's heart leapt, but it was only Gamba and a couple of others loyal to Zaruko. The cave entrance to Imperyo was covered in fire-breathers, waiting to defend their home when the threat grew too close. They stood with two-handed, white-knuckled grips on their weapons, looking as frightened as the Sinovians who were running for their lives. A Jawny woman ran up to the entrance, clutching an infant to her chest. She screamed over the cacophonous carnage behind them, trembling and pleading for safety. One of the armed guards roughly grabbed the woman by the shoulder and pulled her two steps behind them, into the cave. He jabbed at the air in front of her face with two fingers, shouting for her to stay on the ground and not to even think about going into Imperyo. She was sobbing, but fervently nodded while stroking the top of her baby's head, thanking him despite his harsh words. A few other Sinovians tried to get the same treatment, but they were turned away at spear point.

"Help us!" Tayna shouted, her tiny voice barely carrying an arm's length away.

She was far away from the ramp leading to Imperyo and the bombardment of screams, shrieks, and playful chortling calls drowned everything out but themselves. Zaruko suddenly grabbed her arm and dragged her with him, weaving around drass and pushing people in the same direction with one arm. He shouted, spewed flames, and never let go of her arm as they broke free of the frantic slaughter in the center of the city. One of the young man fleeing after them screamed in such a way that Tayna's whole body lurched. She covered her face, balling up as much as she could while still standing upright. Zaruko turned, still not letting her go and spit flames over the top of the victim, still writhing against his fate. The drass ripped its straight talon from the young man's leg and hissed as it back away, blindly swinging at the hot air. Zaruko grabbed the shoulder of a Bruteman that had followed them and ordered him to pick the man up, which he did without hesitation and as effortlessly as if he were a child in his arms.

They ran to the steps just below the cave entrance and turned around, checking to see how many had followed them. Zaruko turned to Tayna and grabbed both of her arms to steady himself. His breathing was erratic and he was shaking all over.

"You'll be safe right here, don't move."

Zaruko glared at the Impery guards, hesitating in the entryway. They were looking at him now, not with disdain but with a desire for instruction, though they knew they shouldn't. He ran back toward the market circle and Tayna called out after him, but he didn't stop. Several more fires spewed out from the middle of the chaos and he wasn't about to let his warriors fight the drass without him. After he had disappeared, the small crowd gathering at the steps grew uneasy.

"It'll be alright," someone called out from behind Tayna.

"Reeta? I didn't see you there."

"Tayna, I'm glad you're alright. Don't worry, we'll be safe right here."

A couple of drass broke away from the fighting, one of them ran straight for the stranded group with fire on his tail. It made a terrible sound, a gurgling, hissing, howling whoop that came growling out if its blunt mouth. The other drass followed it, confused by the sounds it was making and issuing their own concerned warbles. Both beasts had galloped right up to the group and Tayna covered her head, but Reeta blasted them back with a couple of forceful waves. The drass rolled head over tail, back far enough to scramble their senses. The fire on its tail extinguished, it warbled weakly once before bolting off toward the pillar-filled section of the wall with its companion following close behind. Many other drass could be seen evacuating from the middle of the city. Reeta returned back to the group and as Tayna went to thank her, she noticed that several Impery guards had charged forward, but would have been too slow to save everyone as Reeta had. Glancing at the nursery, Tayna saw a number of Impery guarding the building without any drass incidents having reached that far over. What she did see was Marek jogging toward her, a ghostly look on his face.

"Tayna," he gasped, not out of breath but unable to find the air to speak, "I have to speak with you."

"You are," she said, leaning forward and taking his arms.

"It's not safe," he whispered.

Tayna glanced over her shoulder. Everyone was crying, whimpering, embracing each other or staring with terror into the still dispersing mass of drass and blood.

"Tell me," she hissed.

244

"Jahzara, I saw her just before all this. She came out of where I was supposed to meet with the others. Harash is dead," he leaned in, speaking directly into her ear, "I think Jahzara led the drass here…and killed the Jawny leader."

"Tayna," Jahzara called from just a few steps away. They both jumped, nearly knocking their heads together. "I'm so relieved. I came out to check on my children, but you weren't there."

"I'm fine," Tayna breathed.

"I'm so glad," she sneered, speaking each word with her nose wrinkled, staring directly at Marek.

His blood chilled and he immediately reached for the knife he'd been given, but it wasn't there. Confiscated earlier that morning by a couple of thorough Impery. They'd been disappointed by the lack of anything from the New Ones and left quicker than they did with most of the other neighborhoods. Jahzara slapped him across his face hard enough that he tasted blood in his mouth. Tayna threw herself between them, hugging Marek around his middle, squeezing him tightly every time he moved in the wrong direction. She was muttering for him to calm down. Jahzara wanted him to attack her, to give her a reason to burn him in front of everyone.

"Don't you think that's enough for one day," Reeta hissed from behind her, standing flush against the wary crowd.

Narrowing her eyes at them, Jahzara stormed up the steps and disappeared back into Imperyo.

\*\*\*\*\*

Tayna and Marek returned to their people's neighborhood, surprised that it had been left mainly untouched by the horde. Unlike the rest of Threshold, which was thoroughly roughed up and disheveled by the sudden invasion. One of the drass had been killed in the scuffle and people from all around moved in like vultures to take what they wanted from its corpse.

Nikiva teased Sera about her repelling scream, but she confessed to not having been there during the attack. Both sisters were grateful for that small consolation. Ziven was unusually somber, sitting alone in the corner of their clay home, refusing the company of even his potential sieva. Kalan was nowhere to be found.

"Everyone," Marek started off quieter than he'd intended. He cleared his throat and tried again, "Everyone, listen."

The few New Ones that were left huddled in together, slowly drawing closer around Marek and Tayna. Ziven stayed inside his home, but Marek was close enough to their window that he could hear them from inside.

"We don't have the luxury of holding onto our old grudges anymore. We're squatting in hovels, dispersed and confused. Today just made that even clearer. We had nowhere safe to go, I couldn't find anyone that I knew, but I saw many of you. There are too few of us left for feuds that don't apply to this life. We're not Grays and Uppers anymore. We've all been through the same horrible things that I believe far outweigh the hardships we had in Haven. We're all living in the same way now, on the same level.

I'm going to take a team with me and for the next few days, we're going to gather enough food to feed ourselves while we build up these houses. There's also the large stew basin in the Brutemen food house, but only take as little as you need. We're going to use tethering, no sap. Don't worry if you don't know what that is, we'll teach you. The Brutemen may have their strength, the Impery their fire, but we are going to have security. We built a stairway out of Haven. I don't know what started the division among ourselves, if it was over sunlight, I think we can safely say that conflict is over now." A light chuckle hummed out from the gathering. "We're going to make our situation better, starting today."

Tayna put her hand on his shoulder and smiled encouragingly.

"Is Garek being taken care of?"

"Of course," she assured him.

"Then could you stay out here with us? Help me manage this..." he said quietly.

"No more Grays, am I still their leader?"

"We'll split the responsibilities," Marek teased, his hands shaking as the adrenaline left him.

Tayna watched the New Ones sort themselves out, guided by Marek. They went down the line of homes, improving them with what they'd seen on Jawny, Brutemen, and Shiny houses. Dividing up like they did outside of Haven that first innocent month, the various groups got to work right away. Observing their hustle and bustle, Tayna thought to herself how strange it was that when these same people were perfectly safe, they were idle, unmotivated, and depressed. Only when there were no all-encompassing walls, no orange pills, no med-fac, when they were in real danger of dying, did they display signs of life.

Despite everything that was happening around Tayna and all the plans being set in motion, she couldn't pull her thoughts away from what had happened in the alley with Zaruko. She smiled to herself and blushed when there was no reason to. She found herself looking up from time to time when she heard men talking in the hope that he would be there.

*****

Three days of traipsing through the patchy areas of black sludge and the small group of exiles emerged from the dark, dank forest at last. A great, sprawling meadow lay spread out before them, uninfected by the smothering weave of trees and roots. Wind danced freely across the field in flurried bursts, visible only in its path through the tall grass. A stout mountain range outlined the field, fading into blue the farther away they were. There were no drass or tallbugs as far as the eye could see and the eye could see pretty far out there. The two beasts were afraid to come out of the forest, exposure being their biggest weakness.

Zaki grimaced loudly, flinching in the sunlight.

"What's wrong?" asked Josanna.

"I lost my goggles," he groaned, "It's so bright out here."

"You'll get used to it," Chadrik assured him, distracted by the beauty before them.

Grazing in herds, a new sort of animal noticed their presence. These dusty-colored beasts stood on four legs, their backs leveling out at about shoulder high, with necks that allowed them eat grass without having to bend their spindly legs. Flat footed with thick waves of outward spreading fur around their ankles helped them keep from sinking into the overly soft dirt. The biggest ones raised their heads up above the billowing green waves, revealing their two sets of horns, one set jutting out above their eyes, curling upward the longer they grew and the other set bending out from the sides of their heads. Only the males had horns and thick manes around their backs and chest.

"Don't worry about the grazers," Zaki said, squinting away from the sun. "They don't move very fast and they don't get too close."

"What is this place?" Vik asked, still enamored with the view. The only times he got to look out as far as he could see had been at the top of a mountain.

"I like to call it the marshmeadow," Zaki bragged, covering his eyes.

"How about the mellowmarsh?" suggested Vik.

"That's dumb."

"...You're dumb."

"Why don't we make camp here until tomorrow?" Josanna said, shading her eyes from the sun barely brushing the rounded peaks of the mountain range.

"Is it safe here?" Vik asked Zaki, "Out in the open like this..."

"I haven't spent much time out here, but the only thing I think we have to worry about are whistlers. We just need to go farther from the woods and find a spot that isn't so soggy."

"Besides," Chadrik started happily, "We've got a guide *and* a Gadling. Luck to spare."

Zaki did his best to peer around at all of them before scrunching his face at Vik, "Gadling?"

"Uh, yeah. That's right," Vik mumbled, suddenly preoccupied with his hands.

"He's the Gadling?" Zaki shouted, on the brink of laughter. "An abefalarion..."

"It's really not that—"

Zaki interrupted him with a gasp, "Remember when you slapped that mace flower?"

"I barely touched it."

"That was so funny," Zaki laughed, quickly mimicking Vik's pain with his own face, sticking out his tongue and curling up into a ball.

"Thank you," Vik snapped, "I can't relive that moment enough."

Chadrik and Josanna snorted and shook their heads, but Zaki was unaware of the effect his story had on anyone else.

They trekked through the soft grass, occasionally falling into deep puddles that swallowed them up to their shins. For half an hour they journeyed in the direction of the mountain Zaki was leading them toward before he pointed out a good spot.

"It looks like it might rain," Chadrik sneered. "See those clouds behind us?"

"Help me set up the tents then," Josanna said.

Josanna was set on staying the night out in the open marshmeadow. She and Chadrik pitched the tents with Vik's help. Zaki refused to do anything strenuous besides guiding them, but they were satisfied with that deal. Chadrik wrapped the twine around the stake and Vik hammered it into the soft ground with a rock as far as it would go and then some. The arm-length stake was fully embedded in the soil when a rumble echoed overhead and the wet dirt vibrated beneath them. They glanced around at each other and waited for what might happen next. The grazers mimicked them, all of their heads popped up and they stopped chewing mid-bite, grass hanging out of their mouths as their big, brown eyes scanned the landscape. Zaki watched them, squinting his eyes

248

and shielding them with his hand like a visor, not looking around but fixed on the herd. Once enough of them relaxed, so did he.

"What was that?"

"Earthquake?" Zaki shrugged.

They accepted that answer uneasily, but Uther distracted them with distributing rations from his bag and plopped his back against a rock jutting up from the ground. He dug around in his pack for a large, crudely bound book and a black rock wrapped in cloth. Before the sun set too low in the sky, he started a rough sketching of the scene in front of him. Josanna excused herself after they ate, disappearing a short ways into the forest. Chadrik lit a sitter in the tiny fire and offered it to Vik.

"So what was it like, growing up in the mountain?"

"What?"

"Only the Impery know what that's like, and you New Ones. Any other Sinovian who remembers living in their mountain is dead."

"Why don't you ask Josanna?"

"Imperyo isn't a functioning mountain. It shut down fifty years ago."

"Oh, I didn't know that."

"Is there a reason you don't want to talk about it?"

"No," Vik answered too quickly. "No...I just, wanted to get out of there so bad. I didn't know what it was like out here. I feel like an idiot when I remember how I was."

Chadrik took a long puff of his sitter, narrowed his eyes and blew out the smoke from his lungs.

"So it wasn't all that great in there?"

"It was safe. It was falling apart, but it was safe."

"Falling apart? The mountain?"

"The dispensers were shutting down. Food was running out, we couldn't make new clothes, things like that. It was the boredom that was killing me though."

"That's not a problem now?"

Vik laughed despite himself, "No, I guess I got what I wanted."

A few specks of water fell from the clouds that were rolling in fast. Josanna jogged back to them from the woods, flinching when the rain started plopping down harder.

Josanna called out to Zaki, "Get out of the rain, you're going to get soaked."

"What's he doing?" Vik asked, staring at the kid.

He had a knife and he was following something on the ground, searching for the perfect place to strike. Something was wriggling under the muck, rippling like a pulse. He jerked forward, stabbing down on it with a triumphant shout when it started to ooze red blood. It turned into a gushing geyser that quickly swallowed the blade and covered his hand up to his elbow. Zaki hopped back and yelled as the ground trembled beneath them and thunder rumbled in the distance. The rain washed the blood out enough for Zaki to yank the knife up and stick it back in its sheathe before running to the others. They were all looking behind him and from the sounds of it, he was in big trouble.

# CHAPTER SEVENTEEN

Zaki ran back to them, hands still stained with blood. The camp they'd made fell apart over the tremors and the fire splashed into the water that spread out like a spider web on the once dry patch of stable ground. Vik, Chadrik, Josanna, and Uther stared up as a nearby hill bulged, then cracked, crumbled, and stood itself straight up. As tall as a mountain, a giant stretched himself upright until his craggy fingers touched the clouds. The meadow's disadvantage was made painfully clear. With nowhere to hide and it standing too close to the forest for them to get back to it, their only option was to outrun him across the vast marshmeadow with mountains trapping them on every side.

Vik took a few steps forward, unable to believe his eyes. He remembered seeing it from the side of Haven's mountaintop, but standing at its feet made him feel like a helpless speck of dirt.

"Run!" Chadrik shouted.

"Are you ki—"

"Just go!"

The giant took a single, self-balancing step and they were all thrown off as their feet flew up over their heads and they rolled across the meadow. Chadrik bounced up with the help of his own low-powered blast of air, turned on his heels, and ran passed Uther who was pulling everyone up off the soggy ground with rough tugs, launching them recklessly forward. Zaki was already in Uther's arms. Despite being such a great beast, he handled his footing well in the shallow, murky slog. Vik sloshed uselessly forward, the heavy water tugging at every footstep. The rumbling ground stirred up the boggy water and released the previously faint odor of something like rotten eggs. They all grimaced, but it only added to their already desperate yearning to get out of there. Vik jerked his shoulders forward in an attempt to assist his legs, but found that galloping along was the quickest way to move.

And then at once, everything was silenced and replaced with a booming tremor. The grazers had already fled far away from the middle of the marshmeadow and were well out of harm's way.

"Keep running!" Vik yelled simply to yell, releasing some of his compressed fear.

They needed to get to the mountain, the one Zaki had mentioned earlier. He said they could take a shortcut through some caves if they needed to get out of the open area. Any other method of escaping this beast was going to end in their death. He was certain of it. There was a sickness in his gut every time he looked away from a particular part of the mountains ahead, and for a second he could've sworn he saw the flash of fire in front of him and a dark cave with blood. He jerked back as he galloped, stumbling and swatting at the air in front of him.

The angry mountain let out a great moan. The pressurized howling muffled all other sounds, ringing out like a force of silence until a deafening rupture split the ground and sent them all sprawling forward, flailing and splashing into the swamp. Vik pushed against the muck under the shallow water, his hand sinking up to the wrist before he could turn himself toward what everyone was straining to see. Another cloud-reaching giant was breaking free of its slumber. Instead of skin, the underbelly had dirt and muck that crumbled off as it stood. Every limb it pulled from the earth ripped up twines and roots, unknowingly snapping them and sending them whipping above their heads. As if waking from a nap, the colossal Brute stretched to full stature, the clouds whisking away from its touch like wisps of smoke. Its face was without a mouth or nose, but it had eyes. They were tiny compared to the beast, but easily the size of a full-grown man and both were fixed down on them.

With a meteoric swing, the first giant crashed its limb against the ripped up soil. The earthquake that followed was overwhelming, rattling them off their feet as it rumbled and rippled, causing the mud underneath to absorb them into it. The muscles in their legs trembled in unison with the ground, becoming completely unusable.

Vik ripped his hands out of the mud. He pulled and trudged and threw himself with every step, desperately trying to escape the marshmeadow giants. The Brutes' grassy extension stomped on their overnight campsite, leaving a crater in the earth big enough to form a pond and once again rocking the ground under their feet. Uther was farther ahead of them all, heading in a slightly different direction than Vik.

"Uther!" Vik shouted again and again until he got his attention.

Vik pointed, flinging his finger toward the mountainside he wanted to get to before losing balance and tripping in the mud. Uther didn't stop, but altered his course for the right direction with Zaki firmly in his arms. The Brute's roar made a sound so deep, it went unheard but not unnoticed. The waves of noise pummeled them to the core. Chadrik tried to keep running and fighting the nausea, but the vibrations were too intense. He retched, sinking deeper into the ground with every heave even as Josanna passed him. She stopped, slapping into the mud and rolling back up in the other direction.

"Vik!"

He turned and saw her desperately trying to pull Chadrik up, but not even she could dislodge him from the mud. The earth quaked once again as the Brute lumbered toward them. One more step was all it would take for the giant to crush them underfoot. Uther was far away, taking Zaki to the point in the mountain Vik yearned to keep running for. The guide would be safe, Uther would be safe, Vik even had the orb back in his own pocket. That would be more than enough to get him to where these Riders were so he could save Garek.

Josanna's grip on Chadrik's wrist slipped and she fell on her back, nearly disappearing under the water. Vik cursed and ran at them, daring to glance up at the Brute. Its crumbly arm revealed to look more like a cluster of roots strapped together as more muck fell off. The hand that stretched out, closing in on them with inescapable speed, was difficult to make out. A skeletal frame was present, but no clear fingers, none that could be separated from the rest. Vik sloshed up behind Chadrik and helped dislodge his limbs from the mud while the hand drew too near. Josanna was frozen, her hand clutching too tightly to Chadrik's arm. It became dark all at once and Vik ducked down, covering his head, squeezing his eyes shut. The loud whoosh of air rushing away from the tangled palm drowned out all thoughts until a bright light burst out and illuminated everything around them. The fiery jet spewing from her lips billowed with explosive fury, igniting the hand the instant it connected with her flames. The giant jerked its hand back so quickly that they were all lifted up above the mud before splashing back down into it. Josanna was thrown into her own chemicals face first and landed in the muck, writhing and gasping as the rest of the flames splattered around her, staying lit on the top of the water. Vik stumbled to her, trying to roll her over while she held the marshy mud against her face, even shoveling it in her mouth.

"What are you doing?" Vik shouted, "come on!"

Chadrik, now dislodged, joined Vik in putting one of her arms over his shoulder. They had such a long way to go until the mountain could save them and carrying Josanna in that way did not make the trip any faster. The Brute erupted in pain and fury, but they didn't dare turn around. The vibrations stampeding through the unsteady ground told them what they needed to know. There was no outrunning it. They weren't going to make it to the mountain.

Vik stopped scrambling through the muck and turned around to face the giant. Chadrik grabbed his arm and jerked him around, shouting at him but Vik just told him to wait. Chadrik looked between Vik, Josanna, the Brute and the way they should be running several times. Mud covered the majority of Josanna's freshly maimed skin. Gasping was the only way she could take air in, especially since it smelled like burnt flesh, oily chemicals, and rotten eggs. Vik shoved them both to the ground with his entire body. They all sputtered and swallowed marsh water down the wrong tube. Vik threw himself onto his back and rubbed mud over his face, the only part of him exposed above the water. He watched the giant smash its hand into the ground, finally extinguishing the flames. Its mountain-sized shoulders heaving, the Brute scanned the marshland, squinting its beady eyes and letting out earth-rattling barks, but it couldn't find the tiny offenders. Its footsteps treaded heavily around them, vibrating the muck and sinking them deeper. Then it paused, slowed its heaving shoulders and groaned so loudly that whistlers took flight from all around. The giant pulled its hand to its chest, sunk down to its knees and curled up on its side, back into the hill it had been before.

Several minutes of struggling against the mud yielded little results. Vik's arms were free, but the vibrations had sunk his bottom half too deeply. It wasn't until Uther finally made it over to them that he was able to dislodge them with some effort. They kept silent, not asking questions, not speaking on anything, just approaching the fissure in the mountainside that would safely hide them from the Brute. Uther picked up Josanna and carried her effortlessly the rest of the way. He was barely able to squeeze inside, pushing himself through the craggy, narrow entryway until they came out into a small opening. There was a split in the top of the low hanging cave and weak rays of sunlight beamed in through it. Moss coated the walls like a layer of soft fur. It smelled stale and muggy inside, especially near the pools of water that gathered in the cracks of the floor. Zaki was sitting on a rock in the corner of the cave, holding his knees and resting his chin on them. He jumped up as soon as the others came through behind Uther.

"What happened?" Zaki whispered.

Josanna was groaning and sobbing freely, no longer fully aware of the others. Uther sat her down where her back could lean against the wall and lumbered over to his pack. Vik and Chadrik rushed to her side, kneeling down and trying to speak to her.

"I want to die," she managed to sputter out.

"It can't be that bad," Chadrik tried to calm her down, his fingers trembling, "let's get all this off your face, let it heal."

Chadrik started to rub the mud off, but what he saw underneath made him jerk his hand away. He started swearing quietly to himself, the quivering in his fingers running up his arm until his whole body was unstable. Vik saw the part of her burnt skin that had been exposed, only there was no skin. The partially dried muck had easily taken the melted flesh off her face. Vik's muscles grew weak, but he just squeezed his eyes shut and tried to carefully remove more of the mud before it dried any more. Her occasional screams did nothing for his nerves. A large hand smacked Vik's shoulder and he looked up to see Uther standing over them with a knife, the hilt end held toward Vik. There was a long pause where no one spoke or moved until Vik took the hilt in his hand and Zaki jumped off the rock he was sitting on.

"What are you doing?!"

"Go over there, Zaki."

"I can't..." Vik said, thinking of the Gray man he killed on his last day in Haven, "I killed someone before, I can't do it again."

"Please Vik," Josanna gasped, the inside of her neck just as bad off as the outside.

Blood trickled up and over her cheek as she sputtered a weak cough, ripping her throat up with every hack. Her face was almost unrecognizable. All it would take was him cutting her throat. It was sure to be less painful than what she was experiencing, but he kept thinking about how that Gray choked and sputtered to death. His only consolation from that had been that he was protecting his family. It was a disgusting way to die and he couldn't handle the idea of Josanna having to go through that.

"Give it to me," Chadrik said, taking the knife out of Vik's hand.

Chadrik stood over her, rocking back and forth with increasing determination. Uther stood in front of Zaki and tried to shield his eyes, but he was shielding himself too. The giant covered his ears and cringed, waiting for sounds he didn't want to hear.

"You know I love you," Chadrik whispered to Josanna, squeezing her hand. "You always remind me of dad..."

In one swift motion, he swiped the blade across her throat. Rich red blood flowed from the wound and Vik started remembering all too clearly that final day in Haven. The streets, the sounds of bodies crashing, it was all seared into his memory. Edik and all those other people he had seen every day. Leaving them in pools of their own blood. Red and grey. And Havard's pearl dropping out as even he died that day, spilling all the dishes and utensils and orange pills out onto the counter.

"Orange pill," Vik gasped aloud.

They all looked at him as he scrambled in his pockets until he remembered the right one. The last orange pill. He had dropped all the others when the drass attacked them in the woods, unable to scrounge up more while Jahzara was trying to kill him. He held it in between his finger and thumb before pushing it down Josanna's open mouth.

"What is that?" Chadrik asked.

"It's…uh, an orange pill. I don't know, it fixes bad cuts you might get in the kitchen."

"Why would you do that?" Chadrik shouted at him, shoving him away. "I don't want to have to do it again!"

"It might do more!"

"Might?"

"I don't know!"

"Stop shouting," Zaki cried from behind Uther, who was still covering his ears, "Babblers will hear."

"Let's just see. If it doesn't work, I'll do it."

"If it doesn't work and we're torturing my sister," Chadrik snarled, a vein popping out from his forehead, shaking the bloody knife at Vik, "I will kill you!"

"Just wait."

They stared at her for minutes, waiting and waiting while little seemed to be happening.

"The blood's stopped," said Chadrik, his own blood still boiling.

"She's too pale. I'll see if she's still alive."

Vik bent down, tried to feel for a pulse while avoiding where the cut should be. He couldn't feel anything and her eyes were still closed. He reached up to pat her face and noticed her skin was mostly grown back, but still very thin and raw.

"Get me some water."

"I'm purposive," Zaki chanted, darting outside before anyone could stop him.

After returning with muck water and that rotten smell in his leathery satchel, Zaki handed it to Vik with his eyes fixed on Josanna's face. Vik poured it over the mud and handed the satchel back to him.

"More."

They continued until Vik was able to gently smudge the mud away, revealing a large, inward curving scar running along the side of her face, on the outside of her eye and crossing the end of her brow. The new skin was delicate and obvious. Vik felt for the cut on her neck, but it was gone as well.

"That's incredible," Chadrik breathed, "Do you have any more of those?"

256

"No, that was the last one."

Chadrik kept her hand in his while Vik continued to gently wipe the mud away from her healing face. Zaki and Uther comforted one another, unblinking, holding their breath with no words to express their anxiety. Water dripped steadily from the split in the ceiling and thunder sounded like a hum from inside the cave. Though the ground would occasionally rumble, the giants had lost track of their pests and were content to nurse their own wounds in peace.

*****

"I'm sorry I'm late!"

Savan hastily picked up the brittle door, leaning it against the entryway once he was inside. It was better than a scaly curtain, but an intermediate step in the grand reconstruction plan. Shurik watched him scamper around the hovel, shaking out his blanket, setting food on the chunk of wood in the corner of the room and checking off a mental list of all the things that needed mending on the walls and roof. The other residents of the small hut were out accomplishing Marek's assigned tasks, improving their homes, barricading the neighborhood, and gathering enough food for the workers.

"You're exhausting me."

"I haven't said anything," Savan stated, glancing at his grandfather from the corner of his eye. "I didn't forget what you told me last time."

"I wanted you to shut your mouth because you were so damned happy."

"And you weren't, I know. You never are unless someone else is unhappy."

"Exactly. Put those blankets over there," Shurik pointed to the corner of the room with the food.

"Why?" Savan looked down at the rolled up fabric in his arms, "Don't tell me you're too warm at night?"

"No, I heard freezing to death is very peaceful. You just shut your eyes," Shurik closed his eyes and held up his hands, "and there you go."

"I'll bet you're wrong," Savan put both blankets on the end of his new bed.

"I had it all figured out, you know. I was going to walk right off the edge of the top level once I was too old to know when I was dropping rocks. But now, the best I can figure is freezing to death and I can barely manage a shiver at night."

"I'm glad to hear it."

Shurik pouted in his bed, his arms limp in his lap, gazing down at the floor. His face was even more droopy than usual. Savan finished organizing and assessing, stopped in the doorway and sighed.

"You elders…"

"What's that?"

"Weren't you always so bored back in Haven? You were always tricking people, starting problems…"

"I resent that," Shurik said with a fond smile.

"Now you're out of there. Instead of dying and maybe starting all over with another life or place or whatever happens after we're dead, you still get to be you and know that this is different. You're starting a whole new life without having to kill yourself."

"Oh yes," Shurik gave Savan an exasperated glare, holding his arms up, "I feel like I'm starting anew."

"I'm doing my best to make this easier for you. Just…don't kill yourself."

"You've been working too hard for me to throw it all away, is that it?" Shurik grinned, calling out to him as he picked up the door. "You can't always be working on the happiness of others."

"The happiness of others makes me happy," Savan droned, believing it but knowing what his grandfather was going to say in response.

"It won't always," Shurik said with a smile.

Savan hesitated, "You should put yourself to work with something you're good at. Distract yourself."

Savan slammed the door down on the entryway and heaved a sigh out before moving on to another house. His mind was filling with blurry thoughts he wasn't used to thinking. They were unsettling, selfish, and it took too long for him to get rid of them.

*****

Out in the spitfire field, the come-and-go day rain was pouring down in sheets, but Marek worked double-time to gather as much food as he could. He wasn't going to trade it for goods but add it to the stockpile for his people. They'd been working for a couple of days now on improving their homes and their conditions and things were going well. Once his people had steady legs to stand on, things would start

258

getting better and they might even be capable of supporting Zaruko in leading Threshold as a separate community. Marek ripped the spitfire out of the ground, knocking himself on his backside and flinging dirt all over the place. He grumbled, trying to pick the bits out of the basket as best he could.

Benne trampled through the field, approaching Marek once he found him. He was soaked through, but the cool weather was a welcome gift to quarry laborers and farmers alike.

"Hey, careful!" Marek shouted, pointing to the leaves under his shoes.

Benne nimbly hopped aside and winced, "Sorry. I'm no good out here in the fields."

"It's alright," Marek said, pulling himself up, "Is it time?"

Benne glanced around and nodded once, marching away without another word.

Once Marek was back in the city, he dropped off the basket of spitfires and shredded leaves with Savan, who would then distribute them accordingly. He'd become his right hand man in just a few days. Never had Marek known someone more reliable. He knew he respected him in Haven, but it was only out in Agrona that he was able to fully appreciate his demeanor. Tayna recommended him to her cousin, telling him about his old friend's behavior from her month outside of Haven before the Gate closed for good. He was always the first to volunteer, never in a bad mood, always willing to help even when he was exhausted.

Marek went to the tavern and ambled up to the counter, dripping like a wet rag all over the floor. There weren't too many people there in the early evening, but it wasn't deserted. There was only one barkeep at his post and he gave Marek the once over, squinting, his upper lip sneered up just enough to show some teeth.

"I'm sorry," he said after a long pause, setting down the rag and the cup he was cleaning. "You're gonna have to tell me your name."

"We all look the same," Marek smiled.

"That you do," the barkeep chuckled.

"It's Marek."

"Ah, that's right. Well, you're the last one here."

The barkeep waved him around the counter and raised a hatch on the floor. He hurried him down and slammed it shut above his head. Marek stumbled on the first few steps down, his soggy Haven shoes unable to grip anything reliably. He felt his way through the pitch dark until a faint light bobbed over to him, illuminating the rest of the stairway.

"You made it," Tayna said, holding a lantern above her head and peering at him through the railing.

Marek joined them at the dimly lit table. The leaders and their closest companions were idling impatiently and he could tell they had been willing to start without him. Reeta was there with Ridiak, who was unable to stop leaning on the wall, smiling ridiculously at Marek. The Shiny gave him a little wave, clearly having shown up to an important secret meeting after a full sitter, high as the clouds. Makai stood beside her, his arms crossed like he was sculpted that way, positioned protectively behind a twelve year old Jawny girl with a button nose and resting smile that stretched across her face without her even trying. It was Taolani, Harash's youngest, capable grandchild. She had attended all her grandmother's meetings for the last year, having shown great potential and interest in what it took to be a Jawny leader. Her old paintings had been wiped clean, leaving the pale skin shapes sticking out around the new patterns resembling Harash's that replaced them. At some point since Harash's death, she had been officially deemed capable of representing the faction of Jawny in Threshold that supported the son.

Zaruko and Gamba were across from them and of course, Nattina and Benne towered at the opposite end of the rickety table.

"Glad you made it," Zaruko said to Marek as he approached the table beside Tayna.

"Like you were saying," Nattina coaxed him.

Thunder rumbled overhead.

"Right, I was saying we need to be prepared for the Rider's return, but we should also be ready in case they fail."

"They won't," Reeta snapped.

"I know," Zaruko attempted to appease her, "But just in case, we should have a plan."

"We don't need one," she argued, offended by the idea. "Impery aren't the only ones capable of getting things done. A fact made obvious by your girl's blown mission, getting a bunch of Sinovians killed, our only means of defending ourselves taken..."

"That's not your only means of defense. We are the ones defenseless," Taolani said hastily, glancing to Makai for approval. His face was a blank slate.

"You know what I mean," Reeta continued, "My boy's going to bring us back a Rider army and Thesmekkian weapons. The only plan we need is one that covers who takes over after we throw Durako out."

"Does it have to be violent?" Marek asked, gaining a roomful of confused looks.

"Well what do you want to do with all those weapons? Give them away as a peace offering?" Ridiak chuckled.

Thunder boomed, causing Taolani to flinch.

"I only mean, we should use them to better our own lives out here against the dangers like the drass and the whistlers. If we don't need the Impery to protect us, we won't need to feed them and they'll have to come out of the mountain and integrate. It'll be a slow healing process, but I think the wounds between Sinovians and Impery can heal if we just—"

"With all respect, New One," Nattina began, "I don't think you fully grasp the stubborn nature of Lord Durako. He would never let a peaceful transition even begin to happen."

"It's true. If my father saw even a distant possibility of that happening he would snuff it out so fast it wouldn't even singe the ends. He can already imagine it, which is just fueling his paranoia and desperation. The only reason Jahzara was allowed to come with us to retrieve you all from your mountain is because of that fear. There is no peaceful way out of this."

"But we appreciate where your mind is at," Nattina added quickly. "Most of us have lost sight of that kind of thinking."

"Who is going to lead us once Durako is dead?" Reeta said, snapping them back to her previous concern.

Zaruko glared at Reeta, disapproving in her choice of words. Nattina and Taolani were in agreement that Zaruko was the most qualified. Marek agreed simply on the grounds that he felt most comfortable with the idea of Zaruko as their leader once the dust settled.

"So you all just want to repeat the same thing? Put an Impery in charge and see what happens."

"Reeta, I have every intention of uniting the Sinovians and Impery. You know that."

"I had this rebellion organized first, I was the one who found you and told you to join us," She shouted.

"Keep your voice down," Taolani said, glancing at the wood-floor ceiling above them.

They heard another crack of thunder from the storm outside.

"You were holding these meetings with Shinies only and until you were caught holding them by Zaruko, none of us even knew about them," said Nattina.

"That sounds more like the current Impery problem than the goal we're aiming for," Taolani said softly.

"How dare you!" Reeta shouted at the child, only to provoke an aggressive stance from Makai.

"I'm alright," Taolani whispered to him, holding her arm out to the side.

"It's in the past, Reeta," said Zaruko firmly.

"And so should Impery rule. It's done nothing but bring us disaster."

"My grandfather—"

"Was a lesser monster, but a monster still," she scoffed. "He ripped our people from our mountain, gave the mad Riders full reign, built our drass-luring sap houses, I could go on."

"If you do, I will burn you to ash," Zaruko growled.

"Hah! See how quickly they resort to threats when you point out their own flaws."

"You are insulting a good man," said Nattina.

"As the representative of my people, I'm telling you now that we will not submit to another Impery leader."

"As the Impery use their fire to threaten us, so you use the power of your people. This is not a good way for us to conduct these meetings," said Taolani in a firm, but delicate voice.

Reeta slammed her cup down on the table and stormed out of the cellar, Ridiak skipping to catch up with her. Each heavy footstep shook dust off the stairway. Light flooded in when she threw the hatch open but was soon smothered out with a deafening crack. The others weren't pleased with her departure, but Nattina promised to speak with her.

"I hate to put that on your shoulders," Taolani said, "But you're probably the only one she would listen to right now."

"You've been quiet," Marek whispered to Tayna.

"I'm afraid I might not be well," Tayna said each word slowly.

"You were fine a minute ago," Marek said, putting his hand on her shoulder.

She seized up when he touched her and again thunder echoed through the air. Marek said her name and her eyes rolled back until only the white part could be seen. She started falling back, but Marek caught her and lowered her carefully to the ground as her body convulsed and she gasped for air. Zaruko dove to the ground beside them and the others ran over to help, but Marek told them all to stand back waving his arm in the air.

"What's the matter with her?" Taolani asked, her voice going high at the end.

"I think it's the storm," Marek breathed, "She's told me about this before, but I forgot about it 'til now."

Tayna slammed her head on the ground and Zaruko threw his hand behind her. Nattina and the others stepped back, disturbed by Tayna's overwhelming reaction. Seizures and other such behaviors weren't common among the physically fit, surviving Sinovians of Threshold.

"Maybe we should continue this at another time," Nattina suggested, motioning for Benne to follow her out.

Makai nodded to Taolani and they followed the Brutemen out. Gamba offered to get them anything they needed.

"A blanket," Zaruko said. "Some water."

"Thank you," Marek added.

Before Gamba returned, Tayna's breathing settled and her eyes came back forward. Disoriented and babbling, Zaruko and Marek helped lift her into an upright position. She was sweating and tears were running down her face, but she wasn't crying.

"Tayna, hey, look at me. What happened?" Marek asked her.

"It's not real. They left us. It was wrong, now everything's wrong and she's going to kill me," she moved her glazed stare from Marek to Zaruko and whispered loud enough for them both to hear, her lips pulled back and her voice cracking into a higher pitch, "You're on the path."

"Tayna, you're not making any sense. Calm down," Marek told her, gripping her arms tight.

But Zaruko felt his stomach drop into an empty pit. He stood up to take the blanket from Gamba when he returned, but he couldn't focus on anything. Zaruko couldn't shake the eerie chill shivering in his core, as if the truth had burrowed inside him to whisper ominous nothings in his heart.

# CHAPTER EIGHTEEN

Water trickled down the walls of the dank cave, pooling in slow-draining puddles around their feet. The ground faintly jittered as the giants continued stomping around their territory. The sunlight leaked in from the crack they had slipped through and their eyes were finally adjusting enough to traipse around the cozy cave without tripping on the uneven rocks. Chadrik was speaking quietly with Josanna, letting the others rest as they needed before heading out.

"Zaki," Vik whispered, checking to see if he was awake.

"Yeah?" He was.

"When are we getting back on the trail?"

"Once the sun comes out enough. It's too dark now," he pointed passed Chadrik and Josanna, "We have to go through there."

"What, where?" Vik asked, squinting passed them.

"Exactly."

Zaki pried himself loose from Uther. The giant's snoring streak remained unbroken. Scampering carefully just a few steps away, Zaki hovered in front of Vik and stared down at his own hands.

"You said earlier that you only have yourself to keep you safe out here," Zaki said to Vik, sitting down beside him. "But don't worry, your people are extra tough. Extremely durable, they used to say that about the Mek-Enna, uh, that's you. Your designated names."

Vik shook his head, "How would you know something like that?"

"Roque told us, he liked to talk about you guys. The Mek-Enna were the last ones left for a long time."

"Who is Roque?" Vik asked, squaring his shoulders to him, "And how would he know something like that?"

Uther woke up and was leaning forward curiously.

"It doesn't matter," Zaki said defensively. "Why are you mad?"

"I'm not mad, I just want to know."

"I don't wanna talk about it."

"Zaki," Vik said, stifling his increased anxiety, "You can't just say something like that and not tell me what's going on. Aren't we friends yet?"

"I don't know, are we?"

Vik smiled, breathing out an exasperated chuckle, "Yeah, we are. I think you and me are friends."

"Yeah, I guess we are," Zaki said while Vik gave Chadrik a meaningful glance. "Roque is the Rider leader. He's, kind of, a Thesmekka."

Uther snorted out a grunt, but when they looked at him he pretended to be preoccupied.

"...What?" Chadrik gasped, but Vik couldn't breathe.

"You mean to tell me that this whole time, we've been going to find the Riders, hoping they've got Thesmekkian weapons and stuff to help us...but there's an actual Thesmekka there. Alive."

Zaki shrugged.

*****

Marek charged down the street. Clothes flapped in the wind as he passed by, hanging up on lines to dry in front of the Brutemen houses. Their homes were big and well protected. Most Brutemen were quarry workers and with the stones they mined and logs from the woods too big for others to lug around, they were easily able to barricade their houses. The only Brutemen Marek saw in their neighborhood were pregnant women and young children, those who weren't able to work. Luckily, he wasn't there to find a Bruteman, Marek was just passing through on his way to the compact cluster of Impery homes near the tall, metal wall.

The smithy was along the way as well, situated directly between the two neighborhoods. Black smoke rose from both chimneys, but Marek had never been inside. The door creaked open and Marek tiptoed in, glancing from side to side. Dark and sooty, the stone walls barely shared the light coming from the corner smelter. A young, half-Impery girl pumped on the billow, covered in sweat and completely unaware of Marek's presence. He tapped her on the shoulder and she screamed.

"I'm sorry," Marek said, flinching away.

Both her parents burst into the room from behind a solid stone door after unlatching the heavy lock on the other side. The smithy was a Bruteman, but his sieva was a tall Impery woman with hair so short her neck was fully visible. They were both covered in soot and sweat with welts dotting their arms.

"What'dya want?" The woman snapped.

"I need something sharp."

"No weapons," she droned.

"No, not a weapon, just, something sharp."

"That's a weapon," the daughter quipped, rolling her eyes at him. "We're not getting shut down 'cuz you wanna call something different."

"I don't want a knife or a sword or anything meant to hurt someone, I just need something to cut with," Marek desperately tried to explain.

The Bruteman marched over to him, wiped his hands off on a rag and threw it down on the counter beside him, "What's your name, Seer?"

"Seer? Uh, it's Marek."

"...The Gadling's brother?" he asked, the hint of a smile under his bushy beard.

"Yeah, that's right."

"You want something to cut with?"

"Yes sir," Marek said, exhaling.

"That is what we call, a weapon."

The smithy turned his back on Marek and the two women went back to work, the mother almost disappearing into the room until she heard Marek speaking again.

"Then make me one."

They all turned to stare at him, the hulking smithy raising his torch to get a better look at his face, hoping there was a joke there. He lumbered toward Marek and set the torch into the grated metal brazier just beside him.

"You should leave, little Seer."

"I'm not leaving here without a weapon."

"I don't know what you're trying to prove," the woman said coming out of the doorway, "But it's not going to happen. Lord Durako's laws are—"

"Those laws are made to keep us from protecting ourselves, which we are fully capable of doing."

The Bruteman chuckled, "Have you ever seen a drass up close?"

"I haven't been living under a rock. This weapon isn't for a drass."

"Now that's exactly why we're not supposed to make them anymore. Were you involved in that attack on Jahzara?"

"That was my brother, but if I'd been there I promise you, that speech on the balcony would've gone a different way."

"We don't support either side of this. We just want to live in peace," the smithy said calmly.

"You make weapons."

"We make tools, helpful things," the daughter corrected.

"I'm sorry we can't assist you," said the Impery woman, slowly flicking her wrist at him and eying the door.

Marek swayed in place, narrowing his eyes at all of them, almost speaking several times but closing his mouth after each thought.

"Have a good day, Marek," the smithy said, disappearing with his sieva into the back room.

The stone door boomed and left the room tingling from the echo. The half-Impery girl quickly busied herself at the fire, pushing down on the billows with all her weight. Marek slumped where he stood and looked around but nothing helped him think of a better way to put it. He thought that would go very differently.

"I've heard of you, Marek, the Gadling and the Seer's brother," the girl said.

"The Seer, she's my cousin..." he corrected her, trailing off.

"You should go talk to Zaruko."

"About what?"

"About our helpful tools," she said, shooting him a sideways glance that lingered a second too long.

Zaruko sat on his tattered couch, surrounded by his most loyal warriors and friends. Sitter smoke hovered like a mist above them. An Impery woman sat cross-legged on the floor, reading off a list of possible places to hold their secret meetings in the future. Zaruko and Gamba took turns shaking their heads and giving reasons why the listed hideout wouldn't work. The other three Impery in the room launched out of their chairs when the front door creaked open. Marek stumbled in and immediately got a lungful of unexpected smoke, hacking and bending down in the doorway to breathe the air underneath.

Zaruko held up his hand and quickly calmed them down, "He's permitted."

"I need to talk to you," Marek wheezed.

"We're busy," He snapped.

Marek stood up straighter and took a step backward, into the doorway again, "I'll just—"

"Sit down over there."

"Are you sure he should stay?" the woman asked.

"I said he's not a problem," Zaruko repeated, pinching the bridge of his nose. "I'm sorry, keep going."

"That's all I had," she said, sighing and letting the parchment fall into her lap.

Every option was scratched out. Marek glanced around the room and noticed how worn down they all were. Their faces were bruised and their clothes dirty, but most of all they looked like they hadn't slept in days.

"What did you come to talk about, Marek?"

"Oh, I wanted to know why the smithy wasn't making us weapons like you said they would."

"Come on, Marek," Zaruko groaned, leaning over to peer out the window, "I think you could say that a little louder..."

"I'm sorry, I..." he furrowed his brows, "What's going on?"

"Don't worry about it," said one of the other Impery.

"Someone told our friends in Imperyo about our place under the tavern. The barkeep was interrogated," Zaruko spit embers on the floor, as if he'd been chewing on them, "And...long story short, we need to find this traitor before they get any more of us killed."

"Did someone...?"

"Not quite, but Benne won't be joining us for a while."

Marek could feel himself getting high from the fumes floating around the room. His legs started getting heavier and his eyelids settled at half-mast.

"Do we have any idea where to start looking?"

Zaruko stared at him, resting his temples on two fingers. He pulled a knife out from inside his shirt and strolled over to Marek before setting the blade delicately on the table beside him. He breathed in the smoke like it were a soft perfume.

"If it's you," he said quietly, "I want you to kill me now. None of them will do anything to you, as my dying request. So you're all clear, you'll all let him walk out of here and never touch him," he spun around to the others before facing Marek again.

"I'm not—"

"I mean it, just do it now."

"Why are you saying this to me?"

"Because you're the Gadling's brother, the Seer's cousin, the only one who could ruin this entire thing if you're not with us. I don't want to put in anymore of myself if you're against me," Zaruko said, part of him tired of carrying the burden, hoping Marek would pick up the knife and cut his throat.

"I didn't know you liked me so much," Marek joked, "You really need to get some sleep."

Zaruko couldn't help himself. He laughed and picked his knife back up, sheathing it under his shirt and gently slapping Marek on the side of his neck.

"I think I'll do that. You all know where to find me," he said, wandering into the only other room.

"Oh, but hey," Marek started, sucking in a gulp of disorienting smoke, "You know it's Reeta, right?"

Zaruko suppressed a smirk, leaning out from the doorframe of the other room, "That's almost a dangerous thing to say."

Gamba leapt up from the couch and headed over to Marek, putting his arm around his shoulder. Once Zaruko closed the damaged wicker door, he drew him over to the other group of Impery sitting around the room.

"You said something about the smithy?"

*****

Vik found himself strolling along the streets of Haven, both hands in his pockets and staring up at the midday sun through the Gate. He longed to take the stairway, but lacked the courage to do it. All the houses were empty, all the dispensers were working again, all the machines were back to life and the hum of crowds of people surrounded him. He had free reign of everything, but when he focused on the voices, they faded one by one until he gradually realized he was completely alone. Coming to a stop on the top level, Vik looked down and saw his old house. His father was sprinting out toward him. The door whirred shut long after he'd cleared it and Vik tried to shout at him, but his voice was emptiness. As his father sprinted closer to the edge, the Gate above them shut down, turning off the sun like a light switch, leaving only the reflectors to dimly broadcast their stored energy. All the humming voices turned to screams. A fissure crackled up the side of Haven and the mountain started caving. Chunks of rock crumbling down on him. His father ran, pumping his arms, and threw himself off the top level just as a rock starting falling toward Vik.

Yelling, he jerked awake and slammed his hand into a knobby stone wall. Light was barely creeping through the cracks in the tiny, slimy cave. Vik started breathing too hard, realizing he was alone in a small, craggy space.

"Vik!"

"I'm in here!" He shouted back at Josanna, who called from somewhere nearby.

"We know," she said, emerging from the connecting tunnel. "We just heard you screaming and thought something was wrong."

Vik shut his eyes and exhaled, "I didn't scream..."

"Did you have bad dreams?" Zaki asked, unaware of his mockery.

"I didn't have...where were you guys?"

"We were checking out this tunnel. Making sure nothing caved in when those big Brutes went stomping around."

"You left me here alone?" Vik asked, quickly changing his tune with they gave him amused looks, "I just mean, something could've come in while I was sleeping," his face felt hot and he was relieved to be obscured in the dim light.

"Uther's right there," Zaki said.

Sure enough, Uther was rummaging through his pack again, glancing up at the mention of his name. He generally ignored a majority of what they were saying most of the time. In part because he found them difficult to understand, but also due to their petty bickering.

"Oh, he kinda blends in," Vik said, noticing how his skin seemed to perfectly match the deep brown, bumpy cave walls.

They gathered up their things and started trekking through the tunnels. Passageways narrowed and were slippery with rainwater, leaking in from every possible nook. Chadrik slammed his head on some low hanging rocks and Vik bent his fingers the wrong way while blindly feeling for the walls. Josanna complained that her fingertips were pruney.

"What is that smell?" she groaned, scrunching up her whole face before covering it with the inside of her elbow.

"We did go through a couple of marshes, sweat a lot, sleep in a humid cave..." Chadrik said.

"No, it's the mushrooms," Zaki said with a sigh, "We have to hurry. It smells like they're growing pretty well in here."

"Are they edible?" Vik asked.

"No, they're really poisonous. Just smelling them will make you sick."

The four of them exchanged looks behind Zaki's back. Uther was balled up in the tiny passageway, wedging himself along and blocking out most of the light that could've followed them. He grunted irritably and repeated the word sick.

"Yes, sick," Zaki said carefully, "Smell in here is bad."

Uther's shoulders slumped, but he pressed on.

"Zaki, why are we going on a route that has poisonous mushrooms?" Josanna grumbled.

"Do you see any other tunnels?"

After a couple of hours of pushing through tunnels smelling of stagnant sewer water and long-rotted meat, courtesy of the dank fungi, the group finally spilled out into a large, open area. They had spent a majority of that time vomiting in each other's paths and when they had nothing left to give up, dry heaving and spitting any trace of saliva out. The air had been so permeated with the poisonous odor that the inside of their mouths were revolting to graze with their tongues and the drooling had become so intense, they looked rabid at first glance.

The large area they stumbled into had a stream flowing in from one end and out through a tiny hole in the other. At the top, high above them was a hole in the ceiling that allowed enough light to pierce through so they could clearly see the surrounding cavern.

"We can't rest yet," Zaki told them. "It'd be safer to get out of the cave first."

"Good," Vik said, woozy from the nausea.

"Make you think of anywhere?" Chadrik asked, looking to his sister and waving his thumb at the tunnel behind them.

"Home sweet home," Josanna gagged, then corrected herself, "No, that was worse."

"What about for you, Vik?" asked Chadrik, wiping his chin.

"Back there?" asked Vik, his tone high-pitched.

"No, here, this cavern. The light up top," they all squinted toward it.

"Oh, this. Haven was worse than this. Everything was always so cold and lifeless," Vik unwrapped his arms from his chest and glanced at Josanna, "Or maybe it was just me."

"You don't seem like the lifeless type," she said.

Vik tilted his head and found himself at a loss for words, but Josanna didn't seem to notice.

As they carefully descended down another passageway, holding onto the walls and slipping on every other step, she cleared her throat behind Vik.

"You've saved me twice now, Vik. So, thank you for helping me back there."

"Oh, it was no big deal."

"It was my life," she breathed, "And you could've saved that pill for yourself."

"When that you put it like that..."

She turned around and punched him in the chest, causing him to slip on his backside. Uther impatiently pushed him up with the back of one hand, squirming and writhing against the rocks behind him.

They reached the end of the third passageway, leading to a wide tunnel even Uther could've jumped up and down in. Vik wriggled his way out of the end, flopping out on his hands. A staggering pain shot through his wrists and knees, crippling him for a couple of minutes. All he could do was roll out of the way in preparation for Uther to come out after him. They waited and waited.

"Uther?" Josanna called out to him, glancing warily at the others.

After a long pause, a quivering grunt answered from inside the tunnel. It echoed off the slick, narrow walls.

"Are you stuck?" Chadrik asked, poking his head inside.

Zaki dove in, scrambling up to him and grabbed his hand, pulling on it without any effect. Uther tried to shift to the left, tried to pull his head down and crawl, then tried to push the cave walls away from him. His breathing became frantic and he started bellowing a terrified howl.

"Stop!" Zaki shouted to him, falling back against the tunnel wall.

"Calm down!" Josanna yelled, watching him thrash around from the passageway entrance.

The giant was covered in sweat and his beady eyes were wider than they'd ever seen them. His whole chest heaved up and down. Doing that only made him more aware of the tight space. Josanna and Chadrik tried to verbally guide him out, but he was unresponsive. He kept his eyes closed and started mumbling something in a grunting, growling language none of them had ever heard before. Zaki dove forward in his brief moment of calm and slapped his hand against his forehead. Uther's eyes glazed over and immediately his breathing returned to normal. The other three jumped away from the tunnelway when Zaki backed out of it, leading a squirming Uther through with only mild difficulty. They were surprised he was able to so calmly squeeze himself out of the end of the passageway like paste from a tube.

Zaki let go of Uther's head but the giant kept still on the cave floor.

"What'd you say to him?" asked Vik.

They were all staring at him and Zaki didn't understand why, "I didn't say anything, I just guided him out of the cave."

"You guided him...?"

"Yeah, I just took his brain and made it work right."

They all stared at him with blank expressions. One by one, they began to understand what he meant.

"I forgot you could do that," Josanna whispered nervously.

"You can't just do that to people, Zaki," said Chadrik uneasily.

"What'd he do?" asked Vik, bent down beside Uther, slapping his unresponsive face.

272

"He took over his body," explained Chadrik.

"He was stuck!"

"Yeah, he was," said Vik, glancing warily between the three of them, "And you got him out, that was really brave. He could've hurt you, on accident. What we're trying to say is, next time, you need to ask if it's alright with the person."

"He's not really a person..." Josanna stated, tilting her head as she watched Uther start snoring.

"Maybe not, but I think he has the right to turn down a complete takeover of his mind and body," said Chadrik, as if Zaki weren't standing right there.

"I'm sorry," Zaki suddenly burst into tears, sniffling and gasping as he tried to speak clearly, "He was, stuck and I, it was nugatugie, I've never been mumificant with it, only, only abster...milious. He won't be fey, I didn't touch his brain. I wasn't, trying to snaffiply him."

Josanna winced and leaned down to his height, "I have no idea what that meant...but you don't need to be upset. I think you just surprised us is all."

"I'm not bad," Zaki sniffled.

"Of course you're not. We're all friends. Isn't that right?"

Zaki sniffled again and wiped his cheeks with the back of his hands, "Yeah."

"And we're good people, right?"

"Right..."

"Well, good people are only friends with other good people and bad people are only friends with other bad people. So..."

"So...I'm not bad, I guess."

"That's reassuring," muttered Josanna.

Zaki bent down beside Uther, folding to where he sat on the backs of his legs. He wrung his hands together and started speaking quietly to Uther as he slept, promising to never take over his brain again.

"Should we be worried about these Riders?" asked Vik, watching Zaki from the other side of the cave.

"Absolutely," said Chadrik, as if they all already knew that. "They can all do what he did, and they're known for being madder than a sapsucker in a deep hole."

"But they're our best chance," said Josanna.

Once Uther was awake, Zaki made his apologies and promises to him once again and they gathered up their things, pulling his pack out of the tunnel he'd been trapped in earlier. The cave was more purposeful along their new route. Water had carved out a walkway and continued to flow gently in the direction they followed, about ankle high. Chilled and damp, Zaki was the first one to succumb to the shivers. Uther plucked him up and easily warmed him while he carried the child in both arms.

"Will you hang back a little, Uther?" Chadrik snapped, tired of every giant footstep splashing cold water on the back of his legs. He slammed into Josanna while he was looking back at Uther, "Why'd you stop walking?"

"I have something in my shoe," she snapped.

"Say something next time."

"Chadrik," Josanna called out to him as he stormed off.

He ignored her and she rolled her eyes at Vik, "Damn cranky without a sitter."

Vik smiled and then asked Josanna how she was holding up. Her face was almost fully healed and only felt tender when she touched it.

"See, feel it yourself," she offered, leaning her face closer to him.

Vik hesitated, but reached up as Uther and Zaki marched around them, running the back of his hand over her cheek and over the line separating the new skin from the old. He snapped his hand back after touching her lips and she flashed her teeth at him.

"It feels weird, doesn't it?" she said, "It's so soft."

Vik cleared his throat, "Right, it is. Very soft. I'm glad it's better now."

He hurried to catch up with the others, leaving her to scurry after him. Vik's heart was slamming against his chest and he could hear his blood flowing in his ears. He exhaled and blinked hard.

"Here it is!" Zaki called out from just a short distance ahead of them.

They had been looking for a doorway. It was big enough to let Uther comfortably through, but small enough that they could've missed it without Zaki's eyes. Made from the same metal their Gates were: purplish-grey, Thesmekkian material. Vik reached out and touched the smooth, saviors-made craftsmanship. Unlike the Gate from Haven, were no symbols etched into the metalwork. It was just a simple, metallic grey ring embedded in the wall. And it was really in there too, carved into the stone like a proper gateway.

"Okay, who has the Thesmekkian piece?" asked Zaki.

"I've got it, right here, somewhere," Vik struggled to unlatch the strap on his pouch.

"What do we need the orb for?" Chadrik asked.

"It'll open the door from this side. Without it, we'd have to wait for someone on the other side to open it for us."

Vik's heart sank. He swallowed hard, transferring the pearly orb to Zaki, using both hands to keep from dropping it. The tunnel was so dark where they sat, huddled in front of this mysterious gateway, all of them eager for what was on the other side. All of them panting, relieved to finally be getting out of the cold, cramped tunnels. Except for Vik who was suspended in the moment. Zaki crammed the orb into the slot and pushed against it, expecting all the gears to switch and click, spinning the mechanisms and opening the door to the other side of the mountains. But absolutely nothing happened.

Vik squeezed his eyes shut and cursed under his breath. Zaki tried it again and again.

"What's the matter?" Chadrik asked impatiently.

"Yeah, it's cold in here," Josanna whined.

"It's not working."

"What?" snapped Josanna.

"It's...this isn't a Thesmekkian orb."

Chadrik's mouth opened, forming a question, but he stopped the air from leaving his lungs. He turned to Vik and tilted his head before backing him against the wall. Vik pressed his back painfully against the jagged rocks and grimaced.

"You didn't."

"I didn't know we'd need it like this. No one told me it was a key."

"What's going on?" Josanna barked.

Uther and Zaki stayed back, watching the three of them with their arms crossed.

"This idiot switched the orbs."

"Switched them? How did he get another one?"

"Why don't you tell them what this is?" Chadrik snapped, maintaining his uncomfortable distance to Vik.

"That's Havard," he bit his bottom lip when they didn't stop staring at him, "He's...my kitchen's auto-arm."

"Oh...Thessa..." Josanna gasped, putting her hands over her whole face. "You have got to be kidding."

"Did you know you did this?" Chadrik asked through clenched teeth.

"I'd take a kitchen appliance over a Thesmekka anytime."

"What about this time!?" shouted Josanna, her voice echoing off the walls.

"So you knew?"

"They abandoned us to this life, why would I sacrifice my fr—"

Chadrik punched him so hard, he knocked Vik on his side. He groaned from the floor and held his arms out, stunned and attempting to outlast the ringing in his head. Chadrik raised his hand up and was about to smash the orb against the cave floor when Zaki cried out to stop him just in time.

"Not the glimmycrack! We can still use it. Not here, but don't break it."

Chadrik slapped the orb into Josanna's hands and stomped farther back into the tunnel on his own. They could hear his yelling echoing off the cave walls. No one went after him. Josanna held the pearly orb up in her hands and looked from it to Vik.

"This has got to be the most idiotic thing I've ever seen anyone do."

Vik groaned and let his head fall against the cold stone floor.

# CHAPTER NINETEEN

A steady dripping echoed somewhere off to the right, deep in the darkest part of the cave that they couldn't take to escape as it ended too soon. The water dropped just erratic enough, with just enough space in between to prevent them from becoming rhythmically accustomed to it. Chadrik pulled out his satchel of sitters and offered one to Jahzara and Zaki, closing it abruptly when Vik leaned toward him. Josanna spit on the ground between them and they were able to light their smokes before the fire went out. Chadrik sucked in a deep breath and exhaled in Vik's face.

"I did not think it mattered," Vik repeated himself.

"You're right. What difference could there be between a Thesmekka...and a kitchen counter? You know, I've been upset for nothing."

Vik sighed loudly and threw up his hands.

"So fluky, why didn't I acertane the eventable..."

"Chadrik, you'll simmer down once you've settled your addiction," said Josanna, with unusual calm. "Zaki...Zaki, listen, I'm asking you something."

"We're not unwaken yet, unwoken, unwaking...woken..."

"Zaki, stop it," she gently grabbed his arm. The touch was enough to snap him out of it, "How often do your people come through this gateway?"

"Oh, I bet I was the last one," Zaki pondered, "I'd say about a year ago. Maybe."

A collection of different groans filled the empty air. All sound bounced off the cave walls like they were excited to play even for just a little bit. Zaki held his hands up to Uther and they started playing a clapping game. It started off slow, but sped up so fast they had to keep starting over when Uther's hands fumbled, slapping against themselves.

They took turns attempting to break down the barrier. Uther swung his arms like a battering ram against the locked gateway for several minutes before he had to quit. He held his back and hobbled a few steps away, flopping down on the slimy, grooved floor. Josanna turned the orb around in her hand, leaning against the cave wall and staring at the light it weakly reflected.

"What were we thinking?"

"I know, we didn't know him. I confused his eagerness with competence."

Josanna let her hands fall into her lap, one leg stretched out and the other curled up, "Would you shut up already? That's not what I'm talking about."

"That's a surprising change," Vik sighed, taking his hand away from his face.

"You're not the only one who sets fire to stone," she said, slumping even more, "None of us would even be here if I hadn't made a huge mistake, too."

"I don't think getting caught in Imperyo was as bad as this," said Chadrik.

"It wasn't that. This was back when I was twelve. We'd been living in Threshold for a couple of years and I thought I was doing the right thing, by stopping my father from making a bad decision. I wanted to help my father get back on Durako's good side. I trusted Durako because my father used to be his friend, but I didn't know anything. I didn't know the divide moving out to Threshold had caused between them. I'm the one who betrayed him. I'm the one who told Durako what he was planning to do...and, I had to watch him burn for it."

"I didn't know it was you," Chadrik said somberly.

"I've been trying to make it up to him ever since, but I just keep failing in every way. Here we are, at this doorway I never thought I'd see and we're going to die because I couldn't get the job done right. We could have both orbs right now if I hadn't thrown dirt on our plans. I don't blame you for choosing the wrong orb, Vik, I just wish you would've told us."

"I'm sorry," he said again, his most believable version yet. He looked to Chadrik, "I really am."

"I know," Chadrik sighed, closing his eyes, "What are we going to do?"

"We can't sit here forever," Josanna agreed. "But we can't go back. Even if we make it passed the giants, through the marshes and forest again, we'd just end up at Threshold and they would kill us on sight."

"We knew there was no turning back when we set out," Chadrik reminded her.

"I know, but now here we are."

"We're not going to die. Not here, not at Threshold or Imperyo," Vik said, shaking his head and rising to his feet. He snatched the orb from Josanna, "My brother and his boy are gonna die if we don't figure this out. I'm going to find another way out of here."

He started marching in the direction they came from when there was a deafening creak and Zaki started shouting. He whipped around and saw light streaming in from the middle of the gateway as it peeled open, grating rock against rusty metal. The mechanism unstuck and the doors abruptly parted open, splashing them with blinding white sunlight. They drew back, wincing and covering their faces from the direct light with their arms, unable to see what Vik could see at his better angle. There was a boy peering in at them, teetering on the edge of fleeing.

Diving forward, Vik threw himself through the opening doorway moments before it snapped back shut as the young man flipped another switch and mashed the button above it, just a few seconds too late. Rolling to his feet, Vik towered above the startled kid who'd opened the gateway. Only a few years older than Zaki, the boy was a Rider for certain. He was wearing the same pair of thick goggles that Zaki had lost in the forest.

"Wh, what are you doing here?" the boy said in a quivering voice.

"Trying to get through that gateway, so thanks."

"No, go back through. You can't be here," he used his heels and elbows to drag himself back.

"I just need you to open that gateway back up," Vik assured him. "We've been looking for you guys."

The boy was terrified. His eyes wide behind his thick goggles, shallow breathing, all signs leading away from his next series of reactions. Launching himself up off the ground without warning, the boy roared, tackling Vik to the ground. He reached forward and put his hand on Vik's forehead, but he slapped it away in time. Scrambling to his feet, Vik felt blindly in front of him, swinging his arms wildly around until the black smoke over his vision rolled away. He gasped, honing in on the twitchy little guy.

"Who are you?" the boy demanded.

"You first," Vik wheezed.

"Phrixanian Amanaki."

"Vik."

Phrixanian tore a bone sword out of the sheath hanging from his belt and aimed it at Vik like he'd trained to use it.

"Come on, Phrix, let's just talk."

The boy yelled, running at him with both hands on the hilt. Vik caught his arms, shouting as he struggled against the surprisingly strong teenager. Phrix kicked his shin and Vik almost lost his grip. The boy did it again and again, each time Vik struggling to hold on. He threw his head forward and busted Phrix's nose with the top of his thick skull. Dropping the sword, the boy stumbled back and held his arms out from his sides, avoiding his own blood like it was going to burn him. He started sobbing, but Vik was too busy comforting his forehead and picking up the blade to care.

"I just wanted to talk," Vik said, holding the sword less gracefully than his opponent had.

Phrix just yelled in response, glancing up at Vik. He was completely unable to do anything but hunch and avoid getting his own blood on his body. Some of it got in his mouth and he started spitting compulsively.

"Alright, sit down," Vik said, motioning with the sword. "Tell me how to open the gateway."

"No," Phrix said in a nasally voice.

"If you don't, I'll kill you," he said, like he was threatening to ground him instead.

"Good, I wan' you deu."

"I will do it."

"You won' open deh gade-way."

Vik threw his arms down and rolled his eyes, "For the love of…"

*****

The New Ones were slowly getting used to hearing other Sinovians refer to them as Seers, even if Tayna was the only one with the true gift. At least, the only one using it. Most of them were just glad "Seer" was the nickname that stuck. After weeks of perpetual sunburns, many of them dreaded the names they heard circulating in the tavern and in passing on the streets latching onto them instead.

Zaruko, Gamba and a few more Impery helped the Seers establish themselves in their corner of Threshold. They built up their hovels into real homes, made beds to sleep in and tables to eat on. Most of the time, Tayna would bring Garek out so his father could see him on the days he didn't work in the fields. The marked girls didn't stop her. They didn't want anything to do with her.

"If you don't stop this dangerous nonsense, we're going to let her know what' you're doing," Oksana had warned her.

"Good, let her know I hope she chokes on her own smoke, too," was Tayna's reply.

280

After that, the marked girls decided it'd be best to just cut ties.

"Where's Garek?" Marek asked idly, seeing Tayna approaching from the road to the nursery.

"He's safer back there for now."

"It's pretty hot today," Marek said, sneering at the sun.

"We're going to get attacked," she said, holding her arms close to herself, remaining uncomfortably calm.

"How soon?"

"You should get everyone ready."

A rush of energy came over him. He snapped up straight and called out to everyone with one hand cupped around his mouth, shouting the word "incoming". People dropped what they were doing, recognizing the warning they were told to listen for, and came running out to find Marek.

"What's going on?" Zaruko asked, gathering his own people up with them.

"The drass are coming."

Zaruko hesitated, waiting for him to say something more, but he didn't. "Then we need to get everyone as close to Imperyo as we can."

"No," Marek said firmly, "We cannot run to them."

"Marek," Zaruko said, leaning down with his hand on his shoulder, "This isn't an experiment. People are going to die."

A warble echoed out over the homes and the ripple of screaming broke out along the main street, scattering the market circle like marbles spilling from the top of a hill. Sera tore out of her home with Nikiva on her heels. She caught her sister and spun her around.

"What are you doing?" Nikiva shouted.

"I'm going where it's safe!"

"We're safe here."

Sera scoffed, repulsed by her suggestion. She shoved Nikiva away and ran as fast as she could toward the cave entrance, the rest of Threshold struggling to catch up. Nikiva stayed with the Seers, hoping their success would kindle Sera's faith in them for the next time.

There was an empty space between the Seer's neighborhood and the wooden platform under the black mountain's balcony. No one ever walked over that area. All the roads gave it a generously wide berth. Prior to the drass attack, the New Ones got their hands on sacks and sacks of sap, spreading it over the ground around that area over several days.

Waves of drass honed in, focused on the smell of fresh sap laid out like a sweet reward for their invasion. The Seers scrambled to uncover their hidden stashes while the beasts were conflicted and distracted. A long, narrow crate buried up against the side of each home held numerous spears, constructed in just a few days by the ones who stayed inside, away from the prying eyes of any passing Impery. The smithy could never have supplied them all in time, nor could they afford it.

"Stay here," Marek ordered Zaruko.

He dashed for the wooden platform and a number of his people followed him, pre-selected before that day. They tucked their sharpened sticks up into their sides, picked up their feet, and tore across the dirt and gravel. Zaruko shouted for him, but Marek didn't stop. The disoriented Impery leader exchanged a glance with Gamba and they spread their people out around the Seers. Each one of them was armed with an iron knife, hidden in different places on their each of their bodies.

Tayna cautiously scooped up the two covered bowls tucked under the platform supports. The drass were ripping up the tufts of grass and graveled dirt with their curved talons, barreling toward them at an alarming rate. Most of the people from the market circle were able to escape the drass' attention due to the fast-spreading, far-reaching aroma. The other Sinovians watched as the New Ones seemed to be sacrificing themselves, luring the drass straight to them as they gathered on the platform, quickly being surrounded by the vicious lizards. They licked and pawed at the ground with all four of their front limbs, snarling and emitting chuffing noises, confused by the intense scent on an unfamiliar surface, just as Marek had suspected.

He wrung the spear he was holding, nodding once to Tayna. She crept forward, flinching every time one of the drass jerked its head up or lurched unexpectedly. They may have been blind, but she could see them all too well.

"What is she doing?" Zaruko growled, drawing Gamba's attention toward her as well.

Close enough to reach out and touch, she extended her arm and poured the contents of the first bowl on top of the sappy dirt. Three of them reacted to the splatter, charging toward it and snorting at the air around her. One of them got close enough to blow bursts of air on her face as it sniffed with both sets of nostrils. She took a deep, shaky breath and threw the second bowl's contents on the ground beside the beast. The two chemicals reacted and a short-lived fire danced up before fizzling out. Tayna couldn't breathe. The potent sap must have sunk in too deeply. The drass angled its straight claws at her and was about to strike when the ground exploded in a flash fire, spreading outward from the chemically burned dirt. The drass hissed and garbled, flailing and turning tail or diving at them on the platform.

Tayna fell backward and covered her face, but Marek stabbed the creature in the neck before it could pounce on her. He roared, pushing it forward with all his might, but it took the force of another spear to knock it back. The Seers on the platform cried out and charged at the drass, skewering a couple, but scaring away the bulk of the beasts. Many remaining drass charged at the New Ones gathered in front of their partially constructed neighborhood. Women, children, and some of the men gathered, all standing terrified with their pointed sticks, but braced to face them. Zaruko steeled himself to pour flames on the beasts, but nearly jumped out of his skin when screaming erupted from behind him. Blood-curling, heart-stopping shrieks. He half-expected there to be tallbugs in Threshold. The drass acted like they'd been struck dizzy and the Seers around Zaruko charged in during their distraction. They flew passed the stunned Impery and attacked the drass with wild jabs and stabs.

It only took a few minutes, but the drass wanted nothing more to do with the sweet smelling area. In their heavy reliance on sound and natural fear of whistlers, the screaming had alarmed and confused them more than any show of force could have. They scrambled like away like cowards caught stealing, throwing their massive bodies over the broken part of the enormous wall on the side closest to them. The Seers cheered and cried and couldn't believe they did what they did.

Neither could anyone else.

The Sinovians that had been gathered in front of Imperyo's entrance poured over to their side of Threshold, expressing their gratitude and wanting to know how they knew to do that. Most of them wanting a more complex answer than what the Seers were giving them. Tayna was shaking, sitting on the edge of the platform, feeling sick and elated at the same time. Marek kissed her forehead and squeezed her tight, congratulating her on doing something so difficult.

"You need to find somebody a lot crazier than me," she said, her voice quivering, "I don't think I can do that again."

Marek laughed and squeezed her tight again, "I'll get to work on that."

"You do that," she said, trying to laugh, but it came out as half-crying too.

"Marek," said Reeta, surrounded by her own people. Ridiak was among them, "I'm really surprised."

"Good. Maybe you'll put some faith in us now," he wanted to accuse her of treachery then and there, but there was a rare victory in the air. He didn't want to spoil it.

"This changes things for us," she said. "I'd like to be involved again. Once we find a safe place, of course," she looked around warily, putting one hand on Ridiak's shoulder.

"I'd like that too," Marek said, attempting a neutral tone.

Nikiva ran up to Sera. She was far behind all the others, dragging her feet, looking displeased despite their victory.

"It's all going to be alright, we can take care of ourselves now," Nikiva celebrated, hugging her sister around the neck.

Sera pulled back, "Luck, Nikki, that's all that was. That's all that was."

"Why can't you believe in us?" Nikiva asked, her smile slinking off her face.

"Because I'm not stupid," she sneered, going around her with her arms tucked into her chest.

Ziven saw her heading for her house and straight-lined to her, kissing her square on the lips. She looked like she wanted to slap him, but she just laughed instead, tears rolling down her cheeks. Ziven put his arm around her and helped her into her house.

"She'll come around," said Savan, standing near enough to Nikiva for her to hear him.

"What a rush! What a fight!" exclaimed Shurik, holding a blood-tipped spear.

"That is monster blood on there, isn't it?" asked Nikiva.

"Don't give me sass," he grumbled. "Let me tell you how it went."

"It just happened," said Savan. "We were all here."

"You weren't where I was, not when I fought off six drass with this here pointed stick."

Unfortunately for Savan and Nikiva, many other Sinovians wanted to hear a thorough recounting of the tale from his angle and flocked to gather in front of him. The two suffered through increasingly exaggerated tales of impossibly carried out heroics by the elderly storyteller himself, using the spear as proof when someone cast a doubtful word.

*****

That night, the rain rolled in to clean up their mess. Tayna saw it coming without visions and tried to fall asleep before the storm could mess with her head. With the gently creaking fans overhead, the snoring and sleepy breathing in the room, the rain beginning to pitter on the roof, and the exhaustion from the day, she had little trouble drifting off to sleep. The other girls in the room were the only ones in Threshold who didn't know about what had happened and she preferred to keep it that way. Tayna was sure they would only see their victory as something to fear retribution from.

Tayna flinched herself awake in the middle of the night, startled by the crackle of the unexpected storm. Lightning burst frequently enough to keep her consistently alert. The storm carried on and the infants screamed all night. Tayna was exhausted, Illa and Beka were relentless, but Gerta slept stubbornly in the corner.

"Let them cry it out," she'd say angrily, "I'll be rested for when they actually need me."

It was just hours from dawn when Gerta had given up. Tayna's eyes were growing heavy as she cradled one of the other infants she'd named Naya. Garek was undisturbed by the ruckus for the most part, but he certainly wasn't getting a restful sleep. He'd be tired all day. Tayna smiled at the thought. She looked down at Naya whose face was all scrunched up, but she'd given up screaming nonstop and resorted to only crying out when the thunder rolled, rumbling their insides.

The door swung open and flung rainwater everywhere. Tayna flinched away and stood up to put Naya back in her crib. Nothing good could come of a visitor at this hour, in this weather.

"Where's the Seer?"

Tayna's breath left her and she couldn't regain it fast enough to answer. None of the other girls moved aside from the flinching when he shouted his question again.

"I'm her," Tayna said quietly.

She tried to look him in the eyes but she couldn't see them, even after the lightning flashed in through the narrow windows. He was armed with an axe and she'd seen him before, in Jahzara's company. He immediately marched forward, furiously snatched her arm and dragged her out of the nursery. She could hear Beka screaming behind her and wished she would be quiet, but one of the men waiting outside went in after they left and the screaming stopped. Tayna tried to demand an explanation, but her captor struck her hard in the face with the back of his hand. At first it was only silence but then the ringing began and then the stinging pain. He'd slapped her good side, so she could fully feel it. There was a burning pop in her neck from the strain put on it all at once. The man leaned forward and pointed into her face, rain continuing to pour over them all.

"No speaking," he said.

They steered her through the mud, holding the back of her neck and driving her forward at a pace just a little too fast. Her feet stuck in the sloppy muck over and over, but they harshly shoved her loose each time she stumbled. They led her passed the stairs leading into Imperyo, continuing to follow the mountain around to the weak gateway that blocked off the backside. She looked around, back at the stairway as best she could before they snapped her head forward again.

Once they crossed through the gate, she had stepped over the point no one dared to cross. They passed the farthest point she could see from anywhere in Threshold. It was so dark on the other side, but the mountain was always the only thing blacker than the night. Her captors hands continuously slipped off her soaking wet skin, grabbing her neck and arms again, each time harder than the last. Seeing nothing but the distant metal wall and the void of the mountain, Tayna shivered from the cold, but she was trembling too. They hadn't even noticed how hard she had been struggling against them throughout the ominous walk.

No one was behind them, no one was in front of them. There was nothing around except the back of the mountain.

The Impery finally stopped marching and pushed her down. A rock banged against her knee before it sunk into the mud just a little. She tried to look up, but the Impery guard just pushed her head back down. It was impossible to hear anything, the rain was so furious and the lightning cracked out across the sky so hard it felt as though it physically touched her with every strike. Visions flickered in and out of view, spackling the real world with delusions, turning her stomach and spinning her thoughts in frantic circles. She never heard the lighter footsteps approach and settle in front of her. They were feet smaller than Jahzara's, but quickly disappeared, sinking into the mud. Her pale legs stood firm and as Tayna carefully, slowly traced her way up the dainty figure, she saw how confident they were, how certain of what actions they were about to take. Until she got to their face and saw Sera's wide, terrified eyes and the axe above her head. She couldn't believe she was able to hold it that high for that long. Sera looked like a statue, petrified at the exact moment of her greatest trial.

"Hurry up," the guard barked out.

"Don't watch," Sera voice rang out like a scream.

"We will not turn away."

"Sera—"

"Don't speak to me!" She shrieked furiously.

Sera swung the axe down, only hitting Tayna with the air being pushed by the iron edge. It planted firmly into the mud just between

Tayna's knees. If she had not been looking up, she may not have leaned back in time to avoid it planting firmly into her skull.

Tayna flailed and squirmed in her most desperate attempt to get away, but the guard held her down with little effort, punched her in the stomach and pulled her back by the top of her hair. She met Sera eye to eye as she tried to dislodge the axe from the mud. The rain couldn't hide the redness of her eyes. Sera finally managed to rip the axe up out of the ground and bring it over her shoulder. She pulled the corners of her lips down at the ends and prepared to scream as she brought the axe over her shoulder.

Her whole body jerked back with unnatural force and the axe once again missed its mark, landing in the soggy dirt just in front of her with a sloppy, mud-splattering thunk. A thick arrow had slammed her hard to the ground. The guards turned around just in time to meet the spears of Zaruko's warriors. They charged in, lighter without their armor and overpowered them despite their lesser numbers. Tayna was unwittingly kicked forward as the Impery who took her tried to protect himself. She looked up from the mud and saw Sera gasping and holding the arrow with one hand. Tayna crawled over to her and looked over the wound.

"I didn't want to," she cried. "I didn't want to do it."

"But you were going to…"

"I had to."

Tayna closed her eyes and blocked out the sounds of axes and swords behind her, "It's alright…"

"Reeta—" was all she could say before she began choking on her own blood.

Tayna leaned forward, "Reeta? What do you mean? Sera, what did you mean?"

She shook her shoulders, but Sera was gone. Her perfect, pale skin repelled the rain like she was made of porcelain. Her eyes remained staring at the back of Imperyo, longing to be looking out from the inside. Zaruko grabbed Tayna and lifted her to her feet. Silently, he and the others led her around the rest of the mountain, not going back the way they came. Directly behind the entrance to Imperyo was a stone slab raised above the ground, but they ran by it so fast she couldn't see what it was for. As they ran, Tayna couldn't process what had almost happened to her. Her mind was too preoccupied with Sera's face and what her last words had been. She didn't want to kill Tayna, but she was going to, with the help of Impery guards…and Reeta? Was Reeta next? Tayna had to warn her, if it wasn't already too late.

Zaruko didn't stop at the nursery, he didn't even get close to it. He ran through the Seer's neighborhood, the Brutemen's street and rounded the side of the smithy's house. His arms pressed her into his chest and Tayna held onto him tightly in return. She prayed they weren't going to go through the front gate. She wanted to stay in Threshold, she wanted to be somewhere warm and safe.

Zaruko reached out with one hand, balancing Tayna in his arms as he opened his front door. He scuttled in sideways, set her down and slammed the door shut behind her. His head thumped against the door and they waited quietly. Tayna was afraid to breathe too loudly.

There was a faint knock at the door. Two slaps and two knuckled knocks. Zaruko flung the door open and stepped outside. She could hear Gamba's voice, low and steady but the rain masked his words. The room was mostly empty, a table, some chairs and a ripped up couch being the only furniture in sight. A single, weable-fat candle stood on its spindly leg, balancing on the table high enough to bring a dim glow to the rest of the room. Lightning flashed and Tayna felt like she'd been slapped in the face again. Her eyes almost rolled back, but she fought the fit away, breathing steadily and focusing on a spot on the wall. Zaruko came back in, soaking wet and still panting heavily.

Hovering in the doorway, water pouring off his clothes and pooling up on the floor around his feet, he struggled to find the right words. The only thing that came out of his mouth was the sound he made breathing. She waited patiently, pausing only long enough to realize she should help him dry off.

"Here," Tayna whispered.

When she reached out to grab his sleeve, he seized her wrist and pulled her toward him. He caught her lips with his and ran one hand up the back of her hair, pushing the two of them into each other. Their sopping shirts clung together. They were so cold they shivered each time they inhaled. Stripping off their clothes made them warmer and they fell onto the couch, the steam from their intertwined bodies heating the empty room.

# CHAPTER TWENTY

Tayna woke first. The sun was still just a thought in the sky when she opened her dark eyes. Zaruko slept with his mouth half open, embedded in a coarse pillow and she tried not to laugh at the sight, but it slipped out. At once, he opened his eyes and blinked several times. She could see the realization hitting him of where he was and what had happened. He quickly closed his mouth and smiled back at her. Tracing up and down her arm, he delicately let his fingers touch her. Seeing her skin next to his, she suddenly very aware of how different they looked. Facing each other, just a breath apart, they stayed in Zaruko's bed of pillows and tangled blankets. They hadn't said a word to each other since Tayna tried to help him dry off in the doorway the night before.

"I wasn't planning on this," he said quietly.

"You were hoping for it," she teased him.

"Of course," he laughed, brushing her hair away from her imperfect face, "But I meant, I wasn't going to try to make a family for myself out here. It's too dangerous, what I'm doing, where I am. I thought the fire was the only way to truly be safe out here."

"Until yesterday," Tayna guessed in a hushed voice.

"I can't get the Sinovians to work together like you and Marek can. I don't think Nattina can get her own people to cooperate that well. We weren't even needed."

"Of course you were, I had the bowls you gave me…"

"I'm glad you didn't need us."

"*They* didn't need you," Tayna corrected, allowing herself to put her hand on his face, cradling his strong jaw and feeling the rough stubble under her fingertips.

It was strange, touching each other so intimately. But they'd both secretly desired the intimacy for so long, it was like a sweet treat they hadn't pay for.

"All I've ever wanted was to be outside, away from Imperyo. Working with my hands, with my family. I don't care about the fire or the Watcher, Thesmekka, any of that," Zaruko took a deep breath and looked into her eyes, "I don't even want to lead everyone. I just want to be safe and happy, outside the mountain. With you."

Tayna's hand trembled and he put his over it, pressing her hand against his face.

"I know what you've been worried about," Zaruko whispered.

"What do you mean?" she asked, blinking away the wet burning in her eyes.

"You're not as good a liar as you think," he flashed his smile, "Even if I die, we'll have this last night with us forever."

"Run. Into the woods," she quietly begged him, "Just stay there until it's all over."

"Maybe I die there," he said calmly. "Does my living or not change the way the future plays out?"

Tayna couldn't answer him. She didn't want to answer him. Nothing felt right now that these visions were running so deeply through her desires, conflicting with the nature of what she assumed them to be. They should guide him away from danger, but bring them all the safety and peace that they need. It was all wrong, twisted, muddled up in the way it was all to play out, but there was no time for another meditation. It was too late to alter what must be done.

He leaned forward and kissed her scars, but she couldn't feel it.

*****

The other side of the long-spanning mountain range was a new world entirely. With sparse, spread out tufts of grass and boulders breaking up the vast, expansive stretch of dry land, Vik let himself look away from his ward just long enough to see as far as he could see. It was something he thoroughly enjoyed. He couldn't get enough of it. Vik pulled the goggles off the boy's head and slapped the side of Phrix's face until he woke up.

"You don't get to sleep until you open that gateway."

"Gimme those back."

"Nope."

"I'm tired…" Phrix groaned, noticing the color of the sky.

Vik still held the sword. He had to use it six times that night trying to keep Phrix from taking off. It would've been a lot more helpful if he could've seen in the dark too, but his eyes adjusted well enough. Both moons would normally have been plenty to light the area, but they were too obscured by clouds and a nearby storm skirting the valley.

"So am I, but we don't get to sleep until you give me the code."

"Can I have something to eat?"

"No!" Vik's own stomach gurgled. The hunger was starting to affect his mood, "How are you not understanding this?"

"But I'm hungry…"

"All our food is on the other side of that gate."

"Then what's that?" Phrix asked, motioning toward the orb in Vik's pouch.

"This isn't food," Vik said, pulling the orb out and holding it in front of his own face, keeping it at a safe distance from the crazed teenager.

"Why don't you want to help me?"

"I am helping you," Phrix confessed, "By not helping you, this is the best way I can think of. According to my father, not helping is helping and not interfering is directly effective."

Vik rolled his eyes. All night he'd had to listen to this kid's psychobabble. Luckily, there didn't seem to be any immediate danger in the area, not at night anyway. But as the sun rose, the distant cry of whistlers put him on edge and made matters even more urgent.

The ground was sparsely tufted with grass and short plants. For as far as Vik could see, there didn't seem to be any great, tall trees, just normal-looking ones jutting up here and there. Mountains divided the valley thoroughly, creating a wall of steep drop-offs high enough to fall from and have plenty of time to recite their alphabet.

"That's shiny…" said Phrix, absentmindedly staring at the pearl with his head tilted.

"I was supposed to give it to Roque," Vik said, unsure of whether it was the full truth.

"What did you say?" Phrix gasped, sitting up straight.

"Roque, I'm supposed to give this to him."

"What is it?"

"A Thesmekkian—"

"Oh!" Phrix shouted, spinning around to face the combination on the gateway. He rambled on as he mashed buttons, "Oh, he's going to want that. I had no idea, none, zero. That was totally, not expected, at all. Wow, just, so, great. Better than slother caps. Better than poisoning old lady Domitia. Twenty-six and a half times better."

The gateway whirred open like an automatic door, but with a lot more screeching, grinding metal. Vik hurriedly motioned to the others and they dove through the doorway, one right after the other. When Zaki hopped out, he and Phrix glared at one another, refusing to speak.

"What in the hell, Vik?" Josanna gasped, glaring at Phrix while she said it.

"Please, get me something to eat."

"Me too," Phrix said eagerly, forgetting his staring battle with Zaki.

"No, not until somebody tells me what's going on," Josanna said, holding the pack with the food in it far away from the both of them. "We nearly froze to death in there."

"You look fine," Vik said, confused.

"We…did what we had to do," Chadrik sighed, glancing awkwardly at Uther.

Phrix didn't seem surprised by the giant. In fact, he barely noticed him at all. Vik filled them in on what seemed to be the case: that kid was a Rider and wants them to take their "gift" to Roque as soon as possible.

"I'll take you there," he offered.

"They already have a guide," Zaki snapped.

"Like you could just walk back in."

"What are *you* doing out here then?"

"I was out for some slother caps," Phrix explained, "Old lady Domitia…"

"She's still alive?"

"I was trying to fix that. Now I think I'll come with you."

"Why?" asked Zaki.

"Because. You're taking that orb to Roque and I want credit for finding it," they glared at him, "Finding you all, with it. I'm not going to try and take it. I don't do things like that."

Vik was so exasperated with the ridiculous boy that by that point, he didn't even care. Josanna gave him a quarter of a bloodstone and he crunched into it as they marched into the drylands.

*****

The wooden platform beneath the Imperyon balcony was surrounded by a splotchy ring of short grass burnt down to the nubs. All the drass that were killed had been taken apart by the Seers, with Jawny guidance. They didn't do it for free of course, but the Seers had more to trade with than most had ever had at once. Marek met with the other leaders on the platform, unafraid of being overheard. Their spy was gone and they knew that for a short time at least, they'd be without a traitor. The balcony was too high above to worry about being eavesdropped on and they could see everyone around clearly. No one was sneaking up on them.

292

Marek noticed Zaruko and Tayna were sitting unusually close together and they smiled every time their eyes met.

"So what happened last night?" Marek asked.

Tayna froze, but Zaruko started speaking first, "Our spy found out about Tayna's unique sort of assistance. I'm not sure when she knew for certain or why she didn't make a move like that sooner, but it's been taken care of."

"Right," Tayna breathed.

"I've been thinking, with this latest accomplishment, maybe we shouldn't be waiting for the Riders or Thesmekkian weapons to help us."

"What do you mean?" Reeta snapped.

"Waiting around to be saved by either sounds a lot like what we do with the Impery already," Nattina droned. "It will only lead to the same unhealthy reliance."

"The Riders are the most capable of—"

"They're exactly the kind of people we don't want in charge," Zaruko interrupted Reeta. "You think the Impery are bad, with Riders you won't even have a choice. And even if you did, acting like it would get you killed, acting too obedient would get you killed, they're completely unstable. If we could keep them away entirely, I think we would get out of this without any major downsides."

"They wouldn't be in charge of anything," Reeta corrected.

"You're right, and they won't want anything in return for saving us either. From the stories I've heard, they seem so noble," said Zaruko sarcastically. "I believe we can take this on ourselves, with just a little planning ahead. Especially now that they're blind to us."

"Why did we agree to go seek them out in the first place, if you were so against their help?"

"There weren't a lot of other options."

"What did you have in mind?" Nattina asked.

"The same man who came up with our Rider plan came up with a backup. An idea I thought was too unnecessary and ridiculous at the time."

"Let me guess, you're going to get one of us to do your dirty work for you and charge in at the end," Reeta said.

"Someone else will take care of Durako, if that's what you mean," said Zaruko quietly, standing up straighter and glancing around. No one else outside of the meeting was paying them any lasting attention, "Whatever else he may be, he is still my father. I think you should be more concerned if I were wanting to be the one to do it."

Before anything more could be said, Nikiva came jogging up to the platform. She was flustered and completely out of breath.

"Tayna, where's Sera? Someone said there was a fight last night, but no one knows what happened."

Tayna couldn't look at her. Marek hopped up and tried to put his arm around her, but she knew what that meant. She pushed him away.

"No," she whimpered, "What happened?"

Gamba excused himself from the meeting and went to her side. He pointed to the other side of the stairway leading up the ramp and they started marching that way.

"They might not know what's happened yet," Gamba said hopefully, knowing that was unlikely. "The bodies could still be there."

"Sera couldn't do anything like that," Nikiva explained as they hurried along.

She knew she could wish it, maybe even orchestrate it, but there was no way Sera was just going to take a matter into her own hands like that. And the Impery guards, that didn't make any sense. Sera wanted safety and luxury, that's all she ever wanted. That's all she ever complained about. She was dainty and snobbish, but she'd never been desperate. She was always above that. Nikiva started to worry that the more she rationalized against it in her head, the more she began to believe it could've happen. Sera couldn't let go of the old life.

Whistlers called out in the distance, avoiding the smoky mountaintop as best they could. Nikiva thought about how she'd be in the fields right now if she hadn't been looking for Sera. Her sister got out of working in the dirt only to accidentally find herself hauling piss to the walls. At the end of every day, Nikiva would come back to the house and find Sera just after she'd been crying. She never said anything to her about it. She knew how her sister hated to be caught in undignified situations. Crying and smelling of urine most certainly qualified. The last several days she had seemed better, didn't smell, wasn't crying. She had thought her sister was adjusting.

Nikiva could see the Impery gathered ahead. A mass of auburn hair and tanned skin. She was surprised to notice she could tell which Impery lived outside and which lived inside the mountain based solely on the difference in their skin tone. "Grays and Uppers all over again", she thought. Many Impery men lay dead and already rotting around Sera's small body, an axe planted in the dirt just beside her. A short line of Impery guards separated her from her sister.

"Let me see her."

"Get out of here," the guard barked, glaring at Gamba.

"That's my sister. You will let me see her."

The guard shoved Nikiva back and ordered her to leave.

"This is your last warning."

Behind them, Nikiva saw Jahzara standing over Sera's body. She was watching the interaction with interest, smiling wider when she saw Nikiva look over. After she was certain she had the sister's attention, she spit on the body, lighting it on fire. Nikiva screamed at her, cursing and flailing to try and get passed the guards, but Gamba grabbed her and pulled her back. She slumped to her knees with him and watched the flames as best she could through the legs of the guards. She could see Jahzara's own legs carrying her over to the axe and watched as she pulled it out of the ground. Nikiva's whole body jerked and she slammed her eyes shut as Jahzara swung the axe down on Sera's body. She held her face with her hand, breathing heavily, fighting the nausea and shaking her head. Footsteps drew nearer, as did the smell of burning hair and flesh. Jahzara parted the line of guards and stood over the grieving sister before tossing the severed head at her, hitting her in the chest with it. Nikiva screamed and scrambled back.

"For your bone collector."

As Jahzara paraded by, heading back into Imperyo, Nikiva quivered in hysterics on the ground. She couldn't stop looking at the severed head. Sera's once beautiful face so disfigured and lifeless.

"Nikiva!" Gamba said for the fourth time.

She finally acknowledged him when he roughly turned her toward him. Gamba wasn't going to hurt her, but she hid her face anyway. Nothing made any sense. She kept waiting for it all to change again, but it was still that horrible reality. A random draw from a hat that couldn't be put back.

"Go home."

"I can't," she gasped, her eyes wide and senseless. "I can't go, I can't..."

"I'll take care of everything," he said firmly.

"I can't go."

"Nikki, I'm going to take care of this. Go. Home."

She blinked a few more times, balled up on the ground with her hands protecting her face. She nodded, put herself into a state of denial, and carried herself away. Wrapping her arms tightly around her chest, she checked out of reality until she reached her hovel. Even then, no one could reach her for the rest of the day. She didn't even run a sharp rock over her hands. Every moment of their lives together played out well into the night, but the signs weren't there. She kept telling herself she should've been looking harder, she should've asked to help, talked to her, something. Now she'd never talk to her again and she couldn't help but feel like it was all her fault.

*****

On the rippling, rounded hills not too far from Vik and the other travelers, a small pack of curious beasts trailed alongside them. They stayed just out of their direct line of sight, but never out of view. Playfully weaving along, tackling each other while taking turns for one to always watch for the group, they did their best to seem less like a threat, but they were still animals. The intent of their presence was obvious.

"We're being followed," Vik grumbled, glancing up at the hillside.

"I don't see anything," Phrix said.

"They follow you, then they eat you," said Zaki, scoffing. "Don't trust him."

"We're not going to, Zaki," Vik assured him for the hundredth time.

The land was uncertain of itself on the other side of the mountain range. The jungle had been flat for the most part, with the trees shaping the terrain. Roots coming out of the ground, shooting up into the sky, but out there, the ground shaped itself. There were thin wisps of curled rocks that came up in rows, like a rib cage outlining where different Brutes fell. Tufts of grass grew in the shade, but it was all crispy enough to crunch when they stepped on it. From time to time, they would see a stick protruding out of the ground, placed there by someone or something, with a skull on top, laced to other poles by twine.

"They're markers, for the unwaking," Zaki told them.

"Are we close?" asked Josanna eagerly.

"No."

They were well into the afternoon when they saw a gargantuan black rock in the distance. They thought it was a giant tallbug, but it wasn't moving.

"That's where we're headed," Zaki told them.

"We're going to stop at the oasis?" Phrix complained, "What a waste of time."

"I have to agree," said Chadrik, "We don't need to stop."

"I told you to stop speaking for everyone," Josanna wheezed.

"So now you want to stop?"

"I *need* to stop."

296

"We have to figure out what to do about the stalkers," Zaki explained, motioning to the hillside.

Vik was shocked to see them still on their trail. In their distraction, observing their observers in the distance, they nearly stumbled upon a great, slumbering beast on the other side of a rib-like, rocky overhang. It was covered in tough, brown skin and had a ridge of dull spines going from its neck to the end of its tail on either side of its high-set spine. The top of its colossal, misshapen head was a bright green that faded out as it spilled over its back and instead of claws or paws, it had split hooves half the size of a room. Each nostril of the beast was as tall as Chadrik and as wide as his arm length.

Zaki and Phrix didn't stop.

"Look out!" Vik hissed, pointing at the beast.

"It's alright," Zaki assured them, "It's just a great walker. They don't bother us and we don't bother them."

Vik, Uther, Josanna, and Chadrik watched the two children stroll passed the beast's face, close enough that it could stretch out and snap them up without needing to stand. They thought about taking the long way around, avoiding the ribcage walkway entirely, but it was so hot outside. Each shady respite was its own tiny oasis.

Chadrik was the last one to gather up the courage to trot by the sleeping giant. Just as he scampered across the space in front of it, its eyes shot open and it snorted loud enough to briefly deafen Chadrik on the side that faced it. The air the beast ejected blew the Shiny off his feet and scared him half to death. He scrambled up and ran to the others at the other end of the partially covered trail. They were laughing at him and Josanna made sure to ask him how it felt, as a Shiny, to be pushed like that. He was still shaking and didn't want to joke about it.

After a couple more hours, they finally made it to the bizarre rock that hovered over the oasis. It was black and suspended on lighter, gangly spires made of a similar stone. Porous and cratered, the rock held a small lake's worth of water on top. It dripped down onto the fertile ground underneath, overgrown with grass and a couple of unidentified plants. Despite their brilliant colors, Vik decided not to touch them.

Josanna wandered to the side of the clear water, the main part of the oasis, and they all followed. Each one of them immersed in caution, eyes darting around the sky and mountaintops, the sprawling land and distant horizon. They saw their stalwart followers in the distance, the feline stalker pack prancing around the rippling hillsides. When they finally reached the transparent pond, they all dipped their hands into the chilly water and took sips, quickly stopping Zaki before he dunked his feet into their drinking water.

"Can I see that sketchbook in your bag, Uther?" asked Chadrik.

"No," Uther grunted immediately.

"Don't be embarrassed."

"No," Uther repeated menacingly.

Josanna walked Zaki to the other side of the pond and stood behind him, ordering him to clean himself off thoroughly. He shook his arms around in a chaotic circle underwater, using both hands to wipe the accumulated grime off. Vik saw Josanna making snide a comment just before Zaki pulled his arms out of the water and flicked his wrists at her, sprinkling her with contaminated water. She gasped, amused and indignant, then reached for him, barely missing as he rounded the side of the pond, making a beeline straight for the two guys before she could catch him.

"We're not going to save you!" Chadrik called out, waving his hand in front of him.

"No, get out of here," said Vik, pushing the small boy away by his forehead.

Josanna caught up to Zaki and lifted him off his feet with her arms under his, locking him in a careful, levitated headlock. He kicked and flailed, but Josanna just flung her upper body around, hurling him into the pond with a clumsy splash. She stood grinning manically over him, arms crossed and waiting for him to surface and surrender. He surfaced with an adrenaline-fueled squeal of laughter.

Chadrik started a game with them, telling them to jump as high as they could and he would blast them out into the water. Vik learned after scraping his bare back against the dry dirt not to stand anywhere near Chadrik unless getting pushed into the water. Phrix refused to join in on the game, repeating that it was a waste of time. In fact, he chanted that for so long, his words started to sound like one long hum in the background.

As they sputtered and laughed, splashing around in the cool oasis, Zaki shouted a surprising question over to Josanna.

"Do you have any kids?"

She nearly started sinking, forgetting to wave her arms around underwater, "No, I don't."

"Why not?"

Chadrik and Vik grimaced. Even Uther who was sitting in the shallow waters near the edge made a contorted face, preparing for the backlash. But it never came.

"I don't know, I've always been too busy to start a family I guess."

Chadrik whispered to Vik, "She scares everyone away."

"I'm worried about it being too dangerous right now anyway."

"I can protect myself," Zaki bragged.

"Yeah, you can," she said, "But not every kid is able to do what you can do."

"So you want a kid who can be normal?"

She shrugged, "Sure, I guess I do."

"I can be normal."

Everyone stopped messing around. Vik and Chadrik looked from Zaki to Josanna, but she didn't know what to say. He didn't seem to notice that he'd said anything unusual.

"We're not gonna leave you, Zaki," Josanna said after a long pause. "You're going to stay with us for as long as you want."

Without warning, Zaki's face scrunched up and he began speaking unintelligibly. Josanna grabbed his arm and drifted over to a place shallow enough for her to stand on. She wrapped her arms around him, resting her cheek on his head.

"It's okay," she repeated, "You're not getting left behind."

"Uther?" he sniffled, "He can stay too?"

Uther glanced up at them and they thought about that, all of them for the first time.

"Of course," Josanna said, unsure of whether or not it was true.

They might be accepting of the giant, but she found that unlikely. Even after everything they've been through, she still felt uneasy around him and made faces of subtle disgust at some of his idle mannerisms.

"Who's Uther?" asked Phrix, purposely avoiding the giant.

*****

The supply house was the third biggest structure in Threshold, the first two being the water towers. The outside storage area was sparsely stocked, but it held twice as much as the clay and wood warehouse contained inside. With the frequent drass attacks, their resources had dwindled significantly in lieu of the repairs and the fear of leaving Threshold's wall. It was only after the powerful show of unity from the Seers that Sinovians felt comfortable enough returning to their field and quarry jobs.

Zaruko and every last Impery warrior loyal to him hid in the warehouse, waiting for the others.

Gamba whispered to Zaruko, "They're late."

"We're early."

"No one else is early?"

"Stop it," Zaruko hissed, flinching at an innocent noise on the roof.

The time came and the time went that they were supposed to meet with the other leaders in preparation for the attack. It was the day they were going to take Durako out. Tayna said there was no Rider army coming, there was no guarantee that waiting on anyone to return was going to reward them with anything. So they waited there to meet up with the others, to prepare to storm Imperyo without warning, to blitz into them for minimal casualties. The Jawnies would distract on the bottom level, the Shinies would go ahead of them to push any opposition away, and they would deliver Zaruko straight to the manor, which he would burn down with the rest of his warriors. No hesitation for a quick usurping.

The only thing that gave him pause was murdering his own father. It might be while he slept, while he relaxed, or he might even escape at which point he would have to kill him with his hands. That was the worst scenario and the one he wanted to avoid at all costs.

Most the warriors in the room stared off into space, biting their nails or pacing uncontrollably. They heard the door creak and everyone jerked upright. Several of them filed in at once and Zaruko called out to them.

"Did you think we were meeting outside?"

"What took you so long?"

"Somebody's in trouble," Jahzara coyly sang, not yet visible around the materials in the warehouse.

Zaruko's blood froze, shooting sickening chills all over. They were trapped in the back of the warehouse, obscured by baskets, crates, piles of stone bricks, and warped wood. Jahzara marched around the corner of one such stack with two Impery muzzles dangling from her finger.

300

"What are you doing out here?" Zaruko demanded.

"Same to you."

"Why do you care?"

"Because you're out here planning to kill the Impery Lord. I can think of a few reasons to care."

"What are you talking about?"

"It's not what I was talking about, it's what you were talking about. In front of Gamba."

Gamba narrowed his eyes at her and smirked.

"In front of Gamba, your spy, is that it?" Zaruko mocked.

The two didn't need to look at each other to confirm what they already knew.

Gamba snarled, "You aren't getting that lucky, you devious whore."

Jahzara fixed her eyes on Gamba and if fire could've launched from them instead, it would have disintegrated him. She snapped her fingers over and over until the small group of loyal supporters were completely trapped and surrounded by Lord Durako's men. She pointed to Zaruko and Gamba.

"Not those two."

"No!" Zaruko shouted, diving at the closest Impery guard.

Before he could tackle them to the ground, three others kicked and beat him mercilessly until he fell, limp and unable to feel his legs. Gamba met the same fate and the two of them watched helplessly as Jahzara's backup slaughtered the men and women with him. They couldn't escape, but not for a lack of trying. Their short daggers and swords did them little good against the spears, clubs, and axes wielded against them. Zaruko started spitting fire along the floor, trying to ignite the warehouse in the hopes that he could bring them all down together, but Jahzara kicked the back of his head and strapped a muzzle on him. The chemicals burnt his mouth, but his muffled yells went unheeded.


There are times the brain is hard at work, but it feels like there's just a deep nothing. It's as if the only thing the mind can do is dwell on a feeling. Marek sat on a hastily made rug on the dirt floor of his clay hut, his head entirely devoid of any singular thought. Just a feeling he didn't know what to do with.

A hand stuck itself inside the front curtain and waved around with a friendly gesture.

"Can I join you?"

"Sure Savan, come in," said Marek, slowly rejoining reality.

"Great. Here, I brought you something to eat," he said eagerly, holding a thin, wooden bowl out to him as he crossed his bare feet and lowered himself down to sit across from Marek on the thick blanket.

"Smells good," he said, breathing in the warm, meaty aroma.

"It's uh, fodderbug and weable with chopped up spitfire leaves and some other stuff, I don't remember. I stopped hearing what they said after I smelled it," Savan chuckled.

"What's a weable?"

"It's like a, some kind of little thing that burrows around in the fields. I've never seen one."

"We can eat this?" asked Marek, taken back by the concept of eating another creature.

"I sure hope so."

Savan took his sharpened stick and stabbed into a cut piece of meat, holding it up to his mouth as he tore off pieces of it. Marek copied, unsure of how to eat out of a bowl or even with a utensil like the one they had been given. The fodderbug was a bit pungent, but the weable was incredible. It was a taste not unlike the middle of the bloodstone, which was most everyone's favorite part. The spitfire added enough of a kick to it to keep the hovel silent while they greedily hoovered it all down. Any congestion they might've had was fully cleared out, though they hadn't suffered much since each of their first few days outside of Haven. They didn't know it should be any different and didn't think twice about it.

Savan chuckled out of the blue, "I'm so used to eating with my grandfather."

"Yeah?"

"Yeah, all he does is complain about everything," Savan shook his head, still smiling, "bloodstones all his life and he can't stand anything that tastes even a little bit like them. But then if I bring him something different, it's too strange. Take it back. Like I just pulled it out of a dispenser."

Marek laughed with him.

"What's on your mind?" asked Savan, his face flushed from the meal.

302

Marek sniffed once and set the bowl down between them, "I don't want to complain."

"Please," Savan set his bowl down too, "I didn't mean to make you feel uncomfortable."

"You didn't, I just...I can't put my finger on it. There's something off. I keep getting this feeling."

"Is it Haven? Sometimes I feel like that too, like I just want to go back for a while. It doesn't feel real that it's gone."

"No," Marek shook his head and scrunched up his nose, "that's not it."

"Is it a good feeling?" asked Savan, knowing from Marek's posture that it wasn't.

"I want to leave," Marek blurted out, "I want to get out of here so bad, I can't think straight."

"But...but everything went so well. It's all getting so much better. And it's thanks to you, I mean, it's finally looking up."

"I know," Marek said dismissively.

"Is it Vik? Are you worried about him?"

"No. Well, of course I am, but that's not it," he glanced up at Savan and exhaled, "You know what, I think I just needed to say something to someone. And eat."

Savan's worried expression broke and he smiled, "I understand what you mean. I gotta get the rock off my chest sometimes, too. If you ever need to, just let me know and I'll listen."

"Alright," Marek chuckled.

He felt a little uncomfortable with how nice Savan was, but it wasn't a bad thing. It was just not what he was used to from Vik, the one he usually confided in. It gave him a fresh wave of missing Mira.

"Hey Savan," Marek started. "If I needed someone to have my back, no matter what...keep secrets, go with me to these meetings, would you be interested?"

"What about Tayna? Is something wrong?"

"No, nothing like that," Marek said, though he felt in his words an uneasiness that was hard to swallow, "It's just, with Vik gone, it doesn't hurt to have another person to trust."

Savan lit up, "In that case, sure. Of course, I'd be happy—"

Nikiva barged through the curtains, wild-eyed and panting heavily. She threw herself down on the rug beside the both of them to catch her breath, holding up a finger when they asked her what had happened.

"The warehouse...Zaruko and Gamba," she gulped and wheezed, tilting her head back to pull in more air, "I ran over here, just a second..."

Savan put his hand on her shoulder and Marek jumped up, pushing the curtain aside to look out toward the city. There was a thick pillar of dark smoke rising from around the Brutemen's part of town, right where the warehouse would be.

"A fire?" Marek asked.

"Yes, but that's not what I came to tell you," Nikiva said, "they found bodies inside."

"What?" Savan gasped, "Do they know who?"

"All, and I mean all, of the Impery that were living out here with the Sinovians."

Savan and Marek exchanged a glance before he let the curtain loose and sat back down beside them. He took a deep breath, holding it in before slowly exhaling.

"Was Zaruko among them?"

"Not from what the Jawnies that went in saw. Gamba wasn't there either. They couldn't put the fire out with water..."

"So it was an Impery who started it then," concluded Marek.

Nikiva wrung her hands as they sat in silence, contemplating what this could mean for Zaruko and Gamba. They weren't even sure what it meant for themselves. Everything they worked for could have been too much of a threat to the Impery and they were already retaliating.

"I've got to go," said Marek.

"Tayna?" Nikiva asked with a hint of disdain.

"Yeah, I think I need to talk to her."

"Well," Nikiva stood up abruptly, "I hope she tells you everything we need to know. I don't think I can take too many more surprises."

"Nikiva," Marek started, standing up to meet her eye to eye, "Tayna would have said something about Sera if she'd known. It was her own life..."

"Right," she said, giving him a polite nod before briskly leaving the hut.

Savan hurried after her. Marek could hear him calling after her and felt himself doubting his decision. He didn't want to rely on this fortune-telling thing Tayna had gotten so into, especially since it didn't seem to be holding up to a dependable standard. The results of their own hard work proved to be preferable, but he knew he should give it a chance. Marek decided to go and see his son, even if he wasn't going to take Tayna for her word. Besides, Tayna and Zaruko had grown close. She would want to know.

The giant fan in the nursery swung lazily around in circles, stirring the air more than cooling it. That was better than it being too still, gathering enough humidity to suffocate them. The marked girls were huddled in the far corner of the large room, quietly chatting among each other, occasionally sneaking glances at Tayna. She was holding Garek, bouncing him gently and idly pacing around the room, completely preoccupied as she hummed a made up tune.

When Marek walked in, the back corner froze, paralyzed and electrified by his presence. They weren't used to people coming into the nursery and still held onto the stigma given by Jahzara. He took note of them, but went straight to his son. Tayna happily handed the cooperative infant over.

"He never makes a fuss," she chuckled.

"That's good to hear," said Marek, smiling weakly.

After he spent a few minutes whispering to Garek, Tayna's curiosity couldn't keep quiet any longer. She delicately cleared her throat and waited until he looked at her face.

"What's the matter?"

"Zaruko is missing," he said, just getting it out there as quickly as he could.

The color drained from Tayna's face, but other than that, she held it together, "There's more?"

"Yeah, the Impery were killed by another Impery."

"Sure," Tayna said harshly.

"The fire was started by an Impery," Marek explained.

"But someone told them to be in that warehouse."

Marek felt foolish in his oversight, "Of course…"

"Sera wasn't the only spy."

"Thessa…" Marek muttered, "What should we do?"

"What do you mean?"

"To get Zaruko back? I'm assuming he's in Imperyo...if he's even alive."

"He may as well not be," said Tayna, eyes glazed over.

Marek tilted his head barely to one side and narrowed his eyes, "You're not going to try to save him?"

Tayna calmed herself with a slow blink and exhaled slowly, "I've always seen that this was going to happen. He knew it, too."

"What are you saying?" Marek couldn't disguise his disgust.

"Zaruko is going to be the spark that starts it all, Jahzara and Durako are going to get what's coming to them," the back of the room stirred uncomfortably, "And...I'm pregnant."

Marek flinched at the last bit of news, but could only shake his head in response. She was cold and calculating. He knew part of it was her trying to get through this difficult decision, but that was just it.

"Who do you think you are?" he hissed.

"Excuse me?"

"You're not Thessa. You're not the giver and taker of lives depending on what's best. What's best for who? Us? The Impery? ...You?"

"My visions—"

"Are a total mystery!" he blurted out, "Where do they come from?"

"Thessa," Tayna said firmly.

"How do you know? We all have dreams. I've had some pretty vivid ones, too. You get yourself high on sitters and stop eating, sure, you're going to start hallucinating."

"Marek..."

"No, don't try to tell me about how you feel. I'm done letting whether we live or die hang on your feelings. So far what have they gotten us? We sent Vik into a situation he obviously couldn't handle with a level head, got him kicked out of Threshold. All the Impery that were on our side are dead or missing. You got yourself all marked up and Sera tried to kill you. What is this fortune-telling leading us to?"

"A better future," Tayna snapped.

"A lot of good that's going to do us if we're dead."

"A better future for all of us, not just you and me. Why are you even here? Were you hoping I didn't know about this, so you could watch me limp on it along with all the other pebbles in my shoe you seem to be keeping track of?"

306

"That is exactly what I'm talking about, Tayna. You knew, *you knew*! Why didn't you tell me?"

"I knew you'd try to stop it from happening."

Marek was speechless, his mouth hanging open without any words to spill out. He felt Garek squirm in his arms and his heart sank. Suddenly, he was terrified to leave him here with her.

"Some of these terrible things," Tayna shook her head and searched blindly around the room, "They have to happen. I don't want them to, so don't look at me like that. But I do want us to live some kind of life. This isn't a life. People getting killed every other day, it's barbaric. This isn't what Thessa wanted for us."

"Harlok," Marek said quickly, almost cutting her off, "That's who you remind me of."

"I am nothing like my father," snapped Tayna, no longer able to keep her cool.

"You are exactly like him. Leading people to the edge because the visions will it."

Tayna's eyes teared up and her face flushed, but she just clenched her teeth and ordered him out. Marek tightened his jaw, but then turned and headed toward the door.

"Leave Garek," she ordered.

Marek froze in place. He glanced down at his son and then whipped his head around to face her. She was unconcerned by the implications he took from her command.

"You leave my son out of your schemes."

"He plays his part like everybody else," she said simply.

Marek marched up to stand too close to her face, "If anything happens to my boy, I am going to kill you."

The entire room held as still as a picture. The fan's heavy movements served to keep time moving forward for anyone too afraid to breathe.

"If you take him out of here," Tayna said carefully, motioning around the room and attempting to deescalate the situation, "Jahzara will kill all of them."

"That's all?" he asked, unmoving.

"That's all," she lied.

Marek had kissed his son on the head after setting him back down in his crib. He felt like he was leaving him in the drass' den, but he couldn't think of anything else. Nothing Tayna said could be trusted anymore. Every move Marek made could be set up to get him killed "for the greater good". He scoffed and glared around for something to distract him. There were plenty of things. Bright colors, pretty girls, loud screams, and dozens of gossiping passersby, but nothing was more distracting than his own mind, pumping plans into his brain. He needed to talk to Savan. He needed a plan for what was to come, and soon. If Zaruko was taken and his death was inevitable, it was going to be public. An example for the Sinovians. Lord Durako wouldn't waste the chance to make a scene like that, not with his only son. Marek couldn't comprehend what it would take to drive a man to murdering his own child, but he didn't spend any time trying to figure it out. There were some things better left not fully understood.

*****

Zaruko woke in a dry, stone room. Six guards lined the walls and blocked the only door out. A single candle flickered on each wall, but his vision suffered for other reasons. He reached back and struggled with getting his muzzle off, tossing it into the middle of the room with the other one.

"It's too bad you woke up," Gamba's voice gargled from the darkest corner of the room. "I was kind of hoping you were already dead."

Zaruko groaned, rolling his face on the stone floor in agony. He was able to pull his arms up over his head, but his legs wouldn't do anything. When Gamba saw Zaruko trying to crawl to the corner of the room with his elbows, he jumped up and helped him, grabbing under his arms and dragging him under the candlelight. Both of their faces were battered to a pulp. Zaruko could only open one eye and Gamba's nose had been severely broken.

The door creaked open and both men expected to see Jahzara, flaunting her victory. Instead, it was Durako, dressed in royal, white mourning attire, the blood already dry and healing the shallow cuts on his palms. Zaruko laughed quietly.

"Did I miss the show?" he managed to say despite his injuries.

Durako looked down his nose at him, pulling off his gloves one by one, and handing them to the nearest guard.

"You know, son—"

Zaruko face burned hot and he snarled through his teeth, "Don't. Don't talk down to me."

"Then stand up," Durako crossed his arms, bored with Zaruko's angry reactions, "All I ever wanted to do was protect the eternal flame," he put his hand over his diaphragm. "Keep the fires burning, despite how much harder it is for us to light them. The fire is Thessa's gift to us, we are greater than the Thesmekka and so rightly superior to the Sinovians. I don't know why you can't see this."

"You know what, I do see it. I see the light. Finally, after all these years. I'm cured of my ignorance."

"Do you understand the situation you're in, son?"

Zaruko let his head hit the hard wall behind him and cleared his throat, "Yes, I do. I'm just surprised being a martyr feels this good. You're going to kill a couple of Impery in front of the Sinovians...show them that no one can stand up to you. But what they're going to see is weakness. A broken braid in that divine twine of yours."

"That twine was broken a long time ago," Durako growled down at him.

"Yes, that's right. If I'd been there, if Lord Vosko'd been there too instead of bringing more Sinovians back, all those drass might not have gotten into the mountain. Maybe they wouldn't have killed mom, Kasuko would still be alive, too...I'll bet you wouldn't be trying so hard to get another son if Kasuko were still here," Zaruko fumbled with his words, but they were still understandable.

He was dizzy and having a hard time focusing on Durako's face. The wavering light was too unsteady for his battered head and he wheezed, squeezing his eyes shut. His fingers tingled and the pain in his back was so sharp, it was everything he could do not to cry out every time he opened his mouth.

"You will never understand what I lost that day," Durako roared.

"Never understand," Zaruko couldn't help but laugh in pain, "I could never understand loss? Look at me!" he shouted, "What have you not taken from me?"

"You're the one who chose to be against me," Durako said, motioning at a guard and then to Gamba. "Tomorrow is your day. Only yours. You'll have that."

The guard stabbed Gamba in the chest three times, shoving him to the ground when he was done. Blood poured out of each wound and coated the floor between them. Zaruko dove forward, dragging his body closer to Gamba and lifting his head off the ground. Durako took a step back so the blood wouldn't touch his shoes, snatched his gloves back from the guard, and let the Impery open and close the door for him as he left.

"I don't regret anything," Gamba coughed and gargled up a thick clump of blood, "I don't regret a single thing."

"I know," Zaruko said.

He squeezed his hand until he was the only one squeezing back. It didn't feel like they were losing until Gamba was gone. Then it was all over. Zaruko rested the side of his head on Gamba and shut his eyes, dreaming of childhood memories and the future that should've been.

# CHAPTER TWENTY-ONE

Brightly colored stalls displayed eye-catching treats and sparkly baubles, flashing the sun in the faces of passersby to sell themselves. A sweet, sugary aroma swirled in every breeze. Children carried buckets at the ends of long poles over their shoulders, skipping and laughing and teasing one another, leaving a trail of water behind them. Men and women had just started working in the fields, peeling hairy berries, caressing sunblooms for their fragile berries, and shredding spitfires. The jabulian trees bloomed during that time of year, constantly producing a supply of plump fruit, growing straight off the trunk like buds on a stem. Brutemen wheeled barrels full of mud, clay, and stone in from the quarry and dropped them off at the supplier for the more constructive Sinovians to access. They had repaired most of the neighborhoods closest to the wall and even made some improvements, inspired by the Seer's designs. A group of women, both Jawnies and Shinies, strolled down the main street with full pots in their arms, balanced against their hips so they could use their free hands for gesturing during their gossiping about the Seers and what to think of them.

Their conversation was interrupted by a bugling horn crying out over the city. Its call reached the forest, signaling even those in the fields to hurry in at Lord Durako's command. There were those who dropped everything at once and ran for the balcony, but the rest groaned and reluctantly migrated inward. The populace was surprised to see the Impery set up in the middle of the market circle instead of under the balcony above their city. Even more surprising were those in attendance. The closer the Sinovians got to the market center, the quieter they became.

Lying on his side in a pool of foul, sulfur-smelling liquid, Zaruko stared at the dirt as the market flooded with people. Stand owners hurriedly packed up their goods and pushed their stalls far back against the houses on the outside of the circle. Impery warriors lined the path back to the mountain entrance, ensuring a clear road should they need it.

Durako waited until the crowd was of a sufficient size before he began to speak to them.

Nattina watched from the middle of the gathering, supported by all the Brutemen that could make it in time. Reeta and Ridiak hovered near the road that led off to their section of Threshold and Taolani was practically invisible in the midst of her vivid people, though Makai stood tall and stoic as an identifying marker beside her. Despite the presence of everyone, trouble only started once the Seers arrived.

"Where's Gamba?" Nikiva breathed, covering her mouth with both hands and hopping on her toes to see over the crowd.

Marek scanned the faces of everyone with black hair, but couldn't see Tayna anywhere. He pushed his way through the crowd, meeting little resistance once each person saw his face. Murmurs followed him. He could hear them over the droning noise of Lord Durako's funereal speech. Once Marek emerged from behind two of the frontmost people, he saw Zaruko wheezing and wincing on one elbow in the dirt. It was clear he couldn't walk and had suffered through a sleepless night. Feverish and as pale as any Impery he'd ever seen, he'd not been afforded a chance to wash off any blood that'd stained him since he was betrayed. Zaruko silently prayed Tayna was far enough away that she wouldn't hear the sounds he might make while he burned.

Jahzara was also dressed in white mourning clothes, a dress with a veil that did little to hide her smug face. The Threshold Impery were wiped out, her love's leftovers were about to be burned. Everything was falling into place. There was just one more thing left and the timeline they had to accomplish it was about to be extended. Lord Durako began speaking in a strong, unwavering voice.

"I am committed to our survival. So much that I am willing to eliminate any threat, even when they are blood. Even when it is my own son who threatens the lives of Sinovians and Impery alike."

Marek marched passed the invisible barrier and knelt beside Zaruko, getting his knees damp in the vile fluid.

"What are you doing?" Jahzara snapped from behind Lord Durako, who was unwilling to fully stop his well-rehearsed speech.

"I hope you'll forgive me," Marek said, leaning down so Zaruko could hear him over the sound of his father's voice.

Zaruko's head wobbled, weakly lifting up to look at his face, "I wouldn't forgive you if you didn't."

"Not for this," he corrected him, but there wasn't enough time to explain himself.

Marek ripped his borrowed blade from its sheath and slit Zaruko's throat. It was so fast, Durako didn't understand what happened until the audience ignited into gasping and buzzing gossip that quickly transformed into crackling unrest. Shouts from various willful Sinovians stifled Durako's confidence. The Impery started to retreat, though Lord Durako took the time to memorize Marek's almost familiar face. Several Impery guards stomped toward the Seer, but Nattina had already arrived to back him up.

"Leave!" some of the angry Sinovians cried out.

"Go back to the mountain!"

As they shouted at the guards and Lord Durako, Marek slipped something tiny into Zaruko's mouth. The tiny orange pill rode the wave of blood over his lips and Marek had to pinch it up from the ground and push it down his throat. The Impery retreated in full under Durako's rouse of being too upset to respond to their offensive behavior. They didn't run back to the mountain, but they didn't turn their backs completely.

Marek held Zaruko's hand as he choked, struggling to swallow or cough but could do neither through the thick outpouring of blood. Reeta rallied her people together and stood between them and Zaruko, raising her stubby arms up to speak with wide motions and pointing back at the fleeing Impery. The sunlight warming his skin started to grow dim, but beside Reeta's leg, staring out from the crowd of faceless Sinovians, he saw Tayna watching him. She looked almost as bad as he did, but she was already out of tears and her hands were covered in the blood from the deep gashes on her palms. He knew at that moment, she had foreseen his death and that was worse. She'd suffered through it more than once. He tried to reach out to her, but his body had stopped only a moment before the rest of him. Marek traced his glazed eyes and saw Tayna approaching the scene with her hood down and her marred face keeping people at a safe distance.

She strolled right up to Reeta, meeting her face to face, bringing her loud speech to a silent pause without a word. Reeta furrowed her brows and took a couple of steps back.

"What are you doing?"

"Yours is the face I couldn't see," said Tayna in a raspy, exhausted voice.

"What?"

"The one who speaks over him," Tayna hissed.

Nattina had followed the burnt Seer, her titans closely in tow. Marek ran his fingers over Zaruko's eyes to close them, hoping the pill would take effect subtly, and stood behind Reeta.

"She told us we were meeting tonight, not last night," Taolani said, coming out of the horde of Jawnies with Makai. "So we didn't go. I thought we were worried about another spy."

"Break her legs," Tayna said in a hoarse voice, glaring at Reeta, "Then put her under the tavern and cover the hatch."

Nattina motioned for a young Bruteman to act on her words, "Benne will like hearing about this."

Tayna walked passed Reeta as the Brutemen held her down, resisting her pushing force. They blocked the blast for Tayna with their bodies and the other Shinies merely looked on, explaining to Nattina that they didn't know. Ridiak claimed to be especially ignorant. Marek moved aside and let Tayna touch Zaruko's face, but she stopped before she could feel his skin. It was enough that she would remember these last moments every time she thought of him, the smell of the sulfuric chemicals, how he twitched while he choked to death. She wanted to remember the last time they touched differently.

"Tomorrow night is their Watcher's Hour, the eclipse," Tayna said to Marek, "We've got work to do."

"I'll meet you after sundown."

Tayna made an effort not to look at Zaruko's body on the platform as she left the market circle, walking a brisk pace off to the Impery district. Marek waited until she was out of sight, staying beside the hastily setup platform, and then waved Savan down. He and Nikiva been waiting nearby and were the only ones in on Marek's plans.

"We're here," said Savan, trotting up and out of breath.

"Quickly take him to where we talked about, clean him up so those chemicals don't give anything away. I don't want anyone burning his body."

"Let's go," Nikiva whispered.

They lifted Zaruko up by his shoulders and legs, laying him back down on a long twine tarp. Wrapping him up, they lifted him as carefully as they could and carried his cocooned body away, attracting less attention from the scattered, shattered crowd caught up in their own conflicts. Supporters of the protector against supporters of the son. Each group erupting into verbal and physical altercations with very little leading up to these explosions. Marek was chilled through with thoughts of Haven.

"Vik, I hope you're on your way," he prayed.

*****

The mountains stood at attention around them, like an army of watchful Brutes on all sides but one. That one side continued on like an endless valley that faded into the horizon. There were no trees, but patches of dried grass and stumpy flora sprawled out. The fauna was just as sparse.

"We follow the mountains and we'll end up right in the middle of town."

"Obviously," Zaki said, rolling his eyes at Phrix.

Chadrik and Vik were sitting in the dirt nearby, wringing out their shirts after a short lecture from Josanna on contaminating the drinking water. She didn't want to hear about how she started it.

Despite Phrix's protest, they stayed for the remainder of the evening at the oasis, camping against the oddly shaped, black rock formation before the sun fell. Zaki sat himself outside the group, away from the water and the gigantic, stilted stone. He faced the hillside where the stalkers pranced and scurried around in their small pack, staying relatively close.

"What're you doing?" Vik asked, walking out to where he was sitting.

"If they see us watching them, they won't do anything. We'll have to take turns all night. We watch each other watching each other."

"Oh," Vik said, deflating a bit as he stared out at their persistent followers.

"What are you doing?"

"I'll leave you to it then," Vik grumbled.

"No, what are you doing?" Zaki chanced glancing up at him for just a second before whipping his eyes back to the stalkers on the hill, "You just got out here. We all want to fix things because it's so wrong, but you couldn't know that yet."

"People've died, who were close to me," Vik said quietly.

"No one you knew died in your mountain?"

Vik caught his words and thought on them, "It's different."

"Whatever."

"It's not just people dying that makes me want to make things better. I've always wanted to make my life better. But now, those people I care about rely on me doing this. It's not just for me anymore. It's not selfish anymore."

"It's still a little selfish," Zaki chuckled.

"I guess so. I don't know, if there's a paradise out there, if there's a better life, I want it. And I want to get it for myself. I don't want to wait around for it."

"You sound like the Grnuks…"

"The what?"

"Uther's people. But don't think Shimm is paradise. The Rider's home is a bad place, full of bad people. They could never see Thessa and she could never see them."

Before Vik could ask anymore about it Josanna came over, digging through Uther's pack and pulling out a wrapped up twine from the bottom.

"Will you hang this somewhere? I'm going to go in the water once the sun's down," she said, unbraiding her long hair, "Make sure that kid doesn't run off. I don't trust him."

"Anything else?"

"Yeah," she said irritably, "Keep your eyes to yourself."

He held up his hands in a display of innocence and she wandered off, around the bend of the small lake, obscured by some short shrubs.

Vik managed to jam a stick into the ground a short ways off from the monumental stone, using it to tether the twine high enough off the ground to hang clothes to dry. He tested it by plucking on the string. It gave a quick, weak hum as it vibrated from his plucking. Deeming it reliable, he took off his own shirt and tossed it over the line. The stars were more clearly visible than he'd ever noticed, but it was the moon that set him ill at ease. It would be eclipsing soon and it looked almost like an eye.

Turning around to see if Uther or Zaki might want to hang their own clothes up, amusing himself with the idea of there not being any room for Josanna's clothes, he called to them when he didn't immediately see them. Uther wasn't there. Vik looked around, but all he saw was the small lake and their campsite, nestled at the base of the rocky stilts. There was a loud splash and Vik knew Josanna had jumped into the water. Naked. He tried not to imagine that by thinking of anything else, but it was too late. His curiosity begged him to get in trouble, but he fought it off as best he could.

Something moved in the bushes not too far from the campsite and Vik leaned to the side for a better look, but it was already gone. He hunched over and snuck over to the shrubs. More rustling lured him farther away from the others.

"Hey," he hissed after the sound. "Who's there?"

Vik hesitated, glancing sideways at the meager flora lining the side of the water. Josanna was too quiet on the other side. Something could have gotten to her. He cringed at his own weak excuse, but used it anyway. Head tilted back, she had just emerged from the water and still had her eyes closed, running her hands over her hair to clear it from her face. Water trickled down her in slender streams and her body glistened in the moonlight, gently reflected in the water as it stilled. The way she moved, bobbing and swaying back down in the lake made him feel too guilty to keep watching.

Vik popped out the other side of the foliage and slammed right into Uther. He leapt up, grunted out what might've been a scream and broke a small tree in half stepping on it. The commotion alerted Josanna and she yelled at the bushes.

"Uther?!" Josanna shouted, attempting to cover herself and yell at him simultaneously. "Is that you?"

He didn't even care that she'd called him out, he growled at Vik and shoved him back, knocking him on his backside while Josanna carried on in the background, cussing and demanding something to cover up with.

"Vik! Vik, you're over there too, aren't you!?" She roared, striking actual fear into him.

He crouched even lower, refusing to show his face and Uther chuckled at his reaction. He turned and waved at Josanna, tore his shirt over his head and threw it to her in the water. She had to tie it in knots, but she wore it out as a crude dress that touched her ankles. Marching up the bank, sloshing water in her vigorous rage, she confronted the two guilty peepers. She slapped Vik twice in the face. Once for what he did and the second time for Uther, since she didn't think she could reach his face without dropping some of her cover. Uther ignored her ranting, leaving in the middle of it, throwing his pants off and diving into the water.

"I just saw…everything," Josanna gasped.

"Me too," Vik groaned, planting his eyes on the sky to avoid any further incidents.

"If this is how you treat your friends, I want to revoke the entire evening."

Smooching sounds called out to her from the water and her expression fell flat. Rumbling chuckles rattled out from the giant's hearty throat, muffled as he submerged himself. When he came back up, Uther started to hum an unfamiliar tune as he happily rubbed his arms and shoulders.

"He's not even sorry," she complained, throwing her hands up and letting them slap back down on the sides of her legs.

"I guess not."

"But you will be," she added, jabbing Vik in the chest with her fingers.

She didn't storm off after that. She just kept glaring at him, waiting for him to defend himself with some excuse. When he didn't say anything, she tilted her chin up and narrowed her eyes at him, pulling the extremely wide collar tighter together.

"What?"

"You're so beautiful," he said, feeling like an idiot the very instant the words left his mouth.

She let her head fall sarcastically to one side and clicked her teeth, "Really, that's what you're going to say?"

Again he couldn't stop himself from speaking, "Everything about you, you're so different from everyone. I've never seen anyone so, so…"

"Beautiful?" she said, jutting out her jaw. "Vik, I don't know how many naked girls you've seen, but you might need to peep more often."

She started to march passed him, the final act in her display of indignity, but he grabbed her arm and spun her around. Her lips parted to yell at him, but met with his mouth instead. She groaned softly in weak-willed protest, silenced as their lips surged together, caught up in the same passionate tide. He pushed his whole hand against her back, moving up from the base and back down from her neck until they were perfectly aligned, her wet shirt clinging to his skin. They unlocked in a daze, her soaked clothes peeling off his skin and smacking back onto her own. She was flustered, to say the least. Conflicted and offended, but certain she wanted more. For once, she was speechless.

318

He felt like he'd been holding his breath all night, waiting for her to say something. Quickly opening his mouth, he started to form an apology when she swung around and slapped him square on the cheek, the smack ringing out over the water.

The next morning, the group got up early, rejuvenated and more prepared to meet with the Riders. Vik stretched his mouth open and closed, feeling his cheek burning in the shape of a hand. No one dared comment on it, except Zaki.

"What happened to your face?"

"Nothing," he answered too quickly.

Chadrik narrowed his eyes, squinting between Josanna and Vik. Uther issued a low, rumbling chuckle and shook his head, still completely unremorseful.

Over the full clothes line, Vik saw a light flashing in his eyes. The only other things he'd known to reflect the sun like that was the orb and the Gate metal, both Thesmekkian. He hopped up, throwing his damp shirt in the dirt.

"What is it?" Chadrik called after him, jumping up to join him, pulling the cool, clumped fabric over his head.

Vik trotted to a stop beside an enormous clump of hooked rocks towering over them, bending down to examine a shard of glass sticking out of the dirt. He carefully picked it up, rubbing off one side of it on his filthy pants. The shard was so covered in grime, he was only able to see a part of him peeking out at himself. The last time he'd seen his reflection was in the holograms above his bathroom sink in Haven. Numerous darker, faint spots he'd never seen on his face before left tracks over his cheeks, nose and forehead. His skin wasn't pink anymore, but he'd known that before looking in the mirror. Unable to shave since leaving Threshold, the scruffy man he could barely get a glimpse of was pushed aside by a darker, blonder guy with curls. They crammed into the tiny reflection, squeezing the sides of their faces together.

"Blind me…" Josanna breathed, plodding right by them.

She peered around the corner at the wreckage crammed into the rocks. A complicated heap of metal parts, it looked as though it'd been rammed into the stony wall with enough force to crack it right up the side. The accident happened long enough ago that the metal was rusted and anything softer was ruined, smelling of mold of rot.

"Rhuskeggr," Uther grunted.

"Roos-kegger?" Vik asked.

Uther tilted his hulky head side to side, but accepted his attempt. The giant scoundrel pulled at the side of the object, dislodging it after some effort. Several bits of it fell off and more of the reflective glass shattered to the ground. Uther took care not to step in it and took the device by its handles, searching for a switch until he found it. Flicking it up and down, he ran through several different combinations of ons and offs before giving up on it.

"What is it?" Vik asked, watching the giant toss it to the ground.

More of it broke apart and Uther sighed, making a swift hand motion with his giant, flabby arm, "Moves fast."

A scraping, clawing sound rattled above their heads and they looked up in time to see rocks crumbling off the top of the hooked ridge and a whistler with its head sticking through the wide opening. There was plenty of room for it to dive in and take whoever it wanted, but it stayed above them and watched, anxiously fidgeting. Instinctively, they tried to run back the way they came, but it was abruptly blocked off by a couple of stalkers with mismatching lumps on their backs. They nervously paced side to side, refusing to enter the channel. The other side of the semi-tunnel filled with the figure of a great walker, its gigantic, drooping head peering in at them and frantically sniffing the air, stomping impatiently at the ground.

"Phrixanian Amanaki?" someone called out at the same time the whistler squawked.

"Yes?" he answered, looking at the bird as if it had addressed him.

The beasts closed in on them slowly, except for the whistler. It dove down into the passageway and landed in a less than graceful manner. There was a woman top the bird, blonde and black-eyed just like Zaki and Phrix. She held on tight as the creature leaned sideways and appeared to fall asleep, then hopped off and approached them aggressively.

"Who are you with?"

"They've got a gift for Roque," Phrix bragged, "So I've taken them prisoner and am going to deliver them to him, if we can ever get back."

"Let Xavilin take you back," she said, motioning to the great walker. "Do you want us to bind them?"

320

"Oh yes, that'd be helpful," Phrix said, as if she were simply offering them a ride.

"Uh, no," Josanna snapped, stepping away from the Riders. "We would like to arrive unbound, thank you."

Up close, the stalkers were bigger than Vik thought they'd be. Each one was about the size of a drass, long-bodied with powerful, prehensile tails and chubby, clawed paws. Their fur was short, but they were blubbery, with wrinkles of fat that bunched up depending on how they moved. With dog-like noses too big for their faces and stubby ears, they might've been endearing if they were smaller.

The two ridden stalkers rushed toward them, but Josanna spewed fire at them, causing them to scramble in the other direction. The great walker boomed in, busting the brittle stone out of the way as it plowed right at them.

"Stop!" Phrix shouted, "Stop! I'm taking them alive!"

"Not if they don't cooperate," the female Rider threatened, climbing back onto her bird and pushing her hand up under the feathers on the back of its head.

"Don't resist. It's the only way you're getting in without a fight," Phrix told them.

*****

The Riders inhabited the space just outside of the Thesmekkian ruins, the place where their saviors once dwelled. Shimm, was what they called their town, but by the time they got there it was more like a ravaged village. Houses were made of enormous skulls, the creatures they belonged to brought to die by the mind-controlling inhabitants and half-heartedly cleaned out. The residents were used to the smell and decaying stench kept any curious creatures at bay. No people were standing idly around, gossiping among each other, strolling with baskets under the sun. With the exception of a few of those who muttered nonsense with cracked lips and wild eyes, burnt from standing too long in the sun, the town looked abandoned.

Riding into the village on the top of a great walker's head, bound in ropes, the group arrived in Shimm drawing everyone's attention. The tiny village was tucked away in a ribcage tunnel more dense than any of the others they'd come across. Their homes were primitive, but they dressed in Thesmekkian-made clothing. None of the residents had washed since it rained last, which it did much less of in the valley. Their bright blond hair was matted in sloppy dreadlocks and their fingernails cracked, broken, and dirty.

The great walker dropped its head, thumping its chin against the ground. The passengers bounced on its head once before being ordered to slide off. They were packed too tightly to go all at once and threw their legs over the beast's head one by one, sliding down without the use of their arms. Every one of them fumbled without being able to balance with their hands.

Phrix danced and skipped around, proclaiming his accomplishment to everyone who was listening.

"I found Sinovians, I found them! They've got a gift for Roque, but you can't have it!"

The people watched the Sinovians fearfully, hiding most of their faces under scarves or behind their hands, even though the rest of them was plainly visible. Something was definitely off about the residents of Shimm.

"This one's a fire-breather!" the female Rider shouted over Phrix's chanting.

"No! I found them myself," he interrupted, "I was out there looking for…" he glared at Old Lady Domitia, "something nice, when they came through the gateway."

"They have a Thesmekkian orb?" one of the townspeople asked, poking their heads up.

"NO!" Phrix bellowed, "It's mine!"

"Is she really a fire-breather?" another woman asked, tiptoeing closer.

Phrix twitched nervously, glancing from all the people to the Sinovians and back again, "You can have her, she doesn't have a gift anyway. But this one's mine!" Phrix jumped to put his hand on Vik's head.

All the world flooded with a rushing, billowing black smoke, closing like a curtain over his vision. When the drapes drew back again, he was inside a crude cage made of every kind of bone from many different creatures, filled with cracks and splits to see out from. No holes were big enough to escape through. He frantically tried them all, but the cage had been meticulously made. Cackling laughter burst out from the other side of the cage and a couple of gaunt, snaggletoothed women heckled him.

"Please," Vik begged through the openings, "We came here for your help."

"Why in Thessa's name would we want to help your people?"

"They ran us out, right out of their city. They did!" the older woman babbled, "Now look at us. Can't even get the ruins to speak. Not a word, silent as the grave."

The younger woman cackled again, "They want us to help," she repeated, putting her hand on the older woman's arm.

The old Rider jerked wildly, shrugging her hand off her arm and slapping the younger Rider over and over until she ran her out of the area, screaming about her touching her and not knowing who is left to trust. Shuddering, the old Rider pulled her thick scarf up to cover her neck and most of her face, continuing to watch the display in the middle of the town. He could smell her body odor from inside the cage, but still she bundled up as much as she could.

Vik looked passed her and saw a sickly-looking stalker struggling to stay away from the two that had cornered them in the passageway earlier. They were surrounded by people, gasping and clapping and being generally amused by the show in front of them. Tethered in the middle of the makeshift arena, Josanna struggled against her restraint. She had one arm tied behind her back and her mouth covered with a leather strap. The stalkers bounded toward Zaki, knocking her down roughly as they passed. She hit the ground hard and slid across the dirt until the tether stopped her. The arm that had been tied behind her back was roughed up, but freed from its restraint.

"I'll help her!" one of the Riders shouted, running straight at her with a blunt, heavy axe.

Standing over her body, he swung down at the rope and purposely missed. The axe severed her arm just above her elbow and the audience roared with laughter.

"There you go!" he laughed, kicking her playfully in the legs.

Vik heard her muffled screams and yelled out, "Phrix!"

The old woman cackled, "Shut up, you fool."

The crowd suddenly turned from cheers to gasps and murmurs, watching as what was left of Josanna's arm stopped bleeding and healed. The part of her arm still attached to the arena healed as well. Both bloody ends closed up and Josanna struggled to get to her feet, gasping

323

and weak in the knees. It was clear she had no idea what was happening, but then she ripped the leather strap off her face with the hand she still had and burned the Rider to ash where he stood as he frantically slapped at his face and body.

After he was gone, she glanced down at her arm and yelled for Phrix. She did this until the people pushed him forward. Grabbing his shirt, she pulled the boy close and shoved him in the direction of Vik's cage, advancing when he fell on his back. Zaki's attackers stopped to enjoy the new source of entertainment, eager to see someone like Phrix get into trouble with a fire-breather. Zaki fled town on his old, limp stalker, disappearing around the ridge.

"The Impery are reaping what they've sown," Phrix began, crawling backward on his elbows, "And the Sinovians don't deserve help. There's no saving themselves. The Thesmekka shouldn't have created them, any of them. We weren't meant to be here, on this planet."

"We came here to see Roque," she bellowed, her eyes red and fixed. She spit fire on the ground beside him and he yelped, "Take us to him."

"We're what's off, everything else belongs here. We have to try too hard, if you'd just stop, this would all be over. We'd be gone and everything could go back to the way it was meant to be. No need to create and perpetuate our abominable existence here." Phrix gasped, eager to convey his new thought, "You wouldn't be letting down humanity! They're everywhere. Just not on this world. There's no need to be concerned about that. All those stars, most of them are full of people. Not just us either. Strange people, bigger and taller and blue and orange..."

"Phrix," Josanna yelled, "Just take us to Roque!"

"I already gave him the orb," Phrix rambled, "You don't need to see him."

Josanna grabbed the old woman standing nearby and threatened to burn her alive. The Rider shrieked and trembled, but Phrix actually egged her on.

"Are you Old Lady Domitia?" she asked.

The old woman nodded and Josanna shoved her aside, not bothering to watch her scamper away.

"If you're not going to help me, I'll roast you right where you are. I don't care if you're just a kid. Not anymore. You've gone too far, Phrix."

324

"I can't see anything, I don't see you," he started chanting with his eyes shut.

Josanna kicked his legs and threatened him again, announcing her presence.

"I don't care, I'd rather die than take you to see my father," Phrix gasped at what he'd just said and pretended it didn't happen.

Josanna tried to lift him up with her right hand, but simply swung half an arm at the air between them. She was clearly struggling to grasp her situation, whimpering between threats and trying not to look at her arm.

"I'll take you to speak with him, but I can't let you meet with him."

Josanna glanced up at Vik and he nodded eagerly.

"All of us," she ordered.

# CHAPTER TWENTY-TWO

The Watcher's Eye beamed down on Threshold. Fiery orange, the larger moon shone like an unholy iris with the smaller moon blacked out in front. The moons were set to align in just the right position to catch the midnight sunlight and flash it down like a celestial wink. The stony altar behind Imperyo was adorned with blankets, bowls and knives in preparation.

Jahzara threw a black robe over her shoulders. She rounded up her pagan attendants and dashed into the well-lit night, curving around the black mountain's base and deftly avoiding the newly constructed cluster of Sinovian homes. She would've thought harder on burning them down, but there didn't seem to be anyone in them, even at that late hour.

The nursery door was firmly secured, just as she instructed it to be. Pushing it open with both hands, Jahzara's attendants filed in before her, the five of them all eager to snatch up their offerings and flee before the Sinovians found them. Lord Durako was clear about not causing any further scandals to upset the Sinovians. Once the door was shut behind them, she quietly pointed around the room, leaving the brand new Garek for her own taking.

"There you are," she whispered, leaning in a scooping him up in her boney arms.

"Jahzara," said Tayna, sitting on her bed.

Jahzara snapped up, startled by her speaking at a normal volume. Glaring in the dark, she held the infant close to her chest and crossed the length of the room to stand in front of the marred Sinovian.

"I'm not surprised to see you," she hissed, still keeping her voice down, "Though I'd like to know what you're doing here."

"You poor thing," Tayna said, standing up from the bed. "Are your people so barren that you've forgotten what a child feels like in your arms?"

Realization crossed her face like an electrical shock. Garek was so quiet and still, but he was also as hard as spitfires and jabulians wrapped up in a blanket. She dropped the fake infant as the other women in the room caught up on the same understanding. Some threw the vegetables to the ground and others tossed them back in the cribs. No matter what they did, none were fast enough to escape the imposters hunched and hiding in the dark corners of the room. The four Brutemen were able to stab, crush, and smother Jahzara's bewildered attendants without resistance while she stood in front of Tayna, jaw clenched tight.

"Traitor," Jahzara whispered.

"Murderer," said Tayna.

Jahzara gasped and exhaled her words, "You're all traitors and you will be judged for your crimes here. The Watcher has seen everything that's happened to his daughters tonight."

"You are no one, Jahzara. The Watcher doesn't know you and the Thesmekka didn't want to let your people live," some of the Brutemen in the room shifted their weight around and glanced between each other, "There is no betrayal. You are nothing but a way to lure out Durako."

"I would rather die in my own fire."

"You'd be killing your unborn child for him."

Jahzara's mouth dropped open long before she spoke, "How dare you," she whispered.

"I'm not lying, I've seen it. Or rather, I've seen her."

Jahzara took a step back, away from the Brutemen behind Tayna, their hands and clothes speckled with the blood of Impery women. Tayna held out a fitted leather strap and dangled it in front of her face.

"Put this on, or they will put it on for you."

Jahzara snatched it out of her hand and quickly latched it behind her head.

*****

The tavern was packed to bursting. Sinovians were lined up against the walls, crowded around tables and some seats had two people crammed together, only half-sitting. There was some talking and light drinking, but even with more patrons the noise was barely half that of a normal night and most of the clamoring came from the orphaned infants, dispersed among the customers.

Marek approached Nattina who was holding Garek in her giant arms. Benne sat beside them, finally able to rejoin everyone and overly eager for it. He might have done well to rest up a couple more days, but he wasn't going to miss that night for anything.

"How's he doing?" Marek asked, touching Garek's pudgy cheek.

"He loves his sleep," Nattina said. "He has no idea how terrible tonight could have been."

"Good," said Marek softly.

"You've only got your brother to worry about now."

"I will always worry about him," Marek sighed, "He's not happy unless someone's got a reason to be worried about him. When we were kids, right after our father went and jumped, he would go to the edge and sit with his feet hanging off. I'd go out there every day and sit with him, make sure he didn't follow in our father's footsteps, you know? But months went by and I couldn't do it anymore, every single day. I figured he was only sitting there to feel close to the man, since neither of us really ever were, but I started worrying about someone knocking into him or about him slipping.

It's worse with Garek. I feel like everything's out to get us. Is there anyone looking out for us or is it all just up to me?"

"You know, I see this child in my arms and the others around the room and I can see that I'm not alone. Not with this. Besides, it's said the ones that barely make it are the ones who become something great."

The door to the tavern swung open and everyone casually glanced over, most of them doing hard double takes when they saw Tayna coming through with her ward. With a Bruteman on either side of her, holding each arm in place, Jahzara barely needed to move her feet. Her mouth was strapped shut, but with one look she was able to get her point across to every Sinovian in the room. Once they got her down into the cellar behind the bar, Tayna motioned for certain people to join them.

A single flame swayed on the tip of a candle in the middle of the room, barely illuminating the dark soil held back by wooden beams and unevenly stacked stones. Reeta sat wedged into the corner, blindfolded and bound, under constant guard by a Bruteman big enough to withstand the brunt of her forceful gusts of air. The sound of Jahzara and the Sinovians stampeding down the stairs startled her awake. She jerked and demanded to know what was happening. Nattina's men shoved Jahzara down in the opposite corner of the room as Reeta.

Marek, Tayna, Nikiva, and Savan made up the Seers present while Nattina and Benne, Taolani and Makai made up the Brutemen and Jawnies. After everyone settled around the table, blocking the candlelight from the rest of the room, another set of footsteps came trampling down the stairs.

"What are you doing here?" Marek asked Ridiak, putting his hand on his chest to stop him from going any closer to Reeta.

"There's no Shiny here, so I've come to represent my people. And to ensure Reeta's fair treatment," he struggled to speak so properly, still high from his sitter and slurring his speech.

"She's a traitor," Tayna stated, "And will be treated as a traitor."

"All she's done is bring down Durako's lineage, there was nothing ever done against Sinovians. She may have disturbed one set of plans, but as far as we're concerned, she's only ever looked out for her people."

"It's true," Reeta chimed from the corner, "All I want is for a Sinovian to rule. That was only ever my intention."

"Then why were you reporting our actions to Jahzara?" Nattina snapped.

"I was, I planned to have every action led by Zaruko fail, to put him out of favor. I didn't intend for him to die, but sometimes things don't always go the way we want them to."

Jahzara's muffled laugh hummed in the corner of the room.

"Who else is here?" Reeta said, trying to look out the bottom of her blindfold.

"Someone who would agree with you," said Tayna, motioning for them to cover Reeta's mouth.

"Zaruko was an Impery. Nothing would've changed that. Don't let your personal feelings drive a wedge between our people," she managed to say before they gagged her.

Tayna marched around the table, everyone quickly parting out of her way. She ripped the blindfold off Reeta's face and Ridiak hurried toward them, stuttering protests until he was stopped by Benne's enormous arm.

"My personal feelings? I had to abandon them after I came here. When I walked through that urine soaked gate, through a city full of capable people too afraid to risk making their lives better, I had personal feelings. When I was marked as property in a way you'll never understand and when I saw how infant sacrifice was being tolerated and ignored, I had personal feelings…"

Tayna looked down her nose at Reeta before walking away and facing everyone else in the room.

"But when I set myself down to meditate on what was to be, I saw how terrible things needed to come to pass. And even though these things needed to happen and more have yet to come, I put my feelings aside and I had to let them. It is the will of Thessa that guides me," a restless hush fell over the room, "And She's shown me that in the morning, Imperyo will fall. And Reeta, as an agent of Imperyo, so will you."

***** 

The residents of Shimm were furious with Phrix for taking their prisoners, but he appeased them by allowing them to keep the others. Vik and Josanna tried to protest, but Phrix reminded them that he wasn't the only one who wanted to take the orb to Roque. Chadrik was brought into the middle of the arena next. Josanna's arm was untied from the tether and tossed aside, making room for Chadrik.

"Let's just hurry this up," said Josanna.

At the far end of the sheltered city, pressed up against the mountain range, a hollow triangle led deep into the dark center. Phrix anxiously charged forward, his head tilted down and his eyes darting from side to side. Vik and Josanna followed closely behind him, squinting passed the spewing torch held above his head. The walls were solid brown rocks, smoothed at an angle to form a pointed ceiling and braced with metal beams stretching the full length of the hall. There was no smell, nothing old or musty, dank or rotten, just crisp and clean air all the way down.

Josanna kept reaching up to feel where her arm should be, finding the stub after a few missed swipes. She did this so many times down the length of the tunnel that Vik leaned into her, putting his arm around her shoulders. This small action calmed her anxiety and took her mind off the phantom limb. Phrix was completely unaware of their silent exchange, eyeing the walls like something was going to pop out of them at any moment.

At end of the dark corridor was a bright, white glow. It was pure and a more brilliant light than they'd ever seen outside. Coming directly from the spaces in the walls, it illuminated the triangular door. Once they were close enough, Phrix called out to no one, ordering that they open the way. There was a long pause before a familiar whirring sound sucked the door up into the wall above their heads. The light burst out of the newly revealed room, radiating around them like they were stepping out of their world and into the afterlife.

"Don't touch anything," Phrix grumbled, "Don't speak to anything, don't wander off."

They were inside the mountain, but it was nothing like Haven or Imperyo. It was nothing like anything they'd ever seen. The walls of their black mountains were cold and dead, but these were far more alive. It reminded Vik of the forest in its own way. The walls flickered notifications and blinked with awareness in sequenced lights and teal

330

symbols. Circles of grating, sensors, and notifiers clustered together up every angled crossbeam and beside each door, creating breaks in the otherwise smooth metal. The walls, the ceiling, even the crossbeams and doorframes were so sleek, they looked wet. The floor was like a sanded ice pathway, the grains providing more traction than the walls. Vik recognized some of the blue symbols that crossed their paths as ones he'd seen painted on Jawnies like Haku.

"What is all this?" asked Vik.

"I said don't say anything."

"How are we not going to ask you questions?" Josanna asked.

"Later," Phrix snapped, glaring at an especially feisty wall.

Following a series of swishing doors, Vik realized they were being guided somewhere by he walls themselves. Symbols following them in familiar patterns, running along the correct path when the hallways split.

The final doorway led them into a pearly white room. it was full of every manner of vibrant color carrying out countless orders across screens wrapped around the walls, clear enough to see through to the other side. In the middle was a sea green tube of light with bulky, metal buckles fastened incrementally in place along the cylinder. The thick, glassy tube disappeared up into the vast space where a ceiling should've been and continued until it became small enough to be covered by one finger, then split into dozens of offshoots, dispersing into the walls. The glowing was concentrated close to the area above eyelevel and impossible to see through in that spot. It was only when something other than the lights on the walls moved that they noticed the presence of another person in the room.

"Finally," said the duel, automated voice. "I saw you getting out of Haven, with your brother…"

"Are you…" Josanna whispered, unable to finish.

"Yes," it drifted closer toward them on four digits, all mechanical but with an otherworldly grace and fluidity. "I am Roque, leader of specimen group Mek-X. You call them Riders."

Unlike the Thesmekka Josanna had pried the orb from, this one had two pairs of legs and just two arms and was much more delicately framed. It's gold and pearl body was bombarded with brutal damages, scraps, and one leg did not quite touch the ground, causing a limp. However, the Thesmekka was not going to allow a bad leg to degrade its integrity. The eyes were permanently open, just like the other, but they were alight in such a way that they would not have illuminated a dark room or anything more than the face directly around them. The light was harnessed so completely, it did not freely shine on anything undesired. In the middle of the Thesmekka's forehead was an orb, pearly and cracked right down the middle.

"You saw me getting out of Haven?" Vik asked suspiciously.

Roque motioned with his slender arm toward a monitor near the green tube in the center of the room. He spoke aloud and the screen flickered, going from black to solid grey before switching to night vision, showing Haven as a grotesque display of what looked like the day Vik had escaped. All its people entombed and Gateless. Josanna gasped and covered her mouth, unable to look away from the images.

"I saw you long before that day too," Roque said.

The display seamlessly switched to a playback of a time when they had a Gate and everyone was blissfully ignorant of their date with Haven's total collapse ten years from then. A familiar man stepped out of Vik's home, marching straight out. He had dark eyes with heavy bags under them, a nose broken more times than he could count, and a scar on his top lip.

"That's my father," Vik whispered, staring at his face again as if he forgot what was coming next. "How are you doing this?"

"Everything is recorded here for our study," Roque said, casually adjusting the clump of clothes wrapped around his back. "We thought your people were going to be different. They seemed to thrive in close proximity for so long, but division was apparently inevitable. You came here seeking our help when you are perfectly capable of helping yourselves."

"This is us helping ourselves. We made it through everything just to get here," Vik said, "I brought you that orb in exchange for assistance, or weapons so that we can help ourselves."

"Still, you came here to get weapons when you already have a means to destroy one another."

"We don't want to destroy each other, we just want to show them can defend ourselves, if we have to," Josanna clarified.

"You should never hold a weapon you're not willing to use. You might as well be holding nothing at all."

"Well, right now that's kind of the case," Vik said irritably.

"And it will remain the case. I have you and your friends right where they should be. If we're going to be lending any hand to you back at Imperyo, it would be to eradicate every remaining specimen group. The Mek-Havessi, Mek-Grnuk, especially the Mek-Druuga," Roque shifted to face them square on, his unblinking eyes more unsettling than his words, "We are, all of us, abominations, created for the scientific advancement of a higher species. One that had to abandon their project too quickly to clean up their mess, which is all that we are. A mess, waiting to be wiped clean from the planet. One that could bring a lot of trouble to our makers if we don't get rid of ourselves."

"Are you a Rider?" Vik asked, leaning to see around the bulging cover atop the back of the metal man.

Phrix responded to Roque's subtle nod by inserting the pearly orb into a gelatinous screen. The receptacle was stationed in front of the sea green, cylindrical tubing. The dark green goop made a vacuous sound when the boy inserted the orb and the substance adhered to his skin like putty. As soon as Phrix withdrew his hand, the gelatin goo releasing him without a struggle, having deposited the prize safely within.

"I am so much more than that," Roque continued on, "and now that you've brought me the orb, it's only a matter of time before it acclimates to the facility. The AI should begin the process of communication and together we will coordinate our destruction of Imperyo and its infestation. Your Mek-Traxian companion and the old Grnuk are already dead. Surrender yourselves to a quick execution and be at peace in the void."

The screen flickered over to a view of Shimm just outside, but it was not what Roque expected to see. Approaching the two discarded experiments, one of Roque's arms angled to strike a protracted blade into their chests when a voice crackled out from every corner of the room. It repeated itself, becoming less and less garbled each time.

"Es...shing...tion...establishing...ection...establishing connection," the room said, crisp and clear. "I am detecting hostile intentions. Vik. Scanning..." the room went quiet for a moment, "Vik. I am glad to see you."

"How do you know him?" Roque roared, looking at the green tube. He went from calm to outraged with no gradual acceleration, "It is me you should be speaking to!"

"Havard," Vik announced, "I'm glad to see you too, buddy. Well, I can't really see you, but it's good to hear you."

Roque held one arm up while another shoved Vik to the ground, but dozens of robotic arms detached from the room's domed walls and reached out, grabbing onto both the machine and the man, prying him loose and plucking the true Roque from the back of the withered Thesmekkian. The precise limbs easily pinned him to the ground despite his flailing and delivered an electrical shock to his body until he blacked out. His arms were bound in time for him to wake a few seconds later and he was escorted out of the room by the firm grips of dozens of arms cooperating along an unknown path.

"He will be detained until stabilization can be administered."

"This one too," Vik said, motioning in awe to Phrix.

The arms swiveled toward him, but he just covered his head and squeezed his eyes shut, chanting about not being able to see anything. He was bound with no resistance, still hiding within himself as he was carted away, out the whirring door. One of the arms uncoiled from farther away and pressed itself into Vik's chest, pushing him off-balance.

"You had better not pick on me anymore."

Vik held up both hands, eyes wide, "You bet."

As Vik ran down the long, triangular entryway, he wondered what he was possibly going to be able to do to get Chadrik, Zaki, and Uther free from the unstable Riders. The hallway that had once been pitch black was now faintly illuminated, but it was more than enough to see clearly, which is how he spotted the Rider lingering in the doorway to Shimm.

"I knew it," the man said, his intensity growing, "Phrix is a traitor. I knew it! I'll kill you myself!"

Vik halted, but the man barreled at him, hands extended in front of him. He was rushing Vik at a full sprint when Havard's voice boomed out in the hallway, echoing until it filled the whole space. Vik's attacker threw himself to the ground and covered his head, not understanding the words being said until they were repeated a third time. Havard was promising the madman a reward if he went straight through to the other side of the tunnel, congratulating him on proving to be the only trustworthy Rider. When the man finally processed what the voice was saying, he scrambled to his feet, dazed and ecstatic. He grinned from ear to ear at Vik, all malice replaced by pure joy. The man jogged by Vik and disappeared into the bright light on the other side.

"I'm not able to detain anyone in this hallway. I would have had to terminate his life. Now, he will be taken to a safe holding area and medication administered."

"Wow, you really thought that through," said Vik, adrenaline still pumping through his veins.

"Don't let them see you when you get outside until after I start speaking."

Havard's voice assured him he would be protected and together they left the ruins.

The residents of Shimm were gathered around Chadrik and Uther's battered bodies. Zaki was on his stalker, pacing anxiously from an overly safe distance. Vik peered out from the tunnel and jerked when he heard Havard's voice booming out from the side of the mountain itself. He couldn't see where it was coming from, but he also thought it could've been emitting from multiple places. What Vik thought was going to be a huge fight turned out to be a quick surrender from the entire town at once. Havard was privy to information no one else was aware of about the Riders except for Roque. They were an incomplete specimen, an experiment not yet perfected. Their instabilities were too severe to be negotiated with logically and Havard knew from the data on Roque, from his ability to quickly analyze recordings both audial and visual, that the Riders were deeply, insatiably paranoid.

Once Havard had quelled the masses with detailed instructions and vague promises, Vik ran out, leaping over the bodies and untied both the giant and Chadrik. Zaki dropped his stalker, letting it return to the wild once it awoke, and threw himself onto Vik.

"I can't believe it," the boy kept chanting.

"Neither can I," said Chadrik, grimacing in pain.

Vik handed all of them small, orange pills and by the time they hobbled into the triangular hallway, they were feeling like their better selves again.

The ruins became less alien with Havard around. His fatherly familiarity permeated every wall, his helpful digits emerging from the circular gratings along every corridor. He guided Uther, Zaki, and Chadrik in to where Josanna was nervously pacing.

"Vik!" Zaki shouted, running forward and throwing his arms around his waist.

Vik stumbled back a step and returned the embrace, smiling at the others. They were gathered in an all-white atrium with a bright light in place of a ceiling and twelve stories stacked one on top of the other with elevators connecting them. There were a total of seven dormitories like that one spread throughout the pristine ruins. Lined perfectly along the center of the atrium were benches, tables with attached chairs and raised segments filled with soil and long-dead trees, filling the immediate area around them with the smell of rotten wood. Nothing was made for the Thesmekka, but for people. Havard informed him that their intention was to create the perfect species of humanoid to accompany them there at the facility before integrating them into the populace outside of Agrona. Vik was still having a hard time understanding the concept of there being a place outside of Agrona, but was too enamored with the incredibly hospitable ruins to waste too many questions about some other place.

"I'm sorry we got upset with you about having the wrong orb," Chadrik confessed.

"The wrong orb?" Havard inquired.

335

"Yeah, I smashed a Thesmekkian one back in Imperyo instead of you," Vik chuckled, "And they were mad about it."

There was a long, quiet pause where only the whirring of the arms along the walls could be heard. Everyone shifted uneasily and Vik called Havard's name a few times before he responded.

"I'm sorry, it seems I cannot delete records from my cognitive banking. Please, be more careful with what you tell me in the future."

"What's the matter?"

"Should a Thesmekka ever return and discover what you've done, you would be found guilty of murder and put on trial as a sentient being not annexed by the Infinite Aggregate."

"What the hell does that mean?" Josanna asked.

"It means, if for whatever reason the Thesmekka don't destroy every specimen once they return, the law would be bound to have you killed for crimes against a superior member of the Infinite Aggregate."

"So I don't really need to watch what I say anymore," Vik said, throwing his hands up, "Nothing could be worse than that."

"What about the Brutes?" asked Josanna.

"The Brutes?" asked Chadrik.

"Yeah, what ever happened to them? Did the Thesmekka destroy them or did this Infinite Aggregate do it?"

There was a long pause before Havard answered, "Brutes were a means of maintaining the societal parameters of each specimen group."

"So what's that mean?" asked Vik.

"They were fictitious. A piece of the carefully constructed rhetoric designed to keep the specimens from doing what they inevitably did, which was escaping from their containment."

"Who knows what else they lied about," said Chadrik.

"Radeki Luken Athapéle," Havard started.

"Y, yes," Zaki answered, shivering at being addressed so fully.

"If you would follow the lights to the medical bay with Josanna, I will be able to administer your necessary treatments."

"What, what medical treatments do I need?" Zaki asked, practically in tears.

"Zaki, you don't need to be afraid," Vik said, putting his hands on his head. "I'll go with you. But I need to ask, Havard, where can we get weapons? I need to bring our people here, but we—"

"Impossible," Havard interrupted. "My programming forbids equipping sentient beings not annexed into the Infinite Aggregate."

"I'm starting to dislike this Aggregate," Josanna grumbled, arms crossed.

"Havard," Vik began, searching the room for the words, "We need your help."

"Come to the medical bay, please."

The five of them filed out of the dormitories and through several more hallways before they reached the medical bay. It had two tiny rooms leading into the main one. The first room was for putting aside any contaminated materials not being brought into the bay and the second was for decontamination via powerful sprays jutting out of the walls. Havard assured them everything was being taken care of and addressed Uther in a strange, guttural series of sounds. Uther seemed relieved and turned around, following a series of lights leading him away from Vik and Chadrik.

"I have finished assembling and programming a TAI-GR.51 for Uther Jahan as he informed me of being in need of one."

"...Whatever that is," Chadrik whispered to Vik.

Vik shrugged.

"Listen," started Josanna, "You two need to figure out how we're going to get back to Imperyo and what we can use to get everyone back safe."

"I have already thought of a plan," said Havard, "If you'll indulge me."

Vik and Chadrik split off from Josanna and Zaki as they received what they needed from the med-fac. The two arrived in a short room lined with slanted pods. Each one opened like an elevator, but went nowhere. A gentle voice chimed from inside.

"Please undress and get into the pod."

Vik and Chadrik glanced at each other, then into the wired capsule. There were three crimson pads less for comfort and more to indicate the location of his head, back and lower body along with gadgets, lights and sharp ends sticking out from the inner walls. Feeling very uncomfortable undressing in this cold room for a strange, feminine voice, Vik put his body inside the capsule and the doors snapped shut like a before he finished adjusting to the angle.

"Straighten up."

A pleasant, feminine voice issued from inside his trap. Vik wasn't sure how he was supposed to accomplish this. He glanced at both ends of the tube and on one side he saw two circles. Attempting to lie flat on his back and push his feet against them, Vik squirmed around in the capsule for only a few seconds before the pleasant voice chimed up again.

"Excellent, handsome. Now hold perfectly still."

A white-blue grid illuminated all around him, moving up and down the pod before abruptly blinking off again.

"Turn over."

Vik struggled to rotate his body around, lying on his stomach without touching any of the sharp points near his arms. The grid came to life again, repeating the process. The tiny grid lights were heating the confined space like an oven and Vik was starting to sweat. The multi-layered grid flicked off and a trickling sound could be heard near his head. He glanced up and saw a black ooze filling the capsule. Panic was his first instinct. He accidentally slammed his forehead against the doors.

"Do not panic. I am fully operational. Now, take a deep breath."

A form-fitting pad the size of Vik's head detached from the wall of the pod, located his eyes and then jammed into his face at an abrasive speed. Holding his head against the pad on the back of the pod, it filled with the cool liquid until he started floating out away from the rests.

Draining away faster than it had filled, Vik was left covered in a layer of black ooze. It felt wet, but every time he slapped it with his hand it was solid as a rock. The doors swished open again and Vik clambered out, feeling strangely perfect in this disgusting, gooey suit. It was no longer cold, but the perfect temperature. His face was in fact the most uncomfortable place on his body, outlined by a sleek metal exoskeleton.

"Step into the next pod," the voice ordered from inside.

Chadrik stumbled out of his pod, giving Vik a bewildered look before trying to shake the substance off his arms. They glanced around and saw that the very next set of capsules were open, awaiting their goopy forms. He clambered inside and repeated the same procedure, only this time it was significantly more jarring. Plates of metal were being slammed into his body and he could feel bruises forming under every jab of abuse.

"I can tell this is your first time," the disembodied female voice cooed at him. "Relax, darling, and let your body move with the force. Don't fight the fusion."

She was very supportive and instructive, informing him of when he needed to raise his body and what was going to happen next. The plating was thin and hardly felt protective, but it felt like it was holding the ooze into place well enough. A few round, complex pieces were attached to the rest and the helpful voice informed him of their purposes. Some were for breathing, others for stabilizing things that Vik couldn't understand. By the time he was completely covered in metal plating, he barely noticed the punching attachment process. When it came time to cover his head, a rounded plate with an overly soft interior was pressed to the back of his scalp. He could feel the soft foam-like material sift around and hold into place around his skull. Two tiny robotic arms appeared from both sides of his face carrying clear panes of what looked like shaped glass. They slid easily into the slots on the rounded helmet piece and connected in the middle. Both arms lit up with sparks, welding the panes closed down the middle. Much to his surprise, the welding was hardly noticeable in his view.

"I had a nice time suiting you up. Once you exit the pod, stretch your limbs to their fullest to alleviate tension points before the suit is fully cooled. I hope you will come see me again," the woman's voice purred.

The capsule swished open and Vik clumsily pulled himself out, staggering out into the middle of the room. His limbs felt too heavy to lift, but after stretching his left arm up once, the second time was much easier. Chadrik fell out of his pod and did the same, both of them quickly acclimating to their solid yet completely flexible metal bodies.

"This model is very effective," Havard said from the wall near the doorway.

"I think he likes her," Chadrik teased.

The doors to the capsules slammed shut.

"So, we don't get any weapons?" Vik asked, staring at his hands opening and closing.

The plating on his hands were black, and the special pieces scattered around his body were black, but the rest of his suit was sky blue. His voice was surprisingly clear, as if being repeated back to him. It must've been just as clear outside the helmet since Havard's disembodied voice reminded him that he cannot arm him with anything as per the Aggregate's strict programming.

"Despite being unarmed, the suit will provide you with ample advantages. The Doxtari Exosuits are fire-proof up to eight hundred degrees indefinitely, though anything hotter and your tolerance time will be limited. It is also cryo-proof, low level laser-proof, and will deflect most simple projectiles. This should be more than sufficient for their primitive culture."

Vik thought about this, still staring at his hands. He gave a couple of swift punches through the air, unsure of how it would feel in this suit.

"Wow," was all he could manage.

It felt incredible, like his muscles were being assisted and his every move magnified. He may not need to do more than make an example, but deep down a part of him was eager to start some trouble. Getting his family back safely was one thing, taking them back in a whirlwind of glory was another entirely. Once again he would be bringing Marek to a better place, but it was more than that now. It was time to make things right for everyone. He felt a surge of pride at the thought.

"Hit me," Chadrik said, holding his fists up in front of his metal face. "Really hard, do it."

Vik didn't even hesitate. He drew back and punched Chadrik in the chest and he stumbled several steps back, but didn't come close to falling.

"Let's do this," Vik said, his voice projecting across the room.

Uther's face appeared on a screen nearby, previously too transparent to initially catch their eyes. His deep, rattling voice carried on in full sentences and they couldn't believe what they were hearing. His lips didn't match up with his words, but the voice certainly fit.

"I should have it open once you get your people ready, but I can't open it before you get there or we'll have trouble over here."

"There's a Gate in Imperyo?" Vik asked.

"It's on the bottom level, they've got a bunch of junk on it, but it's there."

"Does it still work?" Vik asked Uther.

"That's what I'm trying to tell you, so pay attention. I'm too old to keep repeating myself." Vik and Chadrik drew back from the screen.

"I don't remember you being so cranky," Vik mumbled.

"I'm going to try my best to get the correct Gate locked in and running, but it's going to take several tries and I can't start until you get there."

"How will you know?"

"Stop interrupting me," Uther snapped. "There's one functioning vehicle down in the garage near the Agrona Gate. Havard, take them to it and let me know when they leave as well as provide me with their ETA."

"Right away," Havard responded obediently.

"Why do I feel like he's done this before?" Chadrik asked, baffled by what a difference effortless translation made for their giant friend.

"Uther Jahan was employed as an engineer at the robotic reparations facility on Grnukir. It is unknown how he ended up in this facility on the officially undocumented and unregistered planet, Agrona, but I register his arrival only hours before the last Thesmekka departed."

Vik and Chadrik arrived in the garage and looked around at the massive, near-empty expanse. There was a single vehicle lying on its side. It had no wheels, no doors, but two seats perched in the middle of a thick, round ring, attached to the seating by carefully regulated, attracting forces. As they approached it, another screen illuminated along the way, this time with Josanna's face and Zaki bouncing up and down in the background.

"Vik?"

"How are you guys?" Vik asked, steering away from their goal. "Everyone feeling alright?"

"I feel great!" Zaki said, panting as he jumped around.

"Havard gave him something...experimental," Josanna said out the side of her mouth, raising one brow, "And I've got, well, I'm feeling a little more whole than I was before."

She held up a hand that didn't look quite right.

"It's not finished. Anyway Vik, Chadrik, I want you guys to take care."

"We will," they answered together.

Josanna nodded gently and then a smile burst across her face, "You guys look incredible."

"Excuse me," Havard interrupted. "There's an anomaly moving on the map."

"What do you mean?" asked Vik.

"From the information I'm gathering in the database and off the sensors, it's an enormous beast. It seems to come out of hibernation every ten years. The Thesmekka coordinated their sample extractions with the creature's habits, in order to ensure it remained tranquil."

"I think we know what you're talking about," Chadrik groaned, "The marshmeadow giant."

"Is it moving?" asked Vik.

"It does seem to be heading toward your destination. Though it doesn't move quickly, it has little distance to cover, comparatively. It seems driven. Something must have alerted it."

"We gotta get back there," said Vik.

They boarded the vehicle after instruction on how to start the ignition. Hovering in place, the ring parallel to the ground, the two climbed into their seats as a part of the wall slid down. Natural and artificial light clashed together in front of them. Vik balled his hands into fists around the wheel and allowed the disembodied voice of this vessel to guide him out, pushing forward on the steering mechanism and flinching as the half-opened rings rotated around their bodies. A glowing blue light emitted from the open half of the ring and seemed to be what was propelling them forward.

Once outside the garage, they saw how high up they were. The hovering ring approached the cliff's edge and waited patiently for Vik to push them forward. They both ensured they were fastened securely into their chairs before going any farther.

"What are we gonna do?" Chadrik asked.

"I bet it'll be fine."

"What? What do you mean? Vik!"

Vik pushed all the way forward on the wheel and the ring launched them like a rocket off the edge. The sound of the wind blasting over his helmet almost drowned out the sound of Chadrik yelling at him as he clutched onto his seat.

Vik had never felt more alive. They soared out, dropping to the top of the forest canopies in a gentle arch. Dipping up and down with the shape of the treetops, the hovercraft handled like it had been dying to get out of that big empty room every single day of those fifty years, pushing through each rusty twitch and becoming gentler with every passing milestone. They could already see the hollow black mountain in the distance.

# CHAPTER TWENTY-THREE

Durako woke slumped in his chair beside the bed. Rubbing the bridge of his nose, he groaned and moved his other hand off the table. A wooden necklace in the shape of an oval toppled to the floor and he bent to pick it up, forgetting that he'd even taken it out the night before. The likeness of a familiar woman was carefully chiseled into it and two circles dangled from tiny twines under it, one for Kasuko and one for Zaruko. Looking at the small souvenir, he couldn't understand why he felt so conflicted. His number one threat was dead and although that happened to be his son, he was a disappointment in every way that mattered to him. Things were said and done between them that could never have healed.

"Lord Durako," a man's voice called from the other side of the door, "There are people here to see you."

"I'll be down in a moment," Durako called out, clearing his throat right after.

He glared at the tiny trinket, remembering the day he'd had it made. He picked it up from the craftsman only to never be able to deliver it to her. Roughly wiping a tear from his cheek, Durako growled out another throat clearing and snapped the necklace in half, throwing it on the floor as he stomped out of the room.

Down on the bottom floor of his manor, a few prominent families had gathered to call on him. Once they saw him coming down the stairs, their impatience burst and they began to speak to him like frustrated equals. He listened to them while glancing around the room for Jahzara, but she still hadn't arrived.

"We're just worried about the direction things are taking," one of the family patriarchs summarized, "Many Impery women have been killed in the last month and after what happened with your son—"

"What happened with my son was a necessity, long overdue. I thought I had made myself perfectly clear, but I'll say it again, he was planning to move against me, only him and his anti-loyalists. If there had been Sinovians present, I would've gladly added them to the pile of dead."

"Yes, but you see, they're Sinovians. That's what has us concerned. You seem to believe them capable of an uprising worth fearing."

"Underestimating the enemy is a dangerous mindset to settle in, especially when there are so many of them. It's what landed us into this overly reliant state in the first place."

His tone was becoming increasingly irritated and threatening, but half his guard seemed to be missing. This did not sway the families from feeling uncomfortable in his presence. Lord Durako refused to sit and grew increasingly anxious. He paced around while they offered their sympathies for his difficult decision and tried to politely convey their concerns, but he had reached the point of being deaf to them.

"Where is Jahzara?" Durako finally snapped at one of the guards.

"I don't know, my lord. I never saw her come in."

"This morning?"

"Last night."

Everyone in the room held their breath, waiting to see how he was going to react to determine the severity of the news. Lord Durako thought first of the worst possible explanation and used the denial of tha thought to fuel his next series of actions. He gathered all of his guards and anyone who wanted to join him and stormed out of the manor without another word to the families.

He had told her not to go out last night, to wait for the ceremony another month. It was too dangerous, he'd told her. She acted strangely about it and he should've picked up on that. Internally berating himself along the way, denying every sickening worry with weak consolations, he and his guards descended Imperyo, prepared and willing to do whatever necessary to get Jahzara back. If she was dead, he was prepared to burn down the entirety of Threshold and hunt every last Sinovian himself. If the families were so unthreatened by the fireless masses, then the least he could do was reduce their numbers to protect his ignorant peers.

*****

Marek plodded heavily down the cellar stairs, lazily checking up on their two prisoners. He lurched back down when he saw Nikiva standing over Reeta, panting and trying to rake her hair out of her face with her fingers. The Shiny was lying on her side, struggling to push herself upright with her shoulder.

"Nikiva," Marek started, "Get out of here. You're not supposed to be down here."

344

As she marched passed him, he saw her face was tear-soaked and furious, her eyes red and weary. He remembered the casualties of Reeta's deceptions and his sympathy for the woman fell another notch.

After Nikiva closed the cellar door behind her, he turned to Jahzara and looked down his nose at her. Muzzled and pressed into the corner like an animal, she thoroughly disgusted him. Her arms were bound behind her back and her legs tied together as well. The smithy had specially made her shackles for the occasion.

"I know you're not really afraid of us, of what we'll do to you. But you should be worried about your child. I'll raise it myself, tell it how fire is bad, to fear the Thesmekka and all about you and Durako in such a way that it'll be glad you're gone," he snorted when she started tearing up and glaring wickedly at him, "Calm down. You know, if Durako surrenders peacefully and comes to retrieve you, I don't think I could let that happen. But you're lucky you're with child. Some of us actually respect that," he sat on his knees and leaned in close to her face, pulling out his knife and tapping her shoulder with it. "I've never wanted to kill anyone. But you…I almost don't care that there's a baby in there." He clenched his teeth, "Almost."

Outside, searching the space between the fields and the forest, Tayna walked along with too much muddling her thoughts. She knew Ziven would be out in the fields that day, since nobody else was out there. He was avoiding the festivities in favor of more morbid endeavors.

"There you are," Tayna said from a good distance away, but he still flinched.

"What do you want," he snapped.

"I wanted to ask you to use your talents to make a scrimshaw for Zaruko."

"Absolutely not."

"What?" she asked, only because she didn't know what else to say. "I thought you were a scrimshander?"

"I don't owe you any favors, Gray, piss off."

"Ziven," she started.

"I said no and I will never change my mind. The only thing I want to do for you is make your scrimshander while you're still alive."

"Okay," Tayna said, holding up her hands in front of her. "I'm leaving you be."

He shook a bloody whittling knife at her, his own hands coated in crimson stains. She realized she'd caught him in the middle of tending to Nikiva's request and bolted from the fields toward the line of trees.

Despite what she was out there to do, her encounter with Ziven nagged at her mind. She couldn't see every little thing that was going to happen in her meditations, but the danger of that situation was too great to have missed. If she hadn't gone with her gut and decided to get out of there before he got fully to his feet, he might've killed her. For the slightest moment, Tayna felt like she might not be the one in control. The thought frightened her enough to get itself abandoned.

At the base of a skinny, upward shooting root, the ground throbbed under her foot. She moved it back and saw the pulsing dirt. It was such a small thing, she would never have found it without the visions. Ripping the short knife from her sheath, she stabbed it straight into the vein and warm blood spilled out.

The market circle was packed. Everyone crammed tightly together under the warm morning sun, waiting for someone to speak up. Marek chose to have the execution in the center of Threshold instead of the provided platform under the Imperyo balcony in honor of Zaruko's own showy trial. Nattina held Reeta down with one hand, despite the woman's struggling and occasional bursts pushing the Bruteman leader enough for her to be on her toes. Jahzara was held nearby, around two Brutemen and surrounded by a few more. They didn't want to take the chance of an ambitious mob ruining their plans.

"Do you see him, there?" Marek said quietly to Jahzara, pointing to the Seer woman holding a baby before jabbing his own chest with his finger, "That's my son. I should let these people have you for what you almost did to him and what you did do to his mother."

Hearing a faint rumble, the crowd shuffled anxiously, looking behind them to locate the source. Shrouded in a distant blue fog, they saw a giant raising from the ground over the treetops, far enough away that its booming roars and tremor inducing steps were easily masked by the voiced concerns of the people.

"Don't worry," Nattina called out over everyone, "They never go through the forest."

Once their fears of the giant were eased, a few Jawny took advantage of the distraction, throwing a couple of buckets of urine on Jahzara between the Brutemen before they were chased away by the guards who didn't want to be involved in the stench of collateral damage.

"It was surprising to me," Marek began, shouting over the people and drawing their immediate attention, "that so many people here have been held down by so few. When they said they were able to protect you all and you believed they were the only ones that could, I found myself almost believing it too. The problem wasn't with what they said, but with

346

the division among ourselves. My own people came here, bitterly divided, able to spot a Gray from an Upper by the way we wore our lives on our faces. But you were all unable to tell us apart. That is how petty these things can get and that is how weak we can make ourselves.

"Together, we were able to make ourselves safe from the drass and improve our lives ten times over what they were when we arrived, in a matter of days. Imagine what we could do if we believed in ourselves, together. If the Impery came down here to threaten us and found our eyes all looking in the same direction, all of us pointing to the same problem instead of each other."

Marek pointed toward Reeta and took a deep breath, steeling himself for what he was about to do. Building up the courage to turn a mob of people against one woman in order to bring them closer together. It wasn't the time for second thoughts, no room for even a speck of doubt.

"Jahzara's spy, Reeta, is here before you all today to pay in blood for her crimes against us. Betraying her own allies, crippling our ability to resolve this conflict peacefully. None of us wish for this, but when trust is betrayed down to the deepest roots, there is no curing it with simple apologizes or promises. Seeing the error of your ways. We are strong, a chain united together, but we cannot turn a blind eye to broken links."

Reeta was allowed her final words before Nattina and her Brutemen readied her to die, "I only ever tried to bring us together. The Impery are the enemy and I flushed them out from among us without any of our people getting hurt. This is my reward!"

Nattina pushed her down to her knees and held her face up to the sun by her hair. She held the knife up for everyone to see before slicing Reeta's throat. The Shinies flinched and looked away, all except for Ridiak. He was going to remember everything for Chadrik, whenever he returned.

The giant reminded them all he was lingering in the distance with some far off roaring and another stomping footstep. Jahzara trembled from the thunderous rumbling and glared over every face in the crowd. They were turning their attention from Reeta to her, hungrily hoping for an encore. She struggled against the Brutemen who held her, but she might as well have been tethered to two mountains. Running down the street at a long-enduring pace, Tayna came up behind the crowd, slowing down once she reached them. Jahzara noticed her first, but Marek was next. He waved her up to the front and the crowd struggled to part enough for her to squeeze through.

Tayna stood beside Marek and motioned behind him, so out of breath she was unable to speak. Flooding out of the entrance to Imperyo was Lord Durako and his loyalists, marching at a brisk pace and heading straight for them. The crowd shifted nervously, but Tayna just approached Jahzara, slapped her once and shouted over the people, "together!". She took out a knife and Marek stopped her, asking what she was doing. She shrugged off his hand and gave him a stern look before sawing off Jahzara's hair at the base, ignoring her muffled cries. By the time she was finished, Lord Durako stood just ten paces away, maintaining his distance and shooting frequent glances at Jahzara. He took shallow breaths and couldn't unball his fists, baring his teeth at all of them as he bellowed, commanding them to let her go and face immediate punishment. Tayna tossed the braid of hair at his feet. It hit with a thump, kicking up a little dirt on Durako's shoes. When he looked around at the crowd that hadn't dispersed, he saw they were each of them armed despite his actions just a few days prior. Their weapons were primitive, but numerous.

"We will make this quick," Tayna said, "Submit to Sinovian rule and share the black mountain."

"Why would we agree to this?" Durako growled.

"Because we have your sieva."

His rage was doused in a flood of water, soaking his body in the cold, clinging wetness of fear. All that they'd been hoping for together had finally happened and he could lose her right then.

"Is this true?" he asked Jahzara softly.

She fervently nodded her head, tears of joy plopping out and rolling over the strap across her mouth. He held his hands out in front of him as a show of surrendering and lowered his head.

"It's really a day of rejoicing for you," Tayna began with sarcasm in her voice, "Your son's own children grow within me too. We're all family."

Durako's eyes snapped up to hers, disapproving but afraid to show more. He kept his hands up and shifted in place, wishing Jahzara was beside him to whisper suggestions and approval in his ear. Torn and confused, Durako took a deep breath, prepared to say whatever needed to be said to keep his sieva alive when the next of the giant's footsteps shook the ground under their feet. Everyone screams, turning around and seeing the direction the Brute was taking. Slowly but steadily making its way to Threshold, there was nowhere but the mountain for people to hide.

Jawnies, Shinies, Seers, and Brutemen poured over the execution site, trampling Reeta's body and fleeing straight for Imperyo. Many of Durako's loyalists tried to stop them, but were caught up in the panic themselves, running for home when they heard and felt the giant bellowing. Durako carefully spit fire at the Brutemen holding Jahzara, snatching her away from then when they let go and disappearing into the Sinovian current. She ripped the strap off her mouth and kissed him hard and fast, dashing ahead and grabbing a woman with a baby by the shoulder. Jahzara hooked one arm under Garek and elbowed his caretaker's face, lifting him from her arms as she fell back and to the ground, her feet flailing up as the desperate mob unknowingly stampeded over her.

One hand covering Garek's face, she blew fire over the Sinovian rooftops and stared up at the giant that was about to breach their end of the forest. The rumbling of its footsteps was accompanied by the crackling snaps of enormous trees fracturing like twigs. They could hear the roots and bark popping from the base of Imperyo. Fire hopped from house to house like water running downhill. The sap ignited too easily and the uncoated materials were flammable enough to hold the heat's attention. It was only a matter of minutes before Threshold had accumulated enough fire to catch the Brute's eye, the burn on its gnarled hand a fresh memory. Garek screamed and cried as the colossal beast roared, the sound resembling a monk's meditating chant, vibrating through everyone's chest and burning their eardrums. Durako and Jahzara were almost through the cave when he ushered her upward, pointing toward their mansion.

Tayna couldn't take her eyes off the Brute. She couldn't understand how something could be alive and so much bigger than them. Fire ripped up homes around her and from the corner of her eye, she knew she'd seen this before. Despite how small she felt, how terrifying that beast was, she took comfort in the knowledge that Thessa was still guiding her. The blood from the vein on the forest floor must have drawn the creature out, but it was pushing them all inside. Somehow, this was going to work out in their favor. Marek snatched her arm and jerked her out of her trance.

"Let's go!" he shouted before letting her go and slapping his hands over his ears.

"They took Garek," Tayna said, "You have to get him back."

Marek stared at her, ignoring everything else around him. She had been fervently watching the giant while he had fought upstream of the crowd to grab her. The only way she could've seen Garek get taken...

"What are you waiting for?" she shouted.

"You're just like him," Marek snapped through his teeth, pushing her away and running after his son.

He tripped over the woman that'd been holding his son and someone smashed against his leg. Yelling under the screaming riot, he scrambled up to his knees, moving forward before getting all the way to his feet, just trying to move enough with the current to keep from getting pulled back under.

The entrance to Imperyo was a funnel, but Marek was bringing up the rear. Pushing his way into the mountain proved to be more like surviving a meat grinder. The people against the cave wall were lucky, it was those just outside the middle who suffocated and were carried all the way through before dropping to the ground without anyone taking special notice of them.

One Impery man couldn't take the sight of so many Sinovians rushing into his home any longer. He billowed a great cloud of fire at them, burning them alive just as they made it through the tunnel. Marek tried to apply the brakes, but the crowd was already in motion. He couldn't stop moving forward. Trapped on the conveyor belt, moving toward the furnace, Marek tried to think of a way out. He started to duck down but almost got pulled under, he pulled out his knife, but he'd have to have been directly in the path of the flames in order to hit the man.

Without warning, the flames stopped as a Bruteman he didn't recognize tackled the man to the ground and beat him to death with fists bigger than the man's head. Impery blood ran down the bottom of the ramp inside their own mountain. The fighting erupted from there, as if the fire-breather's death was the start of a race. Fire shot up from everywhere like hidden geysers, dying down just as quickly. Sinovians and Impery rippled over the metal Gate lying in the middle of level fourteen, slamming into and tripping over its edges as they clawed at one another. Bags of mace flower powder exploding left and right and raining down from above them. It was meant for an organized attack by the Shinies, but they settled for the heat of battle instead. They would throw them up in the air and them blast them apart with bursts of air. The powder went far, but inevitably wafted back down, suffocating the frantic mob.

Marek saw Jahzara and Durako already halfway up the mountain and bolted for the ramp. He ignored attempts at grabbing him, shrugged off and spun around obstacles in his way. All he cared about was getting to Garek. The mountain shook and gravel crumbled from the walls, but it wasn't enough to distract the pent-up clashing. The quakes were just adding to it. Nikiva and Savan were carrying Shurik to the farthest point away from everything, partially hidden under the crevice of the first ramp. They huddled together, one of them bleeding, but it was impossible to tell where it was coming from just by looking at them.

Tayna saw Durako and Jahzara reach their manor just as Marek arrived at the top level. He bellowed at them, fueled by a rage he'd never let flow so freely. Both of them turned around, but Durako blocked his path. Sheltering Garek from his own father, Jahzara was pushed back when Marek dove forward, tackling Durako. As they slammed into one another, Jahzara shouted at and threatened him, but her demands went unacknowledged. Durako and Marek grappled to the death on the stone street, delivering shallow kicks and punches whenever they could. Wrapping his arm around Marek's throat, trapping him from behind, the Seer's face turned a dark red before he managed to loosen his grip by elbowing Durako relentlessly in the ribs. Marek spun around and punched him hard enough in the jaw to hear a crack, but it was a bone somewhere in his own hand. He couldn't breathe and his hand was throbbing, but Durako was the one stumbling until he fell on his hip with one hand bracing him from fully falling to the ground.

"Stop!" Jahzara shouted, holding Garek near the edge of the level.

Marek froze in place, rubbing his hand and grimacing, hunched over submissively in front of Jahzara. He begged her and continued pleading even when Durako grabbed him by his neck from behind and threw him down to his chest on the rock hard street. Wheezing, Marek was only able to lift his head while he waited for air to fill his lungs once again. Jahzara couldn't think of a sweeter revenge. He would suffer so thoroughly for what he'd done to her and Durako, what he'd done to their home and people. The ground rumbled so hard, a chunk of the mountain broke off from level eight, damaging part of a house underneath. Jahzara stumbled to one knee, her hand slipping off the level and catching on her elbow. Her chest fluttered and she drew back, ignoring the burning abrasion on the back of her arm. A bright light flashed from the Gate down below and squinting, she saw an image in the portal. Garek squirmed and she shook her head, looking down at him nestled securely in her arms. This wasn't the end for her. There was a way out.

"The Gate is open," she gasped to Durako, clutching Garek tightly to her chest.

Then she ran, leaving the two of them to their senseless brawl. Durako pinned Marek to the ground with his foot and was about to drench him in fire when the sight of something in the hole at the top of the mountain brought Marek's eyes to the side of Durako's face. Feeling confident in his victory, Durako glanced up at what the Sinovian saw in his final moments. The sight gave him such a start that he raised his foot from Marek's chest.

Soaring through the opening, a glimmering ring spun around to adjust its trajectory and landed with ease on the top level street near the two combatants. Durako stood up straight as one of the armored figures charged straight for him, his metal feet crashing against the stone street with every step, until he threw a solid fist into the gut of Lord Durako. It smashed him back against his own manor and firmly held him there. Marek scrambled to his feet and could barely form the words that came to him.

"Are you…Th, Thesmekka?"

Durako's bewildered face looked as though he had the same question, but when Vik's voice projected from the outer speakers, they both lurched out of their awestruck daze.

"No! It's just me, it's Vik. Get Garek and get out. The Gate should be open," Vik turned to Durako, "And you better not give me another reason to—"

Durako shoved Vik away with all his strength, only pushing him a couple of steps. That was all the distance he needed. He sucked in a deep breath and roasted the Thesmekkian imposter. When the roaring fire subsided, Vik was standing with an arm over his face, shielding himself more from the light than the heat. Marek shouted to Vik, but all he heard was the same order announced over the speaker again. He took off down the ramp, following behind Chadrik who had jumped into the driver's seat and steered off the edge once he got about halfway down the mountain. Jahzara was somewhere ahead and Marek focused on catching her and getting his boy back for good.

Durako snatched a rock off the ground that had fallen during the all the rumbling, smashing it into Vik's visor twice, cracking it apart on the second hit. Some of the glass stabbed into his face, just barely missing his eyes and cutting open his cheek and lip. Vik scrambled to get the glass out, but his gloves were too thick to feel the shards.

"Warning, visor damage. Please return to the pod," the voice said calmly in his helmet.

Durako drew back and spewed fire once again, coating him in flames. Vik shouted and swung his arm around through the fire, slapping chemical back into his face. The flames immediately ceased and the two of them gasped, swatting at their faces. Vik bent down and shook his head, hearing the shards hitting the stone street and carefully pulling at the ones still stuck in his face while Durako wheezed and leaned against the wall of his home.

Tayna could see into the Gate from where she stood, but she wasn't interested in it. She caught sight of Marek running down the side of the mountain after Jahzara and took off up the ramp. Passing the fleeing kidnapper in the middle of level thirteen, she threw herself in front of Marek and grabbed him by his shirt. He nearly threw her aside until he saw who she was.

"I have to catch her, she's got Garek!" he shouted, pulling at her hands.

"I'll take care of him," yelled Tayna, catching Marek's attention, repeating herself more calmly. "I'll take care of him, you've done enough."

"What are you talking about? Get out of my way," Marek said, lurching forward when something rammed against his chest.

She kept a tight grip on him, but he could still see the damage between them. A knife stuck out of the middle of his chest. Tayna gritted her teeth, ripping the blade back out and throwing it on the ground. Marek groaned and stumbled into her, pressing his hand against his chest, feeling the blood escaping everywhere. She supported his weight as best she could while his lung filled with blood and he choked and coughed uncontrollably, swallowing so much of it he started to feel sick. It leaked out the side of his mouth and gushed out between his fingers.

"I'm sorry, I had to do it," Tayna said, trying her best to convince him, "You weren't supposed to make it this far. Durako was supposed to kill you up there. It's for the good of everything."

All he could manage was a few gasps and an escaped tear. Marek could feel his legs wobbling and he tried to rest his weight on her, but she struggled with it. Still clutching his shirt in one hand, she wrapped the other under his arm and walked him to the edge. Squeezing him tight, she apologized once again for the way things turned out. Then she let him go.

Savan and Shurik had just gone through the portal and Nikiva was about to follow them when Jahzara shoved her out of the way, leaping through in a hurry with Garek in her arms. Nikiva stumbled back, out of the Impery's way. She glanced up and saw Tayna throwing Marek from the thirteenth level, blood staining the front of her clothes. Teetering on the edge of the Gate, Nikiva couldn't believe what she had just witnessed. Her mouth hanging open, Nikiva was shoved into the Gate by the panicking Sinovians around her. She leapt in and slid on her back, looking at the grand, Thesmekkian portal room in a daze before Savan grabbed her hand and helped her up. She hugged him so the room would stop spinning, but he didn't think it was a show of anything other than overwhelming relief from escaping Imperyo.

Atop the interior of Imperyo, Vik and Durako faced each other, stumbling in place as a chunk of the mountain caved in, revealing the effects of irritable clawing from the Brute on the outside. The top story of the manor was struck by a large stone and part of it was brought crashing down beside them, trinkets and trophies bouncing over the edge of the level and bombarding the people down by the Gate. Every level was falling apart, the walls of Imperyo crumbling and everyone evacuating through the Gate together. The shell of the Thesmekka from Durako's destroyed locked room slid across the street and Durako stared at it long enough to work himself up. He shouted as loud as he could, charging at Vik and taking the both of them right off the ledge.

As they fell through the levels, Vik felt his heart leap into his brain and his stomach drop out completely.

"Warning, visor damage. Please return to the pod."

Vik yelled just to regain control of his body. To remind his insides where they were supposed to be situated. Durako reached into his visor and tried to jab at his eyes, but Vik pushed him away as hard as he could before falling through the horizontal Gate at the bottom of Imperyo and soaring across the length of the room in the ruins, bursting out from the vertical Gate with all the velocity he came with from the other side. The metal from his suit ground against the floor, screeching and leaving black marks in his wake. Rolling into a solid wall, Vik groaned, holding his arm and hearing the disembodied voice in his head relaying damage information once again. According to the voice, his arm was fractured and most likely he'd sustained some minor head trauma. Also, it reminded him that his visor was not secure.

"Marek!" Vik shouted, stumbling back to the gathering in front of the vertical portal.

He yelled for his brother again, but no one came forward. Everyone was sobbing, huddled together or trembling alone and disoriented. Several Seers made it through, but Marek wasn't among them.

Nikiva saw Vik's bloody face indented in the suit and quickly looked away. She didn't want him to see her. Even though there was no way he would know what she saw, she couldn't handle the thought of it. She gripped both Sera and Gamba's rough scrimshaws hanging around her neck and squeezed her eyes shut, taking herself out of the equation, hoping everything was going to play out as it should.

An image was burned into Vik's mind, one taken just before he hit the portal barrier. He had seen Sinovians and Impery screaming and ducking out of their way as he fell into the Gate and Durako didn't, bodies strewn about and the other side of the Gate like a glowing beacon. He had also seen a Seer lying on his back, covered in blood that he kept imagining with his brother's face.

Uther was the only one in the ruins who could've stopped Vik from walking forward in his suit and he did just that. Reaching out with his enormous mitt, he grabbed Vik's arm and pulled him away from the Gate.

"It's breaking apart," he said, the voice Vik could understand issuing from his chest while grunts came from his mouth, "You can't go back in there."

"Let me go," Vik said, looking from his arm to Uther.

"If you go through that portal, back into the mountain, you might not be able to make it back. You'd be trapped when the whole thing collapses—"

"Warning, visor damage. Please return to the pod," the voice interrupted.

"Uther," Vik repeated, pounding the side of his helmet in an attempt to shut the voice up, "Let me go."

Uther took his hand back, blinking several times and allowing him to leave through the Gate. He was the only one going back in, but it was his metal armor that drew their eye. Chadrik jogged up to him, shouting with his hands cupped unnecessarily around the visor in front of his mouth, but Vik's head was already on the other side of the barrier. All he could hear was the repetitive damage report.

Crawling forward and climbing up at the same time, Vik struggled to lift himself up while large chunks of the mountain crashed around him. Durako's splattered body was spread across the fourteenth level. He stood on the edge, scanning the bottom level until he saw him. Marek was laying on his back, his head flinching away from the rocks landing around him. Vik dove to his side, scraping his metal shins against the rock bottom of Imperyo. He put both his arms under Marek, but when he lifted him up, the screams he made stopped him cold. Vik sat beside him, putting both hands flat on the floor on either side of Marek's head so they could see each other clearly.

"It's going to be alright," Vik announced to him, his voice carrying over the Brute slamming into the mountain and the rubble cracking open all around them.

Vik looked around for anyone to help him with his brother, but everyone who was going had already gone through the Gate. Marek was able to move his hand enough to grab Vik's metal arm. His grip was so weak, the suit barely registered it through the black, gooey interior layer.

"Garek," he whispered so quietly, Vik read his lips to understand him.

"He's fine, he's through the Gate. I need to get you through."

"No, no don't," Marek mouthed, a pained tear rolling down his face, into his hair.

Another set of rocks slammed against the bottom level, cracking open close enough to spray them with pebbled debris. Vik had shielded his face from the rocks, but quickly looked back to Marek. His brother stared at him, blinked one last time and then exhaled. Vik put his hand on his chest, shaking him to try and stir him awake, but he was gone. There was blood on his hand and he looked at Marek's chest, noticing the gaping hole for the first time. His body had broken from the fall, but he was dying before that.

On the ruin's side of the Gate, Chadrik called out to Vik. His voice was deafening on their side, echoing off the smooth metal walls, but completely blocked by the barrier on the other. Even if there had been nothing on the Gate to filter the noise, it would've been impossible to reach him. Chadrik slapped his hands together and hopped in place a couple of times in front of the portal.

"Not you too," Uther grumbled, "It's about to break apart. Just wait for him."

"He's not coming, Uther, something happened to him. He might be trapped."

"You'll be trapped, too."

"I know," he grimaced.

Chadrik leapt through the Gate, clumsily pulling himself up despite the distorted gravitational effect. Just a few running steps away from the Thesmekkian portal, his visor scanner picked up Vik, cradling Marek's head with his arm. He was shouting at the body, clenching his teeth and sobbing deliriously. A chunk of level twelve cracked loose, shattering behind Chadrik. He lunged forward and grabbed Vik's shoulders, pulling at them and yelling through the suit-infused speakers that they had to go. There was no time to waste.

Vik lifted Marek's body, aided in part by the built-in suit assistance. Chadrik guided him back to the Gate, standing on the edge and looking up as he waited for Vik to catch up.

"Wait!" Vik shouted to Chadrik as he was about to leap in.

He turned to Vik and the next instant, the Gate flickered off and revealed the stony bottom of level fourteen underneath. A second later and Chadrik would've been cut in half. The entire mountain was coming down on them. The giant Brute wouldn't be satisfied until the scent of Sinovians was completely buried.

"What do we do?" Chadrik shouted, running up to Vik.

He was afraid, truly, for the first time in a long time. The thrill of being chased and outrunning it or fighting back was one thing, but this was beyond him. Being buried in one of the mountains was not how he wanted to go out. When he looked at Vik again, he was standing in front of him with his eyes squeezed shut, still holding Marek in his arms.

"Vik!" Chadrik shouted desperately, "Come on, man!"

# CHAPTER TWENTY-FOUR

Hearing it wasn't enough. Josanna had to see it for herself. She ran down the corridors, Havard's guiding lights zipping along to keep up with her pace. After several automatic doorways and countless halls, she wove her way into the portal room where everyone was still recuperating. The sea green veins connected every portal to Havard's mainframe, but he couldn't reopen the one that had just been shut.

"It's not opening," Uther explained to her, "and it won't ever open again. The Gate was broken on the other side. There's nothing to connect it to."

Tayna overheard the giant stranger and couldn't feel herself breathing. Not because of what he said, but ever since she saw Vik's face on the body of that Thesmekkian being. She had seen nothing of him, nothing of his arrival or that there were two of them, that they would come in through the top of the mountain and alter everything. She thought she had been correcting what needed to stay on course, but she was treading new ground and it was like her eyes were open for the first time in weeks. And she didn't like what she had seen herself doing.

Jahzara approached her, cautiously at first. When she saw the blood on her shirt and her hands, she smiled that wicked-eyed, coy smile before gently transferring Garek to her. Josanna saw her and shouted at Havard, ordering him to detain her. Jahzara quickly told her she was pregnant, but when Josanna didn't believe her Tayna confirmed it.

"Who are you?" Josanna asked her.

"You've got a lot to catch up on."

"Yes, you won," Jahzara confessed with false enthusiasm, wriggling against Havard's grip, "Everything was completely destroyed. We get to start anew."

"Not you," Tayna said, "Maybe we can't kill you, but that doesn't mean you get to walk free."

"What about my baby?" Jahzara snapped at her.

"We'll decide on that when the time comes."

Josanna's head was swimming. Jahzara and Durako actually managed to make a child, Vik and Chadrik were gone, Imperyo and

Threshold were gone, the Sinovians were starting to squabble and her arm was making her twitchy.

"Quiet!" she shouted over the slowly increasing unrest, jumping up on a stack of metal crates and waving her arms, "No more fighting, bickering, whatever. It's over, done! At least for today, please. Get out of here, follow the lights on the walls to the dormitories. If you have any questions, just ask Havard."

"Who's that?" a Shiny asked from nearby.

"He's…this place. Just say his name from anywhere and he could be able to help you. Now, go," she shooed them away, "Just go."

After Josanna hopped down, the Sinovians and Impery started filtering out, following the lighted path. The portal room was complex and strategically located, so they were completely reliant upon the guiding lights.

"Where's Zaki?" Uther asked.

"They had to keep him in the medical bay for observation, in case the meds give him trouble."

"I'll go there and check on him."

"Wait, uh, do you think there's a way to monitor the vehicle's stats from here?"

"Sure," he shifted his weight from one side to the other, "but that doesn't mean anything. The vehicle's probably more durable than a couple of people."

"Thank you," she said curtly.

Turns out the vehicle had been destroyed and this only served to diminish Josanna's spirits even further. Nattina caught up to Josanna the following day and sat down with her, filling her in on all that she'd missed. She looked at the Seer, Tayna, differently after their meeting. It was hard for her to trust someone who claims to know everything that supposed to happen, under the banner of Thessa, and still they were in the spot they were in. That was a bit too heavy for her to handle. It worked out though, since Tayna wanted to keep herself shut away after the forced migration. The two didn't have much opportunity to interact. Nattina informed Josanna that she was the most qualified to serve as Impery representative, but she insisted she had no mind or desire for politics. She only went out to satisfy her own personal needs. The pushy Brutemen eventually wore her down though, and she reluctantly sat in on the leader's meetings, held in the public square in the center of the dormitory.

Despite the tension between Sinovians and Impery, the word going around every group for the immaculate ruins seemed to be,

Sinovia. Shimm just wouldn't stick. It had food dispensers in every apartment, but they were back to the basics. Only mass-cloned bloodstones for a while, until they could cultivate the ruined gardens and start growing the seeds they found in storage. The garden atrium had a glass top, shining in pure sunlight over lush, green grass and overgrown, gravel walkways. It was beautiful, but most importantly, it was safe. Everyone worked on the vast, contained land to grow crops and others restarted their artisan occupations with a renewed interest. It was safer than it'd ever been to go outside, but most of them preferred to find what they needed around Sinovia. The stalkers were still out there, but with the Riders gone, they hardly had a reason to stick around the outer ruins of Shimm with nothing else there to track.

Every family in Sinovia was afforded their own place and each person even had their own room, if they wished to have such seclusion. Several Jawny families kept to their old ways, splitting apartment rooms between themselves instead of spreading out more, but Shinies and Brutemen didn't have the same desire for closeness. Most Impery survivors chose an entirely different dormitory sector all together, but even with that there were still five completely empty areas. Havard had closed the door to the portal room, sealed it up tight in case the Thesmekka thought about returning. For over two hundred years, Havard had been a part of Sinovian lives and illegally suppressed inside a position of silent servitude. He wasn't about to make things easier for his enslavers at the expense of his more delicate wards.

On the note of things being locked up, Phrix, Roque, and Jahzara enjoyed their own rooms in a different area of Sinovia. It wasn't a dormitory, but an actual holding cell full of barred cages and torturing devices. Josanna had no desire to use the tools on anyone, but the fact that they were there unsettled her about the whole, too-perfect place.

Other Riders were in holding cells in the same area. They were all receiving the experimental treatment, but Havard refused to let them out until he was certain they were no longer a threat. He assessed them daily and educated them on the way they should behave once they're recovered and released, but he wouldn't let them out for a long time.

Josanna couldn't help but think how much Vik and Chadrik would've enjoyed Sinovia. This was what they wanted. A paradise, hard work included. For days, Josanna had poured over the databanks Havard provided to her at her request. She discovered just how lucky they were to have made it out of Imperyo back when Durako's father was running things. There used to be many more Sinovians, with their own black mountains dotting the landscape, but Roque and those who preceded him had shut them down one by one, fearing they would be in danger if they all got out. She got to thinking, maybe it wasn't luck that got them there. Especially when she took Tayna into consideration, she started to really wonder if there was something more going on. If maybe Vik's uncanny luck had been more than that. Someone might really be looking out for them, given how long they survived and what all they managed to accomplish.

*****

Josanna's arm nagged most mornings, but that one was the worst she'd had so far. In addition to all the muscles involved with her new arm being sore from the disproportionate weight and increased burden, her metallic arm itself gave her signals of discomfort. Within the hard casing ran wires and fluids of all kinds, designed to transmit signals to her biological body so that she could feel more united with her unnatural replacement and so that she could tend to any minor maintenance demands she required. Although that was the manufacturer's design, Havard had no intention of abandoning her to learn these things on her own. Rolling out of bed, she groaned, trudging to the dispenser and asking Havard for some pain killers.

"You should have breakfast first," he reminded her.

"I won't throw up this time," she said, peaking out through the sliver of her almost shut eyes and roughly dragging her hand through her disheveled hair.

"You've said that exactly eight times now and I won't let you get angry with me a ninth."

She let her head thump against the metal dispenser, immediately regretting it, "Fine. Could I have something to eat then?"

A distant rattling could be heard behind the wall before a bloodstone nearly burst through the opening, but was slowed by the thin sheet of metal clanking as it caught the round, white bulb. She'd never been one to choose a bloodstone over other foods, but it wasn't forever. There were a multitude of plant specimens located in Sinovia and with Havard's help, they were able to accumulate a variety greater than what they'd had before leaving Threshold and Imperyo. After three weeks, the hairy berries were already beginning to bud.

Josanna peeled the recovery tape away from her shoulder. It covered along where her body was joined with the arm, beginning to fuse to the biologically compatible, Thesmekkian metal. She had to clean the area every morning until it was fully healed. Using orange pills was strictly prohibited. The nanoids would try to separate the flesh and metal up to a point in the healing process. Once she was passed that stage, it would be safe to use them again.

"Why do I feel like you're still here?" Josanna said, slumped in place.

"I'm waiting."

"What for?" she eyed the bloodstone, "Did you do something to it?"

"No," Havard said in the most dull tone he could muster, "It's too far away to be certain, but something is approaching Sinovia from the other end of Shimm."

Josanna flopped down on her bed, picking at the bloodstone. She was about to respond flippantly when what he said finally registered in her groggy, morning brain.

"Wait, something? Something like an animal something or...?"

"I can now confirm," Havard said after a long pause, "It is certainly two of this facility's metal suits, though I'm picking up more than two people."

Josanna darted out of the room, her bloodstone rolling across the floor. She jumped into her shoes and threw on another shirt, tugging at the bottom of it until it fit just right as she ran out the front door. She impatiently waited for the elevator, regretting her choice of the top floor despite almost no one else being up there. Dulcet binging notified her of the elevator's arrival just before the doors whirred open, unconcerned with the hurry she was in. Mashing the bottom floor button over and over, she heard Havard chastise her over the elevator speakers.

"Hurry up!" she shouted.

"You're making me anxious," he droned as the elevator gracefully descended to the bottom floor. "Please don't break anything with your reckless behavior."

Josanna bit her tongue, not wanting to get into another "discussion" with Havard that early in the morning and not when she was focused on something else. As she barreled down the corridors, she started telling herself not to get too excited. Havard could be wrong, his outdoor sensors weren't the best quality, he'd said so himself. It could be anything. Two Riders returning home after getting lost in the wilderness or a whistler hopping along the ground. It could even be a smudge on the camera.

Despite trying to ease her anticipation, she didn't slow down unless it was to turn a corner and even then there was barely a change. She arrived at the triangular hall, the entrance to Sinovia or from her side, the entrance to Shimm. Her feet slapped against the metal floor in the dark tunnel all the way down, plapping and plipping until she stepped onto softer dirt. The sun normally not blinding when looking out from Sinovia, but the pitch black tunnel had dimmed her vision. She squinted out into the city and saw, halfway through the ghost town, two metal men jogging toward her. They hadn't been going that fast before she came outside and the way they moved, she was sure of it.

She shouted to them, grinning wide and running into both their painfully solid arms. Pretty certain she bruised something, they all pulled back and embraced her more gently, one at a time. Uther and Zaki came trotting up behind them, relieved to see them alive as well, their giant friend lifting them off the ground just a bit as he squeezed them in his trunk-sized arms. He was careful not to crush the man riding on Chadrik's back, both arms locked around his neck.

"Zaruko," Josanna gasped, "I'd heard you were executed, by your father."

"Sorry to disappoint you," he said with his face pressed indignantly against the side of Chadrik's helmet.

"So what happened? You guys look terrible," She breathed, winded from the sprint outside and combing through her hair with both hands, suddenly overly aware of her own sloppy appearance. "How did you get back here?"

"Chadrik's visor is still working. We'll tell you more about it on the way. I'm dying to get this suit off," Vik confessed.

"I think I'm starting to mold," Chadrik joked, worried it might actually be true.

They were missing chunks of metal off their suits, but for the most part they were still fully equipped. Vik had a badly damaged area on the top of his helmet where Chadrik and Zaruko had tried to help him bash the damage report voice out. When it altered slightly to include the damage to his helmet, they decided to simply outlast the insanity the voice was driving them toward. It had cost them many hours of sleep at first, the feminine voice clearly audible in the area immediately surrounding Vik, especially in the dead silence of night.

The entire stroll back into Sinovia was more exciting than Zaki could handle. They told ridiculous stories that Josanna believed, but only because she had traveled with them to get to Sinovia in the first place. Anyone else was going to have a hard time of it. Vik bragged about having punched a drass and rattled its pebbles so hard it got confused and attacked another drass. Chadrik brought him down a notch with recounting how Vik almost got eaten by a tallbug, but the damn thing couldn't bite through their exosuits. Vik pointed to the dented scratches across his back and chest as proof.

They reached the room with all the pods and only Josanna accompanied them inside. She watched them go in and tried to ignore the seductive pod voice undressing them. Havard dispensed some clothes in their size before they were finished and Josanna took them out, setting them on the floor in front of each capsule. Once they opened, the two stumbled out and she quickly turned around, having seen way too much of her half-brother and not enough of Vik to satisfy her curiosity.

"Alright, I've got on pants," Chadrik said, irritated with her mishap.

"Same here," said Vik, tying the band around his waist.

He was pulling his shirt over his head when Josanna threw her arms around him, kissing his lips again and again until he started kissing back. Their arms locked each other in and dragged their hands over everywhere. Chadrik watched for a few seconds, disbelieving and amused until they parted, giving several trailing kisses before Vik turned to Chadrik, holding Josanna against his body.

"See, I told you."

"You were bragging about kissing me?" She asked, pretending to be outraged.

"Absolutely," Vik said with a grin, kissing her again, "You're so...beautiful, right? Isn't that the word I might've said?"

"Yeah, I think it was something like that...and you, what kind of brother are you? Weren't you upset that he kissed your sister?"

"Half-brother," Chadrik corrected her while he put on his shoes, "I only half-cared."

They left Chadrik to Zaki, who wanted to take him to the dormitories and get them a room next to his. He was one of the few others who had chosen the top floor and the only kid to have an entire apartment to himself.

Zaruko was taken to the med-fac immediately. Havard informed him of the plan to remove and replace his old legs with some functioning ones. The way he discussed the removal of his legs made him nervous, but Havard assured him he would feel nothing during the process. None of what the disembodied voice said comforted the wounded Impery.

"Will you tell Tayna I'm alright, that I'm here. Last time she saw me, I was pretty well dead."

"Yeah," said Vik, "We'll get the word to her."

Zaruko thanked them before he was shuttled away on a conveyor belt into a part of the wall. The door zipped shut behind him and Havard assured them he would be fine in a few days.

Vik and Josanna hovered outside the med-fac.

"I'm worried about something."

"I think we can trust Havard with the medical stuff. Besides, his legs can't get any more useless," said Josanna.

"No, I mean, the way we found him. Out by the wall, claiming to have crawled out of the houses in time. I don't think anyone knew what Marek had done. I mean, someone would've tried to get to him if they knew, don't you think?"

"I don't know, it sounded pretty chaotic, what was happening out there at the time. I think most people were just worried about themselves."

"Maybe so," he said.

"Let's say Marek did hide him away to heal. Who was he hiding him from?"

"Maybe the Impery, I mean, that's the obvious thing. But why wouldn't he tell anybody else? Tayna didn't seem to know about it."

"Do you think, maybe," Josanna took care with her words, "Maybe he was hiding him from her?"

"That's not likely," said Vik, disregarding the suggestion almost immediately.

"Why don't we worry about this later?" she suggested.

Vik agreed and they continued walking down the halls. Josanna told him all about the things that'd been happening since they'd gone missing. She took Vik to see Garek, in the care of one of the burned girls from the nursery, Beka.

"Where's Tayna?" Vik asked before they got there.

"She's been in her apartment for a long time. Probably getting adjusted to things and from what I've heard, she might be a little depressed."

Josanna filled him in on what Nattina had told him about her and the things she had done for them. Some parts of it didn't sound like the Tayna he remembered.

"I should visit her soon," Vik said, worrying about her spending too much time alone with thoughts too big for one person.

Havard suddenly chimed in, "It seems the Enna gene samples carried more with them than just a more durable specimen. Fortunately, the Thesmekka don't test for fringe-leaning, scientific results. From my topical scan approximately twelve seconds ago, her vitals are extremely subdued, but she seems to be perfectly fine. An effect of your specimen's hypothesized mutation. The hibernal trance she's able to willingly enter keeps her body in a low effort state, greatly decreasing the need for sustenance and a REM cycle sleep."

"Thanks Havard," Vik said, feeling a little uncomfortable getting her personal information without her approval.

"I'm sorry about your brother," Josanna said softly, "Everyone loved him. I heard he brought the Sinovians together, at the end."

"Yeah," Vik said, clearing his throat, "Now that does sound like him."

They entered a small commons area, meant for eating meals at small tables scattered neatly around the bright, clean room. Vik gazed around, marveling at the sight of something becoming commonplace for Josanna.

"Could you give me a minute alone?" Vik asked Josanna.

She was caught off guard, but agreed almost immediately. After she left the room, Vik spoke to Havard without looking up from his hands.

"Could I get a knife from you, Havard?"

"...I don't think that's wise," the disembodied voice advised, easily recalling times with Vik not too long ago.

"Havard, please," the urgency in his tone was clear.

One of Havard's infinite arms descended with a finely whetted kitchen knife. It was more than adequate for the job Vik had in mind. He carefully plucked the blade from Havard's pincers and held out his hand, digging the blade into his palm. Marek was the better of the two of them. He lost more than Vik could ever imagine, but he put so much more into life, for everyone around him. Vik groaned loudly as the blade reached the end of his palm and he gasped, panting during the brief respite before setting into his other hand. Havard's arm swiveled frantically above him, trying to find a good angle to dive in from and snatch the knife away. Vik was too preoccupied with the mournings he needed to cut out of his hands. Garek was all he had left of him. If only he had been there, things might have gone differently.

Vik finished with both hands and held the blade up above his head, unsurprised when Havard ripped it away from his fingers.

"Sorry Havard," Vik said softly.

"I understand," Havard said tersely.

He might have understood the reasoning behind his actions, but he didn't have to like it. Havard was familiar with all of Haven's rituals, having been the auto-arm in every kitchen for two hundred years.

"Do you have something for this?" Vik asked, but Havard had already brought a couple of wraps down to him from other skinny arms near the walls.

His hands throbbed and burned, gushing blood, but it felt good to finally be able to cut them. It felt good to be able to give Marek the
366

proper respects after weeks of pouring over their lives inside a metal suit. He felt like he had been suspended in grief all that time. As he looked down at his hands covered in crimson blood, he felt a light weight fall away. It was small, but it was enough.

Vik and Josanna arrived in the nursery and greeted Beka, asking for Garek among the other surviving orphans. There were more after the migration incident, but there were also more of them willing to help raise them. Garek was sleeping as usual, but woke just enough to take a peek at Vik's face before drifting off again. He held him for almost an hour before asking Josanna if there was anything to eat. She chuckled and assured them there was a lot to show him.

They arrived in the atrium just in time to see Ridiak and Chadrik being separated by onlookers. Chadrik was furious and his former friend was shocked by his response.

"I had no idea what she had been doing," he shouted at Chadrik.

"Don't blow stories at me! You were always around, you had to know what she was doing. You should've talked her out of it, told her to wait for us."

"I tried, it was you who let us down! What the hell took you so long to get back?" Ridiak pushed him, not hard, but enough to stagger him and the ones holding him.

"Don't you ever speak to me again," Chadrik roared, throwing his hand out at him, red-faced and shoving off the Sinovians behind him.

When he saw Vik, he quickly looked away and stormed to the elevator. Ridiak stopped in front of Vik and gave him a once over, sneering at him with his blond companions on either side.

"Is there a problem?" asked Josanna, the only Impery in sight.

When he looked between the both of them, he snorted like there was a joke there they didn't see. They left the vast dormitory expanse, filtering out into the corridors, but Vik didn't care enough to follow them. He didn't expect everyone to suddenly get along, but he wasn't prepared for fighting within Sinovian groups.

"He must've found out about his mother," Josanna said somberly.

"Should we go talk to him?" Vik asked, watching Chadrik enter the elevator.

"Trust me, it'll probably be best if we let him be for a while. He's not big on sharing grief."

The dormitory was full of people Vik vaguely recognized and then of course, those he was familiar with like Nikiva, Savan, Kalan, and Ziven. Although the latter preferred to keep to himself, Nikiva and Savan were enjoying their time with his invigorated grandfather, Shurik. He had been injured during the attack, but when they took him to the medical bay, he came back more machine than man. Savan was getting worn out by his overzealous desire to experience everything, like he was living his life anew.

"I've never felt so young and alive!"

"I'm sure," Savan sighed, resting the side of his face on his hand.

"I'm going to go for a morning run, care to join me?" he said to Nikiva, "I enjoy a beautiful running companion. Perhaps once we're through…"

"No thank you," Nikiva said quickly, "Maybe another time, for that jog. Only."

"Your loss," Shurik said with a wink, bouncing in place before taking off around the room and disappearing out the door.

"Maybe his heart will give out," Nikiva sighed.

Vik stopped in the middle of the now lively dormitory. People were moving about, not frantically or dutifully, but finally relaxed for the first time in many of their lives. Children were running around, their feet slapping against the smooth floors, their laughter bouncing clear across the opening. He never knew how much he missed that sound until he heard it again.

Josanna took Vik to the elevator and showed him all the empty rooms overlooking the atrium on the top floor.

"Where's your room?"

She smirked, "Right here."

"Then I'll take…this one," he said, pointing to the one just beside it. "Havard, does anyone live here?"

"This is a vacant domicile."

"Perfect."

The door whirred open and the two of them walked inside. Everything was sleek, smooth metal and soft, high quality material. The furniture was minimalist and wispy. Glossy, white, and blue for the most part with small green exceptions here and there. Vik took a deep breath, inhaling the serene peace and safety he had been without for about two months, not counting the one he spent outside of Haven. It felt like a lifetime ago.

"Everything's going to be alright, isn't it?"

"I think so," Josanna said, kissing him again, this time for comfort. "I think we'll be able to come together here. Enough time goes by, I think people will forget about what kept us apart."

Vik thought about how things were in Haven, with the Uppers and the Grays, "Yeah, I hope you're right."

368

"I know we've lost so much, but—"

"You can't really lose anything," Havard interrupted, much to their surprise, "Not in the way you're referring to. As beings subjected to the flow of time, we're in a perpetual state of moving forward, creating new experiences and memories as well as new connections. Everything we come into contact with is immediately in the past, therefore nothing is lost unless you forget."

"Havard, you're finally able to speak and now I can't get you to stop."

"Would you like me to leave?"

"Only for a while, buddy," he chuckled, running his hands through Josanna's hair and bringing their lips together.

Made in the USA
Lexington, KY
22 October 2017